GRIM LOVELIES

Also by Megan Shepherd

Midnight Beauties

The Secret Horses of Briar Hill

The Madman's Daughter
Her Dark Curiosity
A Cold Legacy

The Cage
The Hunt
The Gauntlet

GRIM LOVELIES

MEGAN SHEPHERD

HOUGHTON MIFFLIN HARCOURT

BOSTON   NEW YORK

hmhbooks.com

The text was set in Adobe Garamond Pro.
Hand-lettering by Luke Lucas.

The Library of Congress has cataloged the hardcover edition as follows:
Names: Shepherd, Megan, author.
Title: Grim lovelies / Megan Shepherd.
Description: Boston ; New York : Houghton Mifflin Harcourt, [2018] | Summary:
When their mistress is murdered, Anouk and her fellow beasties have only
three days until their enchantment ends and they are transformed back into
animals, but in seeking to remain human, they threaten the hierarchy
imposed by the society of magic handlers in Paris called the Haute.
Identifiers: LCCN 2018006637 (print) | LCCN 2017061503 (ebook) | ISBN
9781328809629 (ebook)
Subjects: | CYAC: Magic—Fiction. | Witches—Fiction. | Household
employees—Fiction. | Paris (France)—Fiction. | France—Fiction. |
Fantasy.
Classification: LCC PZ7.S54374 (print) | LCC PZ7.S54374 Gr 2019 (ebook) |
DDC
[Fic]—dc23
LC record available at https://lccn.loc.gov/2018006637
ISBN: 978-1-328-80918-6 hardcover
ISBN: 978-0-358-10823-8 paperback

Printed in the United States of America
DOC 10 9 8 7 6 5 4 3 2 1
4500755786

For my little beastie, S.

Chapter 1

FROM THE FRONT-TURRET WINDOW of Mada Vittora's Paris townhouse, Anouk couldn't see the fountain at the far end of Rue des Amants. She could see, however, the hopeful souls who made their way down the sidewalk, tourists and Parisians alike, some with their noses in guidebooks and others who knew the route by heart, in search of the granted wishes that, according to an obscure fifteenth-century legend (and more recently made famous in a movie from the summer before), they'd receive in exchange for touching a lucky part of the fountain. *What* lucky part, Anouk wasn't sure. No one would tell her exactly what it was a statue of. No books in the house made reference to the legend, and Mada Vittora wouldn't allow a computer or television inside. Perhaps the fountain was a statue of a bubbling mermaid, or a prancing horse or a little peeing boy; maybe wishers were supposed to touch a special hoof or rub a lucky fin or a lucky . . . boy part. Anouk could hardly go outside and look for herself. Mada Vittora strictly forbade her to leave. Her whole life—twelve months and eight days, though she looked closer to seventeen years old—she'd never set as much as her big toe beyond the front door.

A couple made their way down the sidewalk opposite the town-house, and Anouk settled into the window seat, cradling her chin in her hands, and watched. Tourists, doubtless. Americans. Their too-white sneakers gave them away. They were holding hands, which made Anouk smile, but their faces were anxious. It was a look she saw too often. Wishers focused on the one thing they wanted so badly that they took this detour into the outskirts of the Sixteenth Arrondissement, to an area of Paris that had no other draw, no famous patisseries or cafés or landmarks except for the obscure fountain, in hopes that by some chance, the legend was real.

Anouk knew the fountain's magic was only a story, but sometimes, secretly, she wasn't so certain. It was the wishers' faces. Always strained on the way to the fountain but lighter on the return, as though the simple act of wishing had given them part of what they so desperately needed. She'd seen Mada Vittora create incredible things, floating cakes and poison earrings and mirrors that showed far-off places, but she'd never once conjured a look of joy on anyone's face.

She watched the Americans disappear beyond the window, pressing against the glass until she couldn't see them anymore, and then she sighed. A Greek god? Yes, maybe the statue was of a Greek god. Now the view beyond the turret window was the same as always: The row of matching townhouses across the street. The line of parked cars, most of them black and expensive. The sad little tree in the front garden that no one ever remembered to water.

A sleek car slid into the empty space in front of the townhouse, and Anouk sat up. Mada Vittora was back. Anouk quickly checked her hair, her nails, the floors for any rogue specks of dust she might have missed. The driver's-side door opened and Beau appeared, tall and good-looking, in his black suit with his chauffeur's hat shading his eyes, and strode around to the back. He paused to stifle a yawn before opening the rear door.

Mada Vittora climbed out, glaring up at the sun through thick sunglasses. She wore the fox-fur coat that had been delivered last week from Galeries Lafayette. As soon as it came, she'd ripped open the package and clapped her hands together and told Anouk that she simply must try it on, just for fun, and they had giggled together as she had curled Anouk's hair and rubbed blush into her cheeks and paraded her around the house in tottering high heels and the coat.

My pretty girl, Mada Vittora had said, looking over Anouk's shoulder in the mirror. *My pretty little beastie.*

Anouk jumped up to open the front door. Two more figures slid out of the car's back seat, catching her eye, and her good mood soured. Both of them were tall, one with hair the color of sunlight that matched his mother's, the other with hair a dirty shade of charcoal. What were Viggo and Hunter Black doing in the city? Mada Vittora had sent them to handle business in London just last Tuesday. Surely they hadn't arranged everything so soon.

Anouk stepped back silently as Mada Vittora swept up the front steps.

"We're going to have company, my sweet." Mada Vittora ran her nails down Anouk's cheek as she breezed into the foyer, tossing her coat on the entry table. The fox fur smelled of leather and perfume. Anouk smoothed its wrinkles and hung it in the hall closet. "Tomorrow night. A dinner party, and dancing too. You'll have to air out the ballroom. It still smells of sulfur."

"Who's coming?"

3

"The Royals."

A secretive smile played at the witch's lips, and no wonder. The Shadow Royals were the elite rulers of the magical realm that, within French borders, was called the Haute—and they had never dined at the Rue des Amants townhouse. It had only ever hosted the occasional Goblin tea party, the guests with their dusty top hats and garish makeup, even on the men. (*Especially* on the men.) Goblins might look perfectly human, save the almost imperceptible point of their ears, but they were just as likely to gnaw on the table as on Anouk's fruit tarts.

She'd need to order better wine.

"How many?" she asked.

"Six all together," Mada Vittora said, unpinning her hat. "Now, be a dear and fetch us some tea and a drop of whiskey for Hunter Black—poor thing, he's had a devil of a day. We'll take it in the salon. And here. Put this away. Carefully."

She handed Anouk her bag, parting with it as though lending a treasured book. Today it was a black Hermès purse, ostrich leather soft as a newborn's skin, gleaming gold hardware. Yesterday the same bag had been a crystal-studded clutch. The day before that, a crocodile Gadino. The witch's oubliette: Mercurial and magically vast, it held the deepest of secrets.

Viggo strode into the hall next, tossing his hat to Anouk without a glance, but Hunter Black paused long enough to look her up and down with those dark eyes that always made her anxious.

"You've never worn that necklace before," he said.

Anouk's hand flew to her throat, to the small token tucked just beneath the collar of her dress. Leave it to Hunter Black to spot the peek of gold that no one else had. Guiltily, she fished out the charm and worried it between her fingers: an old franc coin, worthless now, with a hole punched in it. She'd strung it on a chain.

"It's . . . it's from Luc," she stammered. "I mean, I found it in his room. He wouldn't mind me taking it."

And he wouldn't. She knew that if Luc had been there and seen her show even the slightest interest in it, he would have tossed it to her with a wink. She'd found it that morning, caught in the crack between two floorboards when she'd gone to his attic to fetch a vial of vervain. His rooms had felt suspended in time without him. The lingering smell of summer on his garden shears, the still-rumpled sheets on his bed, the desiccated herbs tied up in the rafters, English thyme and rosemary and rue, awaiting his hand at the mortar and pestle. It had been a week since he'd disappeared.

She toyed with the franc coin, working her worries into the etchings. It still smelled of thyme; of him.

Hunter Black's gaze went to Mada Vittora in the hall.

"She wouldn't mind either," Anouk said quickly. She tucked the necklace back under her dress collar and cleared her throat. "I'll hang up your coat, if you like." She set down the oubliette and held out her hands.

Hunter Black gave a gruff sort of cough and sauntered off behind Viggo. She let her waiting hands drop. That had gotten rid of him, at least. It could be ninety degrees outside, and still he wouldn't remove the coat unless someone forced it off him at knifepoint. The three of them disappeared into the salon, discussing business and gossiping and speculating over tomorrow's party. She brought them drinks and listened to their glasses clinking as she returned to the foyer.

"Hello, cabbage."

Wet lips brushed Anouk's cheek, and she jumped. She whirled on Beau. The driver's hat was askew on his head, a boyish grin on his face. She smacked him on the arm and then made a show of smearing away his kiss with the back of her hand.

"You're awful, Beau." She picked up the oubliette and turned to the closet. Carefully, reverently, she stepped onto the stool, stowed the oubliette on the top shelf, and then climbed down and dusted off her hands. She lowered her voice. "What are *they* doing here?" She jerked her chin in Hunter Black and Viggo's direction.

Beau let out a long sigh as he tugged off his driving gloves. "Things went sour in London, I take it. The Trafalgar Witch didn't want to agree to the new terms. Sent them packing as soon as they arrived. Viggo's in a mood."

"Viggo's always in a mood."

"Mada Vittora said something in the car about more pressing matters here. I don't think she was referring to just the dinner party."

"Great," Anouk muttered. "The last time we had *pressing matters,* more than one body was found in the Seine. At least Hunter Black wears dark clothes. Viggo's shirts are impossible. Don't they understand how hard it is to get blood out of white linen?"

"Laundry might not be the first thing on his mind, cabbage." He tweaked the strap of her apron with his thumb, using the silly little nickname that always drove her mad. "But maybe it should be on yours."

She looked down to find streaks of dust across the apron's front. "Impossible—this is a fresh apron!" She wiped at the stain uselessly while Beau chuckled. Dust, dirt, crumbs . . . it was her job to clean the house from top to bottom, but even for a maid, she managed to collect a shocking amount of grime in the shortest span of time. She untied the apron's bow at the back of her waist, fighting with the ruffles and ribbons. She pulled the apron over her head and balled it up against her plain gray dress.

"What about Luc? Did they say anything about him in the car?"

Beau's expression darkened. He shook his head. "Nothing."

"It's been a full week. People don't just vanish."

Beau clutched his gloves in one hand and rested the other on her shoulder. "Let me worry about him, okay? I'll figure it out."

Anouk's fingers twisted in the apron's straps. Movement outside the window caught her eye. Another couple strolling down the lane, arm in arm. Parisians, by the look of them. Her hand went to the franc coin at her collar.

"I'd throw a coin in the fountain if I could. Wish him back."

Beau kneaded her shoulder. "You know wishes made in the fountain won't come true," he said softly. "It isn't real magic, not like Mada Vittora's. It's just a silly thing they believe in the Pretty World. Daydreams and fantasies to keep themselves entertained."

Anouk didn't answer, sliding the smooth franc between her fingers. Outside, the sad wilted tree dropped a leaf. The rosebushes along the street were dying too, without Luc there to care for them. From some upper room, the smell of English thyme drifted down.

"Anouk."

Hunter Black had returned to the hallway, his dark hair falling in his eyes. He didn't bother to brush it away. He never did. "Mada Vittora wants a word."

Beau's hand fell off her shoulder. His look said he wouldn't want to be her. "I'll see you after dinner. I've got to wash the car anyway."

"Give the tree some water while you're out there? And the roses?"

"Sure."

Hunter Black inclined his head ever so slightly toward the salon, where Mada Vittora waited, but then he cleared his throat and motioned to her dress. He knew as well as she did that the Mada insisted Anouk always be in full uniform with one of the ruffled aprons. Hair pulled back in a matching ribbon too. Anouk stuffed the soiled apron in the hall closet and went to the kitchen for a fresh one. She looped it around her neck and started to pull her hair back in a black ribbon as she followed Hunter Black to the salon. Mada Vittora's husky laugh mixed with the notes of clinking ice.

". . . business, I suppose. They'll want to discuss new territory lines, and I'll be damned if I let that decrepit Lavender Witch gain any toeholds in Paris. This city is *mine*."

"I assume the lord and lady are coming to dinner, and that girl, the one who plays at being a countess. Who's the fourth?" Viggo's voice lowered. "Prince Rennar?"

A shiver caught Anouk at the prince's name. Rumor was he hardly ever left Castle Ides, the imposing Champs-Élysées mansion from which he governed the Haute, and when he did, it was only to raze some entire country to the ground and then banish its memory from the history books. No one knew exactly how long the Shadow Royals had been working their magic through the world, but Anouk had found references to ancient civilizations—Egyptians and Aztecs and Romans—that contained allusions to *peculiarly* powerful men and women.

8

"Rennar?" Mada Vittora's cheeks were already flushed from whiskey. "No, he wouldn't deign to come. It'll be one of the others, some lesser Royal. A duke, probably."

Now the Royals' kingdoms roughly followed political borders, and the various Royal families tended to keep to themselves except for the odd marriage to strengthen alliances and business dealings for trade purposes. They relied on witches to oversee their industries: food and wines, luxury goods, and, above all, the jewelry that Mada Vittora—the Diamond Witch—kept enchanted.

Behind Anouk, Hunter Black cleared his throat. She jumped. "Was there something I could do for you, Mada?"

"Ah, my dear. Yes." She set down her lipstick-stained glass as a grin sliced between her pretty cheeks. Although four hundred years old, she didn't look a day over forty-five. Sunshine-kissed hair in silken waves to her shoulders. Skin pulled painfully tight over sharp cheekbones. *A fortune in plastic surgery,* some might have said. Anouk knew better. All it took was a weekly bath of lavender-sage tonic mixed with two thimblefuls of Viggo's blood.

On the sofa behind his mother, Viggo wore a similar conspiratorial grin until Mada Vittora stood. The moment her back was turned to him, the smile melted off his face. He took a long, hungry draft of whiskey.

"I have a surprise for you, my pretty girl."

Anouk's hands froze on her hair bow. Half done, one snaking end of the ribbon falling to her shoulder. "Is it about tomorrow's party?"

She couldn't keep the hopeful note from her voice. Anouk was never allowed to attend the parties. None of the beasties were, not even Hunter Black, who usually stalked the shadows of the foyer the whole time, scowling at everyone except Viggo. Parties were for the worthiest members of the Haute, not beasties — mangy animals that had been whispered into the shape of human boys and girls and given brooms with which to serve. Anouk would stay in the kitchen with Beau, licking spoonfuls of strawberry icing from the mixing bowl, or tiptoe to the stairs to peek between the banisters at the beautiful dancing people.

"No, my sweet. Not about the party."

Anouk tried not to let her disappointment show. She cocked her head, a question on her lips. *Then what?*

Mada Vittora placed an icy hand on either side of Anouk's face. Her smile stretched wide. "Tonight, my darling, you go outside."

Outside? Into the Pretty World, where the Pretties strolled hand in hand with the sun on their faces amid cars and mailboxes and traffic signals, walking down the tree-lined block and then the block after that and the one after that?

Outside?

"Do you mean it?" Anouk gasped.

"Oh yes. But first, you'll need a good pair of shoes."

Chapter 2

MADA VITTORA'S CLOSET WAS the stuff of dreams. Anouk knew every inch of it; she had laundered every dress, starched every collar, dusted each pair of shoes. Thousands of them. Golden heels, red leather pumps, satin slippers with little blue bows.

"You'll want a sturdy pair," Mada Vittora said. "Flats. I could swear I had some Chanel loafers in here . . ."

The witch was currently waist-deep in the closet, rooting around like a pig hunting for truffles, her disembodied voice floating back to Anouk, who sat on the bed with her hands clutched in her lap, fingers squeezed together, the pinch of pain assuring her this wasn't a dream. She tucked in her chin in an attempt to hide her smile. "I've never worn shoes before."

"Nonsense," Mada Vittora said from the closet. "Just last week you tried on the Bergdorf heels, remember?"

"I mean real ones. Not just for dress-up." She wiggled her bare toes.

The witch extracted herself from the forest of fur coats. "Here. These will do." Her hair was mussed, her cheeks flushed, and Anouk was struck by how beautiful she was even when rumpled.

She held up a pair of stiff oxfords.

Anouk reached for them, but Mada Vittora shook her head girl-ishly. "Let me. They have tricky laces." She lowered herself to her knees and started to unlace the shoes. Anouk stared at the perfect part in the top of Mada Vittora's hair. It was always the other way around: Anouk on her knees, hemming her mistress's skirt or picking lint off her socks, while Mada Vittora towered over her, godlike. It felt topsy-turvy to have their roles reversed, like a bottle of tonic dropped upside down.

"There now," Mada Vittora said. "Snug, but they'll do."

Anouk bit down on the inside of her cheek. There was a particular tenderness in the way Mada Vittora tied the shoes, teaching Anouk how to lace them with some funny phrase about a rabbit and a hole. The strings of Anouk's heart pulled tighter with each tug on the laces.

Was this what it felt like to have a mother?

Mada Vittora's smile stretched over bone-white teeth. "Are you ready?"

Anouk, afraid to speak, nodded.

Mada Vittora took her hand.

Not even Viggo and Hunter Black, standing in the hallway and snickering to themselves, could dampen her spirits. Nor the fact that the shoes pinched the sides of her feet. Or that she and Mada Vittora were headed the wrong way, not down the stairs to the ground floor but up toward the attic. Luc's rooms? Wasn't this the *opposite* direc-tion of the front door? The shoes clunked awkwardly. As the two of them climbed the stairs, tendrils of drafty air came from beyond Luc's door, carrying scents of thyme, speeding her heart all over.

Mada Vittora walked straight to a ladder that led to a trapdoor to the roof.

"Up you go. Hurry, now, or they'll get away." She held out a burlap sack.

"Wh . . . what will?"

"The birds, my sweet. The birds."

Anouk stared through the open trapdoor in the ceiling, bewildered. It was a clear night; a few stars shone overhead. Fresh air howled down, fluttering the ribbon in her hair. Behind her, the sound of Viggo's snickering grew. Something slowly curdled in her stomach as she realized what was going on. *No, no.*

Anouk spun on Viggo. "A joke." The dry word scraped on her throat. "You aren't letting me go outside at all."

He smirked, tossing a conspiratorial look to Hunter Black, though Hunter Black's face remained as wooden as always.

Anouk choked back the feeling of hot shame. She couldn't cry. She *wouldn't.*

Her hands tightened into fists.

"Oh, my sweet girl, no!" Mada Vittora's silky hands were on her shoulders, turning her around to face her. "A joke? Ah! How foolish of me. You thought I meant outside into the city. Oh, you silly creature." Her soft hands stroked Anouk's tawny hair. "You know that your work is here, in the house. I only meant that there are some crows outside, on the roof . . . Corpus crows, very rare . . . they pass through only once a year . . . breast meat a delicacy for tomorrow's dinner . . . Luc used to catch them, of course, but with him gone . . . oh, you poor, innocent thing. I've upset you."

Her hands drifted to the sagging ribbon around Anouk's ponytail. She gently retied it into a tight bow.

Innocent?

Anouk had heard it before. The sweet one. The innocent one. Beau teased her mercilessly for it, and so did the other beasties when she saw them. They thought that because their tasks took them out into the city—Cricket even lived in an apartment on her own—they were more worldly than she. And they *were,* that was the worst part. Anouk had never seen the things they spoke of—the Eiffel Tower and the patisseries and the bookstore with the sleeping cat—had never been to a bistro, had never been caught in a sudden rainstorm, never taken a shortcut through a graveyard. But innocent? No. They didn't know the thoughts that sometimes wandered into her head late at night. Thoughts of stealing shoes, of sneaking out, of running away and never coming back.

She grabbed the burlap sack and climbed the ladder.

"Anouk," Mada Vittora said. "Wait!"

Anouk paused, hopeful.

"Try to catch at least three," the witch said.

With a burst of anger, Anouk slammed the trapdoor behind her. *Birds!* That was all the Mada wanted.

Her face was hot. Her blood was coursing palpably. Viggo's laughter still clapped against her ears as she paced on the roof. The shoes pinched her feet, *clomp-clomp-clomp*ing on the tiles. The wind chilled her as she stood on the roof, seven stories high. The lights of the city below were like a sea of stars, and . . . and she stopped.

The city.

Paris.

She was—at least in one sense—outside.

Suddenly it hit her: the lights and the wide-open night sky and the squeals of brakes and the rumble of tires and the chatter of voices.

She dropped to a crouch. Steadied herself. Fingertips curled under the tiles as though she might float up to the stars if she didn't hold herself down. She squeezed her eyes shut, but she could still hear the cacophony of Paris, pure and raw, not filtered through double-paned windows.

She drew in a breath. Another. The night rushed down her throat with each gasp. How did this chaos, this vast and crazy world, not drive everyone mad?

Start small, she thought.

She opened an eye.

She looked only at the roof tiles, the errant weeds that bravely grew through the cracks. She lifted her gaze to the edge of Mada Vittora's townhouse, fenced in by iron cresting.

A roosting crow swiveled its head toward her.

Slowly, shakily, she put down the burlap sack and then stood with her arms outstretched for balance, feet unpracticed in the stiff oxford shoes. She cast an uneasy look at the dome of night. The stars shimmered like broken bits of mirror. She'd seen them from inside, but only through the boxy frame of a window. She spun, trying to count them, ten, twenty, two hundred . . . and found herself at the edge of the roof, clutching the wrought-iron cresting with white knuckles, the crow perched beside her. She leaned out farther, transfixed. At the near end of the Rue des Amants, two cars had bumped into each other. The drivers were in the street, throwing their hands up in the air.

She smiled.

And then laughed aloud. *This was Paris.* Out there were thousands —millions—of girls and boys and parents and old people asleep in their beds, or smoking at upper windows, or deep in conversation at corner cafés.

"So pretty," Anouk whispered.

The crow took off in a flutter of wings. Someone was opening the trapdoor. She spun around to see Beau's sandy head pop up between the roof tiles.

"Beau!"

"What in the devil is going through your head, cabbage? Get back from the edge before you fall off."

She dared a glance down to the street below.

He climbed out and kicked the trapdoor closed with his shoe. He had a decanter of scotch in one hand and two glasses in the other. He barely glanced at the city lights as he crossed the roof; he was used to being outside. He handed her a glass. "Viggo told me what happened. It was cruel of them, letting you think you could leave the house." He held up the decanter. "I thought this might help."

"That's the Mada's 1972 Balvenie. She'll skin you."

He herded her away from the edge of the roof, and then poured her a glass. He seemed unconcerned about the possibility of being skinned. "I swapped it out for some Glen Moray from the liquor shop. They won't notice the difference—they're already deep in their cups. Here."

She sniffed the liquid and recoiled. Then she shrugged and took a deep sip. Fire erupted in her mouth.

Beau grinned as she doubled over to cough. He poured himself a glass. "Lovely view up here."

She wiped her mouth.

Beau gazed out over the city. "Mada Vittora's almost succeeded in undermining all the other witches in France. There are only two left who have any real power, the Crémieux Witch and the Rébeval Witch, and they're both far south, along the coast. The Lavender Witch is strong, but she's been banished to Montélimar, cast out of the Haute for insubordination—though there's a rumor that Mada Vittora set her up. I'll bet you the rest of that scotch that's why the Royals are coming for tomorrow's party. The Mada is going to try to convince them to grant her exclusive claim over the city." He waved his glass toward the street. "All those Pretties down there, hers for the swindling. They buy their flower bouquets, sip their coffee and their wine, wear their golden jewelry, and have no idea the Diamond Witch's magic has touched each piece. That they're pawns of the Haute." He laughed darkly. "The Royals' greatest achievement is convincing Pretties they want things that the Royals want themselves."

Below, a fashionable couple were tipsily making their way along the sidewalk. A diamond bracelet glittered on the woman's wrist, a gold watch on the man's, or so it seemed; in fact, they were just common stones and base metals, enchanted to appear desirable. Other witches controlled other industries—fine wines, luxury cars, even the exotic-animal trade—but Mada Vittora oversaw the jewel division of Paris, the most lucrative. Diamonds hadn't been worth a second glance before some ancient Haute queen centuries ago had taken a fleeting liking to their sparkle. But they were hard to extract, and the Royals too superior for manual labor, so she'd had Goblins whisper in the Pretties' ears that *they* wanted jewels, and thus the modern mining industry began. Not for iron, not for copper (those came as fortunate but accidental discoveries later, and the Royals were more than happy to siphon off the benefits), but to suit one queen's whim.

The same with art, architecture, airplanes. The Royals whispered in Pretties' ears, and then they took for themselves the best of what the Pretties produced. All the Pretties in the world worked for the Haute in one way or another. They just didn't know it. And to justify such a system? The Royals called themselves the silent monarchy, gods to a world of children who couldn't be trusted to keep their own politics and technology and economies in balance without the secret hands of benevolent rulers.

The couple disappeared around the corner. Anouk leaned as far as she dared over the cresting, but even from this height, she couldn't see the fountain at the end of Rue des Amants. She sighed.

"It's ironic," Beau said. "Pretties walk by every day in search of fake magic from that wishing fountain and have no idea there's real magic under this roof." He glanced down at Anouk. "Sit with me? Easy there. Careful."

They cautiously settled on the edge of the roof, legs through the wrought-iron cresting. She rested her head on Beau's shoulder.

A nice night, but Luc should have been there. It was always the three of them together, the members of the house staff: Beau, Luc, Anouk. "I miss him," she said.

Beau cleared his throat as though he too felt Luc's absence. "I think . . ." He stopped, then started again. "I think . . . never mind."

Anouk's left hand clutched her glass. Her other hand went to her shoes, and she toyed with the laces, the pretty bow. "You think Mada Vittora has something to do with his disappearance, don't you?"

He didn't answer right away. "We're bound to her as long as she has our pelts locked in that closet. Luc couldn't have run off any more than you or I could. We aren't like the Pretties out there. We can't come and go as we please. She made us and she owns us."

It was true. Cricket had once tried to run away with a Pretty surfer boy from Portugal, and as soon as Mada Vittora had learned of it, she'd gone to the library with the pelts and a tonic of rose-infused blood, and the next day, mystifyingly, Cricket was back in Paris and fuming.

Anouk took a shaky sip of scotch. "You don't think she . . . would have killed Luc?"

"Killed? No." He paused. "She couldn't. The magic would backfire on her."

"You mean the vitae echo."

He nodded. "Besides, if she was going to kill one of us, it would be Cricket or me. We're the ones she can't stand. Luc's always been loyal; he was her first." His face darkened. "But beasties don't just disappear."

Anouk gazed into the syrupy remains in her glass, feeling queasy.

Luc was much more than a gardener to them. He was the closest thing they had to a leader in their misfit household; he was the scholar, the storyteller, the big brother who always knew what to do. The one to resolve the various disagreements that sprang up between them and clean up their messes. Every week, it seemed he was sewing up Hunter Black's latest wounds or sneaking Cricket out the back door before Viggo saw her and got that famished haunt to his eyes. Luc was the light they sought out when things grew dark, there to wipe away tears or tend to scrapes, to sit on the edge of the bed and tell them stories of magical places and beautiful people.

Beau wrapped an arm around Anouk's waist. "Listen, cabbage, I don't think Luc is dead. Mada Vittora has her reasons for everything. Maybe she's sent him off on a mission she wants to keep secret." He lowered his voice. "But just the same, if you think you can do it without risking getting caught, spy on the house. Find clues about Luc. Keep an eye out for anything odd while you're cleaning. Residue from one of her tricks. A note she might have scrawled and thrown away."

She looked at him in surprise. Spy on their mistress? She downed the remains of her scotch and reached for the half-full bottle to pour herself some more.

He glanced at the glass shaking in her hand. "Give me that before you drink too much and fall off the roof."

She rolled her eyes. "You're my brother, Beau, not my nanny."

Beau winced as he scratched at the corner of his jaw. "I wish you wouldn't call me that."

"Nanny?"

"*Brother.*" His hand fell. "It isn't true, not even remotely. We aren't related. Not through blood, not through adoption. We're just . . . just two people who live and work together."

"But that's what you're like to me. You and Luc and even Hunter Black. And Cricket's like a sister. We're family, the five of us." She'd always liked that word, *family*.

He drew in a long breath through his nose, not answering.

"You'd rather I called you coworker? Housemate?" She knocked her shoulder teasingly against him and then snatched the bottle out of his hands and held it up in accusation. "Stealer of expensive scotch?"

Now it was his turn to give her a hard look. He leaned over and slowly took the bottle out of her hand. "You could just call me Beau."

His voice had dropped. The scotch was doing dizzy, heady things to her. Up here, on the roof, it felt almost magically private, as though outside of Mada Vittora's walls they could say anything, be anything. His lips were whisper-close, his breath earthy and sweet from the drink.

He cupped her face in his palm. "Anouk." His thumb brushed over the apple of her cheek, smelling faintly of his driving gloves.

"Yes?" she whispered.

And then he suddenly grinned. "You've soot on your face." He swiped his thumb over her cheek again; it came away with a black stain.

She wiped at her face. "Again with the dust!"

"Maybe we've had it wrong this whole time," he said in mock seriousness. "Maybe Mada Vittora made the rest of us from dogs and cats and birds but you from a dust bunny."

She smeared a sooty finger down his nose. "She probably made *you* from a monkey."

He threw an arm around her shoulder and pulled her close.

She closed her eyes. Her head spun from the scotch. Luc was gone, and if she was being honest, she knew her mistress probably *was* responsible. Mada Vittora, who just moments ago had tied her shoes like a mother would for a daughter.

"What now?" she whispered.

If he'd been there, Luc would have known what to do. Luc always knew what to do. Without him, she felt lost.

Beau pulled back. "Now?" He held up the burlap sack. "Now we catch some crows for a dinner party."

Her face broke into a smile.

Chapter 3

THAT NIGHT, ANOUK CURLED up in her small bed in the turret bedroom. Pasted to her walls were playbills and magazine covers, things Beau had found in the Pretty World and brought back to her. On her dresser was her collection of more found Pretty objects: a single baby shoe, a scratched-off lottery ticket, a man's chestnut-colored toupee. Simple things that were magical in their utter lack of magic. What could be more impractical than a shoe for a newborn incapable of steps? The improbable hopes of million-to-one odds? The charming lie of a full head of hair? The playbill above her bed showed a picture of a prince and a princess, and most nights she'd sigh contentedly as she dreamed of their dashing adventures.

But not tonight. Tonight she dreamed of birds with gold-tipped wings that spoke with human voices, their eyes not inky black but green and hazel and blue, the eyes of children. She woke up shivering.

At dawn, she put on a fresh apron, climbed the stairs to Luc's attic workrooms, and grimaced as she slaughtered and plucked the Corpus crows, her dream still too fresh; it was as though she were plucking fingernails off children.

The flight and tail feathers went into a linen bag to be used later for one of Mada Vittora's tricks. The wispy gray down feathers just made a mess all over Luc's big wooden worktable. His presence in the room was everywhere: in the placement of the knives and mortars and pestles; in the chair's indentation that fit his body, not hers; in a half-cut onion, now shriveled. She smiled as she brushed away a dry husk of onion skin. Luc must have been making more invisible ink —onion, lemon juice, a pinch of bitter herbs. Not long after she'd become a human girl, she'd made a mistake—too much bleach in the laundry—and Mada Vittora had banished her to her turret room for a week with no contact from the others, no conversations, no notes, and Anouk had thought she would go mad. But Luc had slipped perfectly innocent blank pages under her bedroom door, along with a fresh candle and matches, on the pretext that she should write the Mada a note of apology. Only . . . the pages smelled strange, like citrus and onion. When Anouk lit the candle to peer more closely at the paper, the heat from the flame made words bloom across the parchment.

Too bad you didn't make the mistake of pouring that bleach in her shampoo instead. We could have called her the Bald Witch.

A smile had cracked across her face. With those words alone, Luc had made everything okay.

But where was he now, with his secret notes and silly jokes?

She grabbed the last crow and plucked a handful of feathers. She'd asked Hunter Black that morning if he would kill the crows, but he had only scowled and told her to do her own dirty work. As if killing weren't the very task he'd been made for. Magic Is Life; Life Is Magic. The motto of the Haute. In order to do their tricks and whispers, members of the Haute needed to take life; the more complex, the better. The magic from a single Pretty life could theoretically sustain a witch for a year. But magic was tricky. Take a life, and the spell had a way of

23

turning on its caster, causing not outright death, but death in slow little pieces: a liver turned to stone, a heart into wood. It was called the vitae echo. And so Mada Vittora, like all the witches, consumed flowers, herbs, feathers, and blood to work her tricks—smaller pieces of life that carried little or no echo. And if she needed to kill any enemies? Well, beasties couldn't use magic, but they *could* use knives.

It was a useful loophole.

Anouk wiped her forehead with her sleeve and then shook out her apron and watched the downy feathers float away into the air, some catching in the light, hanging suspended as though time were frozen. She used Luc's paring knife to cut out the crows' pink-fleshed breasts, then arranged them in a glass baking dish and rubbed in oregano, rosemary, and sage from Luc's stores.

Ready to pop in the oven downstairs.

She ran a cloth over Luc's table, wiping it clean, then wrapped the carcasses in old newspaper, clutched the bundle under her arm, and picked up the dish.

She padded downstairs and stopped at the landing. Listening. The ticking of the grandfather clock. Otherwise, no footsteps, no conversations. She glanced over her shoulder, Beau's words in her ears. *Spy on the house. Find clues about Luc.*

If any clues were to be found, she knew where to look: the scrying room. But it wasn't as easy as it sounded. The scrying room had an irritating way of moving around the townhouse, appearing behind different doors at different times. Once she'd found it in the guest bathroom. Another time, in the upstairs linen closet.

She walked down the hall, nudged the first bedroom door open with her foot, and looked in, her heart pounding, but it was still just a bedroom, untouched since the last time she'd cleaned it. The next two bedrooms too. The final door was open a few inches. She peeked inside.

It smelled musty, not like a bedroom at all. The reek of old feathers and flesh. There was a chattering of machinery.

Voilà—she'd found it.

She slipped inside, set down the baking dish, and closed the door behind her. She'd only ever glimpsed the scrying room from a distance, catching flashes of Luc's curved back as he leaned over the desk, headphones on his ears, pencil in hand. This had been Luc's job when he wasn't tending roses—not just a gardener, but a spy.

The contraption that took up the entire rear wall of the scrying room was a type of switchboard, only this switchboard wasn't used for two-way communication but for spying: a scryboard. Its operator would connect wires to specific slots in order to listen in covertly on the network of whispers that came from crows and, sometimes, even lowly insects like dragonflies. Scryboards were illegal in the Haute, of course—hence the reason why Mada Vittora had charmed it to keep changing locations around the house —but that didn't mean that every witch didn't have one hidden away somewhere.

Anouk took a step closer, apprehensive. Unlike the Pretties' switchboards made of wood and wire, Luc's scryboard was conjured out of more . . . *organic* materials. The glossy black wires that connected to different hookups were actually dark, ropy veins. A few malformed black feathers grew out of a row of gears near the top. The whole switchboard seemed to be pulsing slightly. In. Out. *Breathing.* Not alive, exactly, but not entirely lifeless either.

She sat on the stool, blowing dust off the log of meticulous notes that Luc kept, the record of who he'd been spying on and what he'd overheard. But that was only the official record he kept for Mada Vittora. He had *another* log. A secret one.

She felt under the desk until her fingers brushed a pad of paper, held there with a latch. She freed the notebook and flipped through the pages, looking for anything that might tell her where he'd disappeared to and why. But it was simply records of conversations he'd overheard—gossip about Goblins, trouble with a former witch's boy turned jewelry broker. She had no idea what she should be looking for. She picked up his headphones, turned them this way and that. Glossy black feathers grew from both earpieces, which were connected by a band of curved bone. She put them over her ears, and when she caught her reflection in the window, she thought they looked like wings on the sides of her head.

For a moment there was only the faint sound of whispering. A man's distorted voice. Nothing she could make out clearly.

. . . These people . . .

She adjusted the headphones.

. . . These people with their little dreams and their little desires . . .

The transmission dissolved into static. She traced the wire. It led to a slot marked *444*, and she flipped through the log until she found the corresponding number. The account for Mada Zola, the Lavender Witch, was 444. Just the night before, Beau had mentioned her banishment. She cocked her head. Who was this man on her wires now, whispering about dreams?

In the official logbook, there were no records for account 444. But in the secret log, Luc had scrawled this:

8 August   *Zola speaking to a man at her estate. A disgraced Royal? Her witch's boy?*
9 August   *Zola speaking to same man again. A partner of some sort. Romantic? Scheming how to break her banishment and return to Paris. Talk of a <u>queenship.</u>*
11 August   *I personally attempted contact. Requested help. No response. Will attempt again.*

Anouk felt a chill. Luc had not only listened in on the Lavender Witch privately—he'd tried to contact her.

Why?

She heard a stair creak downstairs and slammed the log closed, then took off the feathered headphones. She hurried down the hall with the baking dish of crows, headed for the kitchen stairs.

"Anouk," a voice called. "Stop."

She winced. It was Viggo. She'd just walked by his bedroom. She went back and pushed his door open a few more inches. Viggo looked up from his armchair, meeting her eyes. A tube snaked into his left arm's inner elbow, connecting him to a glass pump that was filling steadily with blood, drop by drop. She quickly looked down; he hated for anyone to watch him during a blood harvest.

"Did you want something, Viggo? Water? Tea?" He shouldn't even have been home now. He harvested on Fridays, and it was only Wednesday.

"Come here."

She kept her eyes lowered as she took a step into the bedroom. Viggo wasn't Mada Vittora's real son, of course. Witches didn't have children. The exact reason why was murky in Anouk's mind, but she knew it had to do with the vitae echo: withered wombs, organs turned to stone, nasty things that came with the high cost of doing magic. In any case, witches had no use for children. It was blood they were after. Fresh young blood in copious amounts. Almost every trick and whisper demanded it. And so each witch adopted or stole a baby boy — only ever a boy — to raise. A lifetime of blood siphoned off, pint by pint, in exchange for an upbringing fit for a prince.

Viggo's hand tensed and released, tensed and released. The blood pumped steadily. "Have you seen Cricket recently?"

She shook her head quickly, relieved at such a simple question. "She hasn't come by the house in a few weeks. Your mother's kept her busy with tasks around the city. Thieving books for the library, I think. The last time I saw her was at the Goblin gathering."

Viggo kept pumping his fist.

"Did she say anything about me?"

Anouk paused.

Cricket had had plenty to say about Viggo at the Goblin gathering, all of it heavily laden with profanity. Something about a closet, Viggo making an unwanted confession, breathy whispers of *You're beautiful* and *I hate that I love you*, though he'd never admit to doing it, of course. Viggo was human and young and handsome and richer than a god. Lusting after a beastie girl was beneath him, even one with cinnamon curls and rosebud lips and an easy strut that turned heads as if by magic. Luckily Cricket was a thief with quick reflexes and a quicker wit; she'd gotten back to a roomful of Goblins before his hands had strayed too far.

Maybe being beautiful was a curse, Anouk thought. Beautiful got you cornered in closets with pawing witch's boys. While cleaning the parlor once, she'd overheard two Goblin girls in the next room debating whether Anouk was pretty or ugly. *Pretty: her heart-shaped face. Ugly: the unfortunate nose. Pretty: long tawny hair, though it was often a mess. Ugly: the heavy set of her jaw.*

Ugly, they had ultimately decided.

She'd always been self-conscious about her jaw. It gave her the look of some half-starved creature, she knew, a look that, every time she glanced in a mirror, she feared betrayed her deepest secret:

Animal. Creature. *Thing.*

An involuntary shiver ran down her spine. "No," Anouk told Viggo. "She didn't say anything else."

Viggo grumbled in the armchair. His face was pale; the jar of blood was nearly full. He'd be in a foul temper the rest of the day, moody and drained.

"I want you to send her a message. Tell her my mother wants her here tonight to help with the dinner party."

"But the Mada didn't say—"

"*Tell* her."

Anouk's jaw clamped tight. Mada Vittora possessed their pelts, not Viggo. And yet refusing him was dangerous. One word to his mother, and Anouk might be locked in the cellar for days.

"I will," she said quietly.

She escaped back to the hallway, only then realizing she was still holding the tray of herbed crow breasts and the paper-wrapped carcasses clutched under one arm. She tossed the bird entrails out into the courtyard, calling to the stray cats, trying to entice them. But they never came close.

Anouk exchanged her dirty apron for a fresh one and tied her hair back in a ribbon. She started with the feather duster, humming through each room on all seven stories, and then took the mop and polish to the ballroom floor. She'd read about contraptions the Pretties used, vacuum cleaners and blenders and something called a Mr. Coffee, but those things used electricity, and electricity interfered with Mada Vittora's magic.

The afternoon passed in a cloud of dust motes and wood polish. Only once did Anouk pause; while cleaning the windows, she stopped to gaze out at the city beyond and remember the magic of being on the roof last night with Beau.

She heard Beau and Mada Vittora return sometime in the late afternoon while she was buried under mountains of potatoes and carrots, the cookbook splayed open, apron streaked with peels.

Beau came in, carrying a cardboard box. "Cupcakes from Coquelicot. Lady Metham adores them." He bent over the pot bubbling on the stove, sniffing. "Hot as hellfire in here. Is this a bouillabaisse?"

"Yes. And scamper off, I'm running behind. They'll be here in an hour." It was an old kitchen with poor ventilation, and steam made her hair cling to her face. She pushed it back as she attacked the pile of carrots.

Instead of leaving, he leaned in. "Were you able to find out anything about Luc?"

She paused, knife in hand. "His room was just as he left it. I found the scrying room and a few odd notes in his log, but I don't know what they mean. And then Viggo saw me." She shivered at the memory of the snaking tubes. "He was doing a blood harvest."

"On a Wednesday?" Beau's face darkened. "He harvested twice last week too. Why does the Mada need that much blood?"

They heard footsteps in the hall. Anouk jerked her head toward the door. "You should go. I'll keep looking."

"You'll be careful?"

She hesitated, then nodded.

Beau brushed a curl off her forehead and sauntered out, unbuttoning his chauffeur's uniform. She finished the bouillabaisse and portioned it into teacups with rosemary woven around the handles; for the second course, she'd have a summer salad, for the third, the Corpus crow breasts stuffed with Gruyère and plum, and then the cupcakes and coffee. She laid out the table settings, polished the silver wearing white gloves to avoid leaving fingerprints, and was lighting the candles just as the doorbell rang.

"Anouk, the door!" Mada Vittora called from one of the upper stories.

"Yes, Mada!"

She hurried to light the final few candles, took one last look at the ballroom table, and grinned at the beautiful spread. She ran downstairs, expecting Lord and Lady Metham. She hadn't ever met them but felt as though she had; she'd often seen them, their hair threaded through with glittering silver, their clothes gauzy as spider's silk. Their faces had watched her cleaning daily from the portrait above the drawing-room fireplace. Not just watched her—*spied* on her. The portrait was enchanted. There were real eyes behind those painted ones, though Anouk knew chances were slim that they'd ever bother to spy on a maid when they had hundreds of Goblins and witches and Pretty associates throughout France to keep an eye on. It was a requirement that every magic handler in Europe hang the portrait of the Shadow Royals in the most prominent room of the house. To remind them all of whom they served within the Haute. And to ensure no secret meetings escaped the Royals' ever-watching eyes.

She opened the door and paused, surprised. It wasn't the Methams. A young man waited on the steps, his back to her, looking down at the sad little tree in the front garden.

He wore jeans and a jacket with the collar pulled up against the night breeze, a wool scarf around his neck, and a hat that hid his hair. For a second, hope pulled taut in Anouk's chest. Luc had a hat like that.

He turned.

Pale skin, not Luc's black-brown complexion. It wasn't him.

The young man tugged off the hat. His hair was honey colored, slightly mussed as though he'd combed his fingers through it distractedly.

He wasn't wearing gossamer silks. There was no sign of silver in his hair. But he had the same dark eyes that had watched her from the portrait while she swept and polished the drawing room. His was the devastatingly handsome face of the figure in the very center, flanked by Lord and Lady Metham and the other lesser Royals, a golden crown of briars resting on his perfect hair. Once, she'd even hesitantly dusted some fuzz off his pale painted face, half afraid his beautiful mouth might come alive and bite her.

Now his eyes caught the light, flashing dark tapeta like an animal at night.

"Hello." His voice was deep and not at all unpleasant. "I take it I'm at the right house."

Anouk found she couldn't quite speak.

She hadn't expected the dazzling Prince Rennar ever to wear jeans —or to be standing on her doorstep.

Chapter 4

PRINCE RENNAR'S GAZE DROPPED to Anouk's midsection, and with a blush, she realized she was thoroughly sprinkled with flour. She took a step back, holding the door open with lowered eyes.

He looked at her expectantly. It took her a moment to remember that the house's ancient protection spells required an invitation every time the Royals wanted to enter.

"Your Highness, yes. Welcome to Mada Vittora's home. Please, come in."

He stepped in, uncoiling his scarf, taking in the grand foyer with mild interest. But then his eyes slid back to her with the same eyeshine that sometimes reflected in the drawing-room portrait. It always gave her that neck-crawling feeling of being watched.

She reached back now, rubbing her neck. Came away with an errant carrot peel.

"So it's true." He regarded her with an odd expression. "Vittora does have beasties serving her."

His eyes were too sharp, too piercing, as though they could see through her skin to the bones beneath.

She wasn't sure how to answer this, so she stuttered, "May I . . . take your coat?"

He shrugged out of his jacket and laid it over her waiting hands, but before she could turn to the closet, he grabbed her wrist, quick and firm.

He leaned in.

"You aren't made for sweeping floors, little beastie," he said quietly, not unkindly. "Don't you know that?"

She paused, caught by his words. What did he mean? That's *why* she'd been made, to sweep the floors. The question was on her lips, tickling her tongue, but how did one question a prince? Especially one so handsome?

The sharp click of heels on the stairs interrupted her. She jerked upright and hung up the coat quickly, guiltily, as Mada Vittora swept down the stairs. Prince Rennar was slower to straighten.

"Vittora."

"Rennar." Mada Vittora's smile was icy. "I didn't realize you'd be joining us."

"We have much to discuss, do we not?"

Mada Vittora extended her hand. "Yes. Over wine."

The prince took her hand with the slightest nod, a nod that said that even though he was in her house, even though he appeared decades younger than her, he was undeniably her master. He followed her down the hall, only once looking back over his shoulder at Anouk and her flour-dusted apron.

A sharp voice spoke behind her. "Are you dimwitted, girl, or are you going to invite me in?"

Anouk jumped.

Lady Metham stood on the front steps. Her silver hair was pulled back into a wild twist, and she wore a pale gray gown; it looked like a thunderstorm had landed on the doorstep. Lord Metham was beside her, thin and bespectacled, along with a young woman of Asian descent with short-cropped hair whom he addressed as Countess Quine. Their lips bore the lingering stain of colorful powder, a mixture of finely ground flowers, herbs, dried blood, and butterfly wings made fresh daily by the powdersmiths in the basement of Castle Ides. Around each one's neck hung a glass vial of the mixture. Powder was highly potent, reserved only for the Royals; witches made do with less refined elixirs concocted from their own stores of fresh flowers and herbs. In a pinch, even a plain rose or thorn or housefly swallowed whole could fuel a small trick if more effective means were out of reach.

Anouk invited them in and led them to the salon, where Mada Vittora and Viggo waited and then served canapés and champagne. Not even the drinks washed away the pale blue and green flush of powder on Lady Metham's lips or the pink stain on Countess Quine's tongue, and Anouk wondered what magic they had wrought that day. Prince Rennar's lips weren't stained at all; the vial of powder around his neck was full. She couldn't help but steal glances at him. What had his earlier words meant?

As she filled Viggo's glass with water, he snarled quietly, "I told you to tell Cricket to come."

Anouk spilled the water, then hurried to clean it up with a corner of her apron. She glanced over her shoulder at Mada Vittora and the Royals, who were speaking in low voices by the fireplace.

"I did," Anouk said. "I left a message in Wormly's box, but he wrote back that Cricket had gone to Dordogne on some of the Mada's business. She won't be back for a few days. I tried, Viggo."

But she hadn't. Not at all. Wormly was a Goblin who carried messages for Mada Vittora; Anouk had seen him earlier that day and had only waved from the window. She wasn't about to put Cricket in such a messy situation. As far as she knew, Cricket was fast asleep in bed at the moment and dreaming something sweet.

Viggo's eyes narrowed, as though he sensed the lie.

Mada Vittora clapped her hands and motioned to the ballroom. "Shall we dine?" Her eyes snapped to Anouk and she gave a tight jerk of her head. Anouk ran to the ballroom and pulled out a chair for each of them. Prince Rennar. Lord and Lady Metham. Countess Quine. And at the head of the table, Mada Vittora, whose eyes went to Anouk's apron.

"Change that dirty apron," she hissed. "You're an embarrassment. Oh, never mind, just stay out of the way altogether. We can serve ourselves."

Hot blood burned in Anouk's cheeks. She quickly collected the canapé plates from the salon and dashed off toward the kitchen as Lady Metham proposed a toast.

"To the new territories within the Haute," Lady Metham said. "The Lavender Witch will be furious out there in her flower fortress."

"Let her be," Mada Vittora said evenly.

Glasses clinked.

Anouk returned to the kitchen laden with the soiled plates, still feeling the sting of having displeased her mistress. Beau was perched on a stool, scraping the mixing bowl and licking the spoon.

"I envy them," he said, pointing the spoon toward the ballroom. "Why don't you cook for me like this?"

She put down the dishes and leaned on the counter, closing her eyes, her cheeks still warm.

Beau pushed back his stool and stood. His hand pressed against her back. "What's wrong, cabbage?"

She shook her head. "Nothing." She swallowed down the unsettling bile in her throat. "Prince Rennar is here."

Beau whistled, low and impressed.

She hesitated. "He looked at me like he'd never seen a beastie before. He said I shouldn't be sweeping her floors."

Beau gave the spoon another lick. "What should you be doing, then? The laundry?"

Anouk took the spoon from him and tapped it against her lips, worried. "I don't think that's what he meant. He said it as though I shouldn't be serving her at all." The sugary smell of compote clung to her nose, turning her stomach, and she lobbed the spoon into the sudsy sink. Music started from somewhere deeper in the house, the high strains of a violin. Viggo must be playing. Sounds of clapping came from the ballroom.

"They're dancing," Anouk said.

"They're drunk," Beau answered.

Anouk picked up the plates and dumped them into the sink. She tugged on yellow dish gloves distractedly. Could Luc's disappearance be part of this territory war between the witches? She reached for the soap and a dishrag, but Beau got to the soap first and set it aside.

"Dance with me," he said.

She gave him an impatient look, holding up the dripping dish gloves. "I'm a mess."

"You always are." He wrapped one of his hands around her gloved

38

one. "Come on, I know that look. You'll worry all night over this. You deserve a break."

He held up their hands as though ready to dance. Soapy water ran down his arm, soaking his shirt cuff, but he didn't seem to mind. The tempo of the violin music picked up; Viggo must have been in a good mood. Laughter came from the ballroom.

Anouk rested one hand on his shoulder and sighed. "Go on, then. Show me how."

He grinned. "Step back. Like this. There. Now forward."

She tried to follow his movements, leaving damp footprints on the kitchen tiles. He led her in a clumsy circle around the big oak table, counting, "*One*-two-three-four, *one*-two-three-four." The floor was slick from the water dripping from her dish gloves. Soap bubbles popped in the sink.

"When did you learn how to dance?" she asked.

He spun her in a circle by the oven. "I don't. Know how to dance, I mean. I'm making it up as I go along. Now forward. To your left. Step back." He swept her around the kitchen, past the dirty dishes and the pantry filled with jams and pickled meats. "Twirl. Bow. Now step to the right."

"Beau, you're ridiculous!" She laughed.

He pulled her close, twirling her by the icebox. His shirt was wet to the elbows now. The both of them were a mess, and she felt that same giddiness that she had on the roof, tipsy just from being in his arms, and—

He stepped on her toes.

"Oh!" She grimaced as she pulled her hands from his and clutched at her foot.

"Merde. Sorry about that. Let's see the damage." He lifted her by the waist, set her down on the kitchen table, and knelt to inspect her foot. Her left big toe was red and bore the imprint of his shoe tread, but it wasn't bleeding. He ran his thumb over it gently. "No permanent harm, I think." He paused. "I'd hate for you to have lost another one."

He took her right foot in his other hand and, holding both her feet, ran his thumbs gently over the scars where her little toes had been. It had been six months. Nearly healed.

"One, two, three, four," he said quietly, counting the remaining toes on each foot.

He didn't let go of her feet. His hair was disheveled from dancing and from the steam from the stove. She touched her own. It had fallen out of the ribbon.

"Anouk." Beau's hands tightened over her feet, kneading slightly.

She tugged her feet out of his grasp, embarrassed by the scars and the missing toes and the questions Beau always raised about them. "Don't start, Beau."

She climbed off the table.

"Take these off," he said suddenly, tugging at the dish gloves. "I want to hold your hand. Really dance."

"But we don't know how."

"It doesn't matter."

She pulled off the dish gloves—at least he'd dropped the subject of her toes. "And the apron," he said, digging his fingers into the fabric at her waist. "I hate them, all these stupid things she makes you wear. Dressing you up like a doll." His voice had grown low.

"Beau, are you all right?"

"Take it off," he said, pulling at the ribbons behind her neck. "You

aren't some plaything. It isn't okay, her ordering you around. Prince
Rennar was right. You shouldn't be sweeping her floors."

"But it's my job."

"You get paid for a job. A job with no pay is called slavery." He
tugged at the apron.

"Beau, what's gotten into you? The Mada is . . . she's like our . . ."

"She's not our mother," he said flatly.

The music from the ballroom stopped abruptly. For a moment
the house was silent. No laughter, no clinking glasses, only the slowly
bursting soap bubbles in the sink.

"Anouk!" Mada Vittora suddenly called. "More wine!"

Anouk gave Beau a hard look as she pushed his hands off her
shoulders, then retied the bow of her apron. She smoothed her hands
over it, pulled back her hair, and carried the wine decanter to the ballroom. They had cleared the table, throwing napkins on the floor and
haphazardly stacking the rest of the dirty dishes, and now they leaned
over a map of the city that was unrolled on the table. Prince Rennar
held a dagger over the map, speaking in a low whisper as he made
small, precise cuts. Anouk kept her eyes averted, but she glimpsed
silver powder on his lips. What magic were they doing now?

As she poured the wine, she tried not to make it obvious she was
listening. Rennar was speaking the language of magic: the Selentium
Vox, the Silent Tongue. Members of the Haute spent lifetimes mas-
tering it. Mada Vittora spoke it better than most. The townhouse
library was filled with rare handwritten volumes of Selentium Vox
grammar and vocabulary, books that Anouk borrowed and pored
over at night so that she would be ready to help her mistress if the
time ever came. And it had, once. There had been an evening over

41

the summer when Mada Vittora had guzzled too many limoncello tonics and couldn't remember the words to a love spell she'd meant to cast on some famous Pretty movie star. Anouk had snuck into the library and sorted through the volumes using the bits and pieces of Selentium Vox she'd taught herself until she'd found the right book. She left it out on the bistro table in the courtyard, open to the correct spell; Mada Vittora discovered it and, in her tipsy state, assumed she'd found the spell herself.

When Anouk went back to the kitchen, Beau was gone. Probably sulking in his room on the far side of the courtyard. Was it her fault he and Mada Vittora hadn't ever gotten along? The Mada had given them life. *Human* life. Words to speak their thoughts, hands to do work, clothes to dress themselves, and all the other gifts that came with being human, like music and laughter and fairy tales, things Anouk clung to like precious jewels.

Before Mada Vittora—well, that was only darkness. It frightened Anouk to think about those days. She knew what she had been: *animal.* She didn't know what type—none of them knew—but what did it matter? Animal was animal. Mangy and hungry. Alone and vulnerable. She *knew* she'd been this, but she didn't remember. All she had was a hazy feeling of dread, like trying to rush home before a winter storm strikes, and that's how she'd given her past a name: *Dark thing. Cold place.* It made her first memory all the sweeter: Roses and thyme. Waking on the attic floor with all the rest of them looking down at her. Beau. Cricket. Hunter Black. Luc, the eldest, who looked twenty but had been human for only five years. He'd wrapped a blanket around her and stroked her hair and said, *It will all be well, you're safe now, it's scary now but you'll learn.* A puddle of blood had stained the floor beneath her. Viggo's, though she hadn't known it at the time.

And the Mada. She had been there too, of course, perfumed by the trick's marjoram and wormwood and foxglove, the words of the Selentium Vox whisper still on her lips. When her eyes had found Anouk's, she had tilted her head and smiled.

This one's sweet, isn't she?

Anouk was lost in the memory, elbow-deep in cleaning the dishes, when she heard the click-click of heels on the kitchen floor. Mada Vittora came tottering in, drunk, her cheeks flushed unbecomingly.

Anouk pulled off her gloves. "Is dinner over? Shall I fetch the Royals' coats?"

Mada Vittora waved vaguely. The top button of her blouse had come loose and was dangling. "Viggo's seeing them out. He's going to Castle Ides with them to handle the final paperwork."

An image flashed in Anouk's head of Prince Rennar and she felt a stab of regret that she wouldn't see him again. Why did she care? Honestly, she should be relieved that he and the other Royals were gone. But there had been something about the way he had looked at her so keenly, as though he knew something that she didn't.

"It was a good party, I hope?" Anouk asked.

Mada Vittora took a step and slipped on the soapy water. She cursed and kicked off her heels. Her bare toes were surprisingly pale, like Anouk's. Except, of course, that she had all ten.

"Better than we dreamed." Her eyes glistened with the alcohol. "Big things are going to happen. Just wait and see."

"Oh . . . good." Anouk had been referring to the food.

Mada Vittora saw the unraveling button and frowned. *"Attash betit . . . betit . . . betit . . ."* She couldn't recall the last word of the repair trick.

Anouk feigned a cough. *"Truk."*

Mada Vittora's watery eyes snapped to her. A momentary suspicion wavered in her look, but it was soon drowned out by a tipsy hiccup, and she blinked and flicked at the little button. "Ah, I remember now. *Attash betit truk.*"

The button obediently stitched itself back to the blouse.

A flush of pride warmed Anouk's cheeks. To her surprise, the witch suddenly pressed a kiss against Anouk's forehead. "My sweet girl. My darling girl. *Ma galuk spirn.*" She wobbled away, leaving the heels.

My clever girl. That was what she'd said in the Silent Tongue.

Anouk brushed her fingers against her forehead, the kiss still damp. Her heart was lighter as she finished washing the dishes, dried them, and put them away. She soaked the big roasting pan in the sink to scour first thing in the morning. She cleared the rest of the dishes from the empty ballroom and blew out the candles. She swept the floor and closed the curtains over the tall windows. The moon was high outside. It had to be close to midnight.

A thump sounded from upstairs.

She dropped the broom, which clattered to the floor, and picked it back up in a hurry.

She listened.

No footsteps. No voices calling for her to come clean up a broken vase or fallen books. But something about the silence ate at her.

"Mada?" she called up the stairs. "Is everything all right?"

No answer.

"Viggo?"

But no, he had left with the Royals, and he would have taken Hunter Black with him. They wouldn't be back until the morning. She went to the window and pushed aside the drapes. The black Rolls-Royce was parked out front, as was Hunter Black's gunmetal-gray motorcycle. They must have gone to Castle Ides in the Royals' car.

Now the silence gnashed at her with big, jagged teeth. With a start, she realized the clock above the drawing-room fireplace had stopped. She tapped its face. Nothing. She'd have to reset it.

Her eyes trailed up to the portrait of the Shadow Royals, pulled by some unavoidable force, and she shivered. Were they watching even now? She went to the salon to check the time on the grandfather clock so she could reset the mantel one, but it had stopped too. A chill started at the base of her spine. She checked the hall clock, and the one in the kitchen, and the one on the stairs landing.

Every clock in the house had stopped at exactly midnight.

The chill grew. What was this dark magic? Not like any trick or whisper she had ever seen. The coldness spread up her back as she made her way up the stairs. She realized distractedly that she still clutched the broom in one hand.

"Mada?"

Empty bedrooms, empty halls. She double-checked Viggo's room and the guest room Hunter Black used while he was in town to make sure they'd really left. All empty. She clutched the broom like a weapon, ready to strike. It wasn't until the sixth floor, Mada Vittora's grand bedroom, that she heard the scramble of someone's jagged breath.

"Hello?"

She brandished the broom handle but then let her arms fall in surprise. "Beau?"

He was crouched on the Persian rug at the foot of the bed. The closet door was open. The dressing table's chair was overturned. Bright red wine had spilled and was soaking into the carpet, and Anouk tsked reflexively. The hardest stains to get out.

She set the broom aside uncertainly. "What are you doing in here? Where's Mada Vittora?"

His hair was messy. His chest rose and fell quickly. He met her eyes with a gaze like a caught animal's, a look she'd never seen on his face before, not even the time that Hunter Black had cornered him in the garage and threatened to cut out his tongue if he ever called Viggo a *salaud* again.

"Anouk. Oh God."

The stain wasn't red wine, she realized.

Her mouth went very dry.

Blood.

But whose blood?

Then she saw the knife in Beau's hand.

Chapter 5

THE ROOM SEEMED to spin. Time was doing strange things, as though when every clock in the house stopped, time itself had frozen.

"Beau?"

He stood. There was blood on his hands and staining the front of his white chauffeur's shirt. On the floor beside him, half hidden behind the bed, a pale hand with broken manicured fingernails lay palm up toward the ceiling.

Anouk sank to the floor. She started to call out for help—*Luc!* But his name died on her lips. Luc wasn't here to answer.

"Beau . . . what did you do?"

"It wasn't me." His eyes were wide. "I found her like this a moment ago. I was carrying up her shopping bags from Galeries Lafayette." He pointed the knife vaguely at some packages that had been dropped in a hurry, tissue-paper-wrapped treasures spilling out onto the floor. "I just came in and saw her like this . . . didn't know what to do . . . tried to see if she was still alive . . ."

Anouk's eyes went to the knife in his fist. As if just then realizing how bad it looked, Beau dropped it.

"She's . . . she's *dead?*"

And then she was crawling across the carpet toward that pale manicured hand, almost as though her body weren't her own, as though the blood in her veins was moving her body for her. Closer. Around the corner of the bed. The hand was connected to an arm, long and pale, and a shoulder covered in a cream-colored blouse that bore telltale red stains, like poppies. Something wet and warm soaked into Anouk's palms and she drew back.

Blood.

"I didn't do it," Beau insisted.

She twisted around to him. "Then who did?"

"I don't know. I thought it was only you here."

"It *is* only me."

He paused. There—for a second she saw it on his face. If it wasn't him, and she was the only other one home, then . . .

Anouk scrambled to her feet.

"Someone else must be here," Beau said quickly. "Hunter Black. Or Viggo."

"Viggo wouldn't kill his own mother!"

But there had been that embarrassed, nasty look on Viggo's face during the blood harvest earlier that day. She shook her head— Viggo was a spoiled *crétin*, but not a murderer. And Hunter Black was the shadow at Viggo's side, the loyal hound at his master's call; he wouldn't draw a knife unless Viggo had commanded it. Besides, they had left hours ago.

"Well, I don't know!" Beau said, pacing.

"We . . . we have to tell someone," Anouk stuttered. But who? The police? No, of course not. That was who the Pretties called in detective novels, but this was a house of magic. She tried to think of what

Luc would have done. "We could send a message to Castle Ides. To the Shadow Royals."

"They'll think it was us!"

"Then . . . we have to tell Viggo."

Beau stopped in his tracks. His eyes were wide, sparking fear. "Are you mad? If Viggo sees me with a knife in my hand and his mother's blood on my clothes, he'll have Hunter Black slaughter me where I stand, and you too, probably, for good measure." He started pacing again, this time kneading his forehead with one hand, unaware that he was getting blood all over his face. "*Merde* . . . we've got to get out of here before they come back . . . go as far away as we can."

"Run? We can't. I can't leave the house." But she realized as soon as she'd spoken how wrong she was.

"Yes, you can," Beau said, as though realizing it at the same time. "You don't have to obey her anymore. She's gone. The pelts!" He spun toward the Mada's closet. "I need a bag."

"What are you doing?"

"Go downstairs. Pack whatever you can, quickly. Anything valuable we can pawn. And some clothes, plain clothes, no aprons, for the love of God. I'll meet you by the car. Do you know where her oubliette is? We can't leave it behind."

Her lips parted. His words were a distant buzz in her ears. She remained fixed on the spot. Mada Vittora was face-down. Anouk couldn't see the lips that had smiled at her so sweetly. The hands that put ribbons in her hair.

She sank to the carpet. "We can't leave her. She made us. Luc would say—"

"He would say that we were slaves, Anouk." His hard-edged voice came from the closet, along with the sound of boxes being torn open, coats being pulled from their hangers. "And now we're not, and our pelts are our own again, and we're getting the hell out of here."

She lowered her hand to her mistress's silken hair and petted it gently. So soft. So pretty. She smelled of rosewater—she must have whispered a love spell on someone that day. Why hadn't she done a foresight trick? If she had, would she have seen her own death? Would she be here now, kissing Anouk's cheek, telling her the house looked so clean and tidy?

"Anouk."

Beau was shaking her. She realized she was cradling her mistress's body to her chest, blood soaking through her clothes to her skin. She blinked, still feeling as though time were permanently broken along with the clocks.

Beau shook her again. He had changed clothes and washed his face—how much time had passed?

"Anouk, find her oubliette. And get clothes and any money you have."

Money? Bills and coins? That was something she had only read about. Her shaking hand went to Luc's franc on the gold chain tucked under her dress collar.

The last time Anouk had seen Luc, he'd been working on the coins in the attic—she hadn't bothered to ask him then what they were for. She'd been desperate, distracted; a few days before, she'd lain down on the Mada's bed after a grueling polish of the windows and accidentally fallen asleep. A Goblin named Crumpet had seen her and threatened to tell the Mada unless Anouk stole the witch's good champagne—the Armand de Brignac!—but she couldn't possibly steal from her mistress. Luc had stopped her frantic pacing. *What's the Goblin's name?* he had asked, and she'd told him about Crumpet. *I'll fix it,* Luc had said. *Easy.* And sure enough, the next day, a gift basket of macaroons showed up at the front door, addressed to Anouk, with an apology from Crumpet.

How had Luc managed it?

"Merde," Beau cursed. "There's no time. We'll have to come back for the oubliette."

He had an old burlap sack by his side stuffed with something thick and pungent, like fur coats. He shook her again. This time, his voice was more direct, his tone lighter in a forced way. "Listen, everything will be all right. We have to go. We aren't abandoning her. Viggo will find her here and do what needs to be done. I know she meant a lot to you. And she loved you, that I'm sure of. The rest of us could go to hell, but you were her special one."

Anouk stroked the silken hair once more. A week ago, a Goblin blackmailing her over a nap had seemed like the end of her world. But this . . . this wasn't scrapes and bruises, a ruined soufflé or a torn hem in need of mending. There was no mending this.

Then Beau's hands were on her shoulders, lifting her to her feet. And then she was stumbling down the stairs, and they were running through the entry hall and . . .

He threw open the door and dashed into the night.

She stopped at the threshold.

She'd never set a toe beyond this point in her entire human life. Twelve months and ten days. One year of cleaning and cooking. One year of all the beauty of being human, of happy memories and teasing and Luc and Beau and licking icing out of the bowl. Had she been alive before that? Yes, in a murky, frightening kind of way, but that life was nothing; it was animal, it was instinct, it was just survival.

The cold place. The dark thing.

Her life now — the bright human one, the only one that mattered — had always been within these walls.

She took a deep breath, stepped across the threshold, pulling herself away from the only home she had ever known, and reached for Beau's waiting hand.

Chapter 6

❧

*S*HE WAS OUTSIDE.

Really outside, not just on a rooftop or standing in the mansion's courtyard. Outside, in the night air, with moonlight on her face and the sidewalk underfoot and a woman in a fur coat across the street staring at her bloodstained apron. Beau was at the rear of the Rolls-Royce, throwing his weight against the bag of pelts—*their* pelts—to stuff it inside the trunk, and there was that sad little tree no one but Luc ever watered, and Luc's tin watering can forgotten beside it. She stumbled into the street and a cab shot by, swerving with a squeal of brakes, the driver yelling something she didn't understand, and then a boy on a bicycle flew past her from the other direction, veering sharply so as not to hit her.

She closed her eyes.

Shut out the cars, the lights, the sights of the city. Thought about Mada Vittora's long fingers tying prim knots in her oxford shoes while teaching her a rhyme about rabbits.

"Anouk!" Beau called.

Her eyes snapped open. He was holding the passenger door for her. Her hand went to the gold chain around her neck, to Luc's coin. Hot tears finally rushed at her eyes, tears that, once they started, she couldn't stop.

Beau wrapped a gentle arm around her waist. His voice was softer. "Anouk, we have to go." He steered her toward the car with urgency.

She whipped her head around, looking back down the street. Through blurred vision, she took in the far end, which she'd never been able to see from the turret window, the fountain so close now, just a hundred meters away . . .

"I'll be right back." She tore out of his embrace and started running.

"Anouk, wait! What are you doing?"

The sidewalk bit at the soles of her bare feet. What *was* she doing? She should stop, turn around, but she didn't. She clutched the coin harder.

The alley was just as she'd always imagined. Ivy twisted in the iron gate. Roses climbing the walls. Worn bricks underfoot. The babble of water eased the thrashing grief inside her, and she felt hope rising in its wake. Was this what the Pretties felt like here? Was this why they came to the fountain, for this swell of hope?

But she stopped short when she saw the statue.

It wasn't a Greek god. It wasn't a mermaid, either. Nothing nearly so lovely.

Gargoyle; the word came to her. She'd seen drawings of them in old books, hideous things that clung to buildings like demons, and a pang of disappointment hit her. How could the Pretties wish on something so ugly?

Her heart was thundering. She was foolish, *foolish!* She started to turn back toward Beau, but then the gargoyle's mouth caught her eye. It had an odd curl to the stone. Almost . . . a smile.

She took a step closer, clutching the coin around her neck.

The gargoyle was small, no bigger than a cat, crouching by the fountain's pool, spitting a thin stream of water from its stone lips. Its forehead was blockish and ugly, but its eyes were bright, almost playful. Maybe this was why the Pretties found it so magical: beauty and ugliness in one.

She tugged the gold chain over her head, took off the franc, and held the coin out with a shaking hand.

She closed her eyes.

"I wish for her soul to be at rest."

The babble of water was a balm against her thumping pulse, but it didn't erase the sweat on her brow, the blood staining her clothes.

She opened her fist.

"No."

She felt a hand close over hers, stopping the franc before it fell. Beau. Her eyes snapped open.

"If you're going to make a wish," he said, "make it for us, not her. That we get out of here with the skin still on our backs." He lowered his voice. "There are scrying crows all over the rooftops. Can't you hear them whispering? They'll spread word of what happened throughout the Haute's scryboards—both the official ones and the illicit ones. We need to *go*."

Despite how confident he sounded, his hand was shaking too. He was more worldly than she was, but only barely. He'd been human for two years to her one. His life had been the house and the car and not much in between.

She turned back to the fountain. "I wish for us, then. To be safe."

She dropped the coin in.

Together, hand in hand, they hurried to the Rolls-Royce. Beau had left the key in the ignition, the doors open. Would their wish count? She'd expected Beau to tell her again that the wishing fountain was just a silly thing the Pretties believed in, but he didn't. Maybe deep down he wanted to believe too.

Beau slid into the driver's side and slammed the door. Anouk raced to the passenger's side. She took in the townhouse in one final, heady glance. It looked different from the outside. Only three stories tall, not the seven that it was inside. Where did the ballroom fit? The attic? The courtyard?

A crow landed on the roof cresting, followed by another, and another. Dozens of them. Twice the size of Corpus crows. Peering down at her with sharp glass eyes. The low murmur of whispers carried on the wind. With a flurry of wings, one landed on the chrome hood ornament just feet from her. The bird lunged, moonlight glinting off its sharp beak. The tip of it caught the flesh of her arm. She gasped at the red scratch.

The bird lunged for her again. She jumped back and grabbed Luc's watering can. Tears in her eyes, anger in her throat, she swung it as hard as she could at the bird, slammed the can into it with an explosion of feathers and white shimmering smoke. She waved the smoke away, coughing.

The crow was gone.

But more cawed from the rooftops. Louder. Sharp talons. Sharp beaks.

"Anouk—"

"I know!"

One dived off the cresting, talons aimed for her eyes. She dropped the watering can, jumped in the car, and slammed the door hard just as the crow collided with the window.

Beau hit the locks.

In the car. Safe. Looking out the windshield at the crows. Another one landed on the hood ornament. One pecked viciously at the door handle. Whispers filtered through the air vents, speaking in no earthly language. "They've seen into the windows," she said. "They know she's dead. They'll follow us."

"Like hell they will."

The car roared to life beneath Beau's hands. Anouk clutched the edges of her seat. She twisted to look behind them. The crows were taking wing and swooping down from the rooftops toward them.

"Beau, go!"

He jammed his foot down on a pedal and the car tore into the street. Anouk struggled to keep sight of the birds. Dozens of them glided on the night air, dodging street signs and trees with ease.

"They're everywhere," Anouk breathed.

Beau glanced in the rearview mirror. His face was grim, but there was a confidence in the way he gripped the wheel. He turned down a one-way street, sharply. Anouk's fingers clutched the leather seat harder. It felt like the car was hurtling impossibly fast. He whipped the wheel again, and there was a squeal of brakes. For a second, the skies were clear, and her grip eased. But then the flock of birds appeared over the nearest roof.

"They're still coming!"

The crows weren't limited by streets and traffic signals. They could soar over trees and houses, travel from one city block to the next in seconds. Beau didn't take his eyes off the street, curving sharply around a closed brasserie on the corner, red-and-white awning folded for the night and chairs stacked beneath it. He pressed harder on the gas and they zipped past closed-up shops, then turned onto a cobblestone alley so narrow the side mirrors nearly scraped the buildings, the car bouncing violently. Anouk's heart clattered in her throat with each jolt. *We'll be okay,* she told herself. *I made a wish. We'll be safe. We'll make it...*

Something thunked on the car roof, and she shrieked. The sound of hundreds of flapping wings came from somewhere overhead, along with sharp caws and chilling low whispers like a swarm of bees. Another sharp beak pecked at the roof of the car hard enough that it dented the metal ceiling.

Beau spun the car onto another street, still accelerating. How fast were they going? Eighty kilometers an hour? Ninety? They sped past a bar with thumping music and flashing lights and writhing dancing bodies. Past a supermarket with all its lights on, blindingly bright. And then the car shuddered and the sound of the road changed. Anouk pressed her face to the glass. A bridge. They were driving over the Seine. From here, she could see a wide stretch of the city. Buildings reflecting in the water, and a tower—a soaring metal structure that curved into a point. Hundreds of tiny lights on it, shimmering like champagne bubbles. Her breath fogged the glass.

The Eiffel Tower.

But as beautiful as it was, a dark shadow on the water stole her gaze—a black cloud of flapping wings.

The car shuddered again when the bridge ended. Other drivers were honking at Beau, yelling out their windows as he whipped around them, darting in and out of traffic. The Eiffel Tower disappeared behind clouds. Beau drove faster, taking sharp turns, and her stomach objected. The world was moving too fast. Too many sounds, too many sights. The smell of Mada Vittora's blood on her clothes.

Anouk leaned forward in the seat, covering her mouth with her hands.

"It'll be okay, Anouk." Beau gripped the wheel tighter. "I can lose them. I was made for this. To drive."

She shut her eyes. As the car raced along the dark streets of Paris, it was all she could do not to throw up on the polished silver trim of the Rolls-Royce's floor.

"You can open your eyes now," Beau said. "We've lost them."

Anouk slowly opened one eye, then the other. The world beyond the windshield had gone strangely dark, not the thin black of night, but closed in by some sort of monstrous scales. A loud but rhythmic *whoosh-whoosh* surrounded them as the scales moved back and forth.

On closer inspection, she saw that the scales were made of the same plastic material as her mop.

"We're in a car wash near the Porte de Clichy," Beau said. "We have seven, maybe eight minutes until the rinse cycles are done." He gave a shrug. "I couldn't think of any other place to hide."

She nodded. This was all Beau knew—the world of cars. The brushes helped. They closed off that terrifyingly big world. Water rained down on the windshield like a spring shower, and she felt like she was back in her turret bedroom during a good hard storm. She breathed in the comforting smell of cleansers.

"We lost the crows?"

Beau ran his hand over the steering wheel fondly. "I told you I could drive."

She cocked her head, looked at him a bit differently. Her whole life, he'd been like a brother to her, the kind who teased her about dust bunnies. She'd never seen this side of him: confident behind the wheel, dangerously fast. What else didn't she know about him?

The brushes outside swayed in their rhythmic dance back and forth.

"What now?" she asked.

"The scrying crows' whispers will have spread to Castle Ides. It's only a matter of time before Viggo and Hunter Black go to the town-house and see what happened. And then they'll be looking for us. They'll think we killed her."

A cold feeling returned to Anouk. She looked sidelong at Beau. If he hadn't done it, then who had?

She swallowed. "I wish Luc were here."

"Well, he isn't." It was unlike Beau to snap like that, and it made Anouk realize that he felt Luc's absence as keenly as she did.

She took a deep breath. "We should go to Cricket's apartment. She's the oldest, after Luc. She'll know what to do."

"Won't her apartment be the first place they'll look for us?"

Anouk shook her head. "Not necessarily. It'll take them at least an hour to get to Rue des Amants. Besides, I lied to Viggo today. I told him Cricket was out of town."

Beau raised an eyebrow. "Lied? You?"

Anouk smacked him on the arm.

He feigned being hurt, but then his expression turned grim again. He tugged on a ruffle on her apron. "This will need to go. Your dress too. You can't walk around like that, covered in blood. We'll be stopped by the police."

Anouk tugged off the apron, balled it up, and threw it in the back seat, but the blood had soaked into her dress too.

"I don't have other clothes."

Beau thought for a minute. The soap cycle ended, and another rinse began. Through the snaking watery lines, Anouk could almost make out the city lights beyond. Terror started to claw up her throat again as she thought of the crows, of the danger, of the unknown city, but there was an exhilaration with it this time. Wasn't this what she had always wanted? To be out in the city? To walk among the Pretties? The loud machines of the car wash rumbled to a stop, the final drips rolling off the car.

Beau rested a hand on the gearshift. He eyed Anouk's clothes, tapping a finger against the steering wheel.

"It'll be okay. I know a store we can go to."

"But we don't have money."

"We don't need it at the place I have in mind." He drew in a long breath. "It doesn't open for another few hours, but they might open it for me."

There was apprehension tucked into his voice. Once again, Anouk acknowledged that, as well as he knew the map of the city streets, and the Pretties' traffic signals, and their rules of driving, he was almost as innocent as she was when it came to how anything actually worked in their world.

A green light turned on, and he drove out of the car wash slowly, both of them checking the empty skies, back into the dark streets of Paris.

Chapter 7

ANOUK PRESSED HER FACE to the car window as they made their way through the city. Beau stayed off the wide thoroughfares where the crows might find them again, instead rumbling down side streets through the Porte de Clichy, into Batignolles, past the Théâtre de Paris. Even in the early morning, the city was alive. Street sweepers in green overalls with matching caps pushed plastic brooms. Electric lights illuminated back rooms of the bakeries and patisseries, where Anouk glimpsed women with flour on their arms. The next square was overtaken by open-back trucks overflowing with buckets of multicolored blooms and vendors in thick coats haggling over bouquets of peonies and anthuriums, lilacs and Peruvian lilies. If she closed her eyes, she could almost imagine she was back in the courtyard with Luc.

And then, all too soon, Beau turned down a side street and the market was gone. The lane was impossibly tight, hugged on both sides by squat buildings leaning on one another's shoulders.

"Maybe we should go to Rennar," Anouk blurted out, surprising even herself.

"Rennar? Are you mad?"

"He didn't seem dangerous at the party."

But that wasn't quite true, she thought. He hadn't seemed malicious, but dangerous? She swallowed, thinking of that dark eye-shine.

"Well, he is," Beau said flatly. "We aren't going to the Royals."

The tight lane spilled out onto a curving road, and Anouk checked the skies. Clear. Tall iron fences rose on either side of the street, behind them vast, dark expanses heavy with the shadows of trees.

"Is that a forest?" she asked.

"A garden. Forests are only outside of the city, in the country, I think."

She stared at the iron gates. The garden seemed to stretch on forever; how much vaster must a forest be than this? Luc had told her stories about forests, wild places that were the domain of wolves and bears and hawks. She half expected to see the glint of red eyes watching from beyond the gates. Beau went around a traffic circle and then rolled onto a bridge. Towering trees changed to monuments of white marble that glowed even in the darkness. She leaned forward, trying to take it all in at once.

Beau stopped the car abruptly. "This is it."

Anouk pressed her face against the window and gazed up at a six-story building that took up an entire city block. Dazzling lights lit up the words she had seen on boxes that Mada Vittora brought home.

"'Galeries Lafayette,'" she read reverently. "But we can't shop here. It takes money to buy clothing." She didn't have to mention that Galeries Lafayette was the most expensive department store in all of Paris.

"Wait for me to come around." Beau climbed out of the car, checking the skies again, and opened the door for her. "Mada Vittora doesn't use money here. She has something called an account.

Whenever I bring her here, she takes the clothes and they keep track of everything and send a monthly bill to someone. They know me here. They'll believe me."

"But she's gone."

"They don't know that." He looked anxiously at a giant lit clock face on the opposite building. "And by the time the news spreads, we'll be far away."

Anouk climbed out of the car, scanning the skies for telltale dark wings. None, but her pulse wouldn't calm. Except for a few cars and delivery trucks, the street was quiet. No shoppers. No doormen standing at attention. The department store was dark inside.

"The sign says they don't open until nine."

Beau's eyes scoured the street, slicing back and forth. Looking for crows. Listening for the roar of a gunmetal-gray motorcycle. A jogger ran past them, wearing tight clothes and white headphones. The woman slowed as she approached, jogged in place a few beats, and then turned sharply and started sprinting back the other way.

"It's the blood," Anouk realized, touching her dress. "I scared her. I didn't mean to . . ."

Beau went to the glass door, shading his eyes to see inside. He pounded on the door. "Hello!"

She couldn't shake the image of how the jogger had turned and run. Like she was a criminal. A murderer. Heat started to flush up her neck.

"Hey, you! Let us in!" Beau called to someone inside.

The door was thrown open by an ogre of a man who towered over them with arms like thick hams and no perceptible neck. He wore dark glasses and carried something strapped to his belt that it took Anouk a moment to recognize. A gun? Yes, that was called a gun.

"We're closed."

Beau lifted his hands, taking a step back. "We need help."

The man stared at the blood on Anouk's clothes. "Are you hurt, mademoiselle?"

"Oh, no, it isn't *my* blood," Anouk explained.

"We need to go shopping," Beau added.

The man stared at them like they were playing some demonic joke. But then he took off his glasses and squinted at Beau. "One moment. I know you, don't I? You're Vittora Antona's driver. Apologies, monsieur. I'm just the night security guard. It's my job to keep people out until we open. You understand." He strained his stubby neck back toward the car. His voice fell to a reverent whisper. "Is she here?"

"No," Beau answered quickly. "She's sent me with her . . . her niece. Who's visiting from the countryside. As you can see, we need some new clothes. Immediately. And . . . discretion."

"Of course. Right away." He touched a piece of machinery in his ear, whispered something low. In another few seconds, the click of high heels approached. A slim woman with a tight bun and navy-blue dress came to the door. If she thought the blood on Anouk's clothes or the fact that Anouk was barefoot and missing two toes was odd, she didn't bat an eye.

"Vittora Antona's niece, yes? Very sorry to keep you waiting. Usually if madame wishes us to open the store early for her, she calls in advance. Fortunately I was already here, ordering for our spring collection. Come. Follow me." She tapped the same machinery in her ear and hissed into it, "Round up every sales associate you can. There's a few of them setting up the Cartier display. I don't care if it's early. Now!"

Anouk entered the department store in a state of heady shock.

"Oh!" she exclaimed.

It was more a cathedral than a store. A stained-glass cupola sparkled over four stories, balcony after balcony after balcony after balcony, each packed with dresses and blouses and, oh, the *shoes*. Anouk found herself spinning in a circle to take it all in. Even with half the lights off, it was all glittering glass and marble. And the perfume! Hundreds of delicate little glass bottles, each more glamorous than the last. Anouk grabbed a bottle and sprayed it.

Beau sputtered at the perfume in his face.

"*This* way, mademoiselle." The Pretty in the navy dress waved them toward a contraption that looked like a staircase but was moving, each step climbing above the other, and Anouk stopped short. The Pretty glanced back at her with an odd look, and Beau grabbed her arm and pulled her onto the moving stairs.

"Try to act normal," he whispered.

"Is this magic?"

"Sort of. It's called an escalator."

The stairs moved steadily, lifting them high over the perfume counters into the endless balconies. The lights on the top floor came on. Electricity wasn't magic, Luc had explained to her once, but it worked in much the same way. It had rules to it, just like magic. It could be used only for certain things, and there was always a cost. Anouk gripped the moving handrail, dizzy.

And then the stairs ended abruptly, nearly spilling Anouk off. The Pretty waited primly. Behind her were racks of clothes of every size and color with names Anouk had seen on boxes and bags: Givenchy and Dior and Prada and Louis Vuitton.

"We're in a hurry." Beau grabbed a striped dress off the nearest rack. "This will do. We'll take this."

Alarm crossed the Pretty's face. She snatched up the dress, hung it back on the rack. "Oh, no, monsieur. Oh, no. That won't do at all. It's from last season!"

"Yeah, Beau," Anouk said. "That won't do at all!"

He sighed, glancing back over his shoulder at the front door as Anouk grabbed a skirt with gold trim. The Pretty followed behind her, pulling more clothes off the rack, explaining how *this* would accentuate mademoiselle's long legs, *this* would flatter her fair skin, *this* would hide—if she'd pardon the observation—her meager bosom.

Anouk caught a glimpse of her face in a mirror, gaunt and pale and splotched with blood—*Mada Vittora's blood*—and her stomach lurched.

"This," she blurted out. She grabbed the nearest dress. Black, long-sleeved, with white cuffs and a small, round white collar. "He's right: we really need to go."

The Pretty held her tongue. It was one thing to chastise a driver, but not a client's niece, even if she happened to be inexplicably covered in blood. She smiled tightly. "Certainly. And would mademoiselle be wanting some shoes?"

Anouk wiggled her eight toes. "Yes. Something easy to walk in. Something flat. Oh! Oxfords."

The woman touched the intercom in her ear. "Brigitte? Oxfords.

The Burberry ones. Size nine. To the second-floor dressing room."
She motioned down the hall. "You may change here."

She led them toward a door that had a sign reading SALON PRIVÉ;
it opened into a single dressing room surrounded by crimson velvet
curtains and floor-length mirrors. The Pretty extended a hand to help
Anouk step onto the platform. She cast a withering look back at Beau.

"Surely you'd like to wait outside, monsieur?"

Beau went red. "Right."

"I'll hurry," Anouk promised.

The woman was already untying the bows and buttons of Anouk's
maid's costume. She peeled the bloodstained clothes off Anouk's
limbs and then produced a packet that contained a damp cloth and
scrubbed the blood off her arms.

"I'm sorry. The blood is . . . it's . . ."

"No need to explain, mademoiselle," the Pretty said crisply. "I
assure you, we cater to all sorts of clients with all manner of particular
needs."

She helped Anouk into the black dress and did up the buttons
on the back. It was made of a fine, soft fabric, heavy but not stifling.
Anouk adjusted the white collar around her neck. The dress fit her
slim figure well, and she blinked at herself in the mirror, stunned.
She'd never seen herself in anything but a maid's costume.

"Gorgeous. Yes. And *look* at those legs. Do you have a boyfriend?
You'll have to get rid of him if you do. He'll simply be too jealous. Ah!
Here's Brigitte with the shoes. You'll need socks too. High ones will
balance out the short hem."

The Pretty produced the shoes and a roll of soft black socks that extended all the way above Anouk's knees, leaving only a few inches of thigh.

"Yes. *Magnifique*. Let me write you a receipt."

The woman disappeared while Anouk couldn't stop staring at the mirror.

No silly bows, no frills, no ribbons except the black one holding back her hair. She tipped her chin up. Something about the dress, simple though it was, made her feel bold. No wonder Hunter Black favored dark clothes. She could imagine another life in this dress, envision herself selecting creamy white dahlias at the flower market, climbing into an airplane waiting to whisk her off to somewhere exotic, sitting at a corner café beneath a red-and-white-striped awning, served coffee and macaroons just like anyone else.

But something was missing.

Her eyes fell on a satin jacket on a nearby rack. It was a bold red, made of a quilted fabric that caught the light. Heavy embroidery in dazzling colors hugged the shoulders and arms. There was something undeniably masculine about the jacket, especially the embroidery that wasn't neatly stitched but a little wild, threads running together like spider webs. She stepped down from the platform and walked around to look at the back. The embroidery continued in even more vibrant blues and greens and oranges, cascading along the jacket's soft curves in the shape of some mythical creature with wild curls of mane and wings and thorny teeth. If such a creature had a name, she'd never learned it.

Something beautiful and monstrous.

Gargoyle, she decided.

She snatched it up.

The Pretty came back in, an envelope in hand, with Beau behind her. He stopped cold in the doorway, eyes on the gap of thigh between where Anouk's skirt ended and the socks began. His mouth opened, but whatever he was going to say never came out.

Anouk slid the silk jacket over her shoulders. Yes. *Now* she felt right.

"I'll take this too," she said.

The Pretty looked stunned. "But mademoiselle, that's from the menswear collection. It's a custom piece for an exclusive client coming in later today. It's a Faustine original embroidered jacket. The price is . . . is . . . well, it is priceless. *Non,* it is simply impossible."

Beau snapped back to himself. "You heard her. She's taking it."

"But—"

"She's *taking* it."

Anouk turned away from the infinity of her own face in the mirror and met his eyes, feeling uncertain.

"Yes. I'm taking it," she announced, testing out this strange feeling of power.

She grabbed Beau's arm, pulled him toward the escalators.

"Send the bill to the usual address," he called back to the saleswoman, "and add a tip for yourself. Double the commission!"

Anouk jumped on the escalator, Beau behind her. She stretched out her arms like wings, taking the steps two at a time. The security guard at the bottom held the door open for them.

They tumbled out into the street. The sun was just rising. More people and cars were out now. An engine that sounded like a motorcycle's revved and Anouk jerked around, but it was only a woman riding a Vespa, not Hunter Black.

"Cricket's apartment is in the Eighth Arrondissement," Beau said.

Anouk looked at the busy streets, the flashing traffic signals that kept changing, the eyes that seemed to peek around corners—was that someone in a top hat?—and then down at her oxford shoes. She looked back up at Beau. "We should hurry."

Chapter 8

PARIS LOOKED DIFFERENT during the daytime. At night it had been shadowed corners and grim streets, but now that the sun had risen, Anouk started to notice little things she hadn't before: a horsehead door knocker, a lazy cat blinking in a window, schoolchildren struggling under heavy backpacks. They entered a neighborhood that had fewer monuments and more shops and cafés. It was dirtier, with vibrant graffiti on the walls, but Anouk liked it. Music played from a corner café where couples sat sipping coffee.

Beau found a spot and parked the car.

Anouk climbed out hesitantly, smoothing a hand uneasily over her dress.

In the dress and the Faustine jacket, she looked just like everyone else. *Looked*, yes. But felt? Fear and anxiousness braided together inside her, screaming in her veins that she didn't belong here.

Animal. Creature. *Dark thing.*

Beau hurried around to meet her on the sidewalk. He was still in his chauffeur's uniform but he had lost the bloodstained jacket and rolled up his shirtsleeves. On impulse, she thrust her arm through his.

He tensed in surprise. "This is the Latin Quarter," he explained. "It's mostly students, or at least it used to be. There are a few cheap *chambres de bonne* to rent, and Mada Vittora doesn't give Cricket much of an allowance. This is her street on the left."

His eyes scanned every shadow as they turned down a narrow and winding road with a small café tucked beneath an awning. A young couple sipped tea as they chatted. The man wore a bowler hat set at a sharp angle and a neon-blue cravat. The woman had lime-green makeup on her eyelids and fingernails painted a rainbow of colors.

"Beau, look," she whispered. "Goblins!"

Both the man and the woman wore brass chains hooked to their belts, like the kind Pretties used for pocket watches, but these were linked instead to the dainty china cups they sipped from.

Goblins took their tea *very* seriously.

Beau shook his head and didn't answer until they had passed the strange couple. "Those aren't Goblins. They're Pretties. It's the strangest thing, but the, ah, *nontraditional* style of Goblins has spread throughout the city. It's the latest fashion craze."

Anouk looked over her shoulder at the couple's ears. It was true; not even the slightest point. "I didn't think the Pretties knew about Goblins."

"They don't. They're dressing up like creatures they don't even know exist. The Goblins are just messing with them. You know how Goblins are."

They passed another Pretty girl dressed in garish Goblin fashion. She was winding the pocket-watch chain of her teacup lazily around one finger. Her eyes fell on Anouk.

"Hey, cool jacket."

Anouk beamed. She followed Beau to an unassuming door that opened onto a foyer filled with mailboxes and a narrow staircase. It smelled of something stale and spicy. Beau started up the stairs. The two of them climbed until Anouk was out of breath.

Beau stopped at a door and knocked hard. "Cricket," he called. "It's Beau. Let me in: it's important."

The rest of the apartment building was filled with the gentle sounds of people starting to stir, slippered footsteps and percolating coffee. Morning light poured through the grimy window in the staircase. Anouk wondered if they'd be waking Cricket—she seemed the type to sleep in. But the door cracked open, a chain lock stretching taut, and music with a sharp beat came through the crack. Cricket was dressed in leggings and a white tank that showed her black bra beneath. Her curly brown hair was pulled back with yellow headphones. Her eyes were bleary, like she hadn't slept.

She gave Beau a sharp look. "Whatever that witch bitch wants, tell her to wait until morning."

"It *is* morning," Beau pointed out.

Cricket squinted up at the sunlight coming through the hall window as if she didn't trust it. She started to close the door, but Anouk thrust her shoe in the crack, preventing her.

"Let us in, please!"

"Anouk?" Cricket's voice rose in surprise. "I hardly recognized you! Hang on." Anouk moved her foot, and Cricket slammed the door closed. The chain lock clinked, and then the door opened fully.

Cricket stared at Anouk. "What's going on? How did you get out of the house? And whose jacket is that and where can I get one?"

Everything rushed back to Anouk—the terrible image of her mistress's bloodless hand, the mad dash through Paris. She pressed her hands to her mouth, not sure if she was about to be sick or about to cry. Cricket waved them in, checked the hallway, and locked the door.

The apartment smelled of mint tea and something more pungent, like overripe fruit. It was small, a single room with an unmade bed and a kitchenette with a boiling kettle. A clock in the shape of a black cat sat on the toaster, its circling tail ticking away the seconds. Heavy curtains blocked the windows. Ferns hung from the ceiling, books were stacked on the side table, and there were dirty clothes strewn around that didn't help with the smell. The music came from a desk by the tall front windows out of twin speakers on either side of a laptop computer that flashed with swirling bright images, casting the entire room in a rainbow of neon colors.

Cricket went to the desk and hit a few keys, and the music stopped. She threw back the curtains.

"Whatever happened, it's bad, isn't it?" she said.

Without the music, the black-cat clock's ticking filled the room.

Anouk's fingers itched to pick up the dirty piles of clothes. To run a sponge over the sticky kitchen counters. To do something normal, something routine. Cricket rested her hands on Anouk's shoulders.

"Are you all right?" she asked.

Anouk couldn't help it; the tears started before she could stop them. Cricket pulled her into a hug, smelling of mint and something sharper, coffee maybe, her kinky hair tickling Anouk's shoulders.

"She's dead," Anouk choked out.

Cricket tensed. "I should have known. That's the only way you could be out of the house. What happened? Is Luc back? Did he send you here?"

"He's still missing," Anouk said quietly.

Cricket's eyes widened. "Oh. *Merde*. Give me the details."

Beau turned to Anouk. "Maybe you should go into the bathroom. You don't need to hear this."

"I saw it, Beau. I can handle it."

He looked as though he'd prefer to lock her away somewhere so safe that even unpleasant memories couldn't reach her, but he sighed. "I found Vittora in her room," he explained quietly. "She was already dead. It was ugly. Blood everywhere. We didn't know what to do."

The kettle started whistling. Cricket ran a hand over her face. In the sunlight coming through the windows, her brown skin glowed the color of tea leaves. She jerked the screaming kettle off the stove.

"Murdered? And you don't know who did it?"

Beau shook his head.

Cricket took a step forward, her face suddenly fierce. "And our pelts?"

"In the car."

Relief unwound over her strained face, and Cricket sank into the desk chair. The neon lights on her computer played over her features like something Anouk had read about once. The lights in the north? No. The northern lights. Cricket drew in a long breath. She grabbed a cup and poured herself some tea, hands shaking so badly that water sloshed onto the desk.

Anouk quietly wiped away the drops with her dress cuff.

Cricket set down the cup. "Good riddance."

Anouk gasped. "Cricket!"

Cricket gave her a hard look. Her hands were steady now, more characteristic of the thief Anouk knew. She touched the dangling gold earring in her right ear, the only adornment she allowed herself.

"You didn't know her like we did. You were her pet, her favorite. It's better that she's dead. If Luc were here, he'd say the same thing. You know he would."

Anouk wrung her hands. She went to the windows, looked at the birds on the opposite roof. Crows, but regular ones. If she could go back in time to the night before, would she warn her mistress?

"A flock of scrying crows followed us," Beau said. "When Hunter Black and Viggo find her body, they'll come hunting for us."

"When did it happen?" Cricket asked.

"Late last night. Midnight."

Cricket glanced at the black-cat clock. "Then we have just over two and a half days."

Anouk frowned. "For what?"

"To find another master." Cricket leaned forward, tenting her fingers. "Luc explained it to me in case something like this ever happened: A witch's soul lasts three days after she dies. Once her soul is gone, all her enchantments vanish too." She looked from one to the other as though she wasn't certain they understood. "That means if we don't find another witch to perform the spell again, then by Saturday at midnight . . ."

"We'll turn back to animals," Beau whispered.

Anouk flinched.

Cricket nodded. "It's good that you thought to take the pelts. Beasties' lives are tied to their pelts. If someone burned them, we'd go up in flames. If they were put through a woodchipper, well . . ." She pantomimed being shredded into tiny little bits.

Beau made a face.

"And anyway, if we have any hope of staying human," Cricket

continued, "we'll need those pelts to uphold the spell. We just have to find another witch who can do it, fast. *Merde,* I wish Luc were here."

Beau cleared his throat, still looking slightly green. "There's the Trafalgar Witch. Vittora's called on her for help before."

Cricket shook her head. "She's in England. We'd be stopped at the border." She blew on her tea. "Most witches are out of the question; too far away or too dangerous. Mada Ourselle isn't a complete terror. She might help . . . but she has close ties to the Royals."

"Then we'll need to try something else," Beau said. "Not a witch. In the bird market near Sainte-Chapelle, there's a Pretty broker who has connections to disgraced Royals, an old baroness who still has a bit of magic—"

"No Royals. Too risky."

"Well, what do you suggest? That we go to *Viggo* for help?"

Cricket shot him a dirty look as she drummed her short nails on the mug. *Click-click-click.* She let out a loud sigh. "You say the pelts are in the car?"

Beau nodded.

"Get them."

"They're safe. No one's going to woodchip them. *Are* there even woodchippers in Paris?"

"No, it's not that. I need to check something. A . . . a rumor." She tapped her foot anxiously.

Beau exchanged a look with Anouk, then picked up his keys and headed downstairs. Cricket paced by the windows, sipping the tea, glancing outside. Anouk folded her hands, fighting the urge to mop up the spots of tea Cricket was spilling on the floor.

Cricket dropped down in the seat across from her. "Did Beau do it?" she whispered, her eyes alight.

Anouk nearly choked. "Beau? Why would you think that?" She felt her cheeks burning; hadn't she wondered the same thing?

"Because I'd have done it if I'd known what parts of her were still human enough to bleed."

"Cricket!"

"Did I ever tell you why I don't have fingerprints?" She held out her hands, palms up, the pads nothing but smooth flesh. "Everyone thinks she burned them off to make me a better thief, but they're wrong. I made a mistake—*once*. I kept something I was supposed to steal for her. A rare book. I stole it from the home of a wealthy Pretty and was almost caught. I had to hide in a closet for hours, so I read the book. It was a story of a girl who got a ticket in the mail for a magic train, a train that would take her everywhere, even to the moon, and for years, she just rode everywhere and saw the world. I loved that book. I wanted it. One thing that was just mine. But she knew, of course. The crows. She took the book and burned it in front of me, page by page, and then burned off my fingerprints in their ashes."

Anouk had never heard Cricket's story. She looked away. "She might have given it to you if you'd asked for it."

Cricket snorted. "Not likely. And anyway, what did *you* ever do to earn her ire?" She bent over and grabbed Anouk's foot, tugged off the oxford shoe, and rolled down the sock. She held up Anouk's foot with its four toes, pointing to the scar. "Look at what she did. Look! She cut off your toes on a whim, just so your feet would fit in her shoes.

So she could play dress-up! You didn't make any mistakes. You didn't steal from her, didn't disobey her." Cricket's face went grim. "She was a monster."

Anouk jerked her foot back, quickly rolled up the sock, and laced the shoe. Bunny ears. Crossed in an *x*. Tied in a bow.

Cricket bit her lip. "I'm sorry." She took Anouk's hands. "Listen. We only have each other now. It's the four of us against the world. You, me, Beau, and Luc. No one else understands us; no one else loves us."

Anouk looked out the window anxiously. "Five of us."

Cricket's gaze wavered. "You mean Hunter Black? You know how he clings to Viggo's shadow. If his loyalty was ever challenged, I wouldn't bet on him siding with us."

"But he's still one of us."

"I'm not sure *he* remembers that." Cricket tucked a lock of Anouk's hair tenderly behind her ear. "We'll stick together. We'll find Luc. And who knows? Maybe we don't need a master at all. Maybe we don't need a witch or a Royal. Maybe we could just be . . . human."

Guilt crawled up Anouk's neck. If Mada Vittora had ever heard them talk about not needing a master, she'd have had Hunter Black take their tongues. Her eyes drifted to the desk, to the collection of wires and rubber cables and silver ports. *Electronics.* She hadn't a clue what any of them were for. And a notebook, too, with words in no Pretty language, and illustrations of hand symbols. They made her feel uneasy, like eyes watching from shadows. Anouk slid the notebook around.

"Cricket? These look like—"

"They're nothing."

Cricket grabbed the notebook. That warm feeling spread on

Anouk's neck. She realized where she'd s

were gestures Mada Vittora used for a fi

And the writing had been in the Selent

rotting spells and fire tricks. What was (

—let alone violent ones—when beasties

"Never mind that." Cricket slamme

dragged Anouk by the wrist to the kitche

this. You must. I've only just discovered it . . . . rcıous.

She dug through a glass fishbowl of candy and took out a small paper packet. She poured neon-colored crystals into her palm. Half she tossed in her mouth, and half she gave to Anouk. Anouk sniffed —sweet and artificial. She touched one to her tongue. Cherry. And then it suddenly fizzed on her tongue and went *pop*, and she jumped.

"The Pretties call them Pop Rocks," Cricket said, eyes glinting.

The door opened, interrupting them.

Beau carried the bag of pelts slung over one shoulder to the dining table. Cricket swept the plates onto the floor, and Beau pulled out the pelts one at a time. A musty smell spread throughout the room. They were all different sizes, some the size of small rugs, the fur still matted, others no bigger than dinner plates, and one that fluttered with white feathers. Mada Vittora hadn't bothered to wash the creatures before she'd peeled off their fur or feathers or scales and made them human.

Anouk turned away, feeling sick. She went to the window and focused on the fresh air. Cricket had a dying mint plant on the ledge, and she broke off a few leaves, chewed on one anxiously, hoping it would soothe her stomach, and stuffed the rest in her pocket.

Cricket pawed through the pelts almost hungrily. The one on top,

ate-brown fur. Below it, a tiny one with gray fur and
nk tail. And the one with gray and white feathers, larger
uk had thought at first.

Looks like a dog," Cricket said, "and a mouse. And what's this
one? A swan?"

Cricket rattled out creatures like she was reading from a magazine. Which had been Anouk's? She watched out of the corner of her
eye as Cricket examined them one by one. She didn't feel drawn to
any. None of them pulled at her stomach; she had no fierce pangs of
recognition. She felt something more like revulsion—she had once
been one of these *things*.

"An owl, I think," Beau said. "What exactly are you looking for?"
He too stood back from the pile of fur and feathers as though they
made him fearful.

"Luc had a theory." Cricket ran her hand over the owl's feathered
pelt and then tossed it aside. "That maybe Mada Vittora didn't use
only domesticated animals."

Anouk looked up sharply. "What else would she have used?" Her
teasing with Beau came back to her, that he was half monkey and she
three-quarters dust bunny.

Cricket inspected the next pelt. It was the size of a small sweater
with angel-soft white fur like cashmere. "This one's a cat, I think.
Anyway, Luc wasn't certain. It was something he'd overheard Viggo
saying to one of the Royals. Viggo was there since the beginning, you
know. He was twelve when Luc was made. And then me, and Hunter
Black, and the two of you. He saw it all happen. And he said that one
of us was a . . ."

She reached the last pelt and stopped.

82

A different smell permeated the room. More earthy, like the samples of moss in the townhouse's solarium.

Beau eyed the pelt on the table cautiously.

Cricket slowly reached out a hand and touched it. Anouk stepped forward, her breath coming in odd bursts. This last pelt was different from the others. Not a dog, a mouse, a cat, or an owl. It was much larger, bigger even than the dog's, and the fur was gray and wiry.

Too thick. Too heavy. Too dark.

"Luc was right," Cricket breathed. "One of us is a wolf."

Chapter 9

ANOUK'S FINGERS SANK into the thick pelt while the others argued.

"That's impossible," Beau said. "Where did Mada Vittora find a wolf in Paris?"

"I don't know. The zoo? She *was* a witch. She could have walked through the portal elevator in Castle Ides straight into the Black Forest and trapped one there."

"So what does it mean that one of us is a wolf?"

"What's a wolf if not a traitor? You know what Mada Vittora used to say about wolves: *Wolves in the wood together are good; wolf on its own, expect blood and bone.* It means we can't trust one of us."

"Yes, but which one?" Anouk said.

Beau and Cricket looked at her as though they'd almost forgotten she was there.

"Well, it's Hunter Black, of course," Cricket said. "Isn't it obvious?"

But Anouk kept eyeing the different pelts uneasily. It was impossible to tell. None had Beau's tan skin or Cricket's curly hair. Any of the pelts could have belonged to any of them.

"I guess so," Anouk said.

But it didn't feel right. Hunter Black was decidedly detached, yes —the very picture of a lone wolf. Except for his fierce devotion to

Viggo. Wasn't that more like a loyal hound clinging to his master's heels?

Then her eyes fell on the burlap sack on the ground.

"Beau?" Her head started to feel too light. "Where did you get that bag?"

He toed it with his shoe. "It was in the mistress's closet."

She approached the sack warily. "On the floor? Or on the shelf?"

"I don't know. The shelf, I guess. Why? Isn't it the same one we used to catch the Corpus crows?"

Anouk shook her head. "No. It's not just any bag." She crouched down and touched the sack slowly, as though it might bite. She should have recognized its almost imperceptible shimmer when Beau had first grabbed it to carry the pelts. But she'd been unable to think about anything other than Mada Vittora.

The minute her hand grazed the fabric, it changed, and she jerked her fingers back. It shrunk and folded in on itself, burlap darkening and growing glossy and smooth, silver buckles pushing out from the seams, a snaking black leather strap slithering from the opening.

A beautiful, perfect Hermès purse.

"It's her oubliette."

Beau jumped backward and almost knocked over a chair. "That's it? You're certain?"

"It shimmers, regardless of its form, if you know how to look at it."

Cricket reached out for it, but Anouk held it back protectively.

"Come on," Cricket urged. "There could be all kinds of things in there we need. Money. Gold. Spells we could trade for!"

"It isn't that simple." Anouk opened the bag and turned it upside down. Nothing came out. Cricket's face fell.

"It's empty? That's impossible." Beau grabbed the bag and pawed through the space.

Anouk took the bag back from him. "It isn't empty, but its contents are protected. We'll need a witch to truly open it."

Something outside caught Anouk's ear. A certain familiar rev of an engine. She went to the window. The sun was rising above the tall buildings, casting the city in bright, clear morning light.

The rev came again.

A motorcycle pulled up in front of the apartment, and the driver shut off its engine. The gunmetal color winked in the sunlight. Two figures were on the back, helmets shading their faces. But Anouk didn't need to see their faces. Only Hunter Black's coat.

She spun away from the window. "They're here."

Beau swore as he looked down at Hunter Black's motorcycle. "We have to run."

"Where?" Anouk said. "We're five stories up and there's only one staircase." She went to the door and pressed her ear against its peeling paint. The other residents were up and about now; she heard the canned sound of a radio and the clatter of pans. The downstairs neighbor must be making breakfast.

And then footsteps on the stairs. Two sets.

She recoiled from the door. "They're coming." Her hand went to her necklace, needing the soothing touch of Luc's coin but finding nothing, just skin and bone and an empty chain.

Gone. In the bottom of the fountain.

She dropped her hand. "We have to hide."

"Are you mad?" said Cricket. "Hunter Black was literally made for this. To hunt. He'll find you in seconds."

But Anouk was already searching the room for possible hiding places. She and Beau and Luc had played hide-and-seek whenever Mada Vittora was away and they'd had the full run of the townhouse, a place where entire ballrooms were hidden within closets, staircases led to floors that shouldn't exist, cupboards opened to secret tunnels.

But Cricket's apartment was tiny and sparsely furnished and not magic in the slightest, leaving only a handful of options: Under the bed. Beneath the kitchen sink. In the closet.

"She's right. We don't have any other choice." Beau threw back the shower curtain, eyed the tub. "I parked the Rolls-Royce around the corner, and they didn't see us come in, so they might not know that we're here."

Footsteps thundered up the stairs. One flight down now.

"Zut." Cricket started to throw the scattered pelts into a pile on the floor. "We have to hide these too. Help me."

The musty smell of pelts and *stomp-stomp-stomp* of approaching boots made Anouk lightheaded. "The closet. It's the only place big enough."

The three of them dragged the pelts to the closet and threw them over the messy piles of clothes just as the footsteps stopped short on the landing.

Someone knocked, hard.

"Quick, get in!" Cricket whispered, herding Beau and Anouk toward the closet.

"The oubliette . . . where is it?" Beau hissed. "If Viggo sees it, he'll recognize it."

Anouk scanned the room. "There, beneath the table." She snatched it up just as Viggo jiggled the knob from the outside, trying to force his way in. Beau threw himself headfirst into the forest of Cricket's clothes, sending the coat hangers clattering, and Anouk tumbled in after him.

"Cricket!" Viggo yelled. "Open the door!"

Anouk fought against coats and towels and the musty pelts that sent up a scratchy cloud of dust and made her eyes water. She stifled a cough as Beau eased the door closed.

Darkness.

She heard the little puffs of her own breathing. Clothes rustling as Beau moved closer. Pounding again on the front door.

"Let us in, Cricket. Now!"

Cricket hit the music again.

The low beats blared, pulsing in time with the thumping of Anouk's heart. She pushed a dress out of her face. Her eyes were starting to adjust. The closet door was made of thick frosted glass, the kind that was easier to see out of than into. She could just make out Cricket's blurry figure crossing the room.

She heard the lock slide open and the clatter of a chain.

"What the hell are you two doing here?" Cricket demanded. "It isn't even ten o'clock in the morning."

Anouk pretended she was made of stone, trying not to move an inch. A belt was swinging from a nail, clanking softly, and she cringed and prayed for it to stop.

"You changed your locks," Viggo accused. Anouk could partially make him out through the frosted glass, his unmistakable slouch and fair, mussed hair. He raised his hand, jingling his set of keys. "This apartment isn't yours. It's mine. You can't keep me out."

"What do you want?" Cricket spat.

"Are you alone?" Viggo was leaning close to Cricket, nearly pinning her against the kitchenette sink, while Hunter Black's dark shape set to prowling around the room.

"Of course. Who else would be here?"

"I thought you were supposed to be out of town. A mission in Dordogne."

"Yeah, well . . . I was, wasn't I? Just got in a few hours ago." The music increased a few notches in volume. Cricket must have hit the controls again. Maybe she'd heard the clank from the closet. "Why? What's this about?"

Viggo didn't answer right away. Anouk kept her eyes on Hunter Black's shape moving beyond the frosted glass like some underwater monster as he stalked over to the bathroom. She heard the bathroom door open. The clatter of tin rings as he drew the shower curtain back.

Beau's hand found hers in the darkness; his fingers squeezed hers protectively.

"Hey!" Cricket called. "Tell your trained monkey to keep his hands off my stuff. What does he think he's going to find under that bed, his missing *couilles?*"

It was just a matter of time before Hunter Black looked in the closet. The smell of their pelts was nearly choking. Anouk squeezed Beau's hand back.

Cricket was right. They had to look out for one another. No one else would.

Viggo said something too low for Anouk to hear, but Cricket answered sharply, "Beau and Anouk? No, Beau hasn't been by in weeks, and *Anouk?* I didn't think that little bird was allowed to leave her cage." She paused. "Why, what happened? Is it Mada Vittora?"

Anouk tried to ignore the memory of blood on her hands, wiped clean now, though a little was still caught under her fingernails.

"She's fine," Viggo answered. His voice drifted to a higher octave. He'd always been a bad liar. "In fact, she wants to see you. Tonight. She's summoning all four of you to the townhouse for a meeting. No exceptions."

He tapped her computer and the music stopped.

It was quiet. Too quiet. Anouk could practically hear her heart beating.

"And Luc?" Cricket asked sharply. "Where's Luc? I haven't heard from him in days."

"We don't know where he is," Hunter Black said. "No one does." His hand went to his neck, where, just last week, Luc had had to give him stitches. If Hunter Black had an affinity for any of the other beasties — and Anouk wasn't convinced that he did — it would be for the boy who sewed his wounds and never breathed a word about it.

Viggo shot him a nasty look, like he'd revealed too much. "Don't worry about Luc," Viggo purred, turning back to Cricket. "Pack a bag. You'll need to stay at the townhouse for a few days. Maybe longer. Things are about to get dangerous in the city. There's soon to be changes within the Haute. You'll need my protection." He took his time putting his hands all over her things, her teapot and candy bowl and the black-cat clock and bright yellow headphones. "You're so alone out here. What's it been, four years? Not a lot of time to learn how the world works." He slowly wound the headphone cords around his palm. "All I've ever wanted is for you to be safe."

They were too far from the closet for Anouk to make out much.

Blurry movement of Viggo setting down the headphones and reaching for Cricket's shoulders.

"Get your fingers off me," Cricket hissed.

"You're beautiful when you're angry like this, love."

Anouk squeezed her eyes closed. She hated seeing this. Hated the feel of Hunter Black prowling around, his footsteps so calculated and slow, and hated that possessive note in Viggo's voice. Love? No, what she was listening to wasn't love. Viggo wasn't capable of loving anything, as far as she had seen. Not even his own mother. He must have gone to the townhouse. He must have seen the Mada's body. And yet here he was, pawing at Cricket while his mother's blood emptied into the Persian rug. He was probably already planning how he could take over her empire. If Anouk had to guess, that's what this supposed meeting was about.

Hunter Black's shadow moved away from the bed. He turned toward the closet.

Beau's hand squeezed hers, hard, as though he feared being ripped apart.

Chapter 10

❧

ANOUK PRESSED ONE HAND against her mouth, clutched Beau's hand with the other. Hunter Black was just on the other side of the door. It was so stiflingly hot in the closet. The musty pelts choked her. Fur and particles, their old life, catching in her nose. She couldn't breathe.

But then Beau's fingers intertwined with her own. She could hear his breathing, slower than her own and more steady. He inched over the pile of pelts to wrap his arm around her back. He didn't dare speak.

She leaned her head against his chest.

"I don't need your protection." Cricket's voice in the living room was strained. "I'm not yours. I never will be."

For Viggo's whole life, his mother had showered him with gifts from both the Haute and the Pretty World. Fast cars, expensive clothes, tickets to secret places only magic could access. He'd never been denied anything.

Hunter Black's shadow fell over the frosted glass. Anouk clutched Beau harder, wanting to shelter them both.

Keep us safe, she wished.

Like a coin tossed in a fountain.

Like *magic.*

She closed her eyes, barely knowing what she was doing. How many times had she been dusting the house and overheard Mada Vittora do a simple diversion whisper? Enough that she could recite the Selentium Vox words in her sleep.

"Omni terra das royale oscura, omni figuras das visine etan absconsia," she whispered, lips moving quickly. The taste of mint was still fresh on her tongue.

She felt Beau twist to look at her, but she didn't open her eyes. She *knew* beasties couldn't do magic. But neither could Pretties, and look at how beautiful their world was. Look at all the things they had built, the roundabouts and the cafés and the glittering department stores. What was that if not magic?

"Voc, voc eta commandet suma suspirras." She whispered faster. *"Non avis nos . . ."*

She heard Hunter Black's hand on the closet doorknob, then the metal clicking softly as it twisted. The door opened a crack. She felt a terrible rush of air on her face. The smell of Cricket's tea. The murmur of Viggo whispering declarations of love to Cricket by the sink.

"Non avis nos, non avis nos, spero . . ."

She didn't stop whispering the words.

Don't see us.

Don't see us.

Please.

The door stayed like that, open a crack. And then, just in the moment when she knew Hunter Black would find them, a sharp smack came from the kitchenette. Cricket had slapped Viggo.

Anouk's eyes flew open.

Hunter Black was across the room in three strides to defend his master. The closet door shut, the frosted glass rattling softly. Closed. Anouk stared at the knob in disbelief.

"Hurt him again," Hunter Black snarled, "and I'll put you in your grave."

"No!" Viggo's voice was sharp. "Don't threaten her."

Cricket spat out, "I'll be there tonight. Just get out of here. Just *go*."

Viggo started pacing. He raked his fingers through his flaxen hair. "Did you find anything, Hunter Black?"

"They aren't here."

Not here? Wasn't he going to check the closet? Anouk felt Beau stiffen by her side, as confused as she was. He mimicked the gesture of the slap and shrugged as if to suggest the altercation must have distracted Hunter Black. It was true, Hunter Black always went a little wild at the idea of his master being hurt, but still. He was a hunter, like his name. He didn't get distracted.

Anouk pressed her fingertips to her lips. She was shaking. It couldn't be the magic, could it? Her whisper? It had been only a desperate try. She hadn't expected it to *work*.

"Tonight, then," Viggo said. "At the townhouse. And if either of those little beasties comes crawling to you, you drag them along with you, understand? Or there will be consequences."

Heavy footsteps thumped away, followed by the slamming door. She heard Cricket fasten the chain lock and mutter something unrepeatable.

Had they really not been found?

The closet door flew open. Cricket stood in the doorway. "We've got to get out of Paris. Far away from those dangerous lunatics. Put as much distance as we can between us and them before tonight comes and we don't show up at whatever deranged trap he has set for us at the townhouse." She looked at Anouk strangely. "You must be the luckiest two people alive for him not to have found you in there."

"The f-fountain," Anouk stuttered, feeling the blood hot in her face, her hands starting to shake now that the danger had passed and it was sinking in how close they'd been to getting caught. "In the alley at the end of Rue des Amants . . . the little gargoyle . . . I dropped a coin in the water and made a wish for us to be safe. Maybe it worked."

Cricket scoffed. "That's just a legend."

The muscles of Anouk's arms were twitching now and she couldn't seem to make them stop. "I . . . I also cast one of Mada Vittora's diversion whispers."

Everyone went quiet. A car drove by, honking, and a baby wailed from the apartment overhead.

"That's impossible," Beau said at last. "Even if you know the whisper's words, it takes a magic handler to cast spells." He rubbed his chin for a long time. "It had to have been a coincidence. You saw how he leaped to defend Viggo. His mind was elsewhere."

Anouk expected Cricket to chastise her more; Cricket, who was practical and ironic, who believed in the power of knives, not whispers. But Cricket was oddly quiet. Her long fingers drummed against the desk, *rat-a-tat, rat-a-tat,* as the swirling colors of her computer screen threw rainbows over her features.

She leaned forward, hands tented together. "Do you really think you worked magic just now, Anouk?"

Something about Cricket's firm gaze threw her. "I don't know," she said honestly.

Beau looked from one to the other with a scrunched-up face. "Are you two seriously considering this?"

Silently, Cricket slid her desk drawer open and set out the candle and matches and journal that she'd hidden when they'd first arrived. She struck a match with a sizzle of smoke and lit the wick. She gestured to everything, chewing on her fingernail. "All of this, the drawings in the notebook too. I've been trying to do magic on my own."

Not just any magic. Dark spells.

Anouk searched her face. "Can you?"

"No." Cricket dropped her hand. "Not yet, at least. But—I know this sounds crazy—I can *feel* it. I can feel that it's possible."

Beau scratched his chin, eyeing the flickering candle warily.

Cricket pointed to it. "It's a fire trick. Extinguishing the flame with whispers alone. I'd rather *start* a fire, but I can't find that spell." She gestured to the computer. "I found this one on the Internet."

Anouk had heard Viggo talking about the Internet. It had to do with technology of the Pretty World, but unlike electric lights, which always turned on, and cars, which could be relied on to go forward, the Internet was tricky. Hard to tell what was lies and what wasn't.

"Try it, Anouk," Cricket urged. "I've barely mastered three words, but you're fluent in the Selentium Vox."

"No, I'm not. I've only read some books," she quickly corrected. But she did know the spell—even without looking at the words in Cricket's notebook. Mada Vittora had cast it so often that Anouk could have whispered it in her sleep.

She watched the flame steadily, thought about the light going out, and it spurred a warmth in her body. Her pulse increased. The words took shape in her mouth . . .

"Dreflamos." She murmured so softly that the others leaned forward, uncertain she'd spoken at all.

The flame flickered—just for a second—and then strengthened again.

"See?" Cricket cried. "It worked! Well, sort of."

Beau raised a doubtful eyebrow. "The window *is* open, you know."

"Breeze or not, it doesn't matter," Anouk interjected. "It wouldn't have truly worked unless I'd consumed some life-essence."

Cricket blew out the candle and dropped it back in the drawer. Her gaze was both defiant and hopeful at the same time. "I'm not saying I'm the next great Witch of Paris, or that you are, or any of us. I'm just saying that it's been on my mind." She jerked her head toward the window. "As much as we look like the Pretties out there, we *aren't* them. We've more in common with the Goblins. We were born of magic too, weren't we? Just like the rest of the Haute? So why shouldn't we be able to cast a whisper? Why shouldn't we learn to give those Royals and witches a taste of their own medicine, cut off *their* toes, burn off *their* fingerprints?"

"It's dangerous. The vitae echo . . ."

Cricket paced, stretching and flexing her long fingers. "I know the limits of the Haute. But imagine if we could do even a fraction of what they can. We could stop them from keeping all of us under their thumbs. You've spent more time with Mada Vittora than the rest of us combined, Anouk. You know all her tricks and whispers. If you *could* work them, you'd be as strong as any witch. No one would ever enslave you again. Or any of us."

Anouk looked down at her hands. Torn, broken nails. Short fingers that didn't look suited to do anything but hold a mop.

"If that was true," Beau said, "then it would mean Mada Vittora had been lying to us our whole lives."

Cricket gave him a hard look. "Sounds like her, doesn't it?"

Beau conceded that with a nod.

Anouk kept her eyes on the snaking smoke that, even with the candle put away, didn't quite dissipate. "So what do we do?"

Cricket grabbed her keys and a wad of crumpled bills from a jar on the desk. She pulled on her jacket. Shoved a stick of gum in her mouth.

"We get the hell out of Paris." She took a knife from the kitchen and wrapped the blade in a towel. She held it out to Anouk. "Take this. I've seen you in the kitchen—your skills would give even Hunter Black pause, never mind that the only things you've ever stabbed are vegetables."

Hesitantly, Anouk took it. It was a chef's knife, heavy and solid. The wooden handle nestled in her palm as though it had been molded to fit there. She wrapped her fingers around it and wondered, with a sudden lurch of her pulse, if slicing flesh felt like piercing an eggplant.

Cricket grunted her approval. "Now let's go find someone who will tell us the truth."

"Where?" Beau asked.

Anouk spoke first, surprising all of them. "Montélimar."

Chapter 11

BOTH CRICKET AND BEAU were very silent, until Cricket leaned over the sink and spat out her gum. "I'm sorry," she said. *"But have you gone insane?"*

"Montélimar is where the Lavender Witch lives," Beau said. "Mada Zola."

Anouk thrust her hand in her jacket pocket, rolled the rough sprig of mint between her fingers. "I know."

"Mada. Zola. Is. Our. Enemy," Cricket enunciated as though Anouk had suddenly gone deaf. "Mada Vittora hated her, and the feeling was mutual. Because of their feud, Zola lost all her holdings in central France. She's banished out there to her wilted garden, left to rot like a sack of winter potatoes. Forbidden to have anything to do with the Haute." She reached for another stick of gum as though she needed something to calm her nerves.

"Maybe that's a good thing," Anouk argued. "The enemy of my enemy is my friend, right? If we can convince the Lavender Witch that we served Vittora only because we were enchanted, she might help us."

Neither Cricket nor Beau appeared convinced.

Anouk rested her hands on the table. "Before Luc disappeared, he started spending more time on the scryboard. Yesterday afternoon,

I went through his log. He'd been spying on Mada Zola. Even contacted her for help, though it didn't look as though he ever got a response."

Beau raised his eyebrows. "Did Mada Vittora know about this?"

Anouk shook her head.

"Why would Luc want another witch's help?" Cricket said. "Help with *what?*"

"I don't know, but whatever his aim, he thought he could trust Mada Zola, and I trust him. We should go to Montélimar unless you know a good reason not to."

"Just one? We have *every* reason not to go!" Cricket counted off on her fingers. "One: As far as Mada Zola's concerned, we've always been loyal servants for the witch who orchestrated her downfall. Two: Word has probably reached her that we're potential witch murderers, which I doubt will reassure her when we show up at her door. Three: Even if she does extend the spell, we'll just be trading one mistress for another. Which brings me to four: Have you *heard* the rumors about what she does to Goblins? And five: Montélimar is more than halfway across the country. That's, what, Beau, six hours from here?"

"Seven."

"See? It's almost noon, which means we have only two and a half days left to find a way out of this. We can't spend seven of our last hours on a tour of the countryside." She shook her head. "No. We stay in Paris and go to the bird-market broker."

Anouk turned to Beau for help. "We need a witch, not some Pretty broker. Luc contacted Zola for a reason."

Beau relented. "If Luc trusted her, then it might be worth the risk. I say Montélimar. Sorry, Cricket. You're outvoted."

"Zola is dangerous," Cricket insisted.

"I don't doubt it." He glanced at the black-cat clock ticking away on Cricket's toaster. "Her estate is called the Château des Mille Fleurs. The House of a Thousand Flowers. I drove Mada Vittora there last winter. We could make it before sundown. If we get there and it looks too dangerous, we leave. Come back to Paris and go to the bird-market broker. We'd still have about" — he quickly counted — "forty-five hours."

Cricket didn't answer. She chewed her gum anxiously, and then, grumbling, grabbed a backpack and started stuffing things into it. The yellow headphones. A handful of candy. The cat clock. She slung the backpack over her shoulder and rooted around in a pile of coats by the front door until she found three umbrellas, two of which she tossed to them, saying, "Fine, but take these."

"It isn't raining," Anouk said.

"It isn't for that. It's for the crows. To get us from here to the car without them seeing us."

Cricket didn't bother to lock her door, though she did give the room one final look. Tiny as it was, the apartment was as much freedom as Cricket had ever had in her short life. Cricket turned away sharply, and they descended the stairs into the foyer that smelled stronger now, like curried fish.

Cricket peered through the peephole. "It looks clear. No motorcycles or idiots in slouchy hats." She rested her hand on the doorknob. "Eyes wide. Umbrellas up. Remember, we're in this together."

She shoved open the door and they were awash in daylight. Anouk took shelter beneath her umbrella, ignoring the Pretties on the sunny street who gave their umbrellas odd glances. They rushed to the car,

Anouk's heart slipping and sliding around in her chest. She kept expecting to hear the roar of Hunter Black's motorcycle. The flapping of wings. She dared a peek toward the skies and saw hundreds of dark outlines circling overhead. She dived into the passenger seat and slammed the door.

"The crows are everywhere!"

Cricket was already in the back seat. "The crows aren't our real enemy." She dug around in the backpack until she pulled out the black-cat clock. "This is. Time." She spat her gum into her hand, mushed it onto the clock's base, and then leaned forward between the front seats and affixed it to the dashboard.

Tick.

Tick.

Tick.

Beau climbed in and shot the black-cat clock a doubting look but said nothing as he threw the car into drive, then whipped them through the maze of narrow lanes of the Latin Quarter into the Marais. Eventually, tall buildings bled into countryside: Vast fields of dying grass, dotted with sheep. Villages that clustered together as though for warmth. A train barreled past them in the other direction, and Anouk smooshed her face against the window and watched it grow smaller until it was gone.

"So what exactly do we know about Mada Zola?" Beau asked.

"What's to know?" Cricket leaned forward between the seats. "She's a witch like all the rest. She'll have a houseful of servants, an insufferable brat for a witch's boy, and skin stretched too tight over creaky old bones. If we're lucky, maybe she won't do to us what she did to the Goblins."

"What *did* she do to the Goblins?" Beau asked, though he sounded as though he dreaded the answer.

"Goblins are an old order but an unambitious one; they'd be content living their quiet, bizarre little lives and never amassing an ounce of power. It was easy for witches to exploit them. Last summer, there was an ugly rumor going around that Zola lured Goblins to her estate with the promise of fantastic tea parties, but the ones who attended kept disappearing. And then the ones who went looking for *them* disappeared. Speculation started that she'd been poisoning their tea and burying their bodies in her flower beds. She thought her lavender grew better in blood. More potent. For her tricks and whispers."

Beau looked sideways at Anouk. "This is where you want us to go? An estate with chopped-up Goblins mixed in with the potting soil?"

"It's only a rumor," Anouk offered, though her toes had curled tightly in her shoes.

Cricket snorted. "You still have that knife I gave you, right, Anouk?"

Anouk took it out of the jacket and unwound the towel, wincing at the glimpse of her reflection in the blade. Sunken eyes. Messy hair. Mada Vittora would have had a fit. The thought triggered the memory of blood on her mistress's cream-colored blouse, and Anouk leaned forward, head between her knees.

Cricket rubbed her gently on the back.

"It'll be okay," she said, mistaking Anouk's reaction. "I've got my knives too. And Beau can fight, and—"

"Hang on," Beau interjected. "Me? Fight?"

"You train with Viggo all the time."

"Yeah, as his punching bag."

Cricket dismissed this with a wave. "You know *how* to fight, even if you're usually on the receiving end. This might be your chance to actually throw the punches."

"Let's hope not," Beau said. "Let's hope rumors are just rumors, and when we get to Montélimar we won't need knives or fists or anything else that could get us killed."

Anouk sat up. Cricket squeezed her shoulder in reassurance and then started going through the blades she had hidden in the folds of her clothing, testing the sharpness of each one. On the dashboard, the black-cat clock kept ticking, the tail moving in quick little stabs. Anouk hoped she'd done the right thing in convincing them to come.

Why hadn't Luc told her about trying to contact Mada Zola? Anouk wasn't used to having to guess his logic—she'd always simply trusted him and he'd never let her down. Even Cricket, normally so bold, was chewing her gum anxiously. Luc and Cricket had been around longer than Anouk and Beau and Hunter Black, and from what Anouk had gathered, Mada Vittora had been especially severe with them. She'd let thirteen-year-old Viggo use Cricket as a guinea pig during his phase experimenting with mild poisons until Luc volunteered to take her place. And she'd done worse things. No one ever spoke of it outright, but she'd heard rumors about Mada Vittora long ago forcing Luc into dark tasks that had nothing to do with gardening: late-night massages, having him bring her midnight drinks in bed and not letting him leave until morning. Tasks that she hadn't tried forcing on any of the others—Luc had taken the brunt of the abuse to spare the rest of them.

"We need to stop for gas," Beau said somewhere near Lyon, breaking the silence.

Cricket grabbed a folded map from the seat pocket and wrestled it into submission, then traced her finger along an autoroute. "There's a village called Saint-Désirat ahead. It's tiny. Too small for any scrying crows, you think?"

"I hope," Beau mumbled. "I don't feel like having my eyes plucked out today."

Someone's stomach growled. Someone else's answered.

"Maybe there will be a café too," Cricket continued. "I mean, we can't very well show up at Mada Zola's asking for her to save our lives *and* cook us lunch."

They followed signs to a single-lane road that wound in lazy switchbacks up a hill, past small cottages and vineyards. The narrow road changed to cobblestone as it took them to a mismatch of clustered buildings perched close together. A young man swept the steps of a whitewashed building whose sign indicated it was a café.

Beau pulled up to a gas station and checked the sky. "It looks clear. Go on to the café and order. Anouk, you'll be safe with Cricket. I'll get the gas and meet you there. Keep your eyes open. If anything looks off, leave your pastries and run for the car."

"Hey, now, no one's desperate enough to abandon pastries," Cricket said. "Not yet."

Anouk climbed out, thrusting her hands into her jacket pockets. Her fingers worked anxiously at the mint. Were those two women with a stroller staring at her? Had she missed a spot of blood on her skin? She couldn't shake the feeling that the Pretties sensed the three of them didn't belong.

105

Cricket slid on sunglasses and glanced at Anouk. "Got any cash?"

Anouk shook her head.

"No problem. I got this."

It was a narrow sidewalk, and Cricket swerved to avoid a parking meter, bumping into one of the mothers with a stroller. She made a quick apology and walked faster. Once they were a block away, she pulled the woman's wallet from inside her jacket, took out a handful of cash, then dumped the empty wallet in a potted bush as they walked up to the café.

Cricket grabbed a couple of menus and they picked a table on the patio half hidden by wisteria vines. Cricket snapped her fingers at the waiter, a young man with gold eyeliner and a broken-heart tattoo on the back of his hand—another Pretty taken with Goblin fashion. "Beignets for me, and coffee for both of us. Anouk?"

"Nothing. I'm sorry. I'm not sure I can eat."

A crow landed on the patio railing. Small. Inquisitive. Just a regular crow. But on instinct, Anouk cringed, and at the same time, the oddly dressed waiter flung a plate at it with such unexpected vehemence that she gave him a closer look, perplexed. The plate shattered in the bushes and the crow took flight. The waiter straightened his bow tie and offered no explanation.

Beau appeared on the patio, wiping his hands on his pants, and slid into the seat next to Anouk.

The waiter smiled. "Monsieur?"

"A crepe. Wait, make it two. Three. Okay, four."

"You should order something too, Anouk," Cricket insisted. "Hell, order everything. We might as well enjoy what we can while we can."

"Don't be bleak," Beau said. "I'm sure everything will be fine." He gave Anouk's hand a reassuring squeeze, but she didn't feel reassured. She took her hand back and reached for a napkin.

"It's realistic. We have to be honest with ourselves." Cricket lowered her voice. "What happens if Mada Zola can't help us? Or won't? Then we'll have only two days left as we are. To drive, to wear clothes, to eat pastries. After that . . . well, you know what it was like." Her face soured at the thought, but then she pushed the menu toward Anouk tenderly. "I'm just saying that if there's anything you've ever wanted to say or do, then you'd better say it or do it soon. Because we might not have much time left."

An uncomfortable silence fell over the table. Anouk realized she'd torn the paper napkin into shreds. When the waiter came back, she ordered a chocolate croissant. It came, flaky and buttery and delicious, and something tugged in her chest.

"NASCAR." Beau coughed.

"Are you choking on your crepe?" Cricket asked.

"No, it's a car race in America. That's my dream. To drive in it." He spread jam on his crepe, thinking. "And watch a movie in a cinema. There are so many things I haven't done."

"Ride a train through every country in the world," Cricket said. "That's what I'd do."

"See the northern lights," Anouk added.

"Get a tattoo."

"Oh! Go to a drive-in theater. Movies *and* cars."

"Sing karaoke."

"Eat pasta in Italy."

"Run through a sprinkler."

"Win at Clue."

"Eat sausage in Germany."

"Kiss a boy."

"Kiss a girl."

For a few minutes there was only the sound of clinking plates, of scraping forks and anxious chewing as they all thought of what they'd lose if the worst happened.

Anouk wasn't ready for it to end, the beautiful dream of being human. She wanted to experience everything. See all the places she'd only read about. Sail on a boat. Fly in an airplane. And read—read *everything*. Fairy tales. Romance novels. Only humans could write such pain and love, could make her swoon one minute and cry the next over something that had never really happened to people who'd never really existed.

"We should go," Beau said.

Cricket scooped up the rest of the beignets and stuffed them in her many pockets. Anouk almost hated to get back in the car and face the ticking cat clock whose second-hand tail kept turning and turning, always in the direction she didn't want it to move. As they pulled back onto the autoroute, the nerves crept back into her insides. She wished she hadn't put so much rich cream in her coffee.

Somewhere around Plan-de-Baix, she twisted to look in the back seat. Cricket had lain down and was caught in the throes of an anxious sleep.

Beau cleared his throat. "She's asleep?"

"Yes."

He kneaded the steering wheel with his hands, glancing in the rearview mirror to make sure she was out.

"So, remember what she said at the café about us not having much time left to say the things we've always wanted to say?" His fingers wrapped hard around the steering wheel. "I have something I want to say. I don't know if I'll get another chance." He dared a glance at her.

She shoved her hands in her pockets and suddenly felt a little too warm.

"You know it drives me crazy when you say I'm like a brother, right?"

She nodded. She worked the sprig of mint between her fingers, shredding it into ribbons. She felt the same light, ticklish feeling she had the night they'd danced together in the kitchen, the soap bubbles popping on the floor, such a wonderful moment, and yet at any second they might have tumbled and fallen on their backsides.

"I've never felt we were siblings. In fact . . . *mon Dieu,* this is hard." He paused, chewing on his bottom lip, not taking his eyes off the road. He was driving faster now, though he didn't seem to realize it. "It's like in Luc's fairy tales. The one about a peasant boy who's hopelessly in love with a princess, and there's that monster he has to stab between the horns, only the monster's made of a stronger material than his spear, and I forget the rest, the monster is really his changeling brother, I think . . ." His rambling drew to a close and he glanced at her. "Say something, cabbage."

"I'm still confused about the monster."

"*Merde.* The monster doesn't have anything to do with it. I'm talking about the peasant boy. I'm that boy. And you're the princess."

So many thoughts were tumbling around her mind, giving her a topsy-turvy feeling that was both pleasant and unpleasant at the same time. Her face felt very warm now. She redirected the vents to blow cool air on her.

"Cabbage? Do you understand?"

The speedometer creaked up to 140 kilometers an hour.

"I'm just saying, since we might have only a few days left . . ." He gripped the wheel harder. *"Merde!"* He veered sharply at a sign indicating they were on the outskirts of Montélimar. The tires squealed as he pulled off the road.

Cricket woke with a start.

He slammed on the brakes. They sat on a gravel drive off the autoroute that, just ahead, was blocked by an overgrown hedge. There was no wooden fence, no iron bars. Only a ten-foot-high tangle of shrubs that extended in either direction as far as Anouk could see.

"Is this it?" Cricket said in a hushed voice.

"This is it," Beau answered gravely. "Last chance to turn around. You're certain about this, Anouk?"

The clock kept turning in that endless circle, tick by tick by tick by tick. Anouk brushed a hand at her throat until she found her gold chain necklace. Certain? She'd never been less certain of anything in her life. "I'm . . . sure."

The three of them stared at the green wall. On the other side of the densely woven branches would be the ancient and imposing Château des Mille Fleurs. The fortress of flowers. The Montélimar prison of the second most powerful witch in France.

Well, now the first.

What were you reaching out here for, Luc? Anouk asked silently. *What did you hope to find?*

"When we get in there," Cricket muttered from the back seat, "no one drink the tea. We don't want to end up like the Goblins."

Chapter 12

Two Days and Five Hours of Enchantment Remain

ANOUK ROLLED DOWN HER window and was immediately overcome by the scent of lavender, with its delicate notes of camphor and pine. Luc was always saying lavender had a calming effect, but she didn't feel calmer in the slightest.

Cricket leaned between the front seats, chewing a fresh stick of gum, staring up at the hedge wall. "So how do we get in?"

Beau regarded the hedge as though at any moment branches with woody fingers would reach out and grab the silver hood ornament. "When I came here before, Mada Vittora had me leave her at the gate and wait in town for her signal to pick her up. I can't imagine she climbed the hedges in the heels she always wore. There must be some trick to get through." He patted the steering wheel fondly. "Besides, we can't leave the car. We might need to get away fast."

Cricket opened her door. "Well, we didn't come all this way to get stopped by shrubbery."

She climbed out and Anouk and Beau followed, leaving their doors open, the engine still running, just in case. The hedge extended in either direction, broken only by weeds and a small copse of stunted cork trees near the side of the road. The three approached the hedge as one might a sleeping bear: no sudden movements, expecting the worst, ready to run.

"Anouk, stay back." Beau dug out one of the umbrellas from the car and poked at the closest branch with the pointy end. When nothing attacked him, he grabbed a branch and tried to pry it back, but it didn't budge.

A dragonfly fluttered past Anouk's face, gossamer wings tickling her cheek. She waved it away and watched it fly in lazy circles toward a small, rusted metal box half hidden by overgrown weeds.

"Hey," she said. "Look."

She tromped through the scratchy weeds and pushed them away from the box. It looked like the antique brass call boxes she'd seen on neighboring townhouses, though this one was long neglected. Cricket stomped over, swatting away gnats, and frowned at the box.

"That's Pretty technology," she said. "It isn't of the Haute."

"Well, we might as well try it," Beau said. "We aren't getting past those hedges, that's for sure." He bent to inspect the ornate brass scrollwork. "What do we do?"

"I'm no expert, but I'm guessing we push that button that says Push."

"Wow, thanks, Cricket. I *meant* what are we supposed to say if someone answers? They won't let us in if we tell them we're fugitives suspected of murder."

"So say it's a delivery."

"Witches don't get deliveries."

"How does she get toilet paper, then, genius? She's imprisoned here by decree of the Royals." Cricket shoved him, and he shoved her back.

Exasperated, Anouk couldn't think about anything but the tick-tick-tick of the black-cat clock. She pushed her way between the two of them, stabbed her thumb against the intercom button, and rattled out with barely a breath, "Hello? My name is Anouk. I don't have a last name. I guess if I did, it would be de Vittora. That's who made me. Made us, I mean. There are three of us and we need your help because our mistress is dead and we don't have much time. We're desperate."

She let go of the button.

Beau and Cricket had stopped fighting.

The intercom was silent.

Anouk stared at it, chewing her lip. "I thought we should be honest," she said to them by way of explanation, but now that felt foolish.

"This is wrong," Beau blurted out. Although the sun was setting, he was sweating badly, slapping at gnats. "I don't like the feel of this place. If we do ever find our way in there, we might never find our way back out. We should leave while we still can."

He tried to herd Anouk back to the car, but she shook her head. "Just wait."

She stared at the intercom, willing someone to answer. She'd convinced them to come here, to spend precious hours on the drive. If they were turned away, where else would they go?

Laughter, a little husky and a lot amused, came from a copse of trees on the far side of the car. The intercom was suddenly forgotten. Blades appeared in Cricket's hands, drawn swiftly from the mysterious folds of her clothes. Anouk fumbled for her own knife, realizing too late she'd left it in the glove box.

A girl who looked around eighteen years old came out from the copse carrying hedge clippers in one hand and a cigarette in the other. She was lanky and all angles, like a marionette hinged with too many joints, and strawberry hair pulled into a knot. She wore ripped jeans and a white cashmere sweater two sizes too big for her.

She dropped the cigarette in a patch of mud on the road and stomped it out beneath a black combat boot.

"Doesn't work," she said, nodding toward the call box. "Can't use that kind of technology here."

"Told you," Cricket growled at Beau.

The girl observed them coolly. "You're the beasties everyone's looking for. Every order of the Haute is searching for you, did you know that?"

Anouk bit her lip. "We didn't kill anyone."

"Oh, that." The girl waved away any concern. "Mada Zola doesn't care if you killed Vittora. All the better if you *did*. We got word a few hours ago that she was dead and we've been celebrating ever since." She motioned to a wheelbarrow full of recycling that held more than a few empty champagne bottles.

"I'm Petra," the girl said. "Mada Zola's daughter."

She held out a hand to shake, the hedge clippers dangling carelessly from her other hand. Her sweater looked expensive, but threads were plucked lose and snagged, and a few thorns were tangled messily in the seams. The slouchy collar exposed a bony bare shoulder.

None of them took her extended hand. Cricket eyed the girl's boots enviously.

"A witch's girl?" Anouk said. "There aren't any witch's girls. Only boys."

Petra let her hand fall and raised a thin, unimpressed eyebrow. "Is that so? Well, for what it's worth, I didn't start out a girl." She put down the hedge clippers, dumped the barrowful of recycling in a bin by the gravel drive, turned back around, and took a closer look at Anouk. "Is that a Faustine jacket?"

Anouk nodded.

Petra made an approving sound. She grabbed the clippers and headed toward the hedge wall, combat boots crunching over the gravel. "You all look terrified. Come on inside. I'll make you some cocoa."

Anouk glanced at Cricket and Beau, who both looked as bewildered as she felt.

"Didn't start out a girl?" Anouk whispered.

"Transgender," Cricket whispered back. "Like in Luc's fairy tale."

She meant "The Swan Mirror." It had been Anouk's favorite. She could almost hear his soft voice now: *Once upon a time . . .* It was about a king who possessed a mirror that showed the heart's true desire. When the king's youngest son peered into it, he saw his own face reflected but changed — a young woman looked back, not a man. His heart's true desire was to be a princess, but such a wish seemed impossible. His footman, the son of a seamstress, observed his master's sorrow and offered to help him dress as a lady in the privacy of his chambers. Each night, the footman snuck into the laundry rooms to borrow dresses from palace courtesans, and he taught his master how to sit and stand and dance in the beautiful clothes; each morning, he returned the dresses. And though the prince treasured these secret evenings, he was not content with merely dressing the part. He sought out an enchantress, who told him that only true love's kiss could grant his desire. But the prince had no true love and returned to the castle in despair. His footman overheard his sobs and boldly kissed his tears away. The prince realized that he'd had his true love before him every night, the man who'd danced with him in his borrowed dresses and filled his heart with delight. He kissed his true love and transformed into the young woman he'd seen in the mirror. *You were my prince,* the footman said. *Now you are my princess. In any time, in any shape, you'll always be* my *heart's true desire—I need no mirror to show me this.*

Anouk pressed a hand to her heart, wishing she could hear Luc's soothing voice telling her once more that, just like in the stories, everything would be all right in the end.

Petra stopped before the hedge and squinted at it, then poked at some of the branches. "These are sentinel shrubs. They're enchanted to keep everyone out except who we want in." She looked back at them. "Get in the car and make sure your hands and heads stay inside if you want to keep them." When no one moved, she added, "I thought you said you were desperate."

"Right." Anouk exchanged a long look with the others. They climbed into the car and shut the doors, peering anxiously through the windshield. Petra hunted through the branches until she found a certain one about a foot from the ground that curled in the shape of a corkscrew. She pulled on it, and when nothing happened, she kicked at it a few times with her boot until the hedges shuddered, and she grinned at them in triumph.

Incredibly, the branches started to move. They untangled themselves from one another, drawing back away from the road and then weaving themselves together to form an archway to allow the car passage.

Petra came over to Beau's side and leaned in the open window.

"Follow the drive all the way to the porte-cochère. Don't get out of the car until then. And above all, be careful of your shoes. We have swans. The little monsters crap everywhere." She picked a thorn out of her sweater. "I'll ride up front."

"*Where* up front?" Beau muttered, but she was already climbing on top of the Rolls-Royce hood as if it were the most normal thing in the world, cradling the hedge clippers in one arm, resting a boot on the silver hood ornament. She tapped twice to signal them to go.

Beau didn't move.

Anouk whispered, "What are you waiting for?"

"How about a sign that we aren't about to drive straight to our deaths?" But he put the car in gear and they rolled forward slowly beneath the eerie archway of branches. They all leaned forward to get a good look at the rippling fields of lavender, bursting purple-blue in perfectly spaced rows. Nestled in the nearest valley was the château itself: sun-warmed stone and a terra-cotta roof with gables and a bell tower and a chimney at each end, though there was no smoke now, nor any sign of life in any of the windows. If it weren't for the breeze stirring it all to life, the entire valley would look like a painting.

"I'm no gardener," Beau said, "but didn't Luc grow lavender in July?"

Cricket glanced at the calendar on her phone. "It's October."

None of them said what Anouk assumed they were all thinking: on the property of a witch, anything was possible.

As they inched along the gravel driveway, Anouk eyed the dark soil at the base of each row, half fearing a glimpse of the odd Goblin finger or decomposing foot. But everything was perfectly tended, lovingly cared for. Something as beautiful as these gardens couldn't possibly grow in chopped-up Goblins. Could they?

Cricket sneezed.

As they neared the building, the lavender fields gave way to more traditional gardens dotted with fountains. Anouk cracked open her window and breathed in the smell of roses and lilac, cypress trees and the moldy dark odor of standing water. And the topiaries! Dozens of bushes had been clipped into the shapes of people, larger than life, with oversize leafy hands and heads. Their faces were nothing but green masks, blank, sightless, and yet Anouk couldn't shake the feeling of eyes watching her.

Beau stopped beneath the porte-cochère. His hand hovered over the gearshift, ready to throw the car into reverse at the slightest sign of trouble. "It's been a real pleasure knowing you both. At least before my death I got to eat those nice crepes and drive on the Autoroute Provençale. When we find ourselves churned up into potting soil, don't say I didn't warn you."

Anouk smacked him lightly.

Cricket smacked him harder.

He unlocked the doors and they stepped out into the dying light. The sky was a soft wash of purple, mirroring the fields. Anouk pulled her jacket tighter to block the biting wind. As an afterthought, she grabbed the cat clock and stuffed it into her pocket.

Beau took a step toward the château and something squished under his boot. He groaned.

"I told you to be careful," Petra said, sliding off the hood. "Swans, man. They crap everywhere." She started toward the house.

Beau leaned toward Anouk. "Do *not* drink any cocoa that girl gives you."

He looked back at the car longingly before following Petra through the gardens. Anouk stayed back a moment. There wasn't a single yellowed leaf, not one bruised blossom, and as beautiful as it all was, the place felt wrong. Frozen in midsummer perfection despite the October chill.

Anouk hurried to catch up with the others.

"Where are the gardeners?" she asked, falling in step with them.

"No gardeners," Petra said over her shoulder. "It's only the Mada and me."

And it was true, not a single person was out tending the fields. There was no one around but Petra, and she barely seemed to know which end of the hedge clippers to hold.

Cricket patted her pockets as if reassuring herself she still had her knives.

Petra started up a set of stone stairs overgrown with moss but stopped as the heavy wooden door was flung open.

A woman stood in the shadows of the doorway.

Though Anouk couldn't see her face, it had to be Mada Zola. She felt a strange sort of guilt, as though by being here, she was being disloyal to Mada Vittora. She felt a pang of . . . what? Sadness? Grief? *Anger?*

Mada Zola took a step forward, and the dying sunlight washed over her face. She was beautiful, of course. Witches always were. But there was something about her wine-red lips and deep brown eyes that hinted at some ancient lineage, as though before she was French, she had been many other things with many other names. Her black hair fell in ripples all the way to the hem of her pale blue blouse, untucked over jeans that were rolled up to the ankles.

She took another step forward, barefoot on the stone steps. Her expression seemed both surprised and utterly not surprised at the same time. She made a soft gasp. "You've come back."

Her voice was perfumed yet hardy, like the lavender itself. A delicate gold bracelet circled one wrist, but that was the only ornament she wore, as earthy as her own gardens.

Anouk's shoes crunched in the gravel. This was the woman who could protect them from the bleakness of what they were before — or curse them to an eternity of it.

Cricket whispered, "Um, what does she mean by *back?*"

Anouk's chest felt electric and tense, like she'd swallowed a swarm of bees. As the sun sank behind the purple hills, a fear crept over her that coming here was the exact mistake that Cricket and Beau had said it was.

She hadn't made the mistake of leaving the knife behind again. She dug it out of her pocket and thrust it forward, warning the witch not to come closer.

"Stay back."

Mada Zola stopped in front of Anouk, ignoring the knife. She looked at each of them with shining dark eyes that seemed to hold the kind of knowledge that people had killed for.

Petra, leaning in the doorway, folded her arms and looked away.

"I knew you'd make it back to me," the witch said. "My dearies. My lovelies."

Despite the witch's smile, despite the welcoming arms, Anouk was chilled to the marrow.

"Now, which one of you," the witch said, "is my little lost Cricket?"

Chapter 13

Two Days and Four Hours of Enchantment Remain

N
O ONE ANSWERED, LEAST of all Cricket. Anouk
tried hard not to look at her friend, which might have given
her identity away.

Mada Zola gave a soft laugh. "So serious, aren't you? My poor
dears. My grim little lovelies. What you must have been through.
Come inside and rest. You're safe now."

Safe. A tempting word that Anouk didn't dare believe. From all
directions, the blank faces of topiaries observed her in perfect stillness. She shifted her weight and felt something give way beneath her
left shoe. A crushed rose. Its bruised petals were the only imperfect
thing in this terribly perfect place.

Petra held open the heavy wooden door for them.

Anouk felt a jab in the center of her back. "It was your idea to
come here," Cricket said in a hard whisper. "You go first."

Anouk fidgeted with her jacket, zipping it higher against the evening chill. She closed her eyes and imagined that the wings on the
back of the jacket were *her* wings, gossamer and strong; that the sharp
horns sprouted from *her* head; that she was as rigid and unflinching
as a gargoyle. From somewhere inside the house she could hear the
crackling of a fire.

She stepped across the threshold and ran straight into another topiary. This one was restricted to an enormous clay pot in the center of the château's entrance hall. Branches smacked at her face, and she sputtered and fought them off. The bush was clipped into the shape of a bear, though it was overgrown and shaggy with untrimmed leaves. She eyed its branches warily—bones of wood, claws of thorns, fur of leaves—half expecting it to move.

"Did the bear get you?" Petra asked, turning around. "We've named him Toblerone. Like the chocolate."

"Cute," Anouk muttered. She fought back a cough; apparently no one had dusted Toblerone in ages.

They followed Petra down a hallway flanked with the kind of deep-set windows Anouk had seen in books about abbeys and cloisters. Open doors led to rooms that appeared all but abandoned. Her shoes echoed too loud on the stone floors, and she yearned to kick off the stiff oxfords and walk silently and barefoot, like Mada Zola. But her missing toes had a way of inviting questions she'd rather not answer.

They passed an enormous room that might once have been a chapel, and the smell of thyme wrapped around her. She paused and gave it a closer look.

Empty, the fireplace cold.

But the smell of thyme was fresh, and when she pitched her head to the high rafters, she saw hundreds of bunches of the herbs tied up in clove-hitch knots for drying. The same knots that Luc used. *Were you here, hanging these herbs?* she wondered silently, and then a new question crept into her mind:

Are you here still?

She shot Beau and Cricket a look over her shoulder, but they were both too concerned with checking every corner for something that might attack them to notice herbs.

As they continued down the hall, Anouk realized that no one had dusted *anything* in ages. Cobwebs spanned the exposed wooden rafters, and clumps of curled dried leaves clustered in the corners, skittering in the drafts. Precarious piles of books lined the hallway, as though someone had started to move them from shelf to shelf years ago but abandoned the project. Trying to read the spines, Anouk bumped into a stack and the top book fell open, spilling out dried blossoms that had been pressed between the pages.

She picked up a paper-thin rose.

"You don't have a maid," she said in surprise.

Mada Zola stopped. Her eyes went to the cobwebs in the corner. "Is it that obvious? I used to keep house better. For months it's been just the two of us. I'm afraid we've let things go."

Anouk could think of two things wrong with this statement. First, they couldn't possibly have been maintaining the entire estate alone. The house was neglected, but the garden wasn't. Despite what Petra had claimed, someone had to be out there watering the flowers —tricks and whispers couldn't keep a garden that size going forever. And second, they *hadn't* been alone. Anouk had heard, just two days ago, a person who must have been Mada Zola talking with someone on Luc's scryboard. A man.

"I don't mind the mess," Anouk clarified, even though she itched to attack it all with a feather duster. "It's admirable that you do your own cooking and cleaning. That you don't use servants."

And it was true, the Château des Mille Fleurs wasn't anything like what they'd feared—at least not on the surface.

"That's a kind word for how Vittora treated you," Mada Zola said. "I might have said *slaves*."

She opened a door to a cozy sitting room that was less dusty than the hall, likely because it seemed to be used more often. There was a large banquet table, though it was covered in books and probably hadn't seen a plate in years. And the *portraits*. Every inch of the high walls was covered in ornately framed paintings. Anouk turned in a slow circle, taking in the hundreds of painted eyes, feeling like fingertips were walking up her neck.

She recognized various Royals — there was a painting of Lord and Lady Metham dancing, and one of a rather severe-looking Countess Quine on a horse, and, of course, multiple paintings of Rennar. He was everywhere. It was hard to count exactly how many portraits were of the crown prince, but his handsome face seemed to be looking at her from all angles, from above the mantel, from over the threshold, from at least three corners. She touched her messy hair, realizing she must look awful. Was he watching? Had he taken notice of her? In all the portraits, he was dressed in his frost-gray suit and had a crown of gold briars; in none of them was he the boy with the mussed hair and scarf who'd shown up on her doorstep.

"Mon Dieu," Anouk breathed, staring at the portraits.

"Don't mind them," Mada Zola said. "They don't watch anymore, not since I've been banished. They've nothing *to* watch. Just Petra and me playing cards and pressing flowers."

Anouk didn't feel reassured, and as though sensing her thoughts, the witch followed her line of sight to a life-size portrait of Prince Rennar staring back at them with those cool blue eyes.

"You recognize the prince," she said, somewhat surprised.

"He came to dinner the night Vittora died." She paused, clutching the clock in her pocket. Had it truly been only one day since she'd opened the townhouse door and seen him there? Since her life had changed so dramatically?

Mada Zola folded her arms, studying the portrait. "Don't get swept up in his influence. It's difficult not to, I know. The power he wields, the way he looks at you as though he sees straight to the person inside you, the person you didn't even know you were. Some say he was born of a Spanish duke and a witch during the Louis the Fifteenth wars, but I think he's too patient to bear any witch blood—assuming a witch could even conceive. I'd guess that he came from old Viking royalty. The fair hair. His fondness for the sea." She gazed at the portrait cryptically. "He's been prince for only a few decades. He worked his way up in the ranks over two hundred years. In all that time of knowing him, I've yet to figure him out. Although I've learned that he's not one to be trifled with."

Anouk felt a creeping heat spread up her neck, a shiver that wasn't entirely unpleasant. She took in the other portraits. "You're certain they aren't watching us?"

"I promise." Her voice was a purr. She whispered toward the fireplace, *"Incendie flaim."*

A fire sparked and caught on the dry wood.

"Petra, our guests look shaken to their cores. Why don't you fetch the cocoa and put everyone at ease? Bring a bag of those tiny marshmallows too." She rubbed her hands together briskly before the fire. "Sit, dearies." She motioned to a dusty divan.

Beau looked ready to bolt back to the safety of the car. "I'll stand, thanks." He went to the window, wiped away the grime with his sleeve, and peered out at the gardens. "What kind of security do you have here?"

"Why, who's chasing you?" There was a guarded note in Mada Zola's otherwise gentle voice.

"Who isn't?" Beau answered.

Anouk figured that honesty had gotten them this far—the greatest threat they'd encountered here was being crushed under a falling pile of books—so she might as well continue being truthful. "It's Mada Vittora's boy, Viggo, and the assassin called Hunter Black. They've been following us since we left Paris. Viggo thinks we killed his mother."

"They can't reach you here," Mada Zola assured him. "They can stalk outside the gate and scowl all they want, but they won't set foot on my territory, meager though it is."

Anouk's tight shoulders relaxed, though one hand was still curled around the knife in her pocket. But there was that eternal thumping in her other pocket, the clock. Not so easy to hide from time.

"What did you mean," Cricket said in a slightly high tone, "when you said that we'd come back? And that name you mentioned—Cricket, was it?"

Mada Zola smiled knowingly. "Ah. So you're her."

Chapter 14

Two Days and Three and a Half Hours of Enchantment Remain

CRICKET'S LIPS FELL OPEN. She lifted her hands, feigning ignorance, as Mada Zola searched among the portraits until she found what she was looking for, took it down, and handed it to Cricket.

Cricket made a gargling sound in her throat and dropped the painting. "What is *that?*"

"That, my lovely, is you. Or rather, what you were."

Anouk picked up the frame. It was a simple painting, done by an amateur but one who had a clear fondness for the subject. Maybe Mada Zola or Petra had even painted it. She held it out to Beau.

He left the window and took the portrait. His face wrinkled in confusion as he looked between it and Cricket. It was a cat. White fur and long whiskers, green eyes with a clever kind of look. Anouk couldn't help but think of the pelts in the car trunk. One of them had been white and soft and small, the size of a cat. Judging by the distressed look on Cricket's face, she figured Cricket remembered the same pelt.

"Merde," Cricket cursed.

With her honey-brown skin and light copper eyes, Cricket looked nothing like a cat—especially not this cat. But there were her careful ways. Her ability to move silently. Anouk looked closer at the painting and spied something gold at the cat's neck.

"Did you see this?" she asked hoarsely. She passed the portrait back to Cricket, pointing at the collar.

Cricket's face paled a shade. She clutched the charm earring in her ear self-consciously, but it was useless. They both knew what was stamped on it.

CRICKET

It was identical to the charm in the painting. Cricket's earring, which Viggo had given her years ago but hadn't bothered to tell her what it was, had once been part of a collar. A *tag*.

Anouk had rarely let herself wonder about her past, about that frightening cold place. Certainly not about what animals they had started life as. Whenever she'd looked through the turret window and seen an animal in the street, she'd turned away sharply and dusted, ignoring the fear rising in her throat. It hadn't been until she'd seen the pelts—a wolf, a dog, an owl, a mouse, and a cat—that she'd let herself play that dangerous matching game.

Which was which? Which was *she*?

And now Cricket was the first to learn the truth about herself, and clearly, it wasn't welcome knowledge.

"It's true, then?" Anouk said. "You knew Cricket . . . before?"

Mada Zola replaced the painting on the wall. "Oh yes. Mada

Vittora came here years ago. We got in an awful row. She knew I loved that cat. After she left, I couldn't find it anywhere."

Petra carried in a tray of steaming mugs, and Anouk's stomach tugged—she hadn't eaten much at the café. But she was hungry for more than just chocolate. She wanted *this*—everything the room promised. A cozy fire and warm drinks and a mistress who didn't keep servants, who wasn't bothered that her witch's boy had wanted to become a witch's girl, who didn't care if dust bunnies multiplied throughout the house, who hadn't blinked at Anouk's messy ponytail.

And yet, did she dare trust it?

She wanted to. They all sat, and Anouk took the cocoa with shaking hands. Lavender and honey. Divine. How badly she wanted to drink it. She dared to take the slightest sip. Beau had warned her not to, but Beau was always warning her.

"And Anouk and me?" Beau asked hollowly. "Are we from here too?"

The witch's face softened. "No. I don't know where the two of you come from, or what—*creatures*—you were before. I'm sorry."

Cricket had looked dazed for the past few minutes, but now she suddenly stood, fists clenched. "If what you say is true, then we need your help."

"Yes, I gathered that, my dear."

"You know what she did to us. She made us work for her, and she beat us, and worse." Cricket swallowed. "Now, without her, the spell that keeps us human will expire at midnight on Saturday. We're almost out of time. We need you to recast the enchantment. I can't go back to . . . to *that*." Her eyes flickered toward the cat painting.

For a moment, all were silent. Anouk wasn't sure why Cricket had decided to trust this witch after arguing not to come here in the first place. Maybe because of the painting and the collar that matched her earring. If Mada Zola was telling the truth about that, maybe she was telling the truth about everything.

"Why?" Petra asked, surprising her. She was standing in the doorway with her arms folded tightly. "Why does it matter to you what form you take? Sleep all day, drink saucers of milk. Doesn't sound so bad."

Anouk cocked her head, curious about this girl. She remembered now why witches took sons, never daughters. Only females could become witches, so it was fathomable that a daughter might grow up to become a rival witch herself, whereas a son could never threaten their power. Did those same rules apply to a girl who hadn't been born a girl?

Petra's question seemed genuinely curious, but Cricket's face turned cold. She snapped, "Because my life is worth more than catching mice."

Cricket's stare was vicious, challenging. One more word from Petra, and Anouk had a feeling the blades were going to make an appearance.

"It isn't about whether skin or fur covers us," Anouk blurted out, hoping to avoid a fight. "It's about what's beneath that, even beneath bone."

All eyes turned to her, and she wished she had kept her mouth shut. These were dark thoughts. Thoughts she had ignored her whole life, truths she had looked away from at night, alone in her turret bedroom, when it was hardest to escape them.

Her eyes met Beau's. He gave a small nod of encouragement.

"Before, for all of us, it was a dark place." Her voice wavered as she continued. "A cold place. I don't mean to say that life before was miserable. I mean that it was *empty*. Until Mada Vittora made me into myself, I wasn't *me*. What I am—my memories, my dreams, the people I care about, and the thoughts I think about when I'm alone—it means everything to me. Imagine if one day everything that made you who you are simply disappeared. If all you thought of was filling a hungry belly. If the world was cast in shades of gray, not color. If you lost the ability to express yourself in words. If you never loved. If you never dreamed. That's what we stand to lose. Everything."

Petra was quiet. She looked shaken.

"Restart the enchantment," Anouk said, turning to Mada Zola. "Grant us the chance to remain ourselves. A lifetime of being perfectly normal, that's all we want. The same as anyone."

The witch was quiet for a long time. Her cocoa sat before her, cooled now, the marshmallows melted away. The fire kept crackling. Beau had gone back to stand by the window, but he'd stopped staring out of it, watching for Viggo. Night had fallen at some point; Anouk had barely noticed.

"I'd like to help you." Mada Zola stood. "And I will, as best I can. But the spell you were made with isn't just any whisper. It isn't as simple as making flowers bloom year-round or sparking fire in kindling. Prince Rennar wrote it himself centuries ago. It requires a lengthy whisper with challenging intonations and a tincture of the exact right life-essence. Not to mention a lot of blood."

"I don't mind," Petra said quietly.

Anouk realized that Petra, as a witch's girl, must have a bloodletting chair just like Viggo's. She felt a sudden protectiveness for this girl who was willing to drain pints of her blood for them.

"Thank you, my dear," Mada Zola said, "but without the wording of the spell itself, no amount of blood will keep them from turning back."

"Mada Vittora had the spell," Anouk said in a rush. "We could go back to Paris and fetch it."

Mada Zola shook her head. "Written spells die with their witch. Her copy will be nothing but ash now. The Royals have a copy, but spells of that magnitude are kept in only one place: the spell library at Castle Ides. Only members of the Haute who have invitations can access them. I had an invitation, but it was revoked with my banishment." She motioned to the delicate bracelet on her wrist; it looked like jewelry but was, in fact, the bond of her imprisonment. "One step beyond the fields and I turn to dust." She swiped a finger along the top of a cabinet, coming away with a fine coating of dust that sizzled when she brushed it into the fire.

"But we have only a few days left." Anouk fingered the clock in her pocket with a growing sense of panic. "You mean everything we've risked is for nothing?" She shook her head violently. "It can't all just be lost."

The witch looked at her with pity. "How much time do you have left?"

Beau said quietly, "About fifty-two hours."

"Then it isn't over yet. There might be a way to extend your enchantment without the original spell, some alternative trick."

Anouk found it hard to take comfort from the witch's words. How many hollow promises had Mada Vittora made her? Her mood turned sour, nasty. Witches were tricky. "We can repay you, if that's what this is about. We can serve you like we served our last mistress. I'm a wonder with a mop. I make a good quiche too." She didn't mean for her words to sound as bitter as they did.

A log popped in the fire. Mada Zola eyed the three of them for a long time.

"Quiche. Mops." There was an oddly electric look in her eyes. "You poor dearies. You don't have a clue what you really are, do you?"

Anouk's breathing felt too fast. A distant voice was ringing in her ears, Prince Rennar standing in Mada Vittora's foyer, leaning toward her with those fathomless blue eyes and unsettling words on his lips. *You aren't made for sweeping floors, little beastie.*

From every wall, his face watched, his eyes finding hers over and over. She knew that whatever Mada Zola was about to tell them was what Rennar had been referring to. The great mystery, revealed.

The next few words were about to change their lives forever.

Chapter 15

Two Days and Three Hours of Enchantment Remain

WE KNOW WHAT WE are," Beau said tensely.

Mada Zola gave him an unmistakably pitying look. "Do you?"

She motioned to the walls of portraits, which, in the flickering firelight, played tricks on Anouk's eyes. The skin tones, ranging from pale white to reddish brown, looked more like real flesh than paint. Mada Zola pointed to a small portrait of a woman—an ancient witch, judging by her long blue gown—poised on high castle walls above the sea.

"The beastie spell is centuries old. Until you were discovered, the last beasties that anyone knew of lived in Dubrovnik in the mid-1800s. The Sea-Salt Witch of Babin Kuk enchanted seals into beautiful women whom she used to lure sailors and their cargo to her fortress. She called those beasties selkas. But those all died out long ago. After that, the spell was lost to everyone but the Shadow Royals. I don't know how Mada Vittora got her hands on a copy of it, but she did, and she clearly didn't understand its power. She was a fool to think it was meant for creating house servants. The Royals would have stopped her if they'd found out, but their kingdom is vast and they can be, well, aloof. They aren't in the habit of taking a second look at maids. In any case, they had no intention of allowing beasties to be made again. Not after what happened to the others."

"What happened to them?" Beau asked hesitantly.

"The selkas? Oh, the seal-women weren't the problem. The Royals killed the last selkas before they could turn dangerous. It was the first ones, the original ones Prince Rennar made, that became, over time, *unmanageable*."

The word clouded the air like smoke.

Mada Zola pointed to a portrait of the Shadow Royals that looked just like the one that hung in a gilded frame in the townhouse. There was Rennar and Lord and Lady Metham in the center, flanked by lesser Royals and a witch at the end of each row. They were in a vast library, all leather-bound books and gleaming brass balconies. In the background stood dozens of figures that weren't painted in as much detail as the rest, maids and butlers—enchanted Pretties—dressed in black with their eyes averted. A few mischievous Goblins were peeking through doorways.

"Do you know the three orders of the Haute?" Mada Zola asked.

"The Royals, the witches, the Goblins," Cricket answered. "The Royals and Goblins have been around at least as long as the Pretties have, evolving alongside them but hidden. Born of magic, like the Pretties are born of flesh. Witches are different. They're born Pretty and undergo a change to make themselves magical. It's dangerous. Most don't survive."

Mada Zola smiled—*she* had survived. Anouk noticed that Petra remained close-lipped during all of this, busying herself by picking thorns from her sweater. She was a witch's girl and thus privy to the inner workings of the Haute, but she wasn't *of* the Haute. She'd been born Pretty. Had a lifespan that would last decades, not centuries. That fact had rankled Viggo. Did it eat away at Petra too?

If so, she hid it better.

"And do you know about the vitae echo?" Mada Zola asked.

Anouk felt a shiver as she thought of livers turned to stone, hearts to wood.

"It is the way in which magic stays balanced," Mada Zola explained. "Whenever handlers use magic to, say, heal a burn or open a locked door, they experience an echo. A consequence. A *cost*. Magic comes from consuming life, and life demands a tax in return. If it wasn't for the vitae echo, our magic would be limitless." She crossed the room to a painting of Pretties working with wooden contraptions.

"In the eighteenth and nineteenth centuries, the Pretties developed more advanced technology, and it began to interfere with the Haute's magic. We were able to adapt to most mechanical technologies created before that; there are certain motor engines and clockwork mechanics that do not hinder our spells. But electricity, ah. New technology like that throws our magic completely into chaos. Magic is thinning. And less magic to go around means more competition. Witches vying with one another for what power remains. Territory wars." Anouk thought of how Vittora had fabricated a lie about insubordination to get Zola banished. "Prince Rennar foresaw this as far back as the late eighteenth century. He wanted to create something to rewrite the balance, as he knew technology would continue to grow. Something powerful enough that it wouldn't be limited by the vitae echo."

Her eyes flashed brighter. "Rennar wasn't a prince then, not yet. He was a spell-scribe with an idea. He wrote a spell to create a fourth order: beasties."

None of the portraits showed mice or horses or women with skins of seal, and the witch's eyes shifted to the three of them. As though they were painted figures come to life that needed no gilded frames.

Her lips stretched into a smile. "Prince Rennar's intention was that beasties would look human—*be* human, on almost all counts —but that their souls, as animals, would reside in the natural world. The vitae echo, you see, is uniquely tied to the human world: the world of morals and sin. By contrast, the natural world lies outside of the echo. There is no sin for beasties, because you are not moral creatures but natural ones. And thus you are not bound by the vitae echo. Rennar believed this would make you limitless in his attempts to right the balance of power. He created your kind as saviors."

Anouk studied the portrait of Rennar, trying to discern the truth, but it was only a facsimile of him. His painted eyes so darkly teasing, almost as real as the eyes of the boy who'd stood on her doorstep, but not quite. Only the real Rennar could answer the still-forming questions in her head. A shiver of vertigo washed over her and she touched her brow, felt something like the start of a fever. She rested her forehead against the cool glass of a window.

"You're saying we can do magic?" Cricket's voice was skeptical, but Anouk knew she believed the same thing.

"My dearie, I don't think you understand. I'm not talking about cheap magic that even Goblins can do. I'm saying that beasties are the most powerful order of the Haute. More powerful, even, than the Royals who made them. You can take life without repercussions and thus wield unheard-of magic."

None of them spoke. All those painted eyes. All of *him*. The most powerful order? She was a girl who spent her days dreamily gazing out windows, making frosted cakes just so Beau could lick the spoon, listening to Luc tell her stories. A maid, not a magic handler, and certainly no one's savior.

Had Vittora really never known this?

Beau was facing away from the fireplace, his expression lost to shadows. He seemed oddly distant. He suddenly grabbed his gloves from the entry table.

"Lies," he spat. "She's a liar, just like Mada Vittora. Come on, Anouk. Cricket. We're getting out of here."

He grabbed Anouk's hand and started to pull her down the hallway into the foyer.

"Beau, stop!" Anouk wrested her hand away. "I'm not leaving."

"I'm begging you," he said, lowering his voice. "Don't listen to her. She's just like Mada Vittora. Before he disappeared, Luc—" He stopped short as though thinking better of what he'd been about to say.

"What about Luc?" When he didn't answer, Anouk pressed. "Do you know where he is? Is he *here?*" When he still didn't answer, she hissed, "You've treated me with kid gloves my whole life, Beau. Be honest with me now. I can take it."

Beau looked away as though he didn't like this fiercer version of Anouk. "I only know that Luc didn't trust Mada Vittora. You loved her too much to see it, but Luc saw it, and Cricket did, and so did I. And I'm telling you that I see that same glimmer of scheming now. That witch's words are honeyed poison."

"But I think I *can* do magic," she insisted. "In the closet, I whispered for us to be protected and it worked."

He ran a hand over his short hair. "Listen. I watched Mada Vittora beat Luc. I watched her let Viggo try to put his hands all over Cricket. I watched her cut off your toes, Anouk! And all that time, I did nothing. I let Luc handle it all. But he needed help as much as we did." His eyes were full of ghosts. "In the car on the way here, there was something I was trying to tell you."

The fairy tale of the peasant boy and the princess—she hadn't forgotten.

He took her hand and the tension broke. He was gentle now, and more than a little bit awkward. "I wasted our time together being too much of an idiot to tell you. In Luc's story, do you remember what the peasant boy says to the princess in the end?"

"'Only a fool would risk a monster's impalement for love,'" she recited, "'and I'm a fool.'"

He squeezed her hand, his blue eyes searching hers. "I'm a fool, Anouk."

She wanted to stuff her hands in her pockets, find some charm to tell her what to say. The knife. The mint. The clock. *Useless.* She closed her eyes.

"Beau . . ."

"Like Cricket said, we only have each other now. You're my princess, Anouk. I've loved you since the first time I wiped a streak of dust off your face. And I'm not going to let anything happen to you."

Her hand felt shaky in his. He loved her? He'd joked about such things, always giving her messy kisses on the cheek. She'd never quite realized that it wasn't all in jest.

He cupped her face, leaning in, and for a second she thought he might kiss her. But he whispered, "I'm telling you this so you know why we have to leave."

"She *isn't* like Mada Vittora," Anouk insisted. "There aren't servants here. She's broken the rules to have a daughter, not a son. Cricket trusts her, at least a little."

"Cricket just wants to learn dark spells so that she can slice the Royals into little pieces."

Anouk fingered the mint deep in her pocket, worried nearly to dust. "What if Zola could prove it to us?"

"Prove that we're more powerful than the Haute? How?"

"I have an idea."

He didn't look convinced. In fact, he looked like he might throw her over his shoulder and carry her kicking and screaming to the car. But he didn't, and it dawned on her that something had changed between them in the past few minutes, some subtle shift of power, and she knew without having to ask that he would do whatever she requested of him. It was a power she hadn't asked for, wasn't even sure she wanted.

But it was there.

"Trust me, Beau."

She stood on tiptoe to press a kiss to his cheek and felt him shudder with longing in response. He didn't argue as she led him back to the sitting room. Mada Zola stood from the armchair. For a small woman, she had a way of filling every corner of the room like a clap of rolling thunder.

Anouk pointed to the fire. "Teach me a spell, witch."

Chapter 16

Two Days and Two Hours of Enchantment Remain

MADA ZOLA SMILED SLOWLY. "Very well, but not the fire trick. That one's finicky."

She went to a bouquet of red roses and plucked off the fattest blossom. The firelight cast shadows over half her face, and Anouk felt herself drawn to the witch all the more. Mada Zola held the rose out in open palms.

"Take it, dearie. We aren't allowed powder in this house, but not all spells require such complexity. Sometimes a simple rose can do the job."

Anouk hesitated, but she'd gotten them into this and she couldn't change her mind now. She popped the rose in her mouth. The petals felt wrong against her tongue, like she was eating perfumed silk. She forced it down.

Mada Zola nodded. "A rose alone isn't enough to perform most enchantments, but it can create a light breeze. Make someone forget what he was about to say." She looked at Beau. "Put someone to sleep, like your handsome friend."

Beau grunted. "Why do I have to be the victim?"

Mada Zola ignored him and rested her hands on Anouk's shoulders. "Feel the life of the flower spreading through you. From your stomach to your throat to your tongue to your fingertips. And whisper after me: *Dorma, dorma, sonora precimo.*"

Anouk paused. "Are you okay with this, Beau?"

He muttered, "Go ahead." For all the resignation in his voice, there was a trace of curiosity too.

Anouk's throat felt scratched raw from the rose, and yet the pain had woken her body in some way. She closed her eyes, raised her fingertips, and whispered, *"Dorma, dorma, sonora precimo."*

"I don't feel anything. You—" Beau collapsed to the oriental rug. It happened in less than half a breath. His head hit the edge of a chair as he fell but he didn't cry out, didn't move. It was so fast that Anouk had barely finished speaking.

"Beau!" She dropped to her knees. She held her breath until he suddenly shuddered and let out a raking snore, and she sighed with relief.

"You did it!" Cricket whirled on Petra. "Give me one of those roses."

Petra held her back from the vase. "Who are you going to enchant? We can't have *all* of you passed out and useless." But Cricket was fast enough to grab a rose anyway; she stuffed it in her mouth and coughed out something vaguely resembling the spell. Nothing happened.

Petra smirked. "They call it the Silent Tongue for a reason. Not the Yawping Squawk."

Cricket narrowed her eyes as she spat out chewed-up petals.

Anouk stroked Beau's hair, worried, and looked up at the witch. "How long will he be out?"

"Until morning, I'd imagine," said Mada Zola. "It was a large rose."

Despite herself, a part of Anouk felt relieved. No more of Beau trying to drag her back to the car, and the thought made her feel guilty. She brushed a clump of dust out of his hair.

"We'll put him to bed in the west bedroom," Mada Zola said. "He'll be safe there until he wakes." She rested one hand on Anouk's shoulder and the other on Cricket's. "You should rest, too, dearies, though I know it won't be easy. You look dead on your feet."

"I want to try that spell again," Cricket said.

"Patience, dearie. Patience." The witch made a small *tsk* noise. "You can't do magic properly if you don't have a rested mind."

"But I could help you look through spell books—" Cricket insisted.

"No." Mada Zola's voice was firm, but then she softened it with a gentle pat on first Cricket's and then Anouk's cheek. She turned to Petra. "Show them to the bedroom."

Petra was already picking up Beau's feet. Anouk and Cricket had little choice but to help her hoist him up, and groaning under his weight, the three girls carried him down the hallway and up a flight of stairs to a bedroom. They placed him on the bed.

Petra handed Anouk a gas lamp. "Good night. Try to sleep. Did you know you have a streak of dust on your face?"

Anouk sighed. "Always." She swiped her sleeve over her cheek and then fluffed the pillow under Beau's head. He felt warm. She went to open a window. The clouds were heavy, casting a murky glow over the fields. She sucked in a breath as she caught sight of a tremor of movement in the fields. "Petra, there's something out there!"

Petra, unconcerned, lit another gas lamp for them. "Those are just the gardeners. They tend to the flowers at night."

"I thought you said you two were alone here."

"We are," Petra answered.

A creeping feeling spidered up Anouk's spine as she peered closer at the gardens. A flash of leaves caught in the faint light.

The topiaries.

Their enchanted shapes loomed as they weeded and watered and pruned with their slow, lumbering branches. A gleam in the driveway caught her eye and she jerked to attention, thinking at first it was a gunmetal-gray motorcycle, but it was only a watering can.

"You're certain no one can get through the hedges?" she asked, turning from the window.

But Petra was gone.

A key turned in the lock.

"Hey!" Anouk and Cricket both ran to the door. "Petra, you can't lock us in here!" Anouk twisted the knob, uselessly. Cricket kicked at the door.

"It's for your own safety." Petra's muffled voice came from the keyhole. "I promise, it's better this way. Nights around here can get . . . unpredictable. I'll unlock it at first light."

Anouk and Cricket pounded on the door, calling for Petra, but there was no response. Frustrated, Anouk sank onto the bed. "Our own safety? That's rubbish."

"I'd guess that Zola doesn't want us snooping through her things," Cricket said, sitting cross-legged on the other side of Beau. "Witches, you know. Secretive to the bone. I'm surprised that we're not wrapped in chains in some dungeon."

"Do you think Zola is telling the truth about the spell library at Castle Ides?"

Cricket took out a knife, tapped the hilt anxiously in her palm. "I don't know what to believe."

Anouk lowered her voice. "There's a room here with herbs hanging in the rafters, tied up in the same clove-hitch knot Luc uses."

Cricket considered this. "You think he was here?"

"Yes, or—I know this sounds crazy—is here *now*."

"And, what, Mada Zola has him bound and gagged in a closet? That's what she doesn't want us to snoop around and find?"

"Maybe." Anouk eyed Beau, who was muttering in his sleep. "I think Beau knows more than he's letting on. He promises that he didn't kill Mada Vittora, but I think that he knows who did."

Cricket's expression turned grim. "I still think Viggo did it. He isn't capable of love, not even for his mother. You know what I'd most like to do with what little time I have left? Find him and smother him with that stupid slouchy hat of his."

At the mention of Viggo, Anouk looked back at the window where she'd thought she'd seen the motorcycle. She cocked her head. "Cricket, does Viggo have an invitation to Castle Ides?"

"Why? What are you plotting and why didn't I think of it first?"

Anouk lay back on the pillows, drumming her fingers on her ribs, thinking. "Maybe something. Maybe nothing."

"Well, he does."

It wasn't a large bed and she was pressed against all six feet of Beau. At home, sometimes she and Beau had fallen asleep in bed together, Luc usually snoring in her armchair. But that was before Beau's confession in the foyer. *Only a fool . . . and I'm a fool.* She wasn't sure what to do with those words, which were mixing around in her stomach like champagne bubbles, but she knew that sometime in the past few days, he'd ceased to be like a brother to her. He was something else. Something more. But how much more?

Cricket lay down on Beau's other side, toying with her charm earring distractedly, her foot anxiously jiggling enough to make the whole bed shake. Anouk reached across Beau and took Cricket's hand. Cricket stopped tapping her foot. They interlaced their fingers and held tight. *A mouse, a dog, a wolf, a cat, an owl,* Anouk thought. All predators and prey. If the worst happened, would they turn on one another? She found herself scratching her arm as though fur were already pushing its way out.

"I want to cast magic," Cricket said quietly, a private admission. "I want to show the Royals that they aren't the only ones who matter."

Anouk thought of those dark spells Cricket had found on the Internet and scrawled down. Cricket wanted revenge and that made Anouk uneasy. And yet, didn't Cricket deserve it? Didn't they all?

"You'll learn. I know it. It's easier for me because I already speak a bit of the Silent Tongue."

"Yeah, that and your whispers actually sound like proper whispers, not like someone coughing up a hairball."

She squeezed Anouk's hand. Anouk squeezed back.

The clock was ticking on the table, that black cat's tail always moving in a constant circle. *Tick-tick-tick.* Beau snored softly. She envied him his enchantment. Tonight, she knew, he was the only one who would get any sleep.

Chapter 17

One Day and Seventeen Hours of Enchantment Remain

ANOUK WAS WRONG. At some point, exhaustion overcame her and she tossed and turned and dreamed of awful things: Luc, bloodless and drained, haunting the halls of the château, leaving thyme leaves skittering in his wake.

She sat up with a jerk. Sunlight warmed the window. Beau still slumbered beside her. The other side of the bed was empty.

The door was open, to her relief. Someone had left fresh clothes for her, oversize scraggly sweaters that looked as though they belonged to Petra. She pulled one over her black dress and rolled up the long sleeves and went into the hall. She called for Cricket but got no answer, so she followed the smell of burned toast to the kitchen.

Cricket and Petra were trying to toast bread over an open flame and, judging by the pile of charred ash, failing miserably. Anouk took the tongs out of Petra's hand and dumped their efforts in the trash. "Sit," she said. "I'll cook. Petra, do you have any eggs?"

Obviously relieved, Petra went to the icebox for bacon and eggs and then disappeared into the pantry for more ingredients.

Anouk whispered to Cricket, "Where's the Mada?"

"Supposedly she hasn't left the potting shed all night. She's in there experimenting with different spells."

Petra returned with jars of whole golden honeycomb and canisters of rich black coffee, and they quieted. Once the toast was ready, Petra served herself a generous portion and slathered the top piece with creamy butter.

"Something odd happened this morning." She chewed with her mouth open, licking butter off her finger. "I went back to the hedge to fetch the wheelbarrow and heard a motorcycle pull up to the gate and then what sounded like two boys arguing about how to get in. Then they drove off. I figured it might be friends of yours."

Anouk exchanged a look with Cricket. "Hunter Black and Viggo. *Not* friends."

Petra took a hefty bite of toast. "It doesn't matter. They can attack the hedge with a chainsaw, try to scale it with ladders, but they can't get in." She didn't seem to notice or else didn't care about the crumbs collecting on her sweater.

Anouk returned to making breakfast, this new information stirring in her mind, mixing together like eggs and flour for cake batter. All this time she and Beau had wanted to keep them out, but maybe *out* was wrong. Maybe she wanted them *in*.

She spooned the dough onto a cookie sheet and popped it into the oven, then poured fresh coffee for herself. "I'm going to see what Mada Zola's found." She grabbed a timer and set it. "For the cookies. Take them out in twenty minutes."

She cupped her hands around the mug to warm them as she passed through the halls; it was a drafty old house. In the foyer, she was surprised to find a trail of smudgy paw prints all around Toblerone's pot —had he *moved* during the night? She started for the front door but then stopped, glancing back at the bear.

She'd cast magic last night. Could she do it again?

149

Slowly, almost on a whim, she plucked a leaf off Toblerone's shaggy coat, popped it in her mouth, swallowed it whole, and then cocked her fingers as she'd seen Mada Vittora do.

"Evillate," she whispered. *Wake.*

A row of leaves shuddered along the bear's spine and, just as when she'd put Beau to sleep, the spell worked instantly. She jumped back, dripping coffee everywhere.

"Oh, *merde.*"

She rubbed at the coffee stain on Petra's sweater, then looked back at the bear, wetting her lips.

"Aper tes oculus." Open your eyes.

Incredibly, the bear's head started to sway slightly side to side, his branching bones creaking to life. The jaws opened, showing teeth of sharp briars. Anouk stepped back, ready to run, but the bear only stretched his jaws in a great yawn. The head swung to her, and leaves parted like eyes opening.

He blinked.

She couldn't help but give an amazed sort of laugh. Something fell out of the bear's mouth and clattered to the floor. Voices sounded from down the hall and Anouk quickly whispered a spell to put the bear back to sleep.

She snatched up the fallen object.

A franc coin. A small hole was drilled in the top as though for a necklace—it was just like the one she'd found in Luc's attic. She sniffed it. *Thyme.*

She shoved it into her pocket and went to the window. A light was on in the potting shed. If Anouk was ever going to find out what they were hiding, now was the time.

She opened the front door and closed it loudly so Petra would think she'd gone outside. Then she kicked off her shoes and crept down the hall, past empty rooms, until an oddly bright light in the chapel caught her eye. One of the stained-glass windows was now cracked open. The light from the other side was too low to be the sun.

A secret room.

She peered through the stained-glass window. It was dark beyond except for that one blindingly bright light. Two lights, actually. *Headlights*. She almost laughed. The secret passage led to a garage filled with shiny cars that would make Beau drool.

She kept searching the house, going past the bedroom where Beau slept, past more deserted rooms, and reached one with posters on the wall for bands called Daft Punk and Louise Attaque that must have been Petra's. Anouk stepped into Petra's room, uncertain what she was looking for. She opened a door that led to a bathroom that, like everything else, was in desperate need of a mop. She tried a side door that she'd assumed led to a closet until she heard an oddly familiar sound: quiet, steady breathing.

She took a step into the dark room, tripped on something metal that went clanging across the room, and cursed. She held her breath for a few seconds, cringing, but thankfully didn't hear footsteps or Petra's voice. As quietly as she could, she felt around for a candle, lit it, and found that she was in a windowless room. Petra's bloodletting chair was on one side, along with the usual glass vials and copper collecting bowls like the one she'd tripped on. On the other side of the room was a scryboard.

Its machinery gave that steady breathing sound just like Luc's, and the feathered headphones chattered with unintelligible whispers. She opened the desk drawer, rifled through papers until she found Petra's log, and flipped the pages until she saw his name.

10 August   Received another message from Vittora's gardener. Luka? Luc.

11 August   Wants to make a deal. Gave no response.

13 August   On his way to château—couldn't stop him.
<u>*Tell the Mada.*</u>

Anouk gripped the franc coin—Luc *had* been here! Mada Zola had lied to them and here was proof. She ran downstairs and into the garden, over stone paths that were damp on her feet, realizing too late that she'd left her shoes inside. She banged on the potting-shed door.

"Let me in, witch! Luc is here, I know it!"

Mada Zola opened the door. She had dark circles beneath her eyes. The shed smelled of wood smoke and something bitter, and Anouk spotted a bubbling pot and jars of tonics amid the shovels and clay pots.

Anouk held up the franc coin like an accusation.

"Come in." Mada Zola's voice was calm. She motioned casually to the vials and bottles. "I'm concocting a tonic that I found in a Persian spell book from the fourteenth century. It's used to slow one's aging process. If it works, it might buy you and your friends another few days until your proper age catches up with you. I need thorns and a couple more ingredients from the garden before it will be ready for testing."

Anouk clenched her jaw, focusing on why she'd come. "I found the scryboard logs. Luc—"

"He was here, yes," the witch admitted, cutting her off. "He isn't anymore."

"Then where is he? He disappeared a week and a half ago."

Mada Zola shook her head, returned to her pot, and stirred it slowly. "I'm afraid I can't answer that. He was here two months ago. Long before you say he disappeared." She set down the spoon, and her eyes dropped to Anouk's bare feet, to the missing toes, but she didn't seem surprised. She picked up an empty bottle. "Take a walk with me."

Anouk wasn't inclined to obey, but neither did she want to stay in that reeking shed. She followed the witch into the gardens. "Luc said that you loved your mistress so much that you didn't see the rotten part of her."

Anouk didn't answer. How could she? Yes, yes, she understood now how vile their mistress had been, and yet the memory of her soft hands stroking Anouk's hair was still too fresh.

"Your friend Luc contacted me two months ago, and when I didn't answer, he showed up at the gates with an awful story to tell. He'd overheard Mada Vittora negotiating with a Goblin broker who dealt in small mammals. She wanted four very tame, very mild-tempered rabbits. Young and in good health."

Anouk slowed. "I remember that." She wiped her hands on her sweater, though they were already clean. "Luc thought he was supposed to slaughter them for stew, but he was wrong. Mada Vittora was furious."

"Did you ever wonder why she wanted four live rabbits?"

Anouk curled her toes. "No."

Mada Zola stopped at a nettle plant and pulled off long, spiky leaves to go in the bottle. "According to Luc, she felt that her beasties were growing restless. He and Cricket and Beau were more disobedient every day. And the assassin Hunter Black had become too attached to her boy. So she decided she'd kill her beasties and start over with more docile creatures."

Anouk felt as though she'd been slapped. She pressed her hand to her cheek, feeling a sting she couldn't make stop.

"She was going to keep *you*," the witch continued evenly. "She bought only four rabbits, not five. You were her pet. Her obedient little beastie."

Had the day suddenly gotten darker? Anouk looked up, but no clouds blocked the sun. Was it true? *Of course it was.* She felt like a traitor, like she'd somehow sided with Vittora, that she was complicit just by sweeping floors and serving cake.

"What happened then?" she asked.

"I explained to Luc that whoever possessed your pelts possessed *you*. If he could steal the pelts, then he wouldn't be forced to answer to any mistress. He left and I haven't heard from him since. Of course, that advice was true only as long as your witch was alive. Now you have much bigger problems. Even if you had control of your pelts, the beastie spell would still expire at midnight tomorrow."

They had entered the thorn garden, though Anouk had barely noticed.

"*Do* you have your pelts?" the witch asked.

But Anouk was too deep in her thoughts to answer. Luc had been trying to steal the pelts . . . had Mada Vittora caught him? Had she killed him out of anger?

Mada Zola suddenly took her arm, cupped her chin, and turned her face toward the warm sun.

"Breathe, my dearie. You look on the verge of shattering. You are each so strong in your own way. Beau has a steady strength, like a tree. Cricket's is a bright strength, like lightning. But your strength, ah, yours is quiet. There's a reason magic is called whispers, not shouts. Whispers require a quiet soul, a still mind. I could train you. Teach you to truly handle magic, to be what you were meant to be. You're like these thorns, you know. Dangerous by your very nature."

The wind was picking up, clouds moving in.

"Think about it, little mouse," the witch said. "But think fast. You're running out of time." She broke off a small handful of briars, flinching as one pricked her palm. A few drops of blood spilled out before she pressed a cloth against the cut. She touched Anouk's cheek gently with her other hand, and then went back to the potting shed and shut herself up again.

Anouk stood alone in the garden. Her mind felt whipped like cream, beaten to turn raw ingredients into something new—but *what,* she wasn't sure. She tugged out a rag she'd stashed in her sleeve, knelt by the blood drops on the stone path, and began to clean, but then stopped.

What was she doing?

She cleaned because that was all she knew. Mada Vittora had told her she was a maid, and Anouk would have done anything for a scrap of affection. She thought back to the day Luc had killed the rabbits.

He'd been out flower hunting at the market in the Marais and must have stumbled on Mada Vittora and overheard her plans. But Anouk hadn't known that at the time. She hadn't thought twice to see Luc return from the market and slaughter the rabbits in the courtyard. It wasn't rare for him to bring home live crows for pie, live quail for roasting.

He'd strung up the bodies in the kitchen. *For supper,* he'd told her. *Rabbit stew.* She'd cooked the rabbits without question. But when she'd ladled out the stew, Mada Vittora had taken one bite and slammed the bowl on the floor, shattering it. She'd dragged Luc down from his attic and shoved his face in the scalding stew and broken shards of china. No matter how he'd pleaded that it had been a mistake, she'd beaten him.

Later, Anouk had cleaned up the mess without question.

You knew, didn't you? she whispered silently to Luc. *You knew those rabbits were meant to take our places. You slaughtered them to protect the others, but you couldn't protect yourself.*

She stood sharply. On impulse, she tugged the black ribbon from her ponytail, letting her hair fall loose around her shoulders.

At last she could breathe.

At last she felt free of Mada Vittora — and now she knew what she needed to do.

Little mouse, Mada Zola had called her, as though the truth of what she was were written on her face. Anouk touched her heavy jaw, thinking of those five pelts hidden away in the car trunk. The littlest one, gray and stiff with a ropy pink tail. She didn't feel like a mouse. Not at all. The dark thing inside her wasn't timid and plain, wasn't the type to skitter around the edges of a room, fearful of every footstep.

I'm no mouse.

She stuffed the rag between the branches of a topiary gardener.

"Clean your own damn mess."

She grabbed a handful of roses, stuffed them in her mouth, and swallowed petals down dry as she ran back to the château. She shoved open the front door and climbed up onto the edge of the heavy clay pot in the foyer, then whispered into Toblerone's leafy ear. The bear began to stir with a rippling of green pelt and stretching of creaky wooden joints. On her command, he lumbered down from his pot. He left tiny fluttering leaves in his wake that she followed like a trail of bread crumbs all the way to the sentinel hedge.

She found the corkscrew branch that Petra had used to get in and gave it a twist.

She stepped back, breathless, as the branches began to untangle themselves into the archway. When Viggo and Hunter Black returned, they'd find the gates open. They wouldn't know about the enchanted topiary bear waiting to drag them in his thorny teeth to the château as prisoners.

She left Toblerone to guard the entrance and returned to the château, to the west bedroom, where Beau was still in bed but awake now, groggy, rubbing his head as though it ached. It was cold, and she pulled on her Faustine jacket.

"Anouk. The time—"

She climbed onto the bed and pressed a finger to his mouth.

"For once, let's not think about time."

Then, impulsively, she replaced her finger with her lips.

He stirred awake quickly after that, stiff with surprise at first, but then his arms circled her waist and an exhale slipped from his throat. He kissed her back, sending magic shooting between her two ears, all the way to her ten fingers and her eight dirt-caked toes.

One of his hands found her hair, and she, in turn, found herself touching his cheekbones, his chest, his arms, every inch of him. She felt those champagne bubbles churning like they never had before, going straight to her head, making her feel giddy and thirsty and like she was a fool too, that she should have kissed him long ago, that they had wasted too much precious life already.

"Is this because life as we know it is about to end?" he asked, his forehead pressed to hers.

She couldn't keep her grin from showing. "No. It's because our true lives are just about to begin."

Chapter 18

BY THE TIME ANOUK had tumbled out of bed, grinning like she'd sipped too much wine, combed her fingers through her hair, and straightened her rumpled jacket, it was dark outside. The lumbering shapes of the topiary gardeners dotted the fields, tending to the lavender by moonlight. She squinted toward the hedge wall, but it was too far away to make out the archway or the topiary bear guarding it. Lights burned in the potting shed's windows. She felt her good mood falter—Mada Zola's potion must not have worked or she wouldn't still be out there—but it didn't matter. She was past depending on witches for help.

She closed the curtain and turned back to Beau, who was reclining on the bed, wearing a goofy smile. The cat clock ticked away on the bedside table but he ignored it, continuing to smile, though his eyelids flinched slightly at every tick. As far as the kissing had gone, they hadn't done much beyond short sweet ones on the lips or hands or, once, daringly, a neck; neither of them knew exactly what came after that. Still, Anouk felt as though they had crossed some threshold there was no turning back from. To love, and be loved, and be forever human.

When she at last turned to the clock, she felt a squeeze of panic.

"Midnight is in a few hours. And then—"

"Only one more day. I know."

She took his big hand, pressed her lips to his knuckles, and she knew she couldn't lose this, lose him, lose herself. "Wait here."

She hugged her jacket closer for warmth. There was no sign of Petra or Cricket in the hall—all the better for her to sneak outside to check her trap. Just as she was about to leave the château, something metal clattered at the opposite end of the hallway, followed by a noise like a scuffle.

She stopped. Something felt wrong.

"Cricket?" she called.

There was no answer. Something thunked in the same place and that squeeze of panic returned. "Petra? Is that you?"

She took out her knife, creeping down the dark hallway. The cold bit into the soles of her bare feet. Something thunked again—it came from the direction of the kitchen. The door was cracked open, the smell of nutmeg drifting from it. Would Petra be making more snacks? How much cocoa could the girl seriously consume in one day?

Anouk stepped closer, the knife steady despite her erratic heartbeat. *Not a mouse!* she told herself.

Another step toward the kitchen.

The floorboards squeaked behind her. Wait—*behind her.* She spun around, slashing with the knife.

Her blade crashed against something metal.

"*Anouk.* It's me."

Cricket had two knives raised, blocking Anouk's knife an inch from impaling her between the eyes. Anouk had been fast, but no one was faster than Cricket.

"*Merde,* Cricket, sorry—"

160

"They got inside," Cricket whispered.

They both lowered their knives, and Anouk whipped her head back toward the kitchen, sniffing the air. "Who?"

"Viggo and Hunter Black. I don't know how they got past the gate. Petra's outside in the potting shed with Mada Zola. We have to warn them."

Anouk felt her spine go rigid. *No, no, no.* Toblerone was supposed to be guarding the gate. She'd used magic . . . had her trap failed? Had she made a mistake? A clammy sweat broke out on her skin.

The whites of Cricket's eyes flashed. "Viggo's in the kitchen. I don't know where Hunter Black is. There's a second staircase that runs behind the pantry and comes out by the stove, remember? I'm going to sneak up there and see if I can take him by surprise. You find Beau and then get Petra and Zola."

"Wait." Anouk grabbed Cricket's sleeve. "Viggo might hear you on the stairs. Let me distract him."

Cricket didn't protest or laugh or tell Anouk that it was too dangerous, as Beau would have done. That was what Anouk loved about her. Cricket had never called Anouk a little mouse, not once.

"Yes, all right. Good."

Cricket disappeared into the darkness, and Anouk brandished the knife. Took a deep breath. *Count to ten. Give Cricket time to get to the other stairs.* Then she'd show herself, distract Viggo . . .

She took a step toward the kitchen. Her fingertips grazed the door.

And then something was happening faster than she could process it. The door was thrust open. Viggo's face was there, twisting from surprise to anger and back again in a flash.

"Anouk."

On instinct, she shoved the door wide open, slamming it into his face. Blood spurted from his nose. He let out a cry as she forced her way in and ran to the far end of the table. He pressed a hand to his bloody face.

"You broke my nose!" He started for her with a growl, and she darted to the side, keeping the table between them. He went left; she went left. He stopped; she stopped. He went right; she went right.

"Goddamn it, stop—"

And then Cricket sprinted down the rear stairs behind him and launched off the bottom stair to leap onto his back. He let out another cry as she wrapped an arm around his neck, choking him. For a few seconds it was a scramble between them, a tangle of limbs and feet and even a flash of teeth, but then something silver gleamed in Viggo's hand and Cricket stopped fighting.

A pistol.

No one moved. What were knives against bullets? Anouk had forgotten that Viggo was a Pretty. He could use technology.

"It fires," he said, as though reading their minds. "It's old technology. Purely mechanical; no biometric locks or electric spotting scopes that the magic in this house would interfere with. Almost analog enough that even a witch could fire it. But not quite." He aimed it at Anouk. "Come here, Cricket. Slowly."

Cricket looked ready to spit in his face, but he pulled her close enough to press the pistol to her temple.

Anouk felt rage burning through her. Her mind churned. She could scream for Beau. She could throw a pot from the stove. She could—

Something cold and sharp pressed against the side of her neck. She sucked in a breath.

Oh no.

Hunter Black's breath was hot on her throat. "Drop the knife, Anouk."

She'd forgotten about the shadow that never left Viggo's side. He grabbed her arms, pinned them behind her back. He was so much stronger than her. And Viggo's damn pistol. What weapon did she have? Nothing beside her mind, her hands. *Her whispers!*

"*Dorma,*" she whispered in a rush, "*dor—*"

Hunter Black's hand clamped over her mouth, smothering the whisper. "And don't scream."

Anouk sputtered against his palm, but he only pressed harder. She met Cricket's eyes. A look of understanding passed over Cricket's face as she realized what Anouk had been trying to do. She almost smiled. Cricket didn't have *her* mouth covered, and if magic was what she wanted to do, this was her chance.

She pointed toward Hunter Black.

"*Dorma!*" she yelled. "*Dorma silencia et mada . . . et mada . . .* oh, *merde,* I don't remember!"

Anouk gave a muffled cry. It wouldn't have worked anyway; neither of them had consumed a flower or anything containing life. She needed her mouth uncovered, and she needed something pulsing with life, something like . . . like . . .

Yes.

She bit down on Hunter Black's middle finger. His flesh caught beneath her teeth like a ripe apple; her sharp teeth pierced his skin and warm blood flooded into her mouth. He yelled and let her go, and she felt sick, her mouth filled with his salty, too-warm blood. She tried not to gag.

Viggo looked aghast. "You. *Bitch.*"

Hunter Black clutched his bleeding hand to his chest, reaching for a kitchen towel, and Anouk knew what would happen next. He'd wind back his other hand to slap her and he wouldn't stop hitting until she was broken on the floor.

She swallowed down the mouthful of blood.

"Dorma, dorma, sonora precimo," she choked out.

Hunter Black dropped to the floor—like *that*. It happened so fast, so suddenly, that at first Anouk didn't believe it. She stared at his prostrate body, daring to poke him with her toe.

"Get up!" Viggo looked horribly confused. "Hunter Black, get up!"

"That's what you deserve, *crétin!*" Cricket cheered. She took the opportunity to elbow Viggo in the stomach, and then pressed one of her knives to his jugular and announced gleefully, "Didn't think we could do magic, did you? Thought we were only good for making your bed? Or *keeping it warm?*" She dug the blade deeper and a prick of red appeared, which seemed to delight her. "Now drop the pistol."

He moaned weakly and obeyed.

"We should put him to sleep too," Anouk said, looking around for something else living to swallow. "We could lock them in the wine cellar. Somewhere they can't escape."

She reached for a sprig of rosemary, but Cricket shook her head.

"Let me." She jabbed the blade deeper against Viggo's neck until a line of blood ran down his skin. She licked it, then made a face, but swallowed. "Now what do I say again?"

164

"*Dorma, dorma, sonora precimo,*" Anouk told her.

"*Dorma,* bastard," Cricket muttered, jabbing the knife harder. "*Dorma, sonora precimo,* jerkwad."

Viggo started to mumble a protest but then slumped forward, falling asleep more slowly than Hunter Black, as Cricket's whisper hadn't exactly been quiet *or* precise. As he fell, his head collided with the hard edge of the kitchen sink with a nasty-sounding crack, and Anouk flinched, but Cricket's eyes just gleamed with dark delight.

"That was so cool." She cleaned and put away her blades. "Is there a spell for smashing things? Like stupid boys' skulls?"

Anouk flexed her hands, trying to shake the odd sparking sensation in them.

The gas light over the stove flicked on, and Beau stood in the doorway with wide eyes. "What *maléfice* is going on here?"

"Get Hunter Black's legs," Cricket said.

He still looked confused but helped Anouk and Cricket drag their prisoners down the wooden stairs to the wine cellar. If the upper portions of the château were old, then down there it was practically prehistoric. The walls dripped with unseen moisture; the foundation was crumbled from time. The door to the wine cellar was made of thick oak with a metal grate set into it like a prison cell's. It probably *had* been a prison cell once, Anouk figured. Cricket dropped Viggo unceremoniously on the floor.

Beau shivered. "It's freezing down here."

"They can cuddle for warmth." Cricket kicked Viggo's arm for good measure. "How long do you think they'll be out?"

"Not too long, I hope." Anouk thought of the clock several floors above, its perpetual *tick-tick-tick*. She dusted off a wine barrel and dragged it beside the door, prepared to wait. "And when they wake up, we've got to be ready."

Cricket left to explain to Petra and Mada Zola what had happened, and after a few minutes of shivering next to Anouk, Beau left to fetch blankets and something warm for him and Anouk to drink. Nestling in her jacket, Anouk let out a long-held breath.

They still had time, she told herself. The way she saw it, Hunter Black was one of them, and so that ticking clock meant just as much to him as it did to her. Come midnight tomorrow, he stood to lose not only himself but his abilities as an assassin and Viggo's protector, without which he had nothing.

A moan came from the wine cellar.

She jumped up. "Viggo?" She held a candle to the grate, but the light was too faint to see more than a few feet. "Viggo, wake up. I need to talk to you."

Hunter Black suddenly loomed at the grate, so specterlike that Anouk dropped the candle. She cursed and searched the dusty floor until she found it again, but she had no matches, so she swallowed a briar tangled in her sweater. *Ouch.*

"Incendie," she whispered, and a flame flickered to life.

Hunter Black eyed the candle warily, as though he didn't trust the magic he'd just seen. "What do you want?"

"A deal." It took effort to keep her spine straight. Even though she was on the free side of the door and he was locked inside, Hunter Black still had a way of making her feel rattled. "I have a proposal for Viggo."

He gave a cold laugh. "You have no idea what you're doing without Luc here to hold your hand."

She narrowed her eyes. "Despite all your glowering, you relied on him as much as the rest of us. I think you feel just as lost without him." Her gaze fell to the stitches peeking out from his shirt collar, and Hunter Black clamped a hand over them. Luc had done more than just stitch up his wounds—Luc had shown him kindness when the rest of the world had not.

For a few flickers of the candle he looked as though he wanted to get his hands around her throat, but then his face eased. Grudgingly, he asked, "How is it possible?"

"What?"

He nodded toward the candle. "You cast magic. Just now, and upstairs in the kitchen. Beasties can't cast magic." There was an edge in his voice that went beyond curiosity.

She raised an eyebrow. "I could teach you to cast a spell yourself if you'd stop being such a—"

Viggo shoved his face close to the grate, cutting her off. He'd mostly cleaned himself, but his hair was streaked with dirt. "What's this about a deal?"

"First tell me how you got past the hedge."

Viggo smirked. "I know a trap when I see one—we weren't about to stroll through an open gate. I might not be a magic handler, but I've learned a thing or two from the Haute. Witches know to add a stipulation to wall spells to prevent climbing over, but they always forget about *under*. We followed the hedge for a hundred meters and then tunneled beneath it. And that ridiculous bear? He was only enchanted to keep us *out*. Once we were already in, Hunter Black made quick work of him. *Chop-chop*."

Guilt twisted in her chest. Toblerone was gone because of her.

Viggo touched his throat. "Hunter Black, I'm parched. Open one of these wine bottles. I saw a teacup somewhere in here . . ."

The tunneling at least explained the dirt in Viggo's hair. But now that she looked closer, it *wasn't* dirt. Several streaks of his fair hair were now nearly as charcoal dark as Hunter Black's.

"What happened to your hair?"

He tossed it out of his eyes. "Like it?" His smile was harsh. "A witch's spells last only three days after her death. It's been two. The spell is fading." He cocked his head. "You didn't think my hair just happened to be the exact shade as hers, did you?" He laughed coldly. "She enchanted it afresh every year. Didn't want any reminder that I wasn't really her son but some screaming dark-haired baby she'd stolen out of a pram in the houseware section of Le Bon Marché."

Hunter Black broke open the neck of a bottle of merlot, and Viggo kicked around in the dirt for the teacup he claimed to have seen. Anouk touched her own hair tentatively. If the enchantment that colored Viggo's hair was already fading, then didn't that mean their beastie spell was also fading? That they were *already turning back?* Was her mind playing tricks on her, or did her hair feel coarser? She touched her jaw—was it heavier, more bestial? But she was still just a girl, at least on the outside.

"Now, what's this deal?" Viggo said, tossing back a teacup of wine.

Chapter 19

Twenty-Four Hours of Enchantment Remain

W HEN ANOUK DIDN'T ANSWER, Viggo moved toward the bars, tipping his head forward conspiratorially. "You and I have always had an understanding, haven't we, Anouk? She was like a mother to you too. You and I both loved her. We were the only ones who did."

Anouk eyed him warily. "So do you believe that I didn't kill her?"

Viggo snorted messily and wiped his nose with his sleeve. Not broken after all, but definitely bruised. "You? You turn white when you have to pluck chicken for dinner. You'd never hurt her." His face darkened. "Was it Beau?"

"No," Anouk snapped, but her heart was thumping so hard she was surprised Viggo couldn't hear it. Hunter Black made a slight growl as though maybe *he* heard it. "We don't know who did. But it wasn't either of us."

Viggo grunted noncommittally. "You shouldn't have come here. Mada Zola can't be trusted. You'd be safer with me. Come back to the townhouse. I might not be a witch, but I'm influential among the Pretties. Whatever promises Zola made you, they're lies."

"We need her."

"Ha."

"We *need* her. In twenty-four hours, our enchantment will end. If that happens, we'll turn back to animals, all of us. Even you, Hunter Black. The only way to stay as we are is if we get the beastie spell, which Mada Zola has promised to use on us to keep us human. But there's a problem. It's kept at Castle Ides." She held the candle closer to him, meeting his gaze. "We could never get past their security, but *you* have an invitation."

"He isn't helping you," Hunter Black snarled.

But Viggo held up a hand, silencing him, and eyed Anouk. He'd guzzled a considerable amount of wine in a very short time, but he could hold his alcohol, she had to give him that. "The invitation alone won't get you in. Not without me to present it."

Anouk tightened her jaw. "Then you'll have to come too."

Viggo laughed at the prospect. Hunter Black cursed and went off to the corner to sulk. Viggo leaned against the door, his hair falling in his face. "*You* need *me*. That's rich." He took another sip of wine.

"Don't you want Hunter Black to stay human?" Anouk asked. "And Cricket?"

His only answer was to drink more, though Anouk knew he was toying with her. He lusted after Cricket; perhaps perversely, he'd do anything to keep her safe. His china teacup reflected back the candle-light, and Anouk narrowed her eyes.

"That cup. Show it to me."

Raising an eyebrow, Viggo complied, holding it up to the grate. It was an odd design, not like the Pretties' usual floral patterns. This one had sea-monster tentacles amid delicate little ocean bubbles.

A Goblin design.

Her stomach turned as alarm bells chimed in her head. She thought of those rumors of Goblins invited to the château for tea parties and ending up as potting soil. She glanced again at the wine cellar's heavy door, so like a cell's. Who else had been imprisoned here?

Viggo scratched his chin, his eyes dangerously sober. "I'll help you, but I want something."

"What?"

He leaned closer. "You put me to sleep with a whisper. Bravo, little beastie. And you lit that candle just now with a whisper. I admit, I'm impressed. I never thought beasties capable of magic, especially not you, my little dust mop. If you want my help, I'll give it to you." He paused. "Provided that you make Cricket fall in love with me."

Anouk recoiled from the door. Hunter Black stalked out of the dark corner, a scowl on his face. "Viggo. This is unwise. That girl . . . your *obsession*—"

"I didn't ask you," Viggo snapped, and for a second the scowling mask Hunter Black wore slipped and beneath it Anouk saw real hurt.

Viggo turned back to Anouk, eyes gleaming. "Do we have a deal?"

She didn't answer. It sickened her to think of Cricket gazing at Viggo with adoring eyes, and all because of Anouk. Could she technically even do it? She'd never cast a love spell before, and they were difficult. But she'd heard Mada Vittora cast one; she knew the words to say and the ingredients to use, and Mada Zola could help her. Part of her almost longed to try.

"Forget it." A voice came from the cellar stairs. "She won't do it."

Beau joined them. His fists were clenched and his face looked grim.

"How long have you been there?" Anouk asked.

"Long enough. Go to hell, Viggo. We wouldn't do that to Cricket. Right, Anouk?"

Anouk didn't answer.

Beau spun to her. *"Right?"*

She turned away from his hard gaze and those too-blue eyes that showed his clear conscience, so sure that it was his job to shelter her from the big scary world. Ever since Luc had disappeared, Beau had been trying to fill his shoes, but this was what Beau would never get: Luc understood that doing what was *right* and doing what was *necessary* were two different things.

Her heart was pounding. She gripped the metal grate before she could change her mind. "Get us into Castle Ides and have Hunter Black help us if anything goes wrong, and I'll do it."

Beau's jaw dropped. "Anouk, you can't do this."

Oh, Beau. He couldn't protect her from everything.

"Do we have a deal?" she asked Viggo.

"Oui." Viggo reached his index finger through the narrow grate.

Anouk hesitated, then wrapped her own finger around his. A handshake — or the closest they could manage — between prisoner and captor.

Partners now.

"I need to gather some supplies," she said. "We'll have to work fast. We're running out of time and it's a long way back to Paris."

"Before you say anything," Anouk said at the top of the cellar stairs, holding up a hand to silence Beau, "I'm not really going to do it."

The tense set to his jaw eased, but his fists were still clenched. "You said —"

"I said what he wanted to hear. He'll get a spell, just not the one he wants."

Beau didn't look convinced, kept eyeing her as though she were a different person than the girl in a ruffled apron who'd baked him muffins with crumbled sugar on top, and Anouk rested a reassuring hand on his shoulder. "I would never do that to Cricket. You know that, Beau. But we need Viggo to get into Castle Ides. And we need Hunter Black too. We can't rely on Cricket to be the only one with real fighting skills if things go wrong."

Beau folded his arms across his chest. "So, what, you're going to get Cricket to pretend to love him?"

"*Mon Dieu*, no. She's a terrible actress. I have a better idea, though I'll need a wineglass and some of Petra's blood. Where is everyone?"

"Outside. Zola wanted to close up the tunnel that Viggo dug before anything else could crawl through. Cricket's in the garden. She convinced Zola to lend her a book of spells so she could practice destruction tricks on some poor sapling. She *really* enjoyed knocking Viggo out."

"Good. She'll be distracted for a few hours. Best she doesn't know about this yet. And I need for you to take down all the paintings in the sitting room that show the interior of Castle Ides. We need views of every room, every entrance. Without blueprints, it's the closest thing we have to a map."

"You're serious about this, then? Breaking into Castle Ides?"

"I'm serious about staying human."

Beau looked at the murky line of moonlight that slashed across the floor. "We have twenty-four hours left. If this plan doesn't work, and we're trapped in the city when our time runs out . . ."

"It'll work," Anouk said. "But we have to hurry. It takes seven hours to drive back to Paris and the same to return here so the Mada can perform the spell. That gives us ten hours to figure out the plan and actually go through with it."

Beau let out a sigh to the heavens.

Anouk headed for the foyer. She'd often sat with Luc in his attic rooms as he'd prepared the various potions that Mada Vittora's more complicated spells required. And while a love spell wasn't particularly challenging, it took just the right life-essence ingredients in a particular balance or the nature of love would be thrown off. Too much vervain, the lover would be aggressive. Too little sage would result in a short-lived crush. She needed the real thing. Obsessive love. Consuming love.

She picked up the hedge clippers that Petra had left on the entry table and an old basket and went outside. How many mornings in the townhouse had she yearned to do this one simple act? Step over the threshold without needing anyone's permission? Such a small act, one that everyone else in the world took for granted.

A gust of wind blew her hair back. She worked the franc coin in her pocket between her fingers. If tomorrow night came and they hadn't renewed their enchantment, would Luc, wherever he was, turn back into an animal too?

She found Petra and Mada Zola by the hedge. Fresh soil had been churned up, presumably to fill Viggo's tunnel, and the hedge entrance was closed. She took another step and a branch snapped beneath her foot.

"Has your quarry awoken?" The witch motioned to the fallen branches. "They did a lot of damage getting in here."

There was a hard note to her voice, and with a sick feeling, Anouk looked back at the branches underfoot. Thorns and small green leaves like shaggy fur. She quickly stepped back. It was Toblerone—or what was left of him since Hunter Black had chopped him into firewood.

"Toblerone—"

"You enchanted him. I know. But you attempted a spell beyond your ability and now he's gone."

"I'm sorry. I didn't realize—"

"Let this be a lesson, then. Spells are complex things. Magic isn't something to be trifled with. Members of the Haute spend decades, even centuries, studying the craft of casting. And you've been alive for, what, one year? It's impressive you can even manage a sleeping spell at this point in your young life, but don't get ahead of yourself. You have lifetimes' worth of knowledge still to learn."

Mada Zola gave one final whisper as grass knit itself back over the churned soil, erasing every vestige of the tunnel. Anouk picked up a small branch lined with thorns. A wooden jawbone, or what was left of one.

"I need your help." She let the branch fall. "And yours too, Petra. I have a spell in mind, but I'll need your blood."

Anouk couldn't read Petra's face, but Petra glanced at Mada Zola, and some imperceptible understanding passed between them.

Petra nodded. "I'll be in my bloodletting room." She left Anouk and Mada Zola alone in the moonlight.

Anouk fished a scrap of paper out of her pocket. "It's a love spell. I've heard Mada Vittora whisper it before, but I don't know how to do it myself. I wrote it down the best I could remember it."

Mada Zola took the paper, lips moving silently as she read, and then smiled. "You'll need snapdragons."

They spent the next hour gathering flowers and herbs from the garden—seeking out asters, cutting sprigs of bay laurel, gathering everything carefully to keep the buds intact, and then they took their supplies to the potting shed. Prince Rennar watched Anouk from a portrait hung up by a nail. She let her gaze trail over his slightly crooked nose, the deep-set eyes. It was infinitely easier to look him in the eye, she decided, when she knew he wasn't looking back.

A knock came at the door. Petra handed her a wineglass full of still-warm blood.

"Thanks, Petra."

She shrugged. "More where that came from." But she looked pale.

Anouk frowned in concern. "Those cookies I made this morning—you should eat one. Sugar helps after losing blood."

This brought a half smile to Petra's face. "Not going to argue with cookies." She gave Anouk a nod. "I'm keeping watch over your captives. They're getting very drunk. Viggo is, at least." She motioned to the far gardens. "And Cricket's making sawdust out of our willow saplings."

Anouk poured the blood into a bottle. "That I want to see."

They made their way to the water gardens, where willows lined an artificial stream. It might once have been a bucolic spot, but now shredded limbs and leaves littered the ground; it looked as though a construction crew had passed through. Cricket was attacking two remaining saplings at once. She was using her regular knifework on the tree at the left, slashing and slicing as fast as a crow took wing, while consuming eucalyptus leaves from a pouch at her waist and using their life-essence to cast whispers toward the tree on the right. Mirrored slash marks cut across its trunk, though she hadn't touched it. Leaves rained down, though she was ten feet away. By the time she was finished, both trees had been destroyed with alarming intensity. She hadn't even spared the stumps.

"Exactly *which* Royal is she planning on using that spell against?" Petra asked.

"Um . . . all of them? She's not a fan of the Haute."

"Yeah. I gathered that," Petra answered.

In the glen, Cricket lifted her knives and started in on another sapling.

Inside, Anouk and Petra found Beau guarding the cellar door, sitting on a stool with the plate of cookies on his lap. Beau still looked grumpy about Anouk's plan, but at least he was licking crumbs off his fingers while sulking.

"Have they caused any problems?" Anouk said.

"Viggo's toasted," he said. "He was singing Céline Dion."

"Who's that?"

"You don't want me to try to sing her stuff. You'll go deaf."

They took lanterns and the cookies and went downstairs. Viggo's singing abruptly stopped. Hunter Black appeared at the window. If he'd had any of the wine, he held it better than Viggo. His eyes found Anouk's. He was all glares and a charcoal smear of hair. "If you hurt him, I'll kill you."

Viggo pushed Hunter Black aside and smooshed his own face against the bars. "Anouksh. Good, you're back—*hey*, are those cookies?"

Petra grudgingly shoved a cookie between the bars.

He wolfed it down and dusted crumbs off his shirt. "Thanks. Anouk, you know, when I knew this charming girl years ago, she

177

went by a very different name. You're looking good these days, my friend. New haircut? I can't quite put my finger on it . . ."

Petra smiled tightly. "Don't be an ass."

"Can I have another cookie, *Petra?*"

"Enough cookies," Anouk interrupted. She held up the bottle of elixir and a single short hair from her pocket. She dropped the hair into the elixir and swirled it gently. "Drink this."

The smirk disappeared off Viggo's face. "Is that one of Cricket's hairs? Is that how this works?" He'd sobered up fast.

"You have to drink every last drop," Anouk said.

Viggo's hungry eyes devoured the bottle. Anouk almost felt sorry for him until she remembered his unwanted hands all over Cricket, and then she didn't feel bad at all.

"You'll have to unlock the door," Hunter Black murmured darkly. "That bottle won't fit through the bars."

"Not a chance." With a flourish, Beau produced a curly blue drinking straw. When the others threw him odd looks, he shrugged. "I found it in the kitchen drawer next to birthday candles."

He stuck the straw in the bottle and Anouk held it close enough for Viggo to reach it.

Viggo grimaced at the taste but kept slurping until he reached the *ssss-ssss* of an empty glass. He wiped his mouth. "Doesn't Cricket need to be here?"

"I'm sure she's falling passionately in love with you as we speak," Anouk said. "In fact, Beau, will you go get her? She's in the garden. Careful. Don't sneak up on her."

Hunter Black continued to scowl from the shadows' edge. If he was the wolf, as Cricket suspected, would he be so devoted to one person? Weren't wolves lone hunters? Or else loyal to a whole pack?

"How long does it take?" Petra's fingernails drummed on the cookie tray. "Is this an instant thing or should I make tea?"

Footsteps came from the stairs. The glow of another lamp. Anouk heard Beau's voice explaining something to Cricket, telling her to wait, that everything would be fine.

At the bottom of the stairs, Cricket wiped sweat off her brow from her fighting practice and threw Viggo a glare. "You're still alive? That's a shame."

Viggo didn't answer, his eyes glassy but not from the wine.

"Well?" Hunter Black's arms were folded stiffly. "Go ahead, Cricket. Tell him that you love him. That you'd do anything for him."

"Ha!" Cricket clapped her hands together. "Exactly how much wine have you had?"

The temperature grew colder, as though the cellar stones were sucking up all the heat. Beau looked uneasily between Cricket and Viggo. But Anouk only waited. She felt Viggo's eyes shift from Cricket and slide across the room past Petra, past Beau, to stop on her. She shivered. She'd seen that particular glassiness in a person's eyes. Once, a Goblin girl tasked with delivering charmed necklaces to a jewelry shop had misplaced the package. To punish her, Mada Vittora had enchanted the girl to fall desperately in love with the small yellow postal van that delivered their mail. The Goblin girl was still probably walking up and down the streets of Paris following a hunk of wheeled metal that could never love her back.

"You're supposed to be in love with him," Hunter Black said.

"Him?" Cricket sneered.

Anouk could feel Viggo's hot gaze like sunlight—warm at first, but the longer she was exposed, the closer she was to burning.

"Open the door," Viggo said in a hoarse voice.

Beau clenched his fists. "Not happening."

"No, it's okay. Do it." Anouk's stomach twisted in hitches. Beau grumbled his disapproval, but he unlocked the door.

Viggo staggered out. His clothes were wrinkled, his hair streaked and in disarray, but his eyes were alight. He took a step past Beau. One past Petra. And then straight past Cricket, as though this girl whose love he'd craved above all else had ceased to exist.

He collapsed to his knees at Anouk's feet.

"Viggo," Hunter Black growled. "What are you doing? Get up."

Anouk rubbed the back of her scalp. It still stung from where she'd pulled out a strand of her hair and then cut it so it was the same length as Cricket's. In the dark cellar, no one had noticed the hair that was supposed to be Cricket's was tawny, not cinnamon-brown.

"Oh, *merde,*" Beau cursed, finally understanding.

Cricket realized at the same time and burst out laughing.

On his knees, Viggo bent to kiss Anouk's bare toes. "My love. My angel. My dream. Command me, because my heart is yours."

Chapter 20

Twenty-One Hours of Enchantment Remain

"N O." BEAU DRAGGED ANOUK to the cellar staircase, out of earshot of the others. "Absolutely not. I'm not okay with this. How are you okay with this? I'm not okay with this."

"We don't have a choice."

"You made him fall in love with you. *You!* Not with Cricket."

"Beau, this is a good thing. He'll do whatever I ask. Mada Zola helped me rewrite the love spell so that it's a particularly devoted type of love. He'll fall all over himself to please me. You saw him back there, worshiping at my feet. He's practically our—"

"Our *slave.*" Beau spat the word.

She rested her hands on her hips. "Temporarily. We made the elixir potent but not long-lasting. It'll work two, maybe three days; we need only one. Besides, how long have we been slaves to him? Fetching him tea, polishing his boots, staying awake all night in case he passed out and needed to be carried to bed? Don't you remember how he snapped his fingers at you like a dog? How he pawed at Cricket? It's only fair he gets a taste of what it's like to serve."

Beau folded his arms. "We aren't going to free ourselves by imprisoning others, even *crétins* like him."

But Anouk knew that falter in his voice. Was he jealous? His confession was still fresh on his lips, as were their kisses from the night before. He had to know that this thing with Viggo wasn't real love. Still, he glowered at the wall.

She poked the top button of his shirt and said softly, "Easy, there, or I'll work the spell on you too."

He caught her hand at the collar of his shirt and held it. On flat ground he towered over her, but she was perched one stair higher, and for once they were eye to eye.

"It wouldn't work on me."

"You don't think me capable?"

"Try all you want. Whisper the strongest love spell you know. They'd only be words—I'm already in love with you."

Anouk felt her cheeks burn in that pleasantly unpleasant way. She wrapped her other hand around his, squeezed almost painfully. "Tell me again that you didn't kill her."

"I didn't."

"Then who did? You know something."

His jaw tightened. Something wavered in his eyes, but then he shook his head.

"Who else was in the house that night? Tell me, Beau."

But he wouldn't.

She let go of his hands, frustrated and a little angry. If he'd only tell her the truth, horrible as it might be, maybe she could return those words he'd said to her. *Only a fool . . . and I'm a fool.* For now, all she could do was look at him and see a person she might not know at all.

"We don't have time for this."

She pushed past him down the stairs into the cellar, where Hunter Black was trying to reason with Viggo, who had for some reason collected a small pyramid of wine bottles in the center of the room. When he saw her, his face brightened.

"Anouk! My *trésor*, my *cœur*. Look—for you I have gathered the finest wines. Only the best for you." He collapsed to the ground, then inched forward on hands and knees to kiss her toes. Taken by surprise, she jerked backward and accidentally kicked him.

"Oh! Sorry, Viggo."

He cradled his chin. "Oh, no, my *puce*. No, no. It's my fault. I thoughtlessly let my face get in the way of your foot. A thousand apologies."

Beau sighed. "This is going to get old fast."

"Not for me," Cricket said, popping another cookie in her mouth.

"Get up, Viggo." Anouk felt uncomfortable. She glanced at Viggo's wristwatch. Three o'clock in the morning. "Beau, were you able to make a map of Castle Ides?"

"I tried, but it makes no sense. It's almost like the rooms in the paintings intentionally don't match up. Like the floor plan changes."

"Let me look at it," Cricket said. "You're used to following tidy little road maps where everything's perfectly to scale. Thievery work is often . . . less precise."

"We'll have to hurry," Anouk said. "We don't have long to figure out how to break into the most well-protected structure in the Haute." She couldn't hide her yawn. "And I need coffee."

"Allow me to make it for you, my *chère*." Without waiting for a response, Viggo sprinted up the stairs, taking them two at a time.

"I have to see this." Cricket ran after him, followed by Beau and Petra and Hunter Black, though Anouk grabbed the assassin's arm.

"Hunter Black, wait a minute."

He practically growled down at her small hand on his coat. She was suddenly very aware that they were alone in the dark cellar and that very recently he'd had a knife pressed to her neck.

"I know you don't like what I did to Viggo. But you need this plan to succeed as much as the rest of us do. If we don't get that spell, you'll lose your humanity too. Besides, the love spell is only temporary. It's not real."

"Clearly," he snarled. "He'd never love *you*."

Maybe someone else would have bristled at the barb, but Anouk saw his mask slip another inch. He was like a wounded creature lashing out at anyone but his master.

"We need you, Hunter Black. At the very least, you need to keep Viggo from making an ass of himself in front of the Royals and giving us away. You're one of us. Like it or not, we're a family."

Hunter Black toed one of the wine bottles, sending it rolling across the floor.

She took that as a yes.

She extended her hand. "We only have to work together until midnight."

He grudgingly shook it. "Midnight."

Upstairs, they found Cricket studiously drawing out a map. Every inch of the sitting-room floor was covered with paintings that showed the different rooms in Castle Ides. Cricket had scrawled a rough blueprint on the inside of her forearm, and Mada Zola and Petra were helping her fill in the blanks from their memories.

Anouk picked her way across the floor, holding her arms out for balance, trying not to step on any paintings.

"Breaking into Castle Ides won't be easy," the witch warned. "It looks like a regular ten-story building, but in reality, this same building exists in ten different cities at the same time, a type of portal. The only way to access the upper floors is here"—she pointed to a rectangular chamber on the map sketched on Cricket's arm—"through the building's elevator. Each floor leads to a different city. Rio de Janeiro is the sixth floor. New York is the second. Tokyo is the third. The elevator—"

"Coffee!" Viggo carried in a tray holding a pot of coffee that smelled like burned sugar, nearly stumbling on the paintings on the floor. He poured Anouk a cup. She took a sniff and grimaced.

"The elevator," Mada Zola continued, "is guarded by the Royals' proxies, called the Marble Ladies. You'll need to present your invitation to them at the front desk."

Viggo reached into his pocket and took out an elegant paper invitation, wiggling his eyebrows enticingly at Anouk. She pushed the coffee away.

"The Royals inhabit the penthouse floors," Mada Zola explained. "Once you get there, you'll be closely watched. Guests are escorted at all times by lesser Royals, which will make it difficult for you to get to the spell library. And Beau is correct—the floor plan of the penthouse is set to change every hour, on the hour." She turned to Cricket. "You'll have to keep a close eye on the timing to understand how the rooms rotate."

As Mada Zola explained the rotation schedule to Cricket, Viggo sank onto the divan next to Anouk and begged, "Give me a pistol, *mon amour*. Out of all of us, I'm the only one who can use it."

She eased a few inches away from him. "No pistols. You might be able to use it, but magic in Castle Ides is highly concentrated. There's no telling what bringing technology into that place might do."

Cricket finished writing out the map on her arm and announced, "So, then, while Viggo is distracting the Royals, I break into the spell library and steal the beastie spell. That's it? Easy."

"I'm afraid not," the witch said. "The spell library doesn't contain books but tens of thousands of bound folios holding the spells. It would take days to search through them all."

"They must be cataloged somehow," Anouk said.

"Yes, by magic. And they can be located only by magic." She went to the bookcase and took out a glass jar with something small and spindly inside: a captive dragonfly. "I don't normally use insects — that's dirty Goblin magic — but they have their uses. The Royals use enchanted fireflies to locate the spells, but this will do the job just as well. With the proper whisper, it will lead you to the correct folio."

Cricket reached for the jar, but Mada Zola held it back.

"My darling Cricket, even as a cat, you were prone to recklessness. That might serve you for more action-oriented spells, but this one requires a quiet disposition. Anouk, you must perform the spell. I'll write it out for you. It isn't easy, but I have faith in you."

Anouk carefully tucked the jar in her pocket.

"So all that's left," Cricket said, "is figuring out how to sneak past Prince Rennar's own penthouse apartments and into the library without having escorts. Any ideas?"

The cat clock was ticking. They needed to leave soon, let Beau drive like the wind, make up for some precious lost hours. Anouk paced, stepping around the paintings like puzzle pieces, looking at the haunted faces staring back, the beautiful ballroom filled with dancing Royals and musicians to play for them and —

"Servants."

"What was that?" asked Mada Zola.

Anouk picked up the heavy painting of the ball. "Look — these figures in the background, dressed in black. They're servants, aren't they? And servants don't have escorts. No one bothers to notice the maids. Even in the painting, they're just sketched-in figures. That's how we get from the elevator to the spell library and back — disguised as servants." She turned to Viggo and Hunter Black. "And once we steal the spell, I'll signal to you two that it's time to go. I'll bring a tray of tea to the salon. Lavender tea if everything is good, bergamot if there's trouble."

"We'll need maid uniforms," Cricket said.

Anouk peered closer at the maids in the painting. Each wore a plain black dress, a white apron, and a lace veil covering half her face. The painting didn't show the detail of the specific buttons or hems or shoes, but she guessed that Royals never looked closely at the staff. They wouldn't notice small missing details.

The bed sheets, Anouk thought. *Those are white. And the curtains are dark velvet.*

"Do you have needle and thread, Petra?"

Petra gave a laugh. "Do I look like I do needlepoint?" But then she thought. "We have gardening wire."

"That'll do. We'll have to take down these curtains."

"They're purple, not black."

"A little magic will change that. Besides, no one will be looking at us. They'll be too busy looking at Viggo being . . . Viggo." She waved in his general direction; he was adjusting his ridiculous slouchy hat in a mirror.

She turned to Beau. "And you'll need to stay outside in the car and keep it running in case we need to get out of there quickly."

"Impossible, cabbage. I'm going with you."

She rested a hand on his shoulder. "We all have to play to our strengths. You breathe, sleep, and dream cars. Sorry, but it isn't up for negotiation."

He didn't look pleased, but he didn't argue. "And you? Once you locate the folio for Cricket to steal, what will you do?"

The others' jobs seemed so clear: Beau, the getaway driver; Cricket, the spell thief; Viggo, the distraction; and Hunter Black, their bodyguard in case anything went wrong. Where did she fit into all of this? A maid and a cook—that's all she'd ever been. And yet there was something about bringing them all together that did feel like baking: gathering disparate ingredients—a thief, a driver, an assassin—and mixing them in just the right ways at just the right times while keeping a close eye on the clock.

"What I do best," she said. "Keep things tidy."

She went to the clock on the mantel, counting the hours on her fingers. "We have less than a day to drive to Paris, steal the spell, and return. As long as absolutely nothing goes wrong, we can pull this off."

She started to take down the velvet curtains. There was no time to sew entire costumes by hand, but she'd once seen Mada Vittora cast a trick to stitch a Goblin's mouth shut. She remembered the spell. It wouldn't be perfect, but they were short on time, and the maids' costumes had to stay together for only a few hours.

"As long as nothing goes wrong?" Cricket muttered. "We're so screwed."

Chapter 21

Eighteen Hours of Enchantment Remain

S ITTING IN THE FRONT SEAT of the Rolls-Royce, Anouk slid her hands over the plain dress and white apron. A broom rested at her feet. She adjusted her flimsy veil. The maid's costume didn't fit well, but given that she'd cobbled it and a matching one for Cricket together from curtains and gardening wire in under an hour, that was to be expected. She fought against the feeling that she was going backward, sliding into her old life. The apron was only temporary, she reminded herself. She didn't have to sweep. Didn't have to polish silver. But still, she was startled when she caught her reflection in the side mirror: Hair pulled back in a crisp ribbon. Dress that was blank and forgettable. No golden threads. No gossamer wings.

She folded up the veil and twisted to the back seat, where Cricket sat between Hunter Black and Viggo. Cricket's usual wardrobe consisted of ripped tights and shirts with skulls; Anouk wasn't used to seeing her in a starched apron and prim knee socks with a feather duster in one hand, and she almost had to hide a snicker. Cricket's arms were folded tight to avoid having to touch either of the boys. Viggo, sitting behind Anouk, kept sneaking his hands forward in an attempt to massage her shoulders.

"Stop it, Viggo," she snapped.

"You look tense, my love."

"We're about to break into Castle Ides to steal the only spell that could keep us human. Yes, I'm tense."

They'd stuck the cat clock back on the dashboard with gum, and now it *tick-tick-tick*ed, counting down the hours until they arrived in Paris.

"I hid the pouch of eucalyptus leaves in my bra, but there aren't enough places to stash my blades in this dress," Cricket complained.

"You'll have to leave the big ones behind," Anouk said. "The small ones you can hide in your hair. Speaking of . . ." She motioned regretfully to Cricket's curly mass of hair. "You'll need to pull it back."

Cricket scoffed, offended.

"Maids don't wear their hair loose," Anouk said. "Maids don't wear black lipstick; they don't have rips in their tights. They don't show any personality at all: that's the point. You have to hide everything that makes you *you*. When you move through a room, it should be with quiet steps and small movements. You're not a person, you're a piece of furniture with legs."

She felt a hollow pang inside; she'd never thought about it in these terms before. How long had she spent hiding who she was behind an apron? Scouring floors for hours in the hopes that her work would be so perfect that she'd be noticed? But she was never noticed. She reached for the old franc coin but realized she'd left it on her bedroom dresser, back at the estate.

Beau was looking at her oddly. She had her arms clutched tightly across her chest and was shivering slightly. He handed her the Faustine jacket from the back seat. She laid it over her chest like a blanket, tracing her fingers over the fabric. When she glanced in the mirror again, a piece of furniture with legs didn't look back this time.

The gargoyle.

"Thanks," she said softly, putting the jacket on.

Cricket grudgingly pulled her hair back into a high bun and took off her charm earring, but she refused to remove her sunglasses. She sighed loudly and slid down in the seat. Her boot knocked against Hunter Black and he kicked back.

"Watch it," he snapped.

"*You* watch it." Cricket held up a eucalyptus leaf threateningly. "Or I'll use the cutting spell on that greasy hair of yours."

"I wouldn't do that, Cricket," Beau warned.

But Hunter Black gave her boot another kick and Cricket swallowed the leaf. "That's it. Prepare to be bald. *Incisha coup,* bastard—"

The car lurched hard enough to pitch everyone forward, the engine chugging and struggling. Anouk grabbed the dashboard to steady herself.

"Beau, what the hell?" Cricket cried.

"It isn't me." He fought to regain control of the car. "I told you not to do magic in here. It interferes with the car's technology."

"We shouldn't be fighting anyway," Anouk said. "We're all on the same side now, don't you get that? We're a family." She turned and faced the front. Two hands snaked up to her shoulders and started kneading her tense muscles, and she whipped around again. "Viggo, I said no massages!"

She exchanged an exasperated look with Beau.

"Witch's boys these days," he lamented.

They rode in silence through the French countryside, and Anouk watched the world pass by. Small towns dotted the landscape, and she thought of how each one was filled with Pretties going about their daily lives, to school and offices and grocery stores, never once realizing how precious their very existence was. What a gift it was to be them.

She closed her eyes. What would she lose if she failed? No more beautiful couture jackets. No more fairy tales. No more cooking, smiling, laughing.

Only darkness.

She shivered awake with a jolt. How long had she slept? She glanced at the clock—it was past noon. It was stormy as they returned to the city. On the horizon, the distant lights of Paris lit up the clouds.

Beau adjusted the rearview mirror. "We'll be there soon."

A crow flew by overhead, casting a shadow on the car.

When they had left—had it really been only forty-eight hours ago?—she'd felt as though she were hurtling through some twisted dream world.

And now?

Only two days had passed, and yet those days had changed everything. She wasn't anyone's servant. She stroked the sleeves of her jacket; her battle armor, her second skin.

Rain slapped against the windshield, blurring the city into a kaleidoscope of streetlights. The streets were empty of everything except black umbrellas that hid faces. Beau circled a roundabout.

"That's it ahead."

She jumped as Viggo thrust himself between the front seats, jabbing a finger toward a gray stone building lit up in the rain. The Champs-Élysées was lined with edifices, each more impressive than the last: international banks, luxury hotels, boutiques that catered only to the wealthy. But Castle Ides stood alone. Set back from the street behind a black iron fence, ten stories high, it looked more like a seventeenth-century fortress than a castle, despite its name. The windshield wipers swept back and forth steadily, giving them brief glimpses of the structure before the rain obscured it again. The building looked darker than it had in Mada Zola's paintings.

"Scrying crows," Hunter Black said, answering the question in her head. Hundreds — t housands — of crows perched on every rail and foothold of the building, blackening it with glossy feathers. She had to press her hands against her ears to filter out that incessant chattering. Didn't the Pretties hear it? But the ones outside, hunkered under umbrellas, went about their day as usual. Anouk felt a chill. The Haute wielded power over the Pretties, but the Pretties greatly outnumbered magic handlers. If the enchantments were broken, what would happen? If the Pretties' technology continued to grow, would it render magic obsolete? Would the entire Haute become nothing but a memory?

"Is it always like this?" Anouk yelled above the din.

"No," Viggo answered. "It's because of Mada Vittora's death. The whole city is in chaos now."

Rain pelted the car. If the crows felt the rain, they didn't care. They let it roll off their waxed wings, squawking and whispering and climbing over one another in a tangle of sharp little beaks.

Beau stopped the car. The engine rumbled. The windshield wipers went back and forth. Anouk peered out the window at the imposing entrance with its heavy iron doors. Two crows flew away from a sign that warned away visitors, though Anouk imagined stronger magic was also at work to keep out any curious Pretties. The sign read:

The clock clicked to one o'clock in the afternoon.

"Ready?" Anouk said.

Beau tugged gently on her sleeve, and she realized she was still wearing the Faustine jacket, clutching it hard enough to almost tear the fabric. She shed it reluctantly. Cricket's hair was smoothed back, her face scrubbed of black eyeliner. She looked different; younger, softer. It rankled Anouk—they shouldn't ever have to be anything other than themselves.

"Ready," Cricket said, brandishing the feather duster.

Cricket and Viggo and Hunter Black climbed out the back. She reached for the handle, but Beau stopped her.

"Wait."

The rain kept pelting the car, the windshield wipers sweeping it away. She felt as though they were back in that car wash in the Marais where he'd promised her that everything would be okay.

He reached into his pocket. "For luck."

He handed her the franc coin she'd found in the Château des Mille Fleurs.

She gasped. "Luc's coin."

"You left it on the dresser. I thought you'd want it with you. This way it's almost like he's still watching over you."

She leaned across the dash and planted a soft kiss on his cheek.

"Thank you, Beau."

"Be careful, cabbage. Come back to me."

"Always."

She strung the coin on the chain around her neck, took her broom, and climbed out of the car into the rain. It was cold, and she dashed to the covered porch where the others waited, collars turned up against the rain: a thief, a witch's boy, and an assassin.

The crows' whispers paired with the rain were deafening. Slick oil puddled in the driveway, its swirling colors the only brightness on the gray afternoon. Thunder cracked, and a flock of the crows alighted on a statue by the front door. Rennar's granite face looked out over Paris. She shivered again.

"After you, my love," Viggo said.

He held open the heavy iron door. The others hunched in the rain, waiting for her. She darted inside. The foyer was startlingly bright. White marble floors, white columns, white molding on the ceiling. Even the gaslight chandeliers were glitteringly bright. A wall of glass cut through the center of the room, separating them from the steam-powered elevator and broken only by two small vents at the top and a glass turnstile in the center.

"They must have a good maid," Cricket observed of the pristine room.

"Shh." Anouk nudged Cricket, nodding toward a woman sitting at a reception desk. Another woman stood to the side of the turnstile. They were both very pale—as colorless as the walls—and very still, with identical white-blond hair and ivory suits that were heavily starched. Neither of the women acknowledged them as they approached, and a creeping feeling spread up Anouk's back. There was something wrong with them. They didn't move.

"Don't worry," said Viggo. "Say whatever you like. They can't hear us. None of them are real." He gestured to two more women on the far side of the glass that Anouk hadn't noticed.

"What do you mean, not real?"

He fumbled in his pockets for his invitation. "These are the Marble Ladies. They're enchanted statues. They don't think or care what we say as long as we have an invitation." He found his invitation and presented it with a flourish. The woman at the desk snapped to attention with mechanical precision, inspected his invitation, and then abruptly stood.

Anouk gasped. The woman's back . . . it simply wasn't *there*. The receptionist was only half a person—the front half—like a relief statue carved from a block of stone.

"What if it doesn't work?" Anouk whispered.

"Why wouldn't it?"

Slowly, the receptionist's white eyes lifted to Viggo. "Welcome, monsieur."

Viggo smirked and started to enter the turnstile, followed by his shadow, Hunter Black. But the receptionist slammed a hand into Hunter Black's chest with enough force that the air rushed from his lungs. Another one of the ladies lunged out of the shadows and grabbed Cricket's wrist.

Viggo stepped back from the turnstile.

"Hey, relax!" he said, making a calming motion and gesturing between himself and the others. "They're with me."

"I must inform you that the rules have changed, monsieur," the woman said mechanically. "No guests."

The two other Marble Ladies near the elevator stepped closer to the opposite side of the glass wall, one under each of the vents. They were a foot taller than even Beau and wider by a hand's width.

"But it's Hunter Black," Viggo said. "He always accompanies me. And the others are—"

"This change in policy is a direct order from the head of the Haute," the Marble Lady continued as though he hadn't spoken. "The building is under tighter security. We cannot allow in anyone who does not personally have an invitation."

Viggo glanced back at Anouk. "Any ideas, my love?"

Anouk thought. The glass wall prevented them from making a mad dash to the elevator, and it was too high to climb over. In every good recipe, there had to be adaptation. Room to substitute one ingredient for another, adjustments to be made in the event of a pot boiling over or a shortage of salt. She could do this.

Do you want to hear a story? Luc's voice came to her, and just like that she was back in her turret bedroom, cuddled under a quilt as thunder cracked outside, Luc sitting cross-legged on the foot of her bed with a mug of tea that steamed delicate tendrils around his face. *Once upon a time there was a girl locked in a thousand-foot glass tower. The prince of a warring country intended to keep her there until she agreed to marry him. No way out, no way down, not even bed sheets to tie together for a rope.* Luc had smiled. *Do you want to know how she escaped?*

Anouk thought of the story, of the girl, and inspected the wall of glass keeping them from the elevator. "I have an idea," she said, eyeing the stiff Marble Ladies. "But you aren't going to like it."

Chapter 22

Ten and a Half Hours of Enchantment Remain

AS SOON AS ANOUK told them her idea, both Cricket and Hunter Black scoffed.

"I told you that you wouldn't like it," Anouk replied, then warily eyed the Marble Ladies on the opposite side of the glass wall. "You're sure they can't hear me?"

"No ears," Viggo said.

He was right—their carved hair covered the place where ears would have been.

"Well," Anouk said, "the invitation will let in one person, the bearer of the invitation. But here's the thing—it doesn't specify *who*. So we go in one at a time, then pass the invitation back to the next person."

"We can't pass an invitation through a glass wall," Cricket said. "And the Marble Ladies are too close to the turnstile for us to pass it through that way."

"That's the trick. It's like Luc's fairy tale about the girl in the thousand-foot tower. Remember how she got out?"

Cricket shook her head, looking blank. "Luc never told me that one."

Hunter Black groaned—he clearly knew it, and he knew what Anouk was referring to.

"You and Hunter Black have to work together," Anouk explained. "In the story, the girl is an excellent climber, but she can't escape on her own—the glass walls are too smooth to climb down, and the trapdoor to the tower roof is too high. So she comes up with a plan, and the next time the prince comes to ask her to marry him, she drugs him with willow bark scraped from the bedposts, then leans his sleeping body against the wall and uses it to climb to the roof. She's rescued by something, then. A dragon, I think."

"A griffin," Hunter Black corrected her. "At least get the details right."

Anouk rolled her eyes. "Well, I propose the same. We can't climb sheer glass, but we can climb *them*—the Marble Ladies. You're both in excellent physical shape. Hunter Black, you go through the turnstile, then climb up the Marble Lady on the opposite wall and pass the invitation through that vent back to Cricket on the other side. We don't dare drop it—it could get sucked up in the elevator machinery. She'll give it to Viggo to go through, and we'll repeat everything, and then I'll go through, and then Cricket."

Cricket snorted. "Climb those freaky statues? That's a death wish."

"You heard Viggo," Anouk continued. "As long as we obey the rules, they won't interfere. And we aren't breaking any rules. Besides, I've seen you scale the courtyard wall just to break into the kitchen and steal a slice of cake. You're an excellent climber."

"Fine," Cricket said. She ripped the veil off her head and stuffed it in her apron. "Hold this." She shoved the feather duster into Viggo's hands and then, after flexing her fingers a few times, she grabbed the nearest Marble Lady's shoulders and set a foot in the stiff crook of her arm. She whispered a prayer as she climbed. She stepped on the statue's shoulder, then on her head, and reached the vent.

Anouk took the invitation from Viggo and handed it to Hunter Black. "Your turn."

He presented it to the Marble Lady by the desk, who smiled mechanically. "Welcome, monsieur."

He passed through the turnstile. His grumbles were audible as he rested his hands on the shoulders of the Marble Lady on the far side of the glass and lumbered up on top of her, struggling under the bulkiness of his heavy coat. With a grunt, he took it off. Beneath it he wore a surprisingly plain shirt. He looked younger without his shell against the world. He climbed to the top of the Marble Lady's body and reached toward the vent. He could just manage to pass the invitation through to Cricket.

She grabbed it and tossed it down.

"Your turn, Viggo."

He passed through, and then they repeated the process, and Anouk went through.

"Welcome, mademoiselle," the Marble Lady said.

Anouk was just handing the invitation to Hunter Black when the elevator dinged. The Marble Lady whose shoulder he was perched on suddenly turned toward the elevator, and he wobbled, barely holding on. She took a few strides toward the elevator and stopped there, waiting patiently by the controls. Hunter Black jumped off her shoulders and landed cleanly on the marble floor. Cricket's Marble Lady turned sharply as well and returned to the reception desk. Frowning, Cricket climbed off of her.

"Um . . . what now?" Cricket called.

She was on the opposite side of the glass from the rest of them. With no Marble Ladies standing near the glass anymore, there was no way they could reach the vent to pass the invitation through.

Anouk bit her lip, thinking, but none of Luc's fairy tales offered a solution this time.

Cricket cursed again. "Okay. The vent is too small for me to climb through, but it gives me an idea. Maybe I could make another vent. A hole. A bigger one closer to the ground."

"How?" Hunter Black asked skeptically.

Cricket cracked her knuckles. "I didn't learn that cutting whisper for nothing. I've only cast it on wood, but I don't see why it wouldn't work on glass."

"Even if you can, coming in any way other than the turnstile is against the rules," Viggo pointed out. "They'll stop you."

"Ha, but they'll have to catch me first. You all get in the elevator and hold it open."

Anouk hesitated. "No. It's too risky." But an idea was starting to form in her mind. If Cricket could use magic, maybe she could use magic too. "I'm not powerful enough to prevent the Marble Ladies from chasing you, but there is one simple trick I can do. A diversion spell. The same one I used in the closet to keep Hunter Black from noticing us."

Cricket eyed the glass wall, mapping out the cuts she would need to make. "Worth a shot. Ready?"

Anouk nodded. She, Hunter Black, and Viggo piled into the tight elevator, which was made of mirror that reflected back their faces.

There was a glittering chandelier overhead, and a panel of brass buttons, 1 through 8, and a single button above that labeled PENTHOUSE. ESCORTS REQUIRED.

The doors started to close, but Hunter Black held them open.

Cricket closed her eyes, swallowed a eucalyptus leaf, and began whispering in the Selentium Vox. An almost imperceptible line etched itself in the glass wall, turning at a 90-degree angle and then turning again until it was a rough square.

"Get ready," Cricket told them. She gave the glass a gentle tap with her finger.

It hit the floor and shattered, sending broken glass everywhere.

The spectacle didn't go unnoticed by the Marble Ladies. As one, they stepped toward the glass wall.

"Now, Anouk!" Cricket cried.

Anouk hissed in a breath. She'd seen how fast the Marble Ladies had grabbed Hunter Black. If they seized Cricket with those stone hands . . . She thought of the bird she'd once seen caught under a car on Rue des Amants. Crushed.

"Non avis ila, non avis ila, spero . . ."

The Marble Ladies slowed but didn't stop entirely, as though they had simultaneously realized they'd forgotten something important. Cricket moved fast—first an elbow through the glass hole, then her head, left shoulder, then the right, then torso. Then she was through to her waist and had to suck in a breath to squeeze her hips through.

As soon as she touched the floor, all four Marble Ladies' heads whipped around as though they had felt the vibration. They all focused intently on her. No longer forgetful. Anouk's spell was fading.

"Hurry!" Anouk yelled.

The Marble Ladies moved in a flash. The two by the elevator lunged toward Cricket with startling speed. The one by the desk shoved through the turnstile, coming after her. Cricket dodged the closest one, then jumped up onto the back of the other, using the momentum to spring high enough to reach the chandelier. The receptionist she'd used as a springboard reached for her but she twisted her feet out of the way just in time.

Anouk whispered again. *"Non avis nos, non avis nos, spero . . ."*

But they barely paused this time; the spell didn't work the same on stone creatures as it had on Hunter Black.

Cricket swung back and forth, building momentum, and then let go of the chandelier and went hurtling toward the elevator. The Marble Ladies lunged for her again, but she crashed into the elevator; Viggo and Anouk caught her as they all fell back against the mirrors.

"Hunter Black, let the door close!"

He released it. For a few seconds the steam-powered gears clanked, and Anouk felt her heartbeat pounding harder than it ever had before. The doors were closing too slowly. The Marble Ladies were coming for them too quickly. They were three steps away. Now two. Anouk brandished her broom, her only weapon. The door was still open two inches, then one, then . . .

Closed.

Cricket let out a cry of relief, sagging back against them.

"Quick," Anouk said. "Get ready. Put your veil back on."

"Don't I get an 'Amazing work, Cricket, congratulations on doing magic'?"

Anouk granted her a nod. "Amazing work, Cricket. Now, as soon as the doors open, everyone keep your heads down, your eyes low. Viggo, you distract the escorts so that Cricket and I can slip away and join the other servants."

"Yes, but first, my love, a kiss before we take this risk."

He leaned in with lips pursed and she sputtered and pushed him away. "Viggo, gross! We don't have time for this."

"I must have one—"

"You heard her," Cricket roared. "Hands off." She shoved Viggo, and he fell back against the wall. A low ding sounded. Everyone froze.

"What was that?" Hunter Black snapped.

Viggo's face went slack. He straightened, fixing his knit cap sheepishly, and turned toward the elevator controls.

The fourth-floor button was lit.

"Merde," he cursed. "It's Cricket's fault. She pushed me, and you get only one try, only one floor, you can't just bounce around from one floor to another."

"What do you mean?" Anouk said.

"Wrong button," Viggo said. "We wanted the penthouse."

The round button for the fourth floor glowed brightly.

"What's on the fourth floor?" Anouk asked with dread.

The elevator stopped. Another ding sounded, and the fourth-floor light turned off, indicating that they had arrived.

"The fourth floor?" Viggo said. "That's London."

"Oh, *va te faire foutre,*" Cricket cursed. "London? That means Goblins."

Chapter 23

Ten Hours of Enchantment Remain

E VEN BEFORE THE DOORS opened, Anouk heard
music. It was a blaring mix of heavy metal and accordion
and English lyrics, and the tempo kept slowing down and
then rapidly speeding up, making Anouk's head spin.

The elevator opened.

The fourth floor of Castle Ides was a boardroom with twenty-
foot-high ceilings and vast windows along the southern side; chandeliers hung from the ceiling, and tall bookshelves spanned the walls. It
was filled with overstuffed antique furniture, mahogany tables, and
velvet fainting couches in front of roaring fireplaces. But the richness
of the room was eclipsed by the apparent circus happening within.
One Goblin, dressed in a three-piece suit with a magenta bowler hat,
was hanging upside down from a chandelier, his hat knotted to his
head with a necktie to keep it from falling off. Expensive-looking furniture was stacked haphazardly around the room, and two Goblins
were using chairs as tables and tables as chairs, with a hodgepodge of
teacups between them. Another Goblin very seriously chased moths
with a butterfly net. He had a cup of tea in one hand that he seemed
reluctant to set down, which made catching the moths nearly impossible and sent tea sloshing everywhere.

"Wrong floor," Cricket said. "Definitely wrong floor."

Anouk heard a bus honking. On the other side of the tall windows, a double-decker red bus circled Piccadilly Circus. London was just a single magical breath away. London was where the Goblins had consolidated what remained of their society centuries ago, when witches had launched a bloody campaign to round up the good-natured creatures and force them into servitude. Those few Goblins left had hunkered down in London basements and sewers and other places where it came in handy that they could see in the dark. Even the Goblins Anouk had known in Paris, who likely had never set foot in England, had been almost violently Anglophilic in their devotion to London. She'd seen Goblin girls with their fingernails painted like the British flag, and Goblin boys wearing neon cravats with patterns of Big Ben, and every time a David Bowie song came on the radio, they all stopped and saluted.

"We shouldn't be here," Hunter Black warned.

He banged on the penthouse button, but the elevator didn't budge. Cricket pounded on the other buttons uselessly.

"There must be an emergency staircase, right?" Anouk said.

"If there was," Cricket muttered, "I'd be afraid it would lead to Antarctica."

"They've noticed us," Viggo announced, seemingly amused.

Anouk whirled back toward the boardroom. Two Goblins in velvet armchairs were looking up now, teacups poised mid-sip. Even the Goblin hanging upside down from the chandelier watched them. A pair of Goblins leaning over a table glanced up; each wore a monocle, making one eye look twice as big as the other. Their pointed ears wiggled slightly. With a start, Anouk realized they were sorting dead insects: grasshoppers, flies, spiders, and moths, like the ones the

Goblin with the butterfly net was trying to catch. They were filling glass jars with their wings. Anouk looked down at her feet. A spider inched toward her oxford shoe. She used her broom to nudge it away.

Abruptly, the music stopped.

A particularly colorful Goblin appeared seemingly out of nowhere, grinning. He was short, with light brown skin that had a golden undertone and eyes that seemed too big, and he was wearing a maroon three-piece suit with a blue cravat. Fastened to his belt loop were at least a dozen brass pocket-watch chains attached to various objects tucked in pockets.

He sipped from a teacup that was also secured by a chain to his belt. He had a broken-heart tattoo on the back of his hand, and Anouk thought she remembered seeing that somewhere before.

"Lost, are we?"

He had a British accent, a diabolical grin, and a pet rat perched on his shoulder.

"Y-yes," she stuttered, clutching her broom. "We meant to get out at the penthouse."

He took another slow sip of tea, mouth curled in a knowing smile. "A witch's boy, an assassin, and a pair of maids get out at the wrong floor." Another sip. "That's the start to a good joke, don't you think? Or maybe a bad one."

Behind him, the Goblin hanging upside down from the chandelier let out a high-pitched giggle.

"We were . . . requested," Anouk sputtered, thinking fast. "A . . . big mess. Something about an accident in the kitchen. Soup everywhere. Lots of extra hands needed to clean it up."

"A soup explosion! My, how *dire*."

Anouk gripped the broom tighter. One word from the Goblins could sound the alarm. Their plans could be ruined. Cricket's hands were flexing; she was ready to reach for her knives if needed.

"Perhaps I may be of assistance." The Goblin drained his teacup, then produced another object from his pocket that was also fastened by a chain to his vest.

A golden key.

The Goblin leaned into the elevator, slipped his key in an upper slot, twisted it, and pressed the button for the penthouse. He replaced the key in one of his many pockets. The doors began to close, and Anouk felt a flutter of uncertain relief—had it really been that easy? —until the doors were nearly shut and the Goblin in the blue cravat shot out a hand to hold them open.

He pressed his face to the narrow crack.

"The name's Tenpenny, by the way. I run the London Room. Stop by on your way out. We're having a party. All are invited."

A fly landed on Tenpenny's cheek and his bulging eyes slid to it. He smiled, his makeup giving him a somewhat maniacal look, and petted the rat on his shoulder. He stepped back and offered them a little toodle-oo wave as the doors shut.

The elevator jerked and then started to rise.

Cricket let out a breath. "Is it just me, or did that feel too easy? Like, they're-sounding-the-alarm-right-now too easy?" She shuddered like she'd walked through a cobweb.

It wasn't just Cricket. And something about the Goblin had seemed familiar—had he visited the townhouse? Anouk ran a hand over her hair and the veil, straightened her dress, tried to look normal.

"Don't worry, my love," Viggo breathed in her ear. "Goblins don't care for inserting themselves in politics." He tried to put his arms around her, but she swatted him away.

"Cricket, what's the time looking like?"

"Nine hours till midnight."

"And seven hours to drive back to Montélimar. We have to hurry. I don't trust that those Goblins aren't going to give us away."

In that moment, she yearned for the simplicity of Mada Zola's estate. Rich soil and lavender. The hallways in need of a good dusting. She smiled to herself, thinking of it. All those open country roads for Beau to race his cars on, and endless shiny objects for Cricket to pilfer, and Luc — when they found him — such a beautiful garden for Luc to work in. And for her? She wanted all of it. The kitchen, where she could cook whatever she wanted, or not cook at all. The library, with its books. The fields, where she could spend all day in the sun, all night beneath the stars.

Her hands were sweating on the broom.

"My love," Viggo purred in her ear. "Before we reach the top, I must declare that I love you as the grass loves rain, as the birds love the wind —"

"Can it, Viggo!"

The elevator stopped.

They all went silent. For a second, no one moved. The elevator's mirrored walls reflected the faces of misfits and nobodies.

The doors opened onto an eerily calm foyer.

Anouk could hear voices and footsteps in distant rooms. Mahogany panels lined the walls, along with chandeliers and fine sconces, nothing electric, just like in the townhouse. The floor was made of intricately inlaid wood, and everything was spotless, not a single cobweb or speck of dust.

Cricket rolled up her sleeve to reveal the map she'd penned on her forearm. "We're here." She pointed to a place at her inner elbow. "The elevator foyer. It's near the start of the hour, so the floor plan won't change for about another fifty minutes."

"The Royals will be in the west salons," Viggo said. "They retire there after lunch." Out of all of them, he was the only one who didn't look terrified, though his eyes held that feverish, enchanted sheen. *His* life wasn't at risk, despite all the protestations and promises he'd made Anouk. He wasn't in danger of turning into anything but what he already was: a spoiled boy, richer than a king, who'd never had to do a true day's work his entire life. "I think the salons are that way, if I have the time right."

He jerked his head toward the opposite hallway.

Cricket rolled down her sleeve as another maid approached the elevator, but the enchanted Pretty girl didn't look up, her head cast down, eyes half hidden by the lace veil.

"I'm to take you to your escort," she said quietly.

"Go," Anouk said to Viggo and Hunter Black, but she muttered quietly to Hunter Black, "Make sure Viggo doesn't do anything stupid."

"If he doesn't, they'll know for certain that something is wrong," Cricket added under her breath.

Viggo opened his lips, probably to recite some love poem to Anouk, but Hunter Black slammed a hand over his mouth. He gave Anouk and Cricket a grudging nod. "Be careful."

"Aw, it's almost like you care," Cricket said.

He scowled and dragged Viggo down the east hallway after the maid. They disappeared around a bust of Prince Rennar.

"Right," Cricket said. "Let's get the spell before the two of them screw everything up, as they inevitably will."

They hurried down the west hallway, past more marble busts of bygone Royals with plaster eyes that seemed to follow them. They turned at the corner and entered a hallway that was lined with glass cases holding treasures. Cricket's fingers twitched as they passed by golden robes and jewels and oddly mundane objects too: a threadbare stuffed rabbit, an empty soda bottle, a dented watering can.

"What are they?" Anouk whispered.

"Artifacts," Cricket replied, her eyes gleaming. "This was how the Royals took power over the great Pretty leaders, not with wars or jewels, but with regular objects imbued with magic. Objects no one suspected. That pair of scissors—it was slipped into Napoleon's suitcase and inspired him to wage war against Russia."

They passed more objects: a postcard from Egypt, a bird's nest, a pair of red socks. A butler came down the hall and Cricket feigned cleaning the cases with her feather duster, but she needn't have bothered; the enchanted butler paid them no attention, his lips moving in silent whispers to himself.

Cricket consulted the map on her arm again. "*Merde*—I'm sweating and it's making the ink run. It looks like the library's down this hall on the left. On the right here, these big doors, this is . . ." She blanched. "Prince Rennar's private apartments."

Anouk felt a wave of apprehension, but it was mixed with curiosity. There, through those ancient doors, not gilded like the others, was where Prince Rennar laid his head at night, where he looked over his city, where he hung the scrying portraits through which he watched his private world and maybe had even watched her dusting . . .

She tripped on her shoes and bumped into one of the glass cases. It didn't topple, but the gardening wire she'd used on her uniform snagged and tore. Part of her apron ripped and she cursed. The costume needed to last only a few more minutes, just long enough to—

"This door," Cricket said. "Wait, no, that's a freckle. That one."

She pointed to an opulent gilded door with rich blue trim. Anouk gave a fleeting final glance at the opposite doors, the ones to Rennar's apartments, and then slipped her hand into her apron pocket and clutched Mada Zola's jar with the dragonfly. The finding spell's whisper was poised on her lips. *Trouva, trouva, incantatio bestia.* The dragonfly would lead them along the shelves, past folios of love spells and healing whispers, of potion recipes and invisibility chants, right to the very folio, one of ten thousand, that was the means of their existence.

"This is going to be a theft for the ages," Cricket said, rubbing her hands together in delight. She started to push the door open, but a voice spoke at their backs.

"You two. Turn around."

Anouk froze.

She knew that voice. The deep tone that was both casually unassuming and undeniably powerful. A voice that had once whispered into her ear that she wasn't made for sweeping floors, didn't she know that?

Her lips parted. She gripped the broom hard.

Prince Rennar had given an order, and no one disobeyed the prince.

Chapter 24

Nine Hours of Enchantment Remain

H E WASN'T DRESSED IN jeans and a scarf this time. He looked as though he had stepped straight out of the portrait hanging above Mada Vittora's mantel; he was wearing a frost-gray suit with threads as fine as spider's silk. A crown of golden briars circled his head, the points catching the hallway lights as though he'd managed to ensnare little pieces of the stars themselves. And those eyes that had seemed to follow her as she had cleaned — not flat chips of paint now but the blue-gray shade of the sea where it dropped into unknowable depths. Impossible to capture with a paintbrush.

His hair, though, was still the slightest bit mussed.

Cricket lowered her face so that the lace veil hid her features and nudged Anouk, who quickly did the same. "Your Majesty," Anouk whispered.

She clutched the broom close to her chest. Cricket, never an adept actress, halfheartedly fanned the feather duster over the doorway as though sweeping for cobwebs, but the way it flopped in her hand made it clear she'd never used one before. Anouk thought it impossible that the prince wouldn't notice such a glaring detail, but he only brushed a wrinkle out of his suit distractedly.

"We've guests," he said offhandedly. "A witch's boy and his associate. Fetch a tray of tea and éclairs and bring it to the east salon."

Another second passed before Anouk moved. She loosened her grip on the broom, her palms slippery with sweat. Cricket fanned the duster too hard and sneezed.

The prince leaned closer. "Be certain there's a sharp knife on the tray." He paused. "For the éclairs. They can be difficult to slice."

It took every ounce of Anouk's concentration not to shoot a look at Cricket.

A sharp knife?

She dared the slightest peek at the prince from beneath the veil, and for a second, he met her eyes. A dangerous thrill went through her. She should have looked away to keep her identity safe, but for this one instant, though it was incredibly foolish, some part of her wanted him to see beyond her apron. She yearned for him to recognize her, to tell her once more that she was made for greater things.

And for the briefest second, she thought he did recognize her. But then he looked away, bored and distracted, and the moment was gone. "You understand?"

"Yes," she whispered. "A sharp knife."

His footsteps echoed down the hallway as he left, reverberating off the glass cases. She didn't dare breathe until he had disappeared around the corner.

Cricket touched her shoulder and she jumped.

"That was close. I was afraid he'd recognize us, even with our veils."

Anouk folded up her lace veil. "All men like him ever see are aprons. I could be Mada Vittora risen from the dead, but if I had a mop in my hand he'd still just ask for tea."

Her voice was bitter.

Bitter because it was true. She'd had it in her head ever since the night of the party that the handsome prince was different, that he judged the worth of a person not by his or her clothes but by something deeper. And to admit that he was just like all the others — the witches and the Royals whose gazes skimmed over her like she was a forgotten old lamp — sharpened her anger.

"He asked for a knife," she said. "What do you think that means? It's not for éclairs, I can promise you that."

Cricket's fingers involuntarily went to the folds of her uniform as she checked her own blades. "It means their top witch is dead and they want answers from her witch's boy. And that they aren't going to waste the energy to use magic when knives will do."

Anouk drew in a sharp breath. "You think they're going to torture Viggo?"

"I hope so."

The thought sat with Anouk uneasily, like she'd eaten too much sticky icing. Viggo and Hunter Black had just walked into a room full of the most dangerous magic casters in Paris — no, she'd *sent* them into the room — and the handful of defensive skills between the two of them would mean nothing against the Royals' tricks and whispers.

Cricket thrust the feather duster accusingly in Anouk's general direction. "You look dangerously close to caring."

"Well . . ."

"*Incroyable*. We needed Viggo to get us into Castle Ides, and here we are. Let Rennar carve him up into a ham, for all I care, and serve him with pineapple at Christmas."

"And Hunter Black? I gave him my word that the five of us would stick together. And besides, Viggo is here only because *I'm* here. I'm responsible for him. I can't leave him to be tortured."

Cricket mumbled a curse under her breath. "Fine. We get the spell, and then — only then — rescue their pathetic derrières."

Anouk grinned.

"Now." Cricket ditched the feather duster and cracked her knuckles. "Prepare to watch the greatest thief in all the Haute perform the trickiest heist in history. *Et voilà,* the scene of the crime: the spell library of Castle Ides."

With a flourish, she opened the pair of gilded doors.

Anouk felt a prickle of magic as she crossed the threshold. *What* a library. Nearly every inch from floor to ceiling was lined with shelves containing folios of every color: dusty reds and sea-green blues, faded yellows and darkest blacks. The ceilings must have been thirty feet high, buttressed with wrought-iron arches that made her think of the Eiffel Tower's latticed curves. A balcony ran the full length of the room, and dozens of rolling library ladders stretched up to the very highest shelves. It smelled of crisp paper and older, mustier things: leather and long-held secrets. Rain pounded at the windows — she'd forgotten about the storm.

Spaced evenly in the library were three enormous glass cases. They emitted a mottled blue glow that gave the room a dreamlike cast, like it was underwater. Anouk rested her fingers on the closest case; inside, thousands of fireflies floated on gentle wings, locked in by a magic far beyond her ability to break.

"Blue ghosts," she said, remembering a book she'd read. "They're only found in the Americas, and only for two weeks each year. They glow blue, not yellow. The light leads the Royals to the exact folio they're looking for."

Cricket pressed her face to the case, looking unimpressed. "You've got the dragonfly?"

Anouk held the jar to the light. The trapped dragonfly inside, its only movement a slight pulsing of its elongated body, might not have been magical or rare, but it had its own beauty.

Anouk pulled out a chair at one of the mahogany library tables. "We'll have to be fast. Rennar will be suspicious if we don't deliver tea soon. Are you ready?"

Cricket stretched her neck. "Always."

Anouk set her supplies on the table: the glass jar with the dragonfly, the pouch of floral herbs, the scrap of paper that contained the finding spell. This wasn't like the simple whispers she'd cast before, sleeping spells so easy that even clumsy Beau could learn to do them. This was higher-level magic. Magic reserved for those who were born magical, like the Royals and the Goblins, or who were made magical through unendurable pain, like the witches. She'd heard rumors of the bleak, severe academies where human girls were trained to become witches. Only a small handful survived the final test, the coal baths, where excruciating black flames tore apart and rebuilt Pretty flesh into magical flesh. Who was she, an untrained, untested neophyte, to dare such a spell?

She cleared her throat. Pinched the dusty floral herbs between her fingers and choked them down raw.

She began the whisper. *"Trouva, trouva, incantatio bestia."*

Nothing happened. The dragonfly rested immobile in the jar, its fractured eyes revealing nothing.

Cricket glanced back at her with a raised eyebrow.

Anouk cleared her throat. "Um . . . I must not have gotten the intonation right."

"I'd say take your time, but we don't have any."

"*Thanks.*" Anouk swallowed down another pinch of the dry herbs. She closed her eyes and focused on the tastes: the sweetness of fennel, the bitter tang of bloodroot. They mixed with the library itself—the moldering paper of the spells, the waxed floors—and for the briefest instant, there was only one taste. Only one moment. Only one sensation, and it was *magic*.

She whispered, *"Trouva, trouva, incantatio bestia."*

The dragonfly started buzzing madly in the glass jar. Anouk's eyes snapped open just in time to see the insect thrash so hard that the jar toppled over. The lid came off. Freed, the dragonfly shot into the air.

"It's loose," Anouk cried, and then, "It worked!"

The dragonfly flew straight up toward the arched ceiling, thirty feet high.

"Merde," Cricket cursed. "Keep an eye on it!"

The dragonfly was a grain of sand tossed in the ocean; if they lost sight of it for even a second, they'd never find it again.

With a burst of energy Cricket bolted for the closest ladder, climbed it two rungs at a time, then swung herself up and over the balcony railing like a trapeze artist.

"Where did it go?" she yelled.

"There!" Anouk pointed toward the east window. "To the upper windows."

"I'm on it. *Holà*, if I just knew a flying spell, this would be a breeze."

Cricket sprinted the length of the balcony, folios rustling in her wake. Anouk paced on the lower level, eyes fastened to the dragonfly as it whizzed as fast as a shooting star. Outside, the rain droned harder, in ripples of water like a typhoon. "There," she cried. "Now it's behind you!"

Cricket dropped to all fours on the balcony, pushed off, and ran back the other way. Her pace was breakneck and yet she was almost completely silent. She moved like a ghost through a graveyard. Anouk would have felt awestruck if she hadn't been so focused on not losing sight of the dragonfly.

The insect swooped down over the tables, and Cricket grabbed the iron railing, jumped up and over, and landed gracefully on her feet.

No wonder the Royals used the blue ghost fireflies. They'd be slow and ethereal, lazily lighting the way straight to the folio in question, not doing the mad chaotic dance of the dragonfly. Anouk glanced over her shoulder for a split second. Was Rennar consulting his watch and wondering where the two maids were with his tea?

A chair toppled as Cricket leaped onto one of the tables, and Anouk spun back around. She searched the vast library space with a plunging sense of panic.

"I lost it!" she gasped.

"I haven't," Cricket answered, her attention focused eight feet off the ground near a set of shelves. She leaped on one of the golden ladders and climbed swiftly. "It's fast. *Holà*, Anouk, give me a shove."

Anouk ran to the ladder and pushed it on its rolling tracks as

Cricket focused intently. "Faster! No, wait, it's going the other way. Back, back, back!"

Anouk heaved the ladder in the other direction.

"Stop!" Cricket yelled sharply.

Anouk dug her heels into the floor, braking the ladder so fast that Cricket nearly lost her balance. But her reflexes were sharp; she climbed another rung and then held her hand over a dusty red folio seven shelves up. Anouk could just make out the dragonfly resting on its spine.

"That's it," Anouk breathed. "The beastie spell."

Cricket shooed away the dragonfly, took down the folio, and hugged it to her chest as though it were some living, delicate thing. The blue ghost fireflies in their glass cases pulsed steadily, and as rain pelted the windows harder, Anouk once more felt overcome by that underwater sensation. Cricket climbed down, and Anouk took the folio from her with shaking hands. Such a simple thing. Bound red casing. A single page within. And yet it felt heavy in her arms.

"People are going to write songs about this theft," Cricket boasted. "Wait and see. *Songs*."

Anouk's fingers itched to open the folio. She wanted to silently mouth the words that had made them. And yet it was already growing darker outside. A wet, stormy night was coming. She sniffed the air —she smelled citrus and onion and, oddly, it made her think of Luc.

She couldn't resist. She cracked open the folio. A single page. Here was all that separated them from a lifetime of humanity. She'd cast magic before—why not now? Zola herself had said beasties contained a vast magical ability, so why must a witch cast the spell and not her?

A crow suddenly flapped against the outside window, cawing in sharp calls. "Time to go," Cricket warned.

Anouk ripped out the spell and rolled it into a tight cylinder that she stuffed into the hollow shaft of her broom. To even attempt the spell, she'd need herbs, wings, blood . . .

The crow pecked sharply at the window outside. "We'd better get that tea," she said. "And see if Viggo's been turned into someone's Christmas dinner yet."

Chapter 25

Eight and a Half Hours of Enchantment Remain

THEY DARED NOT RUN. *Maids don't run,* Anouk reminded herself. And that's what they had to be now, furniture with legs, faceless girls concerned only with dust. But she clutched the broom hard in defiance.

Maids didn't steal either. Or cast magic, or rescue idiot witch's boys, and yet here she was. They'd done it! She held their very lives in her hands, hidden in the hollow broom shaft. What would Beau say when she pressed the spell against the windshield? They'd fly back to Montélimar as if the car had wings. Let the crows chase them. Let the whispers and rumors nip at their heels. It didn't matter. As the stars came out, they would stand in the Château des Mille Fleurs' gardens, and Mada Zola would take these stolen words and make them human forever, one by one. Wherever Luc was, he would feel the magic of it too. And she'd find him. She *would*. If she could steal this spell from Castle Ides, she could do anything.

Little dust bunny, Luc would say, and he'd lick his thumb and wipe away the perpetual streak of dust on her cheek. *You saved me when I thought you were the one in need of saving.*

She had to lower the lace veil to hide the smile on her face. "Which way is the kitchen?"

Cricket discreetly rolled up her sleeve and consulted the map on her forearm. "The hallway on the right, beneath the arch, second door on the left. Unless it's past four o'clock. Then it's the third door."

An ancient grandfather clock sat beneath an arch, and Anouk checked the hour, but for once she didn't feel shackled to its ticking and tocking. They had the spell. They had enough time for Mada Zola to cast it—though only just. All that was left now was to warn Viggo, get to the elevator and down to Beau.

The familiar aroma of baking bread and garlic led her to the kitchen. The penthouse kitchen was massive, and so crowded with cooks and maids and butlers that she and Cricket had to squeeze their way in. Steam rose from large pans on monstrous twin ovens. A gaggle of girls rolled dough, stamping Rennar's crest into the crust. Cricket slowed, uncertain of the unspoken rules of a kitchen, but Anouk threw herself into the mess, expertly ducking pans, swerving around butlers carrying crates of wine. She spotted a stack of copper trays and grabbed one, hunted up a teakettle, sniffed out the éclairs, and arranged them prettily on the tray. She pulled a sharp knife from the wooden butcher's block, hesitating only briefly before setting it next to the éclairs. Her hands knew the motions by heart: boil water, collect sugar cubes and cream, scoop out the tea—

She paused at the row of labeled tea canisters.

Lavender.

Bergamot.

Lavender to signal that they'd successfully stolen the spell and they should all meet at the elevator. Bergamot to mean that something had gone wrong and it was every beastie for himself. Her instinct was to reach for lavender, yet the scoop didn't move in her hand. She whistled Cricket over, who narrowly ducked a piping-hot tray of madeleines to join her.

"Lavender or bergamot?" Anouk said quietly.

"What are you talking about?"

"It should be your choice, not mine. Viggo's been awful to you. A brute." She handed Cricket the scoop. "So you pick. I'm your friend above all else, Cricket. If you say screw the jerks, then we'll give a tray of bergamot tea to the closest butler to deliver and sneak off to the elevator on our own. Leave them to their fates."

Cricket was at a rare loss for words. She took the silver scoop and tapped it anxiously against the palm of her hand, leaning toward one canister, then the other.

At last, she scooped out a hefty spoonful from one and dumped it into the pot of boiling water, then picked up the tray and shoved it in Anouk's direction. Anouk lifted the lid to catch the aroma.

"Lavender. You're sure?"

"If anyone is going to torture the *salaud*, it'll be me."

Anouk adjusted her lace veil to hide as much of her face as possible, and Cricket did the same, then Anouk carried the tray into the hallway, Cricket right behind her with the broom and feather duster. Cricket glanced at the map on her arm and whispered directions to the salon. The door was cracked open. Anouk could feel heat within and hear the crackle of a fire and voices. A woman's biting hiss, and then Viggo's petulant moan.

"In and out," Cricket whispered, hand on the doorknob. "Like thieves."

"Like ghosts," Anouk agreed.

Cricket nodded solemnly and opened the door. Anouk tried to

hide the slight shaking of her hands as she entered the salon. She kept her gaze low, taking in the room out of the corner of her eye: Viggo sitting on the sofa, Hunter Black at his side. Countess Quine —she of the hissing voice—towering over Viggo with a blade-capped fingertip an inch from his face. Lord Metham in a leather armchair, stuffing a pipe. His wife by the window, looking drearily out at the rain, lips stained green and pink from powder.

Where was Rennar?

His absence made her falter, and she nearly tripped on the heavy fringe of the salon's rug. The teacups clattered and Countess Quine shot her a look. Fear rippled all the way to Anouk's toes. Rennar hadn't recognized her earlier, but Countess Quine had been at the townhouse that night too, and so had the Methams.

"Pardon me," Anouk said quietly. "I've brought tea at the prince's request."

She bent forward to set it on the coffee table and was able to catch Hunter Black's eye. His face was as growl-some as ever, his posture tense and folded in on itself, but when he smelled the lavender tea, she saw that mask slip.

Was that—could it possibly be—*a look of trust?*

"My love!"

Anouk's short-lived optimism came crashing down. Viggo, the *imbécile*! He was already pitching himself toward her, almost knocking the tray out of her hands and looking inclined to throw his arms around her. Countess Quine stopped talking and stared at Viggo as though he were speaking in tongues. Lady Metham turned from the window with a quizzical expression. Anouk felt the blood drain from her cheeks, but they were saved by Hunter Black. He slammed his elbow into Viggo's side, knocking the breath out of him before he could say one more incriminating word.

Viggo collapsed back on the sofa, clutching his side.

"Have you lost your mind?" Countess Quine asked him. "Do you even *know* this maid?" She started to look more closely at Anouk, her eyebrow rising.

Hunter Black leaned in as though to help Viggo, and Anouk heard him whisper something low and fast. Viggo blinked with understanding.

"I loved," Viggo choked out. "I meant to say that *I loved* her. Mada Vittora, of course. I loved her as a mother; how can you think I had anything to do with her death?"

Countess Quine lowered her metallic fingernails one at a time as her suspicion shifted away from Anouk and onto Viggo. "Then who did?"

Anouk set down the tray and quickly poured the tea.

"How am I to know? She wasn't short on enemies! *Mon Dieu,* I'd never have come here if I knew I'd be subjected to these accusations. My own mother murdered in my house, and you're supposed to be the law of the Haute, you're supposed to find out who did it and bring that person to justice—"

"What about your lapdog?" Countess Quine asked, looking at Hunter Black.

"Hunter Black, like myself, has been trying to solve this murder. What have *you* been doing? Sipping your tea and . . . and putting pomade in your hair and no one thinks about me, about what I'm going through. Don't you understand how hard this is for me? Adopted children have attachment issues!"

He stood dramatically. "Hunter Black, we're leaving. I refuse to allow myself to be abused in this manner. It's unconscionable, really, treating us like Goblins. Worse—like Pretties! You there, you two maids, fetch my coat at once and escort us to the elevator."

Perhaps he wasn't a complete idiot after all. Anouk picked up the tea tray.

He started for the door, and then a look of minor terror crossed his face. A figure blocked his path.

Prince Rennar had decided to join them.

"Viggo, may I suggest that you sit back down, drink your tea, and shut your mouth before it gets you into even more trouble?"

Prickles tickled their way up and down Anouk's spine. Thank goodness for her veil—she doubted she could have hidden her shock. Viggo, however, was as poor at acting as Cricket was. He stared, open-mouthed, searching for something to say.

"Your Majesty, really, it isn't fair—"

Rennar slapped him across the cheek.

Viggo gasped. "You *hit* me!"

He started to protest more, but then wisely shut up. Hunter Black jumped to his feet, and from the way his eyes narrowed, Anouk guessed he must be fighting the urge to defend his master. Viggo slunk back to the sofa, cradling his cheek, sitting as ordered. Anouk could feel Cricket's uncertainty as palpably as her own; the four of them were so close to escaping. An elevator ride was all that separated them from freedom.

No, not just the elevator—Rennar.

"These people," Rennar muttered as he crossed to the fireplace to warm his fingers. "With their little dreams and their little desires."

Such a simple phrase, thrown out like day-old bread crumbs for the birds. And yet a cold feeling washed over Anouk that was frigid enough to turn her blood to ice water.

Those words.

The voice was different—it had been raspy before, filtered through the wires and speakers of Luc's scryboard, but it was the same.

She almost let out a cry.

Prince Rennar had been the man she'd heard through the scryboard.

Her mind started to whirl. Prince Rennar and Mada Zola were the scheming pair that Luc had written about in his secret log. But if that was the case, why would Mada Zola have sent them here, to the den of her accomplice? To the very man whom she conspired with to take control of the Haute?

She felt the prickly sensation of eyes on her and saw that Countess Quine was subtly watching her from across the room. Her sharpened fingernails *click-click-click*ed anxiously on the glass vial of powder around her neck. Her lips were now stained with a pale blue color. She'd swallowed some powder.

She knows, Anouk realized. *They all know.*

What a fool she was.

Prince Rennar *had* recognized her. Of course he had—he'd even been expecting her. He had known she was coming because Mada Zola had told him, probably as soon as they'd left. And now they had done his work for him, rounded themselves up tidily like pigs trotting together to the slaughter pen.

Shocked, she let the tea tray slip from her hands.

Beau.

The tray seemed to fall impossibly slowly, as though time were broken; she was distantly aware of Viggo jumping in surprise, but her eyes were on the window. Rain pounded against it, and beyond was the incessant flapping of crows.

Beau.

And then time resumed and the tray smashed to the ground with the crashing of china. Hot water scalded her feet. Countess Quine cried out, and Lord Metham choked on the smoke from his pipe, but Anouk didn't flinch.

She didn't care about the boiling water at her feet. The smell of lavender, sickening now.

Prince Rennar looked at her.

Really looked at her. No casual glance, no side-eyed peek. He saw her for what she was, what he had always known she was: the prey that had walked straight into the trap he had set for her.

For all of them.

She turned to Cricket and Hunter Black and Viggo.

"Run."

Chapter 26

Eight Hours of Enchantment Remain

IT WAS TOO LATE.

Lady Metham lifted her hands up and, with a single whisper, made the salon doors slam shut. Cricket threw her shoulder against the joists, then fiddled with the lock, but not even she could pick it.

"A trap," Cricket said. "A *putain* trap."

Viggo shoved himself to his feet, tugged his hat off, and raked his hand through hair that was now streaked with black. His eyes found Anouk's. She knew that look—he was going to do something stupid. Heroic, but stupid. Her heart pounded. It was wrong, all of it. Especially that heartsick expression. If a boy ever looked at her like that, she wanted it to be real, not the result of magic.

"If you touch her," Viggo threatened the prince, "I'll break every bone in that pretty face of yours."

Rennar raised an amused eyebrow.

Anouk ripped off the veil that hadn't disguised anything anyway. "Be quiet," she whispered to Viggo. "You'll get yourself killed."

Through all of this, Hunter Black remained perfectly still on the sofa, hands resting on his knees, his expression masked by the high collar of his coat and the dark hair falling in his eyes. But ice-cold energy radiated off him. A winter storm on the horizon, building in strength, and for an uncertain second, she wasn't sure which she dreaded more — the wrath of the Royals or Hunter Black.

Rennar tented his hands together and turned to Lady Metham. "The driver?"

"The Marble Ladies captured him and brought him upstairs. He's locked away."

Anouk felt the air rush out of her. *Beau.* The only one who might have escaped, but it was too late now. Dizzy, she became all too aware of clocks ticking from all sides. On the mantel. The grandfather clock in the hallway. Lord Metham's pocket watch. Every clock in the penthouse simultaneously chimed five o'clock.

A cry rushed up her throat.

Too late.

There would be no drive back to Montélimar now. What had she been three days ago? A starry-eyed girl who'd dreamed of grander things. And now all those beautiful dreams would be within her grasp, if only midnight wouldn't come.

She grabbed the broom from Cricket and brandished it like a weapon.

"You set us up," she spat at Rennar. "You and Mada Zola. She was never on our side. She sent us here knowing she was delivering us straight into your arms."

He smiled, but there was no pleasure in it. "Everyone in the entire Haute is searching for you — you must know that. And you've done well. But there's only one certain way to catch something that doesn't want to be caught: they have to willingly trap themselves."

Anouk's knuckles were white on the broom. Why had she ever thought of him with any reverence? The light caught the edges of his briar-thorn crown, flashing like stolen pieces of stars, but he was no god.

"Put down that broom, little beastie." Rennar beckoned with long, graceful fingers. "The spell inside won't help you without someone to whisper it to life."

"You said I wasn't made for sweeping floors."

"You weren't. But you should never have been made at all — none of you. It was a cruel, stupid twist of fate, what Vittora did to you. Gave you human life, and now I must be the one to take it away. Believe me, I take no pleasure in it." He went to the rain-streaked windows, gazing out over the city. "You've evaded my crows, you made it past the Marble Ladies, you proved that you are just as capable as you were intended to be. But it's over now, Anouk."

And then he was next to her. Had it been magic or had he crossed the room that fast? He touched her arm. There was no violence in the gesture; rather, it was the contact of a herdsman on a skittish horse. His skin was cold from being near the rain-chilled windows.

"I. Said. Not. To. Touch. Her."

Prince Rennar seemed to have forgotten Viggo's existence. Viggo wasn't a beastie, and the Royals had no use for a witch's boy with no witch. But Viggo refused to be ignored. He threw himself hard at the prince, and his fist connected with the prince's jaw with a resounding crack.

For a few startled seconds, no one moved.

Had anyone ever struck the prince of the Haute? Probably not, if that person valued his life and had any sense. But it wasn't clear that either case applied to Viggo.

Lord Metham swallowed a smear of orange powder and jabbed

a spindly finger in Viggo's direction, his stained lips already moving in a whisper that would no doubt cause blood to erupt from all of Viggo's orifices. But just as fast, Hunter Black was on his feet.

To the Royals, Hunter Black was nothing but a lapdog in a black coat.

Their mistake, Anouk thought.

This was what Hunter Black had been waiting for, Anouk realized. A distraction. And Viggo, God love him, excelled at causing distractions. Hunter Black moved like a rolling clap of thunder. One second he was shoving Viggo to the floor, out of danger; the next he was stepping onto the sofa, one boot on the cushions, the other resting on the sofa back, then using its momentum as it toppled over to hurl himself at Lord Metham. He struck so quickly that the lord hadn't even lowered his finger. Unfortunately for him. Hunter Black grabbed the man's finger. A snap sounded as the bone broke, but it was lost amid Lord Metham's howls.

Hunter Black whirled on Lady Metham next, who had more sense and speed than her husband and ducked behind a desk just as Hunter Black flung the teapot at her head. It smashed into the fireplace, sending sharp china pieces raining down.

"They can't even cast spells, you idiots!" Countess Quine cried.

She aimed her hands in Hunter Black's direction. The sharpened blades at her fingertips sparked with energy as her pink-stained lips moved in whispers. Bolts of white-hot light crackled out of her hands and struck Hunter Black on the shoulder. He grunted, barely acknowledging the pain, and ducked to evade the next strike, but Lady Metham was coming at him from the other side of the divan.

"Lancae, lancae, scintilla morta . . ." she whispered.

233

"Oh, shut up." Cricket leaped onto the coffee table, darted out a nimble hand, and grabbed the long pearl necklace around Lady Metham's neck. She jerked it backward, pulling it taut to choke the woman before she could finish the whisper.

Hunter Black snatched up the shards of broken teapot and hurled them at Countess Quine. Half of them caught her sparks, deflecting the magic away from him. One spiraled off and struck Lord Metham, who howled louder.

Hunter Black turned to Anouk. "Get Viggo. Run."

"We'll be right behind you," Cricket added. "Find Beau and get to the elevator. Hold it open for us."

With a cry, Countess Quine brandished her sharpened metal claws at Cricket. Cricket jerked back and drew her own blades but was a second too late. The countess's claws slashed at Cricket's side, but something caught them. They both frowned. The metallic claws had glanced off the gardening wire holding her dress together, and now both the countess's metal claws and Cricket's blades were tangled in the wire.

Without taking a breath, Cricket whispered, *"Incisha coup . . ."*

A red line of blood appeared on Countess Quine's left cheek. Her eyes flared as she pressed a hand to it but her expression became confused when she saw her hand coming away with blood. Cricket whispered again and another cut sliced down the right side of the countess's face.

Cricket cried out in triumph.

Anouk fell to her knees next to Viggo, touching his back. He'd hit his head when Hunter Black had pushed him down, and now he held his hand to a nasty cut on his forehead.

"My love . . . I have to . . . get you out of here," he said.

"I think it's the other way around, actually," she said. "Can you stand?"

She wrapped his arm around her shoulders and helped him up, but just as they turned toward the door, Rennar took a step and blocked their path.

He was touching his jaw. Part of him still seemed shocked that anyone had dared to strike him; the other part looked poised to turn Viggo to dust. He held the knife from the tea tray but didn't come closer. His lips started moving. Anouk heard the start of a whisper she'd heard before.

"Versik, versik sang . . ." Bleed, bleed.

He jabbed the knife in the air in precise movements. And though half the room separated the two men, Viggo gasped and clutched at his face. A thin line of blood poured down his cheek. Rennar slashed the knife in the air again, and Viggo clutched at his stomach. The tang of blood filled the room. Rennar was going to drain Viggo of the only thing he'd ever been valued for — his blood. And maybe Cricket was right, that Viggo had made his own bed. He wasn't part of their pack. *But maybe he is*, she thought. Even now, he didn't seem to fully process Rennar's vicious whispers aimed at him. His eyes, glassy and lovesick, were on her. But it wasn't real love. Only a trick she'd played on him.

"No," she whispered.

Her whisper might not have been a spell, but it was powerful just the same. She did the only thing she could think of: she swiped a finger over the blood dripping from Viggo's face and licked the blood off.

"Incend comme lapis."

235

Her voice was as soft as moth wings, and yet all the Royals whipped their heads around as though she'd shouted. The knife in Rennar's hand turned bright orange, the smell of flesh sizzled in the air, and he dropped it and clutched at the burn mark on his palm.

He seemed confused. He kicked at the knife as though unable to determine how it had burned him, but then he looked from Anouk to the knife and back.

Lord Metham took the opportunity to swallow a draft of powder and whispered with blue-stained lips, *"Lancae, lancae—"*

Magic was still crackling in Anouk's skin. It tore through her, possessing her, consuming her thoughts, twisting them into one single demand: *Stop him.*

"Ak ignis bleu." She cast the whisper without thinking. It was a spell buried deep in her memory. It shot out of her in the form of blue fire that blazed across the carpet straight to Lord Metham. Flames licked up his fine suit. He whispered protection spells, but the blue fire moved too fast. Though the flames didn't burn fabric or flesh, they robbed the oxygen from the air around him. He clutched at his throat. Gasped. Collapsed on the carpet. By the time the flames subsided, he was dead.

"Mon Dieu," Hunter Black said, breaking the silence. "I want to learn that spell."

Lady Metham's head was cocked at a too-acute angle, her eyes too wide, as though she were a doll that might break. Countess Quine turned sharply to Anouk, one of her eyes twitching and wary.

Prince Rennar was as much at a loss for words as anyone else, and his eyes settled on Anouk. He searched her hungrily with his gaze, her arms, her neck, her face, the broom she clutched in one hand, looking for something—what?

"My love," Viggo whispered, "we have to go *now*."

He grabbed her hand and pulled her toward the door. The movement made Lady Metham snap back to herself and she let out an anguished cry and hurled herself toward them, but Hunter Black jumped to block her. Cricket fought off Countess Quine, metal fingernails to knives, slicing whispers to cutting ones.

But Rennar didn't chase. He only stood and watched Anouk with that curious look on his face, almost the hint of a smile.

And then Viggo pulled her into the hallway. She couldn't catch her breath. She looked one way, then the other, trying to recognize the hallways. But the hour had changed, and with it the floor plan.

"We have to find Beau," she said.

Both jumped at the sound of footsteps. "True, but staying alive would also be ideal."

They ran down the hallway. She clutched the broom tightly. She tried to find some reference point, the kitchen or the hallway with the artifacts under glass. But maddeningly, everything had shifted around, and they ran under a stone archway she certainly had never passed before.

"Beau!" Anouk called. "Where are you?"

Only the ticking clocks answered.

Viggo stumbled, and she caught him before he fell. Her hand slid against his stomach and came away slick with blood—his black clothes had hidden the severity of his wounds.

"Merde," she said. "We have to get you out of here."

And then the faintest sound: *"Anouk."*

"Beau!" With one hand she helped Viggo steady himself, feeling her pulse picking up again. "Viggo, did you hear that? He's close."

She called Beau's name, making her way through the maze of hallways toward his calls as fast as she could help Viggo hobble.

She threw open a glass door she'd never seen before, but then —yes. It was the hallway with all the strange little mundane artifacts under glass. To the left, the wide gilded doors led to the spell library. To the right—*zut*—Rennar's apartments.

Viggo stumbled again and sank onto one of the benches outside the library, clutching his cheek. "Leave me, my love. Get Beau. Just don't . . . forget . . . to collect me on the way out."

"I can't leave you," she said, though she could hear Beau calling her name from somewhere close. "I might never find you again."

"Cricket will . . . be able to find the library. Don't worry, I won't . . . go anywhere."

Anouk had never felt any affection for the witch's boy until that moment, but against her every instinct, she pressed her lips to his cheek.

"I'll come back. I promise."

And then she ran past the glass cases, calling, "Beau! Beau!"

"Anouk!"

Closer now. She pounded on a wooden door inlaid with gold filigree. The knob stuck, but it wasn't locked. She slammed the broom handle against it and it opened at last. She stumbled into a dark room and blinked until her eyes adjusted. Heavy curtains were drawn over the windows. She grabbed one and tugged it back to let in light, murky though it was from the storm outside.

A bedroom.

Grander than any bedroom she'd ever seen, even Mada Vittora's. Heavy wooden furniture with red brocade upholstery had been pushed to the sides, and the once-expensive rug was worn where someone had paced back and forth enough to wear it nearly through. Other than the fine wallpaper, the walls were mostly bare. There were no portraits here. No busts or statues. A piece of paper fluttered on the wall, and she took a step closer, smoothed a hand over it. A . . . playbill. For a production in Paris. And beneath it, a branch from a tree with dying orange leaves.

Things from the Pretty World.

"Anouk," a hoarse voice called.

"Beau!" She threw open a small door. He was in the next room —a meeting chamber, by the look of it, but the table had been moved aside to make room for five cages. They were identical in size. Heavy iron padlocks on the bars. Beau was in the first cage, the top of which was low enough to force him to his knees. He clutched the bars. A bruise bloomed on his temple.

She rushed inside and fell to her knees by his cage. She set down the broom. They clasped hands through the bars.

"Those entrance guards, the ones made of stone . . ." He winced. "I didn't even see them coming."

Anouk's stomach shrank as she thought of marble fists on his flesh. The Marble Ladies must have dragged him from the car, their earless heads not even hearing his screams.

"I'll get you out of here." She tugged on the padlock. Rusty. Ancient. Unbreakable, except perhaps by a master thief. "We need Cricket—"

"No—the trunk by the doorway." Beau was breathing heavily, his hand pressed to his head. "Lady Metham put the keys in there."

Anouk spotted the trunk. She crawled over and fumbled with the rusted brass clasps. They didn't want to open, so she slammed the broom handle against them until they broke and then threw the trunk open. It was filled with paper, stacks and stacks of it. From the hallway, the clocks chimed another hour, but she disregarded them. She leaned deeper into the trunk, pushing through the papers to get to the bottom, searching for the key—

But she didn't find the key. She didn't even find the bottom of the trunk.

There *was* no bottom.

The trunk wasn't a trunk at all, but a passageway. A hole. She was pitched so far forward that she tumbled into the trunk. She reached for something to stop her but could grab only the broom, which fell with her. Papers sliced at her skin and muffled her screams as she fell down the tunnel. She kept falling through papers that had no end. The sensation of falling down changed to falling *up*. Being pulled upward by some enchanted force. And then she felt four wooden sides again. She was back in the trunk, only it was a different trunk, and she was tumbling up and out of it and landing on the soft rug of a small room. There was a fire crackling in a hearth. A wide oak desk, carefully organized with stacks of multicolored folios and parchment and squat black jars of ink and other writing implements and ingredients: onion skins, dried eel, lemons. The tools of a spell-scribe. And there was only one spell-scribe in Castle Ides, though he went by a more official title now.

A shadow fell over her.

Prince Rennar looked different as he crouched beside her. He'd removed his crown and his frost-gray jacket. His white shirt was rolled to his elbows, the button at his neck open.

"Little beastie," he said. "It looks as though you've lost your way."

And then she remembered, too late, that the floor plan changed at the chiming of the clocks. Wherever she was, it was far from her friends.

Just where he wanted her.

Chapter 27

Seven Hours and Thirty Minutes of Enchantment Remain

ANOUK CLUTCHED THE BROOM to her chest, protective of the spell tucked away inside. She could crack the handle over Rennar's head. Shove the blunt end into his face. But his expression made it clear that he wouldn't be caught off guard again. The Royals had underestimated Anouk and her friends, and that had given them the slightest advantage in the salon. But the element of surprise was gone now.

She scrambled backward and pushed herself to her feet.

"What do you want from us? You and Mada Zola conspired to get us here. The two of you are . . ." She was almost too embarrassed to say it. "*Amants.* Lovers."

Until that moment, Rennar had worn the mask of confidence that came so naturally to the Royals, but now he gave her a surprised, curious look. "Lovers? Why would you say that?"

"Those . . . those clandestine communications," she stuttered. "Meetings in secret. Talk of a queenship."

A corner of his mouth tipped up, both boyish and arrogant at the same time. "Ah. I forget that you've been cooped up in a broom closet most of your life. You aren't familiar with the ways of the Shadow Royalty. Mada Zola was more powerful than many handlers knew. Her abilities surpassed even Vittora's. I didn't banish her for insubordination—I knew that was a lie—but to keep her power in check. But our world is in danger, Anouk. Every day the Pretties develop new technologies. The ways of magic are fading. I decided that an alliance of her power and mine might be the only way forward. So I offered her a place at my side. A queenship. Though among Royals, marriages are not the romantic storybook things that Pretties tell their children. They are political unions of power."

"A union designed to capture us. Those five cages I saw are for the five of us, aren't they?"

He didn't deny it. He straightened, dusting off his hands. The spell-scribe room was barely large enough for a desk and a chair, and with the two of them in it, the space felt too full. "And yet only four have come. Where is the fifth one, the gardener?"

She paused, surprised. All of her bravado disappeared and she sputtered, "You mean you don't know either?"

"If I did, I would have come for you at Montélimar. We were waiting for you to lead us to him."

"But I don't know where he is," she admitted. "I thought he'd be here. Or at Mada Zola's estate. He's been missing for over a week."

Rennar considered this, and for a brief moment Anouk forgot he was her enemy; it felt as though they were simply two people caught in a mystery. Her dress felt itchy. The heavy curtain fabric, the stiff wires. Or was it something else? The feeling of fur or feathers or scales beneath her skin?

"I suppose at midnight," she said bitterly, "it won't matter anyway."

"That would be true," he said evenly, "*if* I wanted the five of you gone."

"Don't you?"

He shook his head slowly, coming toward her with those eyes that held that tapeta sheen. They caught the firelight like there was something beneath the iris, a stone beneath a stream. She took a step backward but bumped up against his desk. Pieces of parchment fluttered to the floor.

She held the broom across her body. It was all that separated them —a scrap of wood and straw.

"I went to the party at Mada Vittora's home three nights ago to see if the rumors were true that she kept beasties as servants. Imagine my surprise to find that they *were*. That fool Vittora had no sense of the powerful magic she was toying with; to think she was using the most dangerous order of the Haute to clean her cobwebs! But perhaps I speak too harshly of the dead. Few magic handlers know the full dark history of the beasties. And perhaps I share a portion of the blame. I should have seen months ago, through the portaits, that you were more than a girl with a ribbon in her hair and a rag in her hand. But our empire is vast and our numbers are small. We cannot spy on everyone." He turned to a gilded frame on the wall that held only a blank white space. Was this how he spied on his kingdom? "When I returned to Castle Ides after the dinner party, I sent orders to the lesser lords that the five of you needed to be dealt with immediately. They were to come to the house the following day to take all five of you from Mada Vittora, by force if necessary. I had no way of knowing, of course, that she would be murdered and the four of you would flee."

Visions flashed in her mind again of blood blooming on her mistress's blouse.

"Understand me," Rennar continued. "Beasties have not

historically been agreeable creatures. A fact that brings me much regret. They were fundamentally unstable—many innocent people died. As their creator, I was the one who had to destroy them and then shelve the beastie spell indefinitely. And so, despite my wishes, I thought I had no choice but to destroy you as well. Until my spies told me of a different story."

The fire crackled softly.

He touched her hair. Her lace veil was long since gone, her hair once more in tangled knots. His long fingers threaded delicately through her hair, and she felt the brush of his cheek against the side of her face as he leaned close. He breathed in, smelling her hair, and her heart thumped in warning. She squeezed the broom tighter. When he straightened, he held something that had been tangled in her locks.

A thyme sprig.

It smelled woody and of Luc—of Mada Zola's estate.

"They told me of this. Of magic." He motioned to the thyme. His voice was as quiet as dawn, and it felt like magic too. "You have Petra to thank for your lives. She told me—taking the great risk of going behind her mistress's back—what my crows could not see and what Mada Zola didn't want me to know: That you could do magic. Not unharnessed, destructive conjuring like the original beasties. Higher magic. True enchantment. And you, Anouk, showed me that just now in the salon. You took Lord Metham's life with the blue-fire spell, and yet you weren't bound by the vitae echo. If a witch had done that, her eyes would have turned to oak."

The thyme sprig spun in his fingers, the smell making her think of late summer.

"You and your friends aren't like the original beasties. Whatever alteration Mada Vittora mistakenly made to the spell, it was a lucky twist of fate. And so I intended to capture you, but not to kill you. To uphold the spell to keep you human."

He was telling her that midnight didn't have to mean the end for them, and yet she didn't dare believe it. "If you trusted us, you wouldn't need cages."

"Ah, but you see, there are those among us who still wish to see you destroyed. Who don't yet believe you are more stable than the originals. Who claim Mada Vittora must have died at a beastie's violent hand. Hence the cages. As protection until we are certain you won't slaughter the lot of us."

He rubbed the thyme between his fingers, and it smelled alive, awake, reminding her that this wasn't just a dream. "So tell me, little beastie, what am I to do with you?"

"Well, I haven't killed you yet, so you could let me go."

"You killed Lord Metham."

"Not for the joy of it."

He smiled. "The original beasties weren't joyfully savage at first either. They grew unhinged as they aged. You have spent barely one year as a human, isn't that right? You are nothing but virtue, devotion. What of the others, the older ones? Already they are disobedient. Thieving. Traitorous. *Someone* killed Mada Vittora after all."

"It wasn't any of us," she argued. "And you can't blame us for disobeying a mistress who treated us like slaves. And I'm not as innocent as you think."

His eyes shimmered. "I fear that I believe you."

He took a few steps backward. She felt a rush of space—she could breathe again. With a touch of powder to his lips, he whispered a spell and opened the door. Whatever had been behind it moments ago was gone. Now it led to the meeting room with its five cages.

Beau grabbed the bars. "Anouk?"

"Beau!"

Rennar blocked the doorway before she could run to him. "I will make you a promise, little beasties," he said. "I'll keep you from turning back into animals. I don't need the spell hidden in that broom handle; the words are already carved into the flesh of my tongue. And I'll do more than that. I'll use every spy in the Haute to find your gardener friend before midnight, and I'll keep him human too."

Anouk glanced at Beau. "I'm afraid of the price of an offer like that."

"There's no catch," the prince replied.

Beau said from his cage, "There's always a catch."

The prince smiled joylessly. "I've been alive a long time. I have amassed lifetimes of knowledge and experience, but that doesn't come without a cost. I've lost perspective. We need new blood in the Haute. A new way of seeing."

He was looking at Anouk.

The wind had died, and the stillness in the air made the moment feel caught in time, as though they had stepped into a pocket-world that was just large enough for the three of them. She could feel energy thrumming in the prince's movements, but it was tightly contained. Everything about him whispered *control*. Maybe that was the problem, she thought. Too much control made for a rigid heart. Hearts were made to beat steadily, yes, but they were also meant to tremble.

How long had it been since something had caused Prince Rennar's heartbeat to falter?

"I went about this all wrong," he continued. "I see now that you aren't meant to be caged. But you must understand that I had no way of knowing you would be any different from the original beasties. Your magic is everything I ever wanted and more. You are powerful, Anouk. With the right training, you could help restore the balance. If you think I'm out of touch, show me. If you think I am cold, teach me. Make me remember what it feels like to see the world as you do, full of beauty and hope. In return, you will no longer need to fear midnight, not any of you."

He looked as he had the first time she'd seen him, not the handsome prince in a portrait but the boy in a scarf standing on a Paris street. That boy was still there, somewhere, that spell-scribe who had written the beastie spell in hopes of creating a better world.

"As long as we agree to be your monsters," she countered.

"Monsters? No. I want you to be something far more dangerous." Somehow, in the space of a heartbeat, he was by her side, so close that she could feel the crackling energy in his body, not so tightly coiled now. Behind him, Beau was an angry, trapped shadow.

"And what is that?"

"Princess of the Haute."

Chapter 28

Seven Hours of Enchantment Remain

ANOUK STARED AT HIM as though she hadn't heard correctly. Days ago, she'd been on her hands and knees scrubbing biscuit crumbs from between kitchen tiles. Her dreams had felt big and impossible—walking in Paris arm in arm with someone, like the Pretties did, making a wish on the fountain. Dreams that felt childish now that the prince of the Shadow Royals was offering her an entire kingdom.

"A political arrangement," he continued. "The same proposal I had discussed with Mada Zola, but of course, now I see how much more suitable a partner you would be. The ways of the Shadow Royals are ancient but effective; we will rule side by side, equals in all things. I'll teach you to develop your magic. You'll show me how not to misuse my own."

For a second, he looked as though he wanted to take the beastie spell from her broom and fold it between their palms, the spell that would bind them forever. But he didn't.

"Anouk, don't listen to him!" Beau called from the other room. He was gripping the bars with white knuckles, but she couldn't go to him while the prince blocked the doorway.

"No cages," Prince Rennar said temptingly in a quiet voice meant only for her. "No banishments. No chains. Say the word, and the chauffeur is free."

"And what of love?"

He raised an eyebrow. "That's up to you."

She didn't trust him. Of course she didn't. Even if he wasn't intentionally lying to her, his mind was as twisted by the vitae echo as the witches' had been. He might say he wanted equality and mean it, but like shifting winds, he might just as easily change his mind.

And of course, there was Beau. The few kisses they'd shared might mean little to the young Pretties who gave out kisses like corner-store candy, but what they had was more delicate, more complex, like a chocolate soufflé: it was just as sweet, but you had to take your time and pay attention to it or it would collapse in a spectacular mess.

And yet, if she refused the prince, would she—all of them—end up animals forever?

Rennar was offering her a chance to save herself and her friends. Like in one of Luc's fairy tales, where a girl made a deal with Death but found that the deal was riddled with catches. *I thought there was nothing worse than dying*, the girl said. *I was wrong.*

"Don't do it, Anouk," Beau called again.

From somewhere, a clock was ticking. How many hours did they have left? Six? Five?

A spider crawled across the floor. She couldn't stop staring at it, trying to remember what life felt like when the only things that mattered were fear and hunger. She'd led them here. She'd convinced them to risk everything, and now the decision rested in her hands once more. Did she resist and risk returning to that? Or obey and live?

Rennar had his back to Beau; he didn't see Beau reach between the bars for the spider. Anouk felt a flash of danger. What crazy idea had gotten into his head? His fist closed around the spider and he shut his eyes and popped it into his mouth.

She squeaked a gasp of surprise.

Beau made a face as he choked down the spider. He drew in a breath and began to whisper; though he was trying to be quiet, quiet for Beau was like a shout for her. *Too loud,* she thought. *Rennar will hear.*

"No," she spat out. "No, that's my answer. I'll never agree to be yours."

"Dorma, dorma . . ." Beau whispered behind them.

Too late, Prince Rennar heard the whisper. His midnight eyes flashed. A counter-spell was already on his lips, and in a fraction of a breath he would have silenced Beau, but Beau finished his first. Prince Rennar stumbled as though he'd been hit over the head. Beau's whisper had been murmured and unclear, as though he'd spoken with rocks in his mouth. Rennar doubled over and fell on all fours. He was fighting to keep his head up, his eyes open.

He lost the battle to stay conscious and collapsed to the floor.

Anouk stared, unable to believe what she'd seen. "Beau, you did magic!"

"Well, poorly."

Anouk dug through Rennar's pockets for the key and unlocked the door to Beau's cage. As soon as Beau was free, she threw her arms around him. He felt alive. Warm. Almost too warm, as though some sickness was inside him. Something inside her burned in response —maybe not a sickness after all. Maybe their true natures.

"We can't trust the Royals," he said. "But Rennar had a point. If we leave, we'll be running away from the only magic handlers who can cast the beastie spell."

The words of the Selentium Vox conjured themselves behind her teeth, and again, she longed to gather the right ingredients, to *try*.

She grabbed his shirt collar. "I'd rather have one last night as ourselves than a lifetime in cages. Let's get out of here."

She grabbed her broom, and they ran through the labyrinth of Rennar's apartments. His bedroom. A bath with a golden tub. A personal library, the walls lined with books, real books, unmagical stories from the Pretty World. A jacket flung over a chair. A volume with a teaspoon used as a bookmark. Rumpled sheets on the unmade bed told her two things: Rennar didn't let maids into his private chambers (she'd guessed this, given the spider), and his sleep was too troubled for dreams.

They reached an empty antechamber with doors on all sides. Anouk threw open a random door—a linen closet. The next—an exterior garden. Beau started from the opposite side. He opened a door and found a rickety staircase plunging downward.

"Here!" Anouk called. At last, she'd found a sight she recognized: the artifact hallway. They ran into it and Anouk stopped short at the row of empty benches outside the spell-library doors. "Viggo's supposed to be here."

The sound of approaching footsteps came from down the hall.

"Merde," Beau cursed. "The other Royals are coming."

It was too late to run for the elevator, so Anouk and Beau started to hustle the other way but stopped when a voice called out: "Wait! It's us!"

They turned as Cricket and Hunter Black came around the corner with Viggo hobbling between them.

The five of them clasped hands, delighted at their small reunion, but then they heard more footsteps. The smile fell off Cricket's face.

"About two dozen duchesses are right behind us," she said.

"Let's not make it easy for them." Anouk raised the broom. She remembered how, in the salon, Hunter Black had used the broken shards of the teapot to deflect Countess Quine's magic. And there were a *lot* of glass cases. She swung the broom against the nearest case.

"Smashy!" Cricket said. "I love it!"

She leaned hard on a case until it toppled over. Anouk slammed the broomstick into another case and then started on another as a fleet of Royals rounded the corner.

"Right," Beau said. "Time to go, cabbage!"

Anouk pulled the beastie spell from the broomstick's handle, put it in her pocket, and then tossed the broom aside. They ran. Anouk could hear the shushing sounds of whispers behind them, but she didn't dare glance back. The clinking of broken glass meant the duchesses were close. They charged through the maze of hallways. Rain pelted the windows. Crows flapped their wings just beyond the glass, cawing and screeching.

"Which way?" Anouk cried.

Cricket held up her forearm as they ran, consulting the map, trying to figure out the calculations based on the shifting rooms. "Left. No, right!"

They skittered around a corner, dragging Viggo with them as fast as they could.

"There," Anouk cried in relief. "The elevator's just ahead!"

But she heard the start of a whisper behind her. Not just any whisper, but one she recognized. One to shut doors—permanently. And ahead, the wide-open doors of the elevator gave a sudden shudder and began to close. *No.* Her muscles burned. Her face felt hot. She ran as fast as she could, Cricket on her heels, Beau and Hunter Black practically carrying Viggo between them, but it was too late. The doors were closing.

Nearly shut.

They wouldn't reach it in time.

"No!"

Then a shadow moved in the elevator. Someone was there. *Inside.* She couldn't see who—but whoever it was, that person was their last chance.

"Hold the elevator!" she cried.

The doors continued to close. All that remained was four inches.

Three.

Two.

"Please! Hold the elevator!"

At the last possible second, a hand shot into the narrow space between the doors. A hand with black fingernail polish and a tattoo of a broken heart on the back. A bell dinged. The elevator doors paused. Then, slowly, they began to open again.

It was the Goblin, Tenpenny, his rat still on his shoulder. He grinned at them with his maniacal smile, but then his eyes shifted to the army of Royals pursuing them and he frowned. Anouk crashed against the half-opened elevator doors and shoved her way between them enough to slip in. Cricket pushed the doors open wide enough for Hunter Black and Beau to help Viggo hobble inside.

"Close it, close it!" Cricket yelled once they were all on board.

Anouk threw herself against the buttons, pounding on anything that would ding or light up, but the doors didn't close. No lights came on. She felt panic clawing beneath her skin. The Royals were almost on them. Close enough that she could see the smeared blue powder on Countess Quine's scowling lips.

Tenpenny inserted his master key in the controls. "Going down, I assume?"

"Yes! *Dieu*, yes!"

He twisted the key and at last the doors began to close.

Chapter 29

Six Hours of Enchantment Remain

ANOUK SLUMPED AGAINST the closed doors, her flushed face reflected in endless succession in the mirrored walls. She'd never been so thankful for a brief moment of peace. The elevator descended slowly, rumbling beneath her. Beau rested his head against the mirror, face tipped toward the lights that illuminated the bruise across his face, which was turning a nasty shade of plum.

"Look, man," Viggo said to the Goblin. "I know you wanted us to go to your party and all, but—"

Tenpenny grabbed Viggo by the collar and jerked him downward until they were eye to eye. "Look, *boy.* You can't possibly be stupid enough to think this is about a party. I wouldn't risk incurring the ire of the Royals so that you could cut a rug." He released Viggo's crumpled collar before smoothing a hand over his own blue cravat. "We've had our bright little eyes on you, beasties. Wondering, like everyone else in the Haute, if you're as powerful as the rumors say."

Bright little eyes . . .

Anouk gasped as she remembered where she'd seen him before, though his hair had been covering the tips of his ears. "You were the waiter at the café in Saint-Désirat. You've been following us!"

"Naturally." Tenpenny replaced the golden key in his left breast pocket, then sorted through his dozen or so other pocket-watch chains, muttering to himself, until he found the one he was looking for. It connected to a monocle, which he cleaned with his cravat and held to his eye. The swipe of gold eyeliner on his upper lid glittered beneath the magnification. "We had to be certain of two things. First, that you could indeed do magic. Second, that you weren't a puppet of the Royals."

"We're nobody's puppets," Cricket asserted. "And the Royals can *va se faire foutre.*"

Tenpenny turned his monocle on Cricket and inspected her from head to toe. "What positively foul words from such a beautiful mouth. I'm of a mind to fall in love with you, my dear." He put away the monocle and consulted the elevator's floor dial. Its brass arrow dropped to the fifth floor. "Time is short. As soon as we disembark, the elevator will return to the penthouse to collect the Royals. We have only a few minutes' head start on them. I can get you to safety, but there is a cost for my assistance."

The elevator dial's arm dropped to the fourth floor. Then the third. The more distance between them and the Royals, the more Anouk felt the tightness in her chest ease, but they were far from being out of harm's way yet.

"We'll pay whatever it takes," she said, "if you can keep us human."

Tenpenny stroked the pet rat perched on his shoulder, considering this. "I have a few ideas. None of them pretty, mind you, none of them guaranteed. But there's a chance."

"We only have until midnight."

"Oh, then it'll *certainly* not be pretty." He waggled a finger at

257

them. "Listen closely, my beastie friends. For the past three years, the five grandest witches of Britain have been clearing London of Goblins. They call themselves the Coven of Oxford. Chasing us out or slaughtering us—they don't care. A few months ago they succeeded in ridding the city of the last of us, and we came here to Paris in exile. We need you to help us retake our city."

The elevator reached the bottom floor with a sudden lurch. Anouk's heart leaped; she grabbed a brass sconce to steady herself.

"Well, beasties? Do we have a deal?"

Ding.

Anouk, thinking of the vicious Marble Ladies, sputtered out, desperately, *"Yes."*

Tenpenny danced eagerly from one foot to the other. The pet rat mirrored him, scampering from one of his shoulders to the other. The doors opened to the foyer, and Anouk took everything in: The gleaming white walls. The ivory desk. The wall of glass with the single turnstile. And the Marble Ladies. *Not* immobile now.

Four alabaster faces turned like clockwork when the elevator rumbled open. All too fast, they came striding toward the elevator, arms raised, stone hands reaching.

"They're coming!" Anouk cried.

The Marble Lady in the front slammed one stone hand against the doorjamb, holding the elevator open. Another behind her swiveled her head toward Anouk. Her features remained motionless, but her hands curled into fists. Anouk shrieked and scrambled as far back into the elevator as she could.

"Tenpenny!"

The Goblin unlatched his pet rat's collar and held the creature up so they were nose to nose. With a great sigh, he said, "I'm sorry, old friend, but we both knew it would come to this."

Just as Anouk was about to yell again for him to *do something*, the rat made a heart-wrenching final squeak and Tenpenny bit its head off. A revolting crunch as the spine snapped. Someone—one of the boys—screamed. Blood sprayed from the rat's neck, decorating the elevator's mirrored walls with garlands of red. Anouk couldn't get away in time. Blood speckled her apron. A vile-tasting bubble pushed up her throat as she pressed a hand to her mouth, staggering backward into the corner of the elevator. Viggo tried to go to her, but a Marble Lady grabbed him by the back of his shirt. Hunter Black hurled himself against her arm, but he might as well have been fighting iron bars. The Marble Lady didn't flinch.

Tenpenny spat the rat head on the gleaming floor and then tipped the little furry body over and gurgled down its blood.

"*Transfixa petrifie,*" he whispered. "*Transfixa . . .*"

The third Marble Lady stepped into the elevator. Cricket dodged her just as the lady's fist smashed into the mirror, sending broken bits of glass raining down. It happened so fast that Anouk wasn't sure if she'd been cut or not. All she could feel was shockingly solid fingers clamp down on the back of her skull, gripping her painfully by the hair.

The Marble Lady had her.

It's too late, Anouk thought.

But then Tenpenny dabbed blood from the corner of his mouth with a handkerchief and pronounced the final word of the whisper.

"*. . . Petrifie.*"

The Marble Lady clutching Anouk's hair froze.

All four of the Marble Ladies were as still as the statues they should have been. Except, of course, that Anouk had never heard of statues that were posed for a fight with clenched fists. She winced; even frozen, the statue's fingers coiled painfully around her ponytail. She disentangled herself with care, tugging the last few strands out by force, and rubbed her stinging scalp.

The other beasties looked equally stunned and equally spattered with blood.

It was perfectly quiet in the foyer, with the Marble Ladies suspended in time like a drawing in a book, never to break their poses, until Anouk exclaimed to Tenpenny, "You killed your rat!"

"Yes, my dear, that's what Goblins do."

Beau started for the exit, but Tenpenny tsked. "Not so fast. It's raining."

"So?" Beau said.

"These boots are suede!" The Goblin poked at a collection of black umbrellas in a stand by the door until he found the one he was looking for and pointed the end toward Beau. "*Now,* dear boy, we make our escape."

Beau rolled his eyes as he shouldered open the door. The rain was coming down in sheets against the pavement. It seemed impossibly dark—too dark. *The streetlights are all out,* Anouk thought, until she heard a sharp caw.

"Crows," Beau said.

There were hundreds of them. On each awning. On every branch. Perched so thick on the streetlights that they blocked the light.

"Never mind them," Tenpenny said. "Hop on, beasties!"

Five motorcycles stood in the driveway. Four were manned by Goblin drivers in rain slickers and galoshes, each clutching a large black umbrella identical to Tenpenny's. Tenpenny mounted the fifth motorcycle, not letting go of his umbrella, and revved the engine with one hand.

Anouk gasped. "Wait, we forgot about the oubliette! We left it in the car . . . our pelts . . ."

The driveway was empty; no sign of the Rolls-Royce. Anouk's thoughts were a storm. *Who had the pelts? What if they were destroyed? How could they uphold the spell without them?*

"No, we didn't." Beau ducked through the rain toward the bust of Prince Rennar and rummaged through the bushes until he extracted a few objects.

"The oubliette," Anouk cried. "And my jacket!"

Beau grinned. "I'd never let that bag fall into the wrong hands. I stashed it in the bushes as soon as we arrived."

Anouk pressed the Faustine jacket to her face. A ticking sound came from somewhere, and she rooted through the pockets until she found the black-cat clock. Her stomach dropped as she saw the time. *Five hours until midnight.*

As though he sensed time slipping away too, Tenpenny called through the rain, "Quickly now, beasties."

Cricket leaned toward Anouk. "Are we seriously trusting Goblins?"

"Do we have a choice?"

"Maybe not," Hunter Black growled, "but *I'm* driving." He jerked his thumb at a driver, indicating that the Goblin should scoot to the passenger's place, and climbed in front.

Cricket threw her hands up, exasperated. "I'll take Blondie." She climbed on behind a Goblin girl with long blond pigtails who flashed her a golden-toothed smile. Beau and Anouk helped Viggo climb onto the third motorcycle behind a boy with spiky green hair, and Beau joined a driver wearing a top hat.

"Now you, dearie. Hold on tight." Tenpenny patted the empty place behind him. Anouk hiked up the torn hems of her maid's costume to climb on. What exactly was she supposed to hold on to? This was even more terrifying than riding in a car for the first time. She gripped a metal bar behind the seat, searching for a place to rest her feet, when suddenly Tenpenny peeled out and she shrieked, nearly tumbling off.

"I said hold on," he called back to her.

The tires squealed in the rain and threw up sheets of water behind them. She wrapped her arms around his middle. This was *not* like flying. This felt more like *dying*. Tenpenny accelerated down Boulevard Saint-Germain at breakneck speed, still clasping the umbrella in one hand. She dared a look behind her: five motorcycles in all—and four umbrellas; Hunter Black scoffed at the idea of rain protection—roaring through the stormy streets of Paris. Crows took off from every street lamp as they passed, causing each light to glow brightly, illuminating their path as though to say, *Here they are, Rennar, they're right here!* The din of wings was deafening, louder even than the peals of thunder and the honks of cars as the line of motorcycles weaved through traffic. Ahead, two delivery trucks drove impossibly close together, but Tenpenny revved the engine and aimed for the narrow space between. Anouk shut her eyes. Then instantly changed her mind and opened them. The weaving motion made her even queasier when she wasn't watching the road. She squeezed Tenpenny tighter.

"Where are you taking us?" she shouted into his ear.

"Where the crows can't follow!" He cackled.

She pressed her forehead into his back. His suit had threads of metallic gold woven in it, and she thought of her hastily sewn maid's uniform, practically in tatters now. Large patches of skin on her back and shoulder were visible through the seams, barely held together by garden wire. She thought briefly of Petra giving her the wire. And Mada Zola. She had thought she could be happy at the Château des Mille Fleurs. What a fool she'd been. Beau and Cricket had warned her, and yet once more she had fallen for a witch's promises.

Never again, she vowed.

Petra, at least, had helped them. Because of her, Rennar had decided to keep them alive. She felt a stab of affection for the witch's girl. It couldn't have been easy to go behind her mistress's back to share information with Rennar. Did Zola know of what she'd done? Had Petra been punished?

She looked over her shoulder again. Cricket was holding the umbrella for her Goblin driver, who was using her free hand to take a swig of something from a flask. Hunter Black brought up the tail end, weaving through the traffic just as skillfully as the Goblins. Beau caught her eye and shook his head as though to say, *What in the world are we doing?* Riding on the back of motorcycles, teamed up with Viggo and Hunter Black—and Goblins!—with only hours left before their spell wore off.

Rain streaked down his hair, matting it to his face, and he looked scared—terrified—but, even more than that, determined. They were in a serious mess, yes. It was doubtful they could trust the Goblins, true. *But they were alive.* They'd escaped Castle Ides, eluded the most powerful members of the Haute, and they were still human. They could still feel rain on their faces, could still yell overhead at the crows, "Go *se faire foutre.*"

It wasn't over yet.

And then, suddenly, she was falling forward. She gasped and clung hard to Tenpenny. The world had gone darker. The rain abruptly stopped. She was bouncing wildly, her teeth chattering in her head. *Thunk-thunk-thunk-thunk-thunk.* It took her a second to realize that they had plunged down the stairs into a Métro station. People shrieked and jumped out of the way as the procession of motorcycles jostled down the steep stairs. Signs flashed by her. Belvédère station. At last they reached the platform and she no longer felt like her teeth were being jostled loose, but then more screams rang out as Tenpenny roared straight through the crowd of passengers awaiting the next train. The platform ended ahead in tiled wall.

Where were they going to go?

A second before they would have crashed spectacularly into the tile wall, Tenpenny jerked the bike to the left and jumped it straight off the platform and into the Métro tunnel. *Bum-bum-bum-bum-bum*—the bars of the Métro track beneath them. If the motorcycle had a headlight, Tenpenny didn't turn it on, and they plunged into pure blackness. A rumble from somewhere deep. The whine of the other engines behind them. She tightened her hold, biting her lip. And then, at last, she saw a light up ahead. She could see graffiti covering the walls, names and phrases: *Bye-bye, Paris. L'amour est mort.*

The light grew brighter. She had to shade her eyes.

Something big rumbled and squealed. Something headed for them.

A train.

"You're going to kill us!"

Tenpenny's only answer was to rev the engine. He leaned forward, driving even faster. The incoming train let out a prolonged honk. A warning. The light was growing even brighter. She felt a scream hurtling up her throat as the train grew closer and closer, almost on them, and then, a moment before impact . . .

Darkness again.

Tenpenny had turned down a side tunnel at the last second. She glanced back, saw the glint of four other motorcycles with relief. They'd all made it. The tunnel wasn't like the greasy-smelling Métro line. There were no lights, which wasn't a problem for the Goblins, who could see in the dark. But *she* couldn't. She felt rough walls pressing in. A low ceiling. It smelled of stale air and ancient stone. Water trickled from somewhere. The old aqueduct might be nearby. Or, at the least, sewage pipes. A faint light shone at the far end of the tunnel, a warm, flickering orange like fire. As they neared she could make out that the tunnels were of hewn limestone, briny with lichen, twigs and trash pushed to the sides — and bones. She'd never seen a human bone before, but there was no mistaking the length of those femurs, the curve of a cracked skull. They were in the catacombs.

The tunnel spat them out into a large chamber that was lit only by a roaring bonfire. She'd thought the catacombs were all twisting narrow mazes with low ceilings, but this was cavernous. How could such a large space exist beneath the city?

Tenpenny parked next to a structure that, on further inspection, appeared to be an abandoned Métro train. Someone had spray-painted THE BLACK DEATH on it, and the windows had been pushed out to make a bar filled with bottles of colorful liquids; music with a thumping bass pumped out of speakers where the engine had been. Dozens of Goblins were gathered around, most holding teacups, and at the sound of the motorcycles, more poured out of smaller tunnels and tombs and crypts into the cavern.

Tenpenny dismounted with a flourish. "Welcome, dearies, to the Catacomb Club. Let's get some lights in here for our guests!"

Torches appeared and lit up the cavern. The Goblins crowded around. She felt swept up in a twister of bright colors, bowler hats, glittering makeup, and clinking teacups. The music blasted over the chatter of excited voices. On every wall was graffiti, but not like in the Métro tunnels. This was beautiful but strange: Grinning bared teeth. Sea-monster tentacles. Patterns of neon spider webs. Anatomical hearts.

The Goblins swarmed her. She heard Cricket yell a warning, but the crowd didn't stop until they had dragged the five of them off the backs of the motorcycles and to the raging bonfire in front of the Black Death railcar. Anouk fought and twisted against the many hands holding her, but the Goblins threw out whispers that made her fingers just slip off them. Their whispers were different than the witches', not softly murmured but almost spat out. And then more arms were lifting her until she'd been dragged to the top of the Métro car onto a sort of makeshift stage. Cricket and Beau and Viggo and Hunter Black were dragged up beside her. From here she could see the entire cavern of the Catacomb Club. Art deco lanterns had been stolen from abandoned Métro stations to decorate various smaller crypts, and they came on one by one, the light glistening off skulls that lined the ceiling like grinning macabre molding. Someone had made a throne out of bones.

Tenpenny jumped up beside them, grinning proudly. He still had traces of rat blood on his cravat.

"Goblins in exile," he said. "I promised you a means to return to London. These beasties have agreed to undertake a task against impossible odds. A risk of the deadliest proportions. A quest of untold dangers!"

Beau leaned toward Anouk. "Um, what exactly did we agree to?"

Standing unsteadily on top of the abandoned railcar, she felt tipsy. Hundreds of Goblin faces peered up at her with wide grins and hopeful eyes and slightly pointed ears. Their makeup made them look like people you'd turn away from on a dark street, but they weren't vicious. Goblins loved little pranks and fabulous clothing; these were the lowest of the Haute, magical only in the most basic ways, just magical enough to do the dirty work for witches. She thought of the Goblin girl whom Mada Vittora had made fall in love with a mail truck. These weren't their enemies, she knew.

That was a start, at least.

"Now," Tenpenny said, patting her on the back. "I believe there was talk of a party." Someone cranked up the music. The whole train car started vibrating to the beat beneath her feet.

"About this dangerous quest . . ." Anouk started.

"Yes, yes, we're grateful for your selfless sacrifice, all of you, but first let us celebrate. London shall soon be once more the heart and home of the Goblins!"

He shoved Anouk, then Cricket, and then the rest of them off the stage and into the throngs of exuberant Goblin revelers.

Chapter 30

One Hour of Enchantment Remains

A NOUK TUMBLED OFF THE RAILCAR straight into the waiting hands of dozens of Goblins. Hands pressed against her back, holding her up and passing her along through the crowd. Gaudy faces grinned at her. Rats squeaked. The music roared even louder.

"Put me down!" she cried, but they only bobbed her higher. She managed to lift her head enough to see Beau being hoisted onto a heavyset Goblin's shoulders. She tried to call out to him, but he was being carried in the opposite direction. She couldn't see Cricket or Hunter Black or Viggo, but judging from the curses and screams coming from the crowd, they were as tangled as she was. For the length of a few throbbing songs, Anouk let herself be carried around the eager crowd, gradually passed farther and farther from the Black Death, until the Goblins lost interest in her and she managed to fight her way to the ground. She dropped down, hid in the midst of dancing boots and stomping feet, and climbed over random bones until she was able to crawl out from the partying mass and into sweet freedom at the edge of the cavern. She collapsed against an empty copper kettle, gulping fresh air.

"Tenpenny!" she called angrily, catching sight of him.

He was standing next to an odd assortment of animal cages made from wired-together rib bones, sipping a cup of tea, tapping his foot to the music. She stormed over, shaking out the dust from her clothes.

"Listen, I don't know what promise you think we made, but there won't be any dangerous quests if midnight comes and we turn back into animals."

He consulted his pocket watch casually. "You worry too much, dearie."

She felt the push of frustrated tears at the corners of her eyes, and she kicked at a skull. What on earth had made her think she could put her trust in Goblins?

Tenpenny bent to inspect the nearest cage, which was full of rats. "What a lovely coat on that one. Though I've always been partial to white."

She spun on him angrily. "Stop picking out a new pet and help us!"

"But I require another rat."

"So you can bite its head off too?"

"No, dearie. So *you* can."

This shut her up. He returned to inspecting the rats and at last settled on a small black one that he fed a piece of cheese and then set on his shoulder. "I haven't forgotten my promise. I told you I would help, and, if you'd stop screeching in my ear, that is what I will attempt to do. Now, pick two more rats and follow me."

She looked around for the others. Beau was still being carted around on someone's shoulders, and there was no sign of the others in the crowd. She reached toward a rat, but paused. She thought of the small mouse pelt they'd taken from Mada Vittora's closet.

"Do we have to use rats? It's a little, um, personal."

Tenpenny drummed his fingers on the rib-bone bars. "Do you feel a kinship with roaches? No? Good. Come on. We can find some privacy in the Skull Crypt." He grabbed a jar of cockroaches and thrust it in her hands.

She followed him down a small side tunnel and into an old crypt with a limestone sarcophagus on top of which was someone's half-finished dinner. Tenpenny swept the plates to the ground and started humming as he set down the jar of cockroaches and several messy-looking containers that reeked of rotten, dead things. In the distance, she could still hear the whir of the party.

She took a step back and tripped over a dry, brittle skull. "We're *really* running out of time," she pointed out.

"You can't rush magic. We're already working outside the rules as it is. You know about the vitae echo, yes? Magic Is Life; Life Is Magic, and so forth and so on. The witches in their grand estates prefer to take life from flowers and butterflies and rosebuds. *Hmph.* You'll find none of those pretty things in the dank holes they've relegated us to. Worms, slime, rats. Those are our ingredients."

Anouk made a face.

"Don't recoil so, my dear! There is nobility in the rat. Beauty in the moth. Though the rest of the world might not respect the dark creatures of the night, within these catacombs they are prized. Each rat cherished . . . until its death. And if we must sacrifice our crawly friends, we pour out a cup of tea in the deepest tunnel and say prayers for them."

"And you can keep us human with slime?"

"Absolutely. Doubtlessly." He bit his lip. "Maybe."

She dug the beastie spell out of her pocket and fanned the dust from the sarcophagus before laying the paper down reverently and smoothing out the wrinkles. "I hope you're right. We risked a lot to get this spell."

He cocked his head curiously, stroking the rat on his shoulder, then pushed the spell back her way. "Ah, perhaps you misunderstand. Such a complex spell is beyond Goblin capabilities."

Alarm bells went off in her head. "But you said you'd help us!"

"And I shall. I cannot cast the beastie spell, but one thing we Goblins excel at is working around the rules."

She sighed in frustration as he started pulling down jars and old tea tins from among the bones, humming to himself as he poured it all into a porcelain teakettle.

She turned away while he worked, watching the party, trying to spot the others. Beneath their makeup, the Goblins looked worn and tired. Some had mascara-streaked faces. Almost all had thin, malnourished arms.

It wasn't anything like the beautiful world of the Haute that the portraits showed, mischievous Goblins peeking around corners. Goblins hadn't fallen to the bottom of the Haute by chance; it was a system designed to make them powerless.

"Almost ready, dearie," Tenpenny called. "Fetch the others."

She made her way back into the heart of the revelry, searching the made-up faces for her friends. She found Beau assessing stores of insects and bitter herbs next to the blond-haired Goblin girl with gold teeth. Cricket was inside the Black Death with two Goblins who were showing her the art of summoning tricks with hand gestures. Hunter Black was in a small crypt, sharpening a bone into a weapon. And Viggo—

"There you are, my love, my soul, my heart." He pushed through the crowd and smacked into her hard enough to make her shoulder sting. His face was wan and lovesick. She led them all to the Skull Crypt, where Tenpenny was mixing together the final ingredients with a curved rib bone. He gave the concoction a sniff and tossed the bone aside.

"Now then, beastie friends. This won't cure you, but it will do the next best thing."

"What's that?" Beau asked suspiciously.

"Kill you."

"*What?*"

At their horrified looks, he added, "Only temporarily." He poured off four teacupfuls of the potion. "This elixir has a powerful malignant effect that will, by and by, stop your hearts from beating. A stopped heart cannot age, can it? Time will halt for you. And if time stops, so does the countdown to the end of your enchantment."

"Yes, but we'll be dead!"

"*Technically* dead. But that doesn't mean you have to stop living. You'll still have use of your bodies, just like always. The elixir works slowly. It will take twenty-four hours to stop your hearts entirely. You can take an antidote before then."

Cricket stared at the elixir. "So that's it? You're giving us poison, and it'll grant us only one extra day?"

"I told you it wouldn't be pretty."

Hunter Black scowled. "You tricked us, Goblin."

Tenpenny acted offended. "It's one more day than you would have had without me."

Anouk sat heavily on the sarcophagus, loose brittle bones skittering at her feet. She coughed at the cloud of dust and tried to brush it off her clothes but gave up. She was always dirty. Always a mess. Was it so surprising that she'd just led them into another mess? Cricket and Hunter Black continued to argue with Tenpenny, while the blond Goblin who had followed at Beau's heels hung in the doorway, staring at Beau moonily.

"At least Rennar promised us more than twenty-four hours," Cricket complained.

"Rennar? Bah! Lies! Listen closely, dearies. Rennar and that witch told you only half the story. It's true that you aren't affected by the vitae echo, but saviors? Ha! You weren't made to save anything. You aren't heroes."

"Then what are we?" Beau asked.

"Monsters! Oh, come, don't look surprised. Nothing good is ever created from magic. You were made to be the most terrifying thing in the known world. The vitae echo is a safeguard. It is meant to keep handlers from slaughtering whole villages and from taking lives for their own gain. But you don't have that safeguard—don't you get it? Rennar made you as weapons. You can do all the dastardly things that he can't—but only if he can control you. That's why the other beasties were destroyed. They were monsters, yes, which was what he wanted. But their mistake was not answering to him."

"Do we look like bloodthirsty devils to you?" Cricket asked, motioning vaguely to the ribbon in Anouk's hair, to her own less-than-threatening maid's costume.

Tenpenny turned to her. "You thirst for magic so you can exact revenge. You want to destroy, to tear down. I see it in your eyes."

"And what's wrong with that?"

"Nothing, my dear, as long as you don't mind living in a broken world."

Cricket pressed her rosebud lips together tightly.

Anouk glanced at the beastie spell. She felt shaken; in times like this, it was Luc they turned to. What would he do now? Would he trust Goblin poison?

No. He would fix this himself.

She jumped down from the sarcophagus and started digging through Tenpenny's tea canisters. Milk thistle in this one, sorrel in that one, a jug of some poor creature's blood that still had fur floating in it. She grabbed a teapot, threw in ingredients.

"Anouk?" Beau asked.

"Just wait."

Spells—even the most complex ones—didn't come with recipes. It was up to each magic handler to interpret the requirements of a given situation and develop a custom-made brew. Mada Vittora had been partial to roses and goldenseal; her tonics all held an air of romance, even when the spell had nothing to do with love. Cricket was fond of eucalyptus. What would Anouk's signature ingredients be? She would have liked to use feather down, but with only Goblin stores to work with, she had to settle for white dandelion fluff.

She sniffed her tonic and then took a sip. It burned deliciously on her tongue, like spices and licorice. She whispered. She didn't even need to look at the torn folio page; the words were buried deep inside her. They *were* her. Rennar, Zola, and Tenpenny—the most prominent members of every order of the Haute—had all told her she carried great power. And she could *feel* it. A tingle from her belly to her toes to her ears. A tickle on her lips.

"*Skalla animeux . . .*"

"What are you—" Beau said, but Cricket elbowed him.

"*Quiet.* It's the beastie spell, you idiot. Tenpenny can't cast it so she's going to try."

Anouk closed her eyes and let the syllables pour out of her. Gone was the throbbing beat of the party in the other room, the chatter of rats from their cages. It was only her and the Silent Tongue, and she was speaking it, feeling it working beneath her skin; she was no longer the dark thing but a girl, a real human girl . . .

Then, without warning, *fire.*

She cried out as sharp pain burned down her arms. It spread impossibly fast from her neck to her knees to her toes, replacing that delicious tingle with searing agony that made the spell, not even halfway spoken, die on her tongue and her body crumple on the floor.

Beau was immediately by her side, feeling her forehead, but his touch only burned more, and she cried out and pushed him away.

A shadow fell over her. She squinted open an eye.

"That, my dear, was unbelievably stupid." Tenpenny stood over her, tsk-tsking. "Only fools attempt magic so far beyond their ability."

"But . . . you said . . . we're powerful . . ." She grimaced as another wave of pain radiated through her. "No vitae echo."

"The pain you're feeling now? That isn't the vitae echo. That's just your body rejecting the change you were trying to put it through. Don't you understand that there's a world of difference between talent and skill? When I said you had the ability to be more powerful than the Royals, I meant innate potential. Potential means nothing without training. Do you even know the difference between a trick and a whisper? Don't answer that. Of course you don't. Poor dearie. How brave of you—and how absurd—to try."

He crouched over her, holding out the teacup full of his own poisonous elixir. "We've been at this a long time, my friends. Since practically before Pretties could clothe themselves. I don't care if you're saints or monsters. You can be whatever you want to be as long as you help us retake London. I believe that was our deal, yes?"

Still shaking, Anouk reluctantly accepted the noxious brew. A dead dragonfly was floating in it. She sighed. What other option did they have now?

He smiled. "Splendid."

Each of the others also took a teacup, and, wincing, they all drank down the poison. Anouk felt it spread down her throat, coating it like tar. She expected it to sink to her stomach in a heavy way, but it remained eerily in her chest. She rubbed at the skin over her heart. The beats came slower, slower, slower, and then stopped.

"Congratulations," Tenpenny said. "You're officially dead-ish."

Chapter 31

Fifteen Minutes of Enchantment Remain

THE FIRST ORDER OF business, according to Tenpenny, was to get them clothes that weren't made of tattered curtains and gardening wire. The blond Goblin girl with gold teeth, December, led them into a tomb that served as a communal closet: piles of dusty top hats in one corner, ties and cravats in another, and skeletons set up around the room as dress dummies, arrayed in various British-punk clothes. For Anouk, December rustled up boots and a pair of slim tuxedo trousers that looked great with The Faustine jacket; for Cricket, she found a tweed suit with the pockets stylishly ripped out.

Anouk ran her fingers along the smooth trousers, worn at the hems. A hand-me-down, maybe, or stolen from a shop years ago and mended over and over. The Goblins had so little and yet were more than willing to share. Why had she ever believed that the Haute was a beautiful world of magic and grace? Everything had a darker side, magic most of all.

"Midnight is in five minutes!" Tenpenny said, admiring their improved fashion. "Come, join the partiers. Tonight we celebrate not only our fortune but yours. Let midnight come and dare it to change you."

Anouk felt herself caught up in a wave of giggling Goblins who herded her and Cricket to the dance area in front of the Black Death bar. Someone had stolen a giant clock from one of the Métro stations and suspended it from the ceiling on a heavy chain. Now it swung back and forth, sweeping over the crowd, a Goblin straddling the top of it and waving at them all.

The clock read four minutes to midnight.

And then the Goblins were dancing around her, and someone passed her a delicious warm drink, and she felt herself smiling.

Three minutes to midnight.

She grinned widely now, jumping up and down with Goblins on either side of her. Someone started counting down and she thought of a tradition among the Pretties, a New Year's countdown sealed with a kiss at the end. Her eyes searched the crowd for Beau. Shouldn't they celebrate? Midnight was coming but it wouldn't take them. Not tonight. And one thing she'd learned was that they had to enjoy every second of life that they had.

In a place where magenta and blue and green hair was the norm, Beau's plain sandy hair stood out. He was about twenty feet away, and he was looking for her too. She started weaving through the tight crowd.

"Five!" Someone counted down the seconds.

"Four!"

Then their eyes met. Beau grinned. It felt like the crowd had faded into the background. She felt herself moving toward him automatically, for once the Goblins parting to let her pass.

"Three!"

The enormous clock overhead swung back and forth, casting a shadow on the revelers. Someone was dancing with one of the old skeletons, blocking her way, and she stood on tiptoe not to lose sight of Beau.

"Two!"

There. A path cleared. He was just steps away.

"One. Midnight!"

The cavern erupted in cheers. She took a step toward Beau, feeling like someone in a fairy tale, like a Pretty at a New Year's ball, but then someone else was tugging at her hand, pulling her sharply away from Beau. Viggo — it was Viggo. A second before she realized what was happening, he kissed her. His lips were softer than she'd imagined. He smelled like the sweet hot drink everyone was passing around, and his arms circled her waist as though screening them from the crowd, a private moment between the two of them.

"Viggo, eww, stop it!" She sputtered and shoved him away but then softened when she saw the look on his face. Sheer, almost sweet happiness, even if it was because of a spell. She'd never seen Viggo look sweet, not once. He was a twat and she'd sooner kiss a frog, but even frogs deserved little moments of joy. She pecked him softly on the lips.

When she pulled back, Beau was standing next to them. His face was as slack as if she'd slapped him. He turned sharply, pushed his way through the crowd. The smile fell off her face as she disentangled herself from Viggo and ran after him.

"Wait!" she said, catching his arm. "Beau, I was only being nice. You know I can't stand Viggo. And he doesn't love me either, it's the spell —"

"The spell," Beau muttered angrily. "I'm sick of that damn spell.

I'm ready for it to wear off, Anouk. Ready for him to stop trying to kiss you. And having you kiss him back!"

"We need him like this."

"You *like* him like this. Your puppet."

"Beau, that isn't true! Listen, we don't have time for stupid arguments about Viggo—"

But he strode away and was lost among the revelers before she could finish. She caught a glimpse of blond hair and saw December sliding behind him through the crowd. Jealousy flared in her. Fine. Let the Goblin girl try to comfort him where she couldn't.

Twin Goblin boys in blue bowler hats pulled her into a swirling dance, but she managed to extricate herself from their arms and slip to the refuge of the blessedly cool, empty tombs. She sank down on a fallen gravestone, hugging her knees. Why couldn't Beau focus on what really mattered? Tenpenny's concoction, vile though it was, had worked. Midnight had come and they were all still human.

But were they *all*?

Luc's disappearance nagged at her like a briar just beneath the skin. Wherever he was, he hadn't drunk Tenpenny's elixir. Had midnight been the end for him? It was a terrible thought, that he was truly lost to her now. What possible hope of finding him did she have when she wasn't even certain what kind of animal to look for? A mouse? An owl? Even if their paths crossed, he wouldn't know her, and she wouldn't know him. Maybe she hadn't understood the first thing about being human if she'd failed her best friend so gravely.

"Oh no, did the poison work too well? Are you actually dead?"

Tenpenny sat down next to her and mocked feeling her forehead.

"Still some breath in you. Why aren't you celebrating? Is that chauffeur giving you trouble?"

She paused and shook her head. "Even if we can find someone to recast our spell, I'm afraid that a spell alone can't make us human. *Truly* human. Only actions make a person human, not magic."

"Yes," Tenpenny mused. "Well, and the fact that you don't have a tail."

She rolled her eyes.

"My darling girl, look at you. Pale as a slug. Drab as pudding. Tonight is not the night to feel depressed at the state of your reality. Here. You need some color."

He produced a sleek tube of lipstick and drew on her left cheek, then her right. He sketched a shape, filled it in, licked his finger, and wiped off a smudge.

"Eh. Not perfect, but what ever is?"

He handed her a mirror. He'd drawn ruby-red hearts on both of her cheeks, though messily. It gave her the look of a performer, and between that and the tuxedo trousers, she blended in a little more with the Goblins.

"There, now. Fashion is art and we are the canvas. Do you feel like a piece of art, my dear?"

"I feel more like that slug you were talking about."

He tsked. "Have you ever heard the story of the Goblin and his shadow? No? Many years ago, a Goblin angered a minor duke by baking his pet peacock into a pie, mistaking it for a chicken. The duke cursed him. Every day, the Goblin started to notice his shadow hung around more, even in the light. It started to grow darker in places, especially around the eyes and nose. *His* eyes and *his* nose. When he looked into the mirror, he found that he was fading. His own shadow was trading places with him, stealing his life. He had to live the rest of his days in pure darkness, where there were no shadows, before his swallowed him whole. What I'm saying is, don't let anything—not shadows, not sorrow, not peacocks—steal your brightest days."

She sighed. "It isn't that easy. There's one of us missing. The fifth beastie, Luc. He was like an older brother to me. He was there when I was first made, and he always protected me even when I didn't know I needed protecting. And now the rest of us have been granted an extra day, but not Luc. We don't know where he is. When midnight came, he must have turned back."

Tenpenny gazed at her with a puzzled expression.

"In a way it's like he's dead," she continued. "If he saw me, he wouldn't know me. Everything between us would be gone."

Tenpenny still looked at her strangely, and she patted her hair self-consciously. "What? Do I have something on my face?" She brushed at the ever-present dust.

"Not that, dear girl. It's the other beastie. The gardener."

"What about him?" An idea struck her and she whipped her head around, searching the Goblin crowd. "Is he here?"

If she'd had a heartbeat, it would have raced.

"Of course he is. You brought him."

"What?"

"That oubliette you had with you, the one that Beau hid from the Marble Ladies. There are two sections, you know. The nonmagical one that is currently holding your pelts. But there are all sorts of interesting things hidden away in the magical part."

She stared at him as though he were speaking some foreign language. "You unlocked the oubliette? How?"

"A little dirty magic did the job. I took a peek while you were in the loo to see if you'd brought anything good."

"And Luc. You mean to say that Luc is . . . that he's . . ."

"He's in the oubliette." He gave her a quizzical look. "Dear girl, don't tell me you didn't know that he's been with you the entire time. Oh my. What a delicious tragedy."

Chapter 32

Twenty-Four Hours of (New) Enchantment Remain

S HE JUMPED UP FAST enough to send the bones skittering across the floor. A cloud of dust rose in their place. "Where's the oubliette now?"

Tenpenny scratched his chin. "Last I saw, December was guarding it."

She ran back into the thick of the party, searching the crowd for the Goblin girl with the blond braids. She spied Cricket dancing on top of the Black Death with a Goblin boy in an indigo kilt and pushed toward them.

"Cricket!" she shouted. "Where's Beau?"

"He disappeared with December. That way, back toward the old Métro tunnels. Is everything okay?"

"Get the others and meet me in the Skull Crypt."

Cricket gave her a curious look but kissed her Goblin boy sweetly on the cheek and climbed down from the top of the Métro car, using the window frames as a ladder. The lights and music were pounding harder than ever. Anouk pushed through dancing bodies to the tunnel that led back to the Métro line. A few Goblins loitered beneath the archway, smoking something spicy and sweet, but there was no sign of Beau. She ran over the damp, dirty stone ground, calling his name.

Low flickers of flame lit up loitering groups of Goblins, some laughing or speaking in low voices, others in romantic embraces of two—or three—people.

"Have you seen December?" she called to a group catching spiders in the dark with a butterfly net, and they pointed farther into the darkness. It was cold here so far from the bonfire. She hugged her arms around her jacket, running her fingers anxiously over the embroidery. Then, in the dim light of an old curved Métro lantern, she saw the back of Beau's sandy head.

"There you are—"

He wasn't alone. He turned and she saw blond braids. December, her lips painted an electric pink, a matching glow to her cheeks. Beau's own lips were the same electric shade.

"Oh."

Not the most eloquent response, but it was all she could think to say. Heat flushed up her neck. They'd been kissing here in the dark tunnel. Beau and December. Was this about that business with Viggo? Some kind of revenge?

Beau's face went a shade paler. He made a quick effort to wipe the lipstick from his mouth. "Anouk. Um . . . listen. Oh, *merde*, I'm an ass."

Yes, he most certainly was, and she was about to tell him as much but then her eyes fell on the oubliette resting at December's feet. That was more important than any kiss. She grabbed the bag and shook off the dust, unable to keep her anger from escaping. "It's Luc," she spat.

Beau's face flickered with uncertainty. "Luc?"

"He's trapped in the oubliette." She hugged the bag to her chest and started running down the tunnel, past the kissing couples and the spider-chasers, hearing Beau and December's footfalls echoing behind her.

"Anouk, wait!"

The cold enveloped her like a shadow, but she barely felt it. Luc was here. He'd fix all of this. She'd soon see him again, those warm brown eyes, that easy grin that said their problems were only hiccups and scrapes. *This?* he would say. *The Royals after us and time running out? This is nothing.*

She ran into the Skull Crypt, where Tenpenny and Cricket were waiting. She clutched the bag close. Beau and December ran up behind her.

"Anouk," Beau whispered insistently.

She waved him away without glancing at him and turned to Cricket. "Where are Viggo and Hunter Black?"

"I couldn't find them." Cricket raised an eyebrow at the smeared pink lipstick on Beau's mouth. "I see where *you've* been, Beau."

Beau swore mildly under his breath and scrubbed at his face with his shirttails, glancing anxiously at Anouk.

Tenpenny snatched up the oubliette. "I'll take that." He laid it on the sarcophagus with a flourish and rolled up his sleeves for dramatic effect. "Now. There is fine skill involved in breaking into a witch's oubliette. Each one is locked with a particular spell that can be opened only by the witch who whispered it. Of course, we Goblins are excellent at lock-picking."

Anouk glanced at Beau out of the corner of her eye. His arms were crossed tightly over his chest, and she couldn't read the look on his face; anxiousness, certainly, and almost a bit of dread, but she couldn't be sure how much of it was because she'd caught him with

December or how much of it was due to the potion they'd drunk. They *were* mostly dead, after all.

"Watch this." Tenpenny shook out a few wriggling worms from a jar, slurped them down, and polished them off with a mug of beer. After a belch, he waggled his fingers over the oubliette.

"Changa, changa, a forma verum et abria." The burlap fabric started to glisten as it transformed from rough fibers to silk. Anouk caught glimpses of the other bags it had been—ostrich leather, the Hermès gold buckles—but it continued to morph until it settled on a well-worn leather sack with primitive stitching.

"The oubliette in its true, original form," Tenpenny said in a stage whisper, and then he flicked off a piece of worm he'd spat out. "Ugly, isn't it? Fashion has improved dramatically in the past four hundred years."

"Just open it!" Cricket cried.

Tenpenny upended the leather sack. All manner of things tumbled out onto the floor: Glass jars packed full with herbs. Old books with titles in a language Anouk had never seen. Oddly shaped wood carvings. And a parrot who squawked and flew away. December chased after it.

"Hey, that's mine!" Cricket cried, grabbing a well-worn book. "The book about the girl on the magic train! I thought Mada Vittora burned it." She hugged the book to her chest, grumbling curses about lying witches.

Tenpenny shook the sack once more, and it grew and expanded, and then something enormous tumbled out of it, something with arms and legs that somersaulted over the dusty floor and landed against the tomb with a painful-sounding crack.

"Luc!"

He looked awful. Grime coated his scalp and shoulders. The white gardener's uniform he usually wore was stained with dirt and long-dried blood. His brown-black skin was more sallow than she'd ever seen it. He didn't sit up.

Anouk shoved past Tenpenny and knelt by Luc's side, touching his shoulder.

"Are you all right?"

His eyelids fluttered and he muttered something unintelligible, but he didn't wake. She shook him. This was wrong. He was supposed to grin at her and wink and say everything would be all right.

"He's been in there a long time," Tenpenny explained. "Cramped space, you know. Not much to eat. I'm surprised he didn't gobble down that parrot."

"Shouldn't he have turned back into an animal?" Cricket asked. "Midnight came and he didn't drink the potion."

"Ah, but time doesn't exist the same way in the oubliette as it does here. He's been in a state of suspended timelessness."

Anouk glanced at Beau. He was chewing hard on his lip. Sweat had broken out on his temples. He didn't say anything. Was this still about the kiss?

"Beau, you don't look very surprised," Anouk said. Come to think of it, he'd been fiercely protective of the oubliette ever since they'd fled the townhouse. She narrowed her eyes, but then Luc suddenly coughed back to life and she turned to him and touched his face.

"You're okay!" she cried.

"Anouk?" Luc's voice was rusty. He licked some moisture into his dry lips. "Where . . ." His eyes were dazed. "You're out of the townhouse. How . . ." He started coughing again. Anouk helped him stand. He was so thin, a boy made of sticks. He had spent almost two weeks trapped in whatever strange world lay within the oubliette's walls.

"I'm so sorry we didn't get you out earlier. We didn't know where you were."

Luc blinked a few times, pressing a hand to his forehead. Despite his weakened state, he had an air of solidity about him. Even on his deathbed, he'd still manage to find the strength to jump up and box the ears of anyone who insulted her.

His hands were smooth and firm and the color of night tulips as he traced a finger over her cheeks painted with red hearts. "I'm supposed to look out for you, remember? Not the other way around." He tried to grin, but it came out as a grimace.

She hugged him hard, feeling tears welling at the trace of thyme on his clothes. She had her North Star again. She let go and then it was Cricket's turn to embrace him. Cricket whispered something in his ear that made him smile. He kissed her cheek. "Always, gumdrop. Always."

Then he seemed to notice the tension between Beau and Anouk. His eyes dropped to the empty bag, then went back to Beau.

"You didn't tell them?" Luc said.

Anouk whipped her head to Beau. "Tell us what?" And then Beau's silence suddenly made sense to her. It was about far more than a kiss. She shoved herself to her feet. "Beau, did you know Luc was in there?"

Beau flinched as though he'd been struck. "No!" She stared at him hard, and he winced. "Well, not the whole time. I only learned that he was in the oubliette the night we fled. And then I didn't believe it was possible to get him out without another witch. Besides, once the Royals were searching for Vittora's killer, I thought it would be best for him to stay in there, hidden, until it was safe to come out."

Anouk gaped at him. "What does Vittora's killer have to do with anything?"

Both Luc and Beau went very quiet.

At last, Luc rested a hand on Anouk's shoulder. "You loved her so deeply, Anouk. I'm sorry."

Anouk still stared at Luc and Beau, uncertain, and then it all came crashing down on her. She leaned against the tomb, suddenly not trusting her own legs to keep her standing.

"You killed her," she whispered to Luc.

Luc sank wearily onto the tomb, dusting the grime from his short hair. He took a deep breath. "It started with the rabbits . . ."

He explained in a rusty voice how he had overheard Mada Vittora's plan to kill and replace all of them but Anouk and that he knew he had to stop her. He prevented it the best he could, having Anouk cook the rabbits before the witch could perform the spell. He even tried to contact Mada Zola for help, not knowing that Mada Zola would turn on him. After he returned from the Château des Mille Fleurs, Mada Vittora was waiting for him. She cursed him into the oubliette.

"It was dark in there, like the world was cast in shadows. I searched for a way out, but there was nothing. No doors. No windows. I had no idea how much time was passing. For all I knew, she was going to leave me there for centuries. But the rest of you were in danger—I had to come up with a way out. And then I found this." He took a vial out of his pocket.

Cricket squinted. "Parsley?"

"Jimsonbane," he said. "It's rare. Most of the world has forgotten about it. I came across a reference to it years ago in an ancient botany encyclopedia. I'm not even certain Mada Vittora remembered she had a vial left in the oubliette."

The distant dance party still raged, but in the quiet of the crypt, Anouk felt like she was caught in that same never-ending timelessness that Luc must have felt in the oubliette.

"Jimsonbane," he continued, "is the only herb known to have ethereal-projection properties. If handled correctly, it can cast an herbalist's spirit outside of the body."

"And out of the oubliette to escape," Cricket guessed.

"Well, that was the idea." Luc frowned as though remembering something unpleasant. "It didn't quite work like that. I did cast my spirit out, intending to escape, but I cast it right into Mada Vittora's bedroom. She was there. It looked late outside—maybe close to midnight. She'd been drinking. When she saw my spirit, she went pale. I saw myself in the mirror. I looked translucent, like a ghost."

"A ghoul, you mean," Tenpenny clarified. "Ghosts don't exist."

Luc gave him a suspicious look. "Um, who are you again?"

"Long story." Tenpenny petted his new rat.

"Right . . ." Luc eyed the rat blood on the Goblin's cravat. "Anyway, I could feel the jimsonbane fading. I could see my spirit flickering, and Vittora saw it too. She thought she'd won. But she didn't know that spirits on jimsonbane have the ability to hold physical objects—one of the reasons why it's so valuable. I took the knife from her dresser and stabbed her. I had to. She was going to kill us."

Anouk looked down at her hands, remembering her mistress's

blood on them. She wanted to feel that hot buzz of anger again. She wanted to feel *something*. But could she condemn Luc for killing their mistress after everything she'd done to them—and was going to do to them? Still, she felt a small part of herself slip away. She'd loved Mada Vittora once. A twisted, misunderstood love, but even the cruelest forms of love were never lost without heartache.

"I didn't have much time after that," Luc said. "The jimsonbane was used up. My spirit returned to my body in the oubliette. Beau came upstairs just as it was happening."

Anouk turned hotly on Beau. "There was no reason not to tell us."

Beau rubbed his scalp awkwardly, wincing at her tone. "Telling you wouldn't have freed him. Besides, what was I supposed to say, that your best friend had murdered the witch you considered a mother? I was afraid it would break your heart. I was trying to protect you."

Anouk stared at him, uncertain what to think. What did it mean that he thought lies could protect someone? Was that how he saw her—as an artless, sheltered girl incapable of facing reality?

She stepped back. Looked at the scattered magical objects at her feet—anything to avoid looking at Beau. Jars of herbs. Scraps of paper with long-forgotten spells. Gold coins. Priceless objects that now belonged to them.

Luc touched her shoulder. "Can you forgive me, Anouk?"

She drew in a breath. "I understand why you did what you did." She paused and then blurted out, "At least you're here now. You can fix this entire mess."

She waited for Luc's confident grin. That knowing wink.

He held out his hands, shaking his head. "I can barely stand, dust bunny. I've been gone. I can't fix anything."

"But you always know what to do," Anouk insisted.

Then she saw that Cricket and Beau and Tenpenny were now looking at *her* the same way she had once looked at Luc. When had she become the one everyone turned to for guidance?

A flicker of hope started to return. She swallowed. "There's nothing wrong with a little dust," she said, blowing a streak of it off Luc's thumb.

Outside the crypt, the dance party had dwindled to a core group of revelers; the rest of the Goblin horde were asleep on the catacomb floor using skulls for pillows. It felt cold — too cold.

Where was Viggo? Ever since she'd cast the love spell, he had been practically glued to her side.

The smile fell off her lips.

"Where are Viggo and Hunter Black?" she asked sharply.

"Um, about that." Beau looked even more uncomfortable. "I was so sick of that love spell that I had December break it. I didn't think we needed Viggo's help anymore."

"Love spell?" Luc asked, bewildered, and then he raised his eyebrows doubtfully. *"Viggo?"*

"I have *so* much gossip to tell you," Cricket said.

"If the spell is broken, then Viggo isn't loyal to us anymore," Anouk said. "He'll go straight to the Royals and tell them that we're here in the catacombs."

"I'll find the prick," Cricket offered, producing a blade.

"We don't have time. They could be anywhere in Paris by now. We have to change our plan."

"To what? We were short on options to start with."

A paper fluttered to the floor and landed amid the detritus. The beastie spell. Anouk knelt down, smoothed it out, and then flipped it over and sniffed. Once more she smelled that familiar odor of onion and lemon, only now, with Luc back, she remembered where she knew it from: the secret messages she and Luc used to write to each other in invisible ink and slide beneath each other's doors.

She met his eyes and smiled.

She dug a match out of her pocket, whispered a flame to life, and held it a careful distance below the spell. Luc might not be able to solve their problems for them anymore, but he had given her an idea.

"There's always another way," she said, "if you're desperate enough."

Chapter 33

S HE BLEW OUT the candle flame.

"Look at this." She showed them the back of the beastie spell. "Rennar didn't only write a spell to turn animals into humans. There's a second spell here, written in an invisible solution of cepa de apa, lemon, and diluted blood. I *knew* I recognized that smell." She shared a knowing look with Luc. "The words are revealed when exposed to fire. It's a contra-beastie spell that can turn humans to animals."

Tenpenny peered over her shoulder at the spell. "It's surprisingly elegant. Rennar does have a way with words, doesn't he? That handsome devil . . ."

"So you can cast it?"

"Goodness, no."

Anouk's lips parted, ready to insist that he at least try.

"But *you* can," he added.

She wrinkled her nose in surprise.

"This spell is, above all, exceptional in its simplicity. You see, it's much easier to turn a human into a toad than the other way around. Even someone with only a basic mastery of magic, such as yourself, could manage the pronunciation. But the ingredients—ah, there's the catch." He pointed to a notation on the spell. "The beastie spell requires no more than a thimbleful of blood, but the contra-beastie spell calls for six pints. That's far more than any Goblin or even Royal could consume. The vitae echo would ravage us. But you, dearie, could guzzle that much and more."

This took all of them by surprise. Finally Cricket broke the silence and said, "I hope you're proposing to turn Viggo into a toad."

"Not Viggo. Mada Zola." Anouk swept aside the bones from the sarcophagus and traced a map in the grime on top. "The Royals haven't yet lifted Mada Zola's banishment. She's still trapped in her estate. If the Goblins will help us lay siege to Château des Mille Fleurs and capture Mada Zola, we can force her to perform the beastie spell on us before midnight tomorrow under threat of casting the contra-spell on *her*."

"You want to return to Montélimar?" Beau sounded uncertain.

"It's our strongest chance, and besides, Viggo doesn't know about it so he won't be able to warn her of our plan. Tenpenny, can we still count on the Goblins to fight for us?"

"A deal is a deal, dearie."

Cricket leaned in the doorway, looking out over the sleeping masses with a frown. "They don't look like much of an army."

Tenpenny scoffed, affronted. "I'll have you know that Goblins have incredible stamina." But then he too evaluated the drunken sprawl of sleeping revelers, and his confidence waned. "Er, cappuccino is a wonder for shaking off fatigue. They'll be fine."

"Once again, we're screwed," Cricket muttered.

"You keep saying that," Beau countered. "But we've gotten out of every narrow scrape. Breaking into Castle Ides. Stealing the spell. Avoiding the crows. Fighting off the Royals. And we're still alive."

"True, except for the fact that, currently, we're actually dead." She kicked at the empty vial of Tenpenny's heart-stopping elixir.

Luc rubbed the sides of his head like he was still caught in some freakish other reality. "Wait, the four of us and some Goblins are going to attack Château des Mille Fleurs?" He let out a long puff of air. *"Merde.* Is it too late to banish me to the oubliette again?"

Anouk smacked him on the arm. "Mada Zola's witch's girl, Petra, went behind her mistress's back to help us. She might help us again. That could make all the difference."

Luc turned to Tenpenny. "If we're doing this crazy thing, let's at least be smart about it. Where's your scryboard? We can listen in on anything Zola and Rennar might be scheming."

Tenpenny cleared his throat. "Scryboard? Never heard of it. Sounds like something illegal." When Anouk gave the Goblin a hard look, he conceded with an eyeroll. He went to the hallway and called for December, who returned with the parrot on her shoulder.

"December, show them the scryboard."

December led them through another graffiti-lined tunnel to a low wooden door. Anouk ducked inside. No bones here, but the smell of something rotting was thick, and she held a hand against her nose. She didn't recognize the scryboard until she heard its whispers. Or, rather, its *hissing.* There were no glistening black feathers here. No ropy, vein-like wires. Instead of being made from organic materials taken from crows, this scryboard was made from insect components. A hard carapace covered the whole contraption. She eyed it uncertainly only to realize it was eyeing her back with a fractured, eight-sided insect eye emerging from one side. Luc sat on the stool, cupping a scaly set of headphones over his ears. She took a step backward and bumped into Beau.

He motioned her into the corner, where they had some privacy. He looked nearly sick with guilt. "You're angry about December."

Her mind went back to the dark Métro tunnel and pink lipstick on two sets of lips. "I hope you don't need magic to tell you that."

"I was jealous about Viggo and Rennar, and she said I had nice hands and you know I'm vain about my hands and . . . and it was stupid. So stupid."

A sigh escaped Anouk's lips. "It doesn't matter right now. We don't have time to argue over smeared lipstick when our lives are running out." She started to turn away, but he stopped her.

"I should have told you about Luc."

Yes. That was the real problem, wasn't it? She looked away before he could see the still-fresh sting in her eyes.

"I'd do anything to keep you from being hurt," he insisted. "You loved Luc and Mada Vittora more than you loved anyone else. How could I tell you that one had killed the other?"

"I'm not a bird with broken wings, Beau. I don't need to be sheltered."

"I was wrong. You weren't naive then, and you certainly aren't now. Through all this darkness, you've held on to love and hope, and that's true strength."

She wasn't sure how to respond to this. The boy who'd spent every day of her human life with her was now seeing her—the real her—for the first time. "I should have seen that there was no love in Mada

Vittora's heart," she admitted. "Luc did the right thing. It's better that she's dead."

Beau didn't answer, but his face showed that he didn't think she believed that. Love was love, even if it had been cruel, and it was like Beau to see that she was still mourning Mada Vittora even if she refused to admit it to herself.

"I won't keep anything from you again, cabbage—"

She pressed a finger to his lips to silence him. She was reminded of the first time they had kissed in Montélimar. She'd held her finger to his lips like this and then replaced it with her own lips. What would Rennar, with his proposal of marriage, think of his beasties in each other's arms?

"You mesmerized him," Beau murmured, reading her mind. "The prince. I could see it in his eyes."

She dropped her finger from his lips. "He wanted to use us."

"It's more than that. He's fascinated by you. You have something he lost long ago—youth. Wonder. He was enchanted by your hopefulness. He has everything under the sun, power and time and riches most people only dream of, but he doesn't have what you have, not anymore." He traced a thumb gently along the red heart on her left cheek. "And he has what you want too. Knowledge. Answers. The confidence that comes from experience. I could feel the pull between the two of you. You're fascinated by him too."

His words felt dangerously close to painting a picture of her and Rennar, and it wasn't a picture she felt comfortable with at all. "What are you saying?"

"Just that I'm damn glad you didn't step into that cage."

Slowly, his arm circled her back, holding her not like a broken bird, but like a slice of cake he wanted to devour whole and then lick up every last drop of icing—but Luc interrupted them.

"Anouk. Get in here and listen to this. See if you can make it out." He took off the carapace headphones and cranked up the external speaker. Anouk and Beau joined him and Cricket at the scryboard. The hisses were very quiet, but she was used to quiet. It was a sound she had heard before.

Dragonflies.

"They're saying that Castle Ides is empty," she said in surprise.

"Empty?" Beau said. "Where'd all the Royals go? Oh, *merde*. It's here, isn't it? Viggo told them we're in the catacombs and every Royal in Paris is on the way down here—"

"No." Anouk cut him off. "They aren't coming here." She clicked off the speaker tensely. "The dragonflies say they're going to Montélimar."

Cricket swore. "How did they know that was our plan? Great, now we're supposed to capture Mada Zola *and* fight off the Royals? There's no way. We're screwed. And before you say anything, Beau, I mean it this time. Royally screwed."

"You're underestimating the effects of cappuccino on Goblins, my dear," Tenpenny said, coming in from the grand hall. "Not to mention the fact that we have the numbers. Even if the Royals bring the lesser court, how many of them are there—nine or ten? Plus one witch. And there are hundreds of us."

He took a calm sip of tea.

Beau massaged the bridge of his nose as though his head ached. "I still don't understand why Rennar and the Royals would bother to go to Montélimar if Viggo told them that we're here. We're literally right under their noses. Seriously. Those pipes are marked Boulevard Saint-Michel, which is a block from Castle Ides."

They all tipped their heads toward the dripping municipal water pipes that fed into the upper city. Anouk felt something cold at her back, a breeze that wasn't there. Why *hadn't* Rennar simply raided the catacombs? Now, with most of the Goblins still yawning and stretching and hunting up clothes, they wouldn't have put up much of a resistance.

"Because I didn't tell him where you were," a voice said.

Viggo stood in the doorway. His hair was entirely black now, a reminder that midnight had come and all of Vittora's spells were broken. For a second, Anouk thought of the Goblin girl cursed to fall in love with a yellow mail van. At least now she was free. Everyone who had been bound by Vittora's spells was.

"Viggo." Her breath quickened. She'd cast a spell on him without his permission—she'd made a slave of him, forced him to do all sorts of humiliating things. The Viggo she knew would have been plotting an elaborate revenge that involved many sharpened spikes. Hunter Black was behind him, the ever-present shadow. She eyed them both closely. "What are you doing back here?"

"If you mean am I going to try to kiss your feet again, no. The spell is done. I'm not happy about that love spell, by the way. I think we all know that I never would have done those things if not under the influence of magic beyond my control. Just so we're all clear."

No one answered. Anouk wasn't entirely positive he wasn't plotting revenge.

"I didn't go to Rennar," he said, guessing at their silence. "I didn't tell the Royals anything. Oh, I considered it. As soon as December broke the curse, Hunter Black and I stormed out of here and I had every intention of returning with an army of crows at my heels. But I didn't."

"Then why the hell did you come back?" Cricket snapped.

His dark eyes flashed to hers. "Because you need me."

"Ha."

"No—you do. If you're going to go through with this insane plan to storm Montélimar and fight off both Zola and Rennar, you'll need powerful magic on your side. Blood magic." He looked theatrically over his left shoulder and then his right. "I don't see any other humans around here willing to siphon off pints of blood for you."

He was right, Anouk realized. They had Goblin numbers, but the Royals were experts in manipulating magic. The few simple whispers she could do would be nothing against them. The contra-beastie spell required powerful ingredients, the most rare of which was six pints of blood. Which meant there was only one way they might prevail: by exploiting the fact that Rennar's and Zola's magic had limits. The vitae echo. *She* didn't have that limit.

"But we'd need half your blood," she said. "That could kill you."

He tossed back a lock of dark hair. "Possibly."

She narrowed her eyes at his cavalier attitude. "Why would you risk that for us? After everything I did to you—the spell?"

"Yes, the spell," he said, his dark eyes cold. "That damn spell that wasn't about love at all, but manipulation. True love has to be as equals. Two people who come together willingly. Love isn't about possession." He paused dramatically. "It's about sacrifice."

He was staring at Cricket, and she didn't look impressed.

She said coldly, "Is this when you tell me that through the curse of the spell, you've actually learned the true meaning of love?"

"Well—*merde*. I've been planning that speech all the way down here."

She rolled her eyes. "He hasn't changed at all."

"I have," he said, and for once, he sounded sincere. "I understand now that what I felt for you wasn't love. It was obsession. It wasn't until Anouk made *me* her love captive that I realized that's never what I'd want for you. Do I really love you? *Alors,* I don't know. I'm not certain I'm even capable of love. Mommy issues and all." He cleared his throat. "Anyway, this is what I'm offering. My blood, maybe even my life. And you'd better say yes before all that wine I drank twenty minutes ago wears off and I stop feeling so damn heroic."

Cricket still didn't smile, though she hadn't reached for her blades, which was at least one promising sign.

"I'm sorry, Cricket. I was an ass."

She narrowed her eyes. "Apology accepted, but if you think there is even a slight chance that I'll love you back after all this is over, you're wrong."

"Well, chances are high that I'll be dead anyway."

"So what does this mean?" Tenpenny said.

Anouk turned to him. "It means you have about an hour to wake the rest of the Goblins and be ready. We have an errand to run. Pick us up outside 18 Rue des Amants in one hour."

Tenpenny consulted his watch.

"One hour, dearie. Tick-tock."

Chapter 34

Twenty Hours of (New) Enchantment Remain

I T WAS STILL RAINING in the streets of Paris. A light mist cast an orb around each of the streetlights, and as they hurried along the thoroughfares, Anouk felt how fiercely she loved this city. All those nights sitting in her turret window and watching the Pretty World outside, she had wondered if she'd ever be a part of it. If her feet would ever stroll these streets, if she'd ever look up at the glowing moon. She had wondered if it could possibly be as perfect as she imagined or if a rock would always be in her shoe on that stroll, if smog would always obscure the moon.

And it was true, there were rocks and there was smog, but there were also stars. The city was like life itself: good and bad, pretty and ugly, kindness and cruelty all in one. But most important, it simply *was*. And that felt like a kind of magic too.

Rue des Amants was quiet in the early-morning hours. A wealthy neighborhood filled with townhouses used only part of the year by residents who also lived in Switzerland and New York and Monaco. It lacked the vibrancy of the Latin Quarter, where students quoted Descartes at all-night cafés and music hummed in the street.

Their footsteps echoed off the quiet townhouses as they passed rows of black cars. Anouk stopped at the sad little tree in front of number eighteen.

"No one bothered to water it?" Luc asked accusingly.

"I couldn't cross the threshold," Anouk reminded him.

It felt strange to reenter the townhouse. She had never come in through the front door, and as she stepped inside with the oubliette in hand, she pictured herself here just three days ago, eager to serve and stow away the oubliette. She marveled at how simple life had been then. How little she'd known. And yet how wildly she'd dreamed.

She bent down and picked up her old hair ribbon.

"Her body?" Luc asked.

"Taken care of," Viggo answered without elaborating. He pushed past them up the steps, heading to the bloodletting room. Hunter Black followed at his heels, but Anouk took her time, looking at the townhouse with new eyes. It had been her home as much as it was Mada Vittora's. She had cared for it. Cooked in the kitchen, swept the floors, convinced Beau or Luc to make any repairs that were needed. Beau went to the kitchen to scarf down whatever leftovers he could find in the icebox, and Cricket went with him in search of a whetstone to sharpen her blades.

"I should change clothes," Luc said, and he climbed the stairs to his attic. Anouk followed slowly, up the turret to her own bedroom, where she ran her hand over the baby shoes, the playbills, the little things from the Pretty World she had so loved. A sheen of dust covered her desk, and she grabbed a cloth to clean it as she'd done countless times, but then stopped. All those little tasks, sweeping and polishing and cooking, belonged to another person's life now. No matter how hard she scrubbed, she'd never be that person again.

She went back downstairs, pausing at Mada Vittora's room. The door was open a crack. A sense of foreboding overcame her as she remembered the last time she'd stood here and mistaken the blood for red wine. She inched open the door. No body, as Viggo had said. Even the bloodstain was gone. She knelt down, ran her fingers over the rug. None of her cleaning products could have gotten it out so well—someone had done this with magic.

And then she whipped her head around to the portrait above the bed. Prince Rennar. She could feel his lingering presence. Smelled a trace of his cologne. He'd been here. Viggo must have invited him in for the day. Rennar had taken care of her mistress's body. She wondered if he'd gone into her room too, if he'd touched her things as she had once touched his.

Could Rennar see her from the portrait now? She climbed up on the bed and turned it around to face the wall. The townhouse was protected by ancient magic that not even he could break—he couldn't set foot beyond the front step without an invitation—but she didn't want his eyes in the house either.

Outside of the bloodletting room, she heard the *hiss-hiss* of the chair's machinery. She pushed open the door hesitantly. Hunter Black was seated on a wooden bench by Viggo's side. Viggo had his eyes closed. His lips were very pale. The jar was fuller than she had ever seen it before—it held four pints, at least.

Hunter Black didn't look up when she came in. His gaze stayed focused on Viggo's pale lips.

Anouk sat next to him. "He's asleep?"

"He passed out after three pints."

"He might make it," she said. "It's possible to survive with only six pints left. His chances of surviving are probably better than ours will be at Montélimar."

Hunter Black didn't answer.

Anouk hesitated, unsure how to ask the question on her lips. "You love him, don't you?"

"Of course."

She considered her words carefully, thinking of Luc's fairy tales, the prince and his footman. "I mean, you're *in* love with him."

His back jerked upright as though he'd been attacked. His dark eyes flashed. He looked ready to deny it, but then he let out a long growl of a sigh. His silence said everything.

"The love spell," she said. "It wasn't real. You know that, right?"

"Of course it wasn't," he snapped. "He would never love *you.*"

She didn't take offense at his words—she knew a wounded animal when she saw one. And she also knew hopelessness. A boy in love with a boy who liked girls. A cruel twist of fate.

"He can't love you back," she said quietly. "Not romantically."

"Thank you for reminding me of such a painfully obvious fact."

"But he cares about you. You're his best friend. His *only* friend."

Hunter Black grunted for an answer. They sat on the bed, watching the machinery continue to pump Viggo's blood. Five pints now. Anouk tried not to think about having to drink it, instead focusing on how strong it would make her. Both Mada Zola and Prince Rennar had told her that she was capable of amazing things. She was going to get her chance to prove it. But as she watched Viggo grow more and more pale, it sat uneasily with her. Beasties weren't susceptible to the vitae echo, but she couldn't shake the feeling that magic would still have a cost. No life was taken without consequences. If Viggo died, that magic wouldn't have come for free.

"That blue-flame spell," she said quietly to Hunter Black. "Do you still want to learn it?"

He looked away from Viggo at last and gave a single nod.

Anouk found a pouch of borage herb in the attic, and they consumed leaves of it and she taught him the words of the Selentium Vox spell and the accompanying hand gestures. Hunter Black tried again and again to master the right tone. As an assassin, he was used to being *quiet*—he wasn't used to being *calm*.

At last the pump clicked off, and Hunter Black stuffed the borage in his pocket and checked Viggo's vital signs. Anouk unbuckled him from the machine. Six pints. When she lifted his arm, it felt alarmingly light, like a limb without bones.

"His pulse?"

"Still there," Hunter Black said. "Weak, but steady."

Viggo suddenly gave a slight moan. "Need . . . wine . . ."

"How about water," Anouk suggested gently. She went to the bathroom to pour him a glass while Hunter Black carried him from the bloodletting chair to the bed, pulled off his shoes, and laid the blanket over his body. Viggo was shivering slightly. She paused in the bathroom door as Hunter Black smoothed Viggo's hair off his forehead. It felt like something she shouldn't be watching.

She cleared her throat and set the water on the side table. "Viggo, how do you feel?"

"Like I'm missing half my blood."

"You are."

"Well, that explains it."

A car horn blared outside—the British anthem, unmistakably

the Goblins. Anouk checked the clock. Six in the morning. The sun would be rising soon. One last day.

"What the hell are you waiting for?" Viggo's voice was raspy, his eyes closed. With a weak hand, he slapped away Hunter Black. "Get out of here already and turn that flower witch into potpourri."

"Hold on until tomorrow. We'll be back," Anouk promised.

"Hopefully without tails," Viggo murmured.

Anouk squeezed his hand. She took the pints of blood, hid them away in the oubliette, and slung it over her shoulder. "Thank you, Viggo."

The car honked again.

Beau appeared at the doorway. "Anouk, Hunter Black. Time to go."

"Give them a minute," Anouk said, and she herded Beau down the stairs. In another second, Hunter Black joined them in the front foyer dressed in his black coat, his hair slicked back and knotted at the nape. If he felt any sadness or worry for Viggo, by now he knew how to hide it.

"You think you've mastered the blue-flame spell?" she asked.

"I learn fast when it comes to new ways to kill people."

They stepped into the front garden. A fleet of Goblin motorcycles filled Rue des Amants. There had to be a hundred motorcycles, most of them carrying two or even three Goblins. There was much honking and cheering, and Anouk thought that maybe cappuccino *was* magic.

Beau, Cricket, Hunter Black, Luc, and her. The five of them together at last. They stood on the front steps as a team, a family. Someone from across the street yelled about the early hour and threatened to call the police, but Anouk just grinned.

If there was anything to fear in the streets of Paris, it was *her*.

Chapter 35

THEY RODE WITHOUT STOPPING, speeding past villages and fields, tearing down curving roads, honking at any car that dared to drive too slowly. Clutching Tenpenny around the middle, Anouk felt distinctively queasy. She had drunk every pint of Viggo's blood, slowly, giving it time to digest. And now it sat heavy in her stomach, and Tenpenny's driving didn't help. But as the hours passed, she began to feel a change. The blood felt less like a greasy puddle in the pit of her stomach and more like sunlight spreading through her body, warm and bright and life-giving. She felt marvelously daring, like she'd drunk too much champagne or was walking on the edge of a rooftop.

Six pints of blood. Enough to cripple a witch.

Mada Vittora had been careful never to add more than a thimbleful of blood to her potions. Any more and the vitae echo would start to take effect. Her skin would turn brittle, her back would stoop, dust would be shed from her clothing and collect in her wake as though she were desiccating from the inside out. But Anouk felt the opposite.

Young. Vital. Alive.

She slid on a pair of black sunglasses, and from the next motorcycle over, Cricket gave an approving nod.

Anouk grinned. Being on the back of the motorcycle *was* a bit like flying. She could feel the pulsing energy of the Goblins, their determination and hope. This battle meant everything for them, too. The first step toward regaining the city they loved. And ever since dancing atop the Black Death with the Goblins, she'd wanted that for them. Throw out the London witches. Install a new leader, preferably one in a top hat.

The sky darkened. She looked up, expecting a cloud, and her mood dimmed at the flock of crows that had moved in overhead.

"Crows!" she called in Tenpenny's ear.

He nodded grimly. "There will be no element of surprise for us. What of the contra-beastie spell? Are you ready?"

Viggo's blood kept pulsing like lightning bugs in her body, making her feel light and strong, and she nodded.

"And the witch's girl of the dubious loyalties?"

It was impossible to guess what Petra might do when they arrived. At first blush, Petra had seemed content living with Zola and tending the gardens, but Anouk knew from experience that just because a witch's servant looked happy didn't mean she was.

"Let's hope that soft spot in her heart extends to Goblins."

She smelled the lavender long before they saw the fields. Pine-like and rich, a smell that was intoxicating even now that she'd learned about the dark secrets that might be buried beneath the soil. They crested a hill and the first lavender rows appeared in long arcs that stretched toward the midday sun. It was a clear day, but there was a chill in the air. She was glad for her jacket. She patted the pockets where she had stashed a knife and the contra-beastie spell.

Beau pulled ahead of the pack and signaled to the others to follow him down the road to the estate. The Château des Mille Fleurs' topiary hedge rose along both sides of the road. The leaves looked sharper, more like slick green blades. Had the hedge always been so high? It was tall enough now to block out the sun and plunge them into shadow.

Beau slowed to a steady crawl as he led the procession of motor-cycles down the gravel lane, but he didn't bother to cut his engine, dismount, and walk his bike. There was no reason for stealth — the crow spies had made certain they would surprise no one. He stopped ten feet from the gate, signaling for the Goblins to go no farther.

"The hedge is dangerous," he called. "Don't let anyone get too close."

"So how do we get through?" December asked.

Beau dismounted and waved over Anouk and the others. In Luc's fairy tales, armies always brought a vast array of weapons: pistols, armored horses, missiles. But the most threatening-looking things in this Goblin army were a few sharp hatpins. They were as bound by the vitae echo as the Royals. This battle would be fought with magic, not firearms.

Anouk and Luc and Cricket and Beau gathered beside the call box. Hunter Black, in typical Hunter Black fashion, had separated himself from the crowd and was inspecting the hedge as closely as he dared. From the corner of her eye, Anouk saw a Goblin take cautious steps to the nearest branch and poke it hesitantly with an umbrella. She was about to call for him to back away when Luc said, "We could dig under."

Beau shook his head. "That's how Viggo got in last time. I saw Mada Zola cast a spell to prevent it ever happening again."

"If we set up a ramp," Cricket offered, "the Goblins could jump it with their motorcycles."

"The spell blocks us from going over too," Beau said.

A sudden scream interrupted them. The Goblin who'd wandered too close to the hedge was flat on the ground with vines wrapped around his ankles. He tried to sit up, but two more vines reached from the hedge and clamped onto his arms. All too fast, the vines dragged him inward.

"Kingsley!" Tenpenny cried.

In a few strides, Hunter Black was by the Goblin's side with his knife drawn. He slashed at the vines, but there were too many of them. For every one he cut, three more appeared. The Goblin cried out, his voice rising in pitch, silenced only when the vines swallowed him into the hedge.

Only a blue bowler hat was left behind.

A stunned silence overtook the crowd.

Tenpenny ran up, breathless, with eyes even wider than usual. He picked up the fallen hat with shaking hands. A vine curled around Hunter Black's wrist, but he sliced it off and stepped out of reach. Tenpenny and the rest of the Goblins took a few steps backward too.

Worry rippled through the crowd. Anouk turned to the trash bins and kicked one over with a frustrated cry. Champagne bottles tumbled out amid a messy tangle of sticks.

She stopped moving.

At first, the sticks looked like any hedge trimmings, but a certain twist of one branch caught her eye. The branch curved almost like a jaw with a row of thorns rising up like teeth.

"Toblerone," she whispered.

"Now is no time to think about chocolate," Tenpenny said sharply.

"No, it's Toblerone!" She held up the jaw branch. "These sticks used to make up an enchanted topiary bear. The branches were his bones. He died—in a sense. He was cut up and pulled apart. Petra must have dumped him out here with the trash."

Luc, still weak from his time in the oubliette, looked aghast. "Who would do that to an innocent shrubbery bear?"

Both Anouk and Cricket looked pointedly at Hunter Black, who scowled. "That was a long time ago."

"It was the day before yesterday!" Cricket yelled.

"Well, a day and a half ago I was trying to tear you apart too, Cricket. And look at us now. One big happy family whose members haven't attempted to murder one another in at least a few hours."

Anouk gathered the branches of the bear and laid them out like puzzle pieces on the gravel lane. "If we can resurrect him, there's a chance he could get through the hedge. He's *made* of hedge. And he's outside the estate borders, which means Zola can't control him."

She put down the final branch and stepped back. She could feel the magic flowing within her, and it felt *right*. Creating, not destroying. But as much as she wanted to resurrect the bear herself, she didn't dare use up any of Viggo's blood. It was a finite supply, enough for only a single big spell, one burst of magic. If she used it now, she wouldn't have enough left to cast the contra-beastie spell on Mada Zola.

"Tenpenny, can you resurrect him?"

The Goblin tenderly handed his fallen friend's bowler hat to

December, who tucked it into her motorcycle bag. He fished a worm out of his pocket, swallowed it, and then held his hands over the wooden bones and whispered.

"Vitae. Vitae ahhora."

It happened slowly. First there was a flutter of leaves. Then a twig fluttered too, moving a little too much to have been caused by breeze alone, and then an even bigger branch rolled onto another. The branches began to graft themselves back together at the places where they'd been cut, forming a wooden skeleton with limbs and a backbone and a heavy skull with thorny teeth. And then it all came together in one beautiful shiver, and Anouk was looking not at a pile of hedge clippings but at a living topiary bear. Toblerone pushed himself up on his trunklike legs, shook out his leafy green pelt, and then swiveled his head to Tenpenny.

"Command him to tear through the hedge," Anouk said.

After swallowing more worms, Tenpenny whispered another spell. Slowly the bear's head swung to face the hedge. He lumbered forward on heavy limbs, swiped at the nearest branches with a massive paw, and shredded them with his sharp thorn-claws like they were made of crepe paper. No vines darted out to snag him; no branches fought back. Beneath his woody paws, the hedge gave way as he tossed branches aside, snapped sticks, and cleared a path wide enough for them to pass through.

"Bravo!" Anouk said.

Tenpenny turned to his Goblin army. "Prepare for entry."

The Goblins dismounted from their motorcycles and checked their belongings one more time, making sure each was safely secured by its brass pocket-watch chain. A few knives glinted in the sunlight, and even an antique sword or two. The air filled with the smell of bitter herbs, rue and horehound and wormwood, and the tang of blood as the Goblins consumed the life-essence they needed for the battle. Anouk winced at the squeals of rats that were dispatched for the cause. A murmuring spread through the crowd as the Goblins thanked their deceased animal companions for the sacrifice they had made.

"Do not forget the dark truth about this place," Tenpenny announced to the crowd. "Beneath the witch's fields are the flesh and bones of our brothers and sisters, Goblins lured here and used to strengthen the witch's powers. We do this as much for their memory as for ourselves!"

With a roar of engines, the Goblin army mounted their motorcycles and swarmed into the Château des Mille Fleurs' outer fields. There were hundreds of them, top hats tumbling off their heads, a fleet of exiled Londoners far from home. Motorcycles zipped and weaved around Anouk and the others, and the danger of it caught in her throat, the roar of engines making her breath quicken. Her hair flew around her head as the last Goblin motorcycles disappeared through the break in the hedge. She ran a short ways after them, stopping at the first fields, watching the dust rise in their wake as they rode toward the château.

Cricket joined her, breathless.

"This is it." Anouk glanced at her friend. "You finally get a chance to tear the world apart."

There had been a time when Cricket would have smiled grimly at the idea of slashing through the highest members of the Haute, but she didn't smile now.

"Cricket?"

Cricket shook her head. "That damn Goblin is right. It can't just be about destruction. After all this is finished, if we succeed in tearing down the Haute, you and I are going to have to put it back together again. Better."

Two more motorcycles roared. Beau and Hunter Black pulled up on either side of them. Luc rode on the back of Hunter Black's motorcycle. He was sweating badly in the sun, blinking with eyes that still weren't quite used to bright daylight.

"Are you sure you've recovered enough for this, Luc?" Anouk asked.

"I am, if you're sure it's worth the risk."

She shoved her fists in her jacket pockets. "There's no turning back now."

She and Cricket climbed onto Beau's motorcycle, and the five of them brought up the rear of the army. As the engines revved, she felt Viggo's blood quicken in her limbs. It made for a heady feeling —almost like having a secret. No Royal or witch had ever consumed this much human blood and lived.

She tried to imagine the look on Mada Zola's face when a simple maid overpowered her. Then, maybe, the Haute would understand that they couldn't play with humans or animals or *anyone*. Living things weren't toys for their pleasure.

But her determination wavered as they approached the château. The beautiful stillness that had enveloped them on their first visit was gone now. There was smoke everywhere. Goblins were screaming. They were fighting against some sort of army that Anouk couldn't make out in the smoke. But what army? It was supposed to be only Zola and Petra and a handful of lesser Royals.

Beau cut the engine and she jumped off, coughing. The smoke was clearing and she wasn't certain what she was looking at. It was a scene from a nightmare. Giant soldiers made of wood were stalking the garden in pursuit of Goblins. They towered ten feet high. Their bodies were formed of spindly branches, their legs powerful trunks, their hands like many-fingered roots. Smoke rose from their wooden shoulders.

She spotted one that was only half burned. His arms and head were bare wooden branches, but his lower half was covered in manicured leafy green.

"It's the topiaries." Her voice was a stunned gargle. "The Royals enchanted them to fight."

"And the Goblins are using fire spells against them," Luc said. "But it doesn't look like it's working."

The burned wooden skeletons left behind were hideous things. They couldn't be stabbed or shot with arrows — there was no flesh to them. She watched, stunned, as one lumbering wooden soldier snatched up a Goblin in a neon dress and twisted her body in a terrible way. Her screams died along with her. As the smoke continued to clear, the horror grew. More bodies on the ground, bleeding out into the soil. Crushed like autumn leaves. Broken Goblins. *Dead Goblins.*

Beau looked stricken. "What about the vitae echo?"

"The Royals aren't doing the killing," Luc said tensely. "The wooden soldiers are killing on their behalf. The right spell could reverse someone turned to stone, but not even the greatest spell can bring back the dead."

"Look!" Beau pointed out a team of Goblins who were fighting back by one of the fountains. They had surrounded one topiary soldier and were throwing out rotting spells to wither its branches. It was working, but slowly.

Without warning, a hiss of magic came from every direction at once. Anouk felt it sizzle in the air and spun around. A chubby Goblin twenty paces away had been turned to stone. One minute he was flesh and blood and gold eyeliner, and then he was an awful granite statue, immobile, a perpetual scream frozen on his lips. She had to blink to make sure she was seeing straight.

Anouk felt a shiver as another wave of magic shot by them. A few paces to their left, another Goblin turned to stone. That was powerful magic. Witch magic. "She's close. The Mada."

She followed the direction of the magic to the château's bell tower. A figure with long black hair wearing a billowing white blouse stood in its open window next to a young man in frost gray.

Zola and Rennar.

"We have to get into the château," she said. More sparking streaks of magic shot out from various high windows. Beautiful faces loomed there: a handful of lesser Royals, counts and duchesses, eager to impress their prince. They wouldn't make it easy.

And then Anouk's eyes caught on the bear. Toblerone. He had followed Tenpenny down the path through the fields and was now standing at attention by a crumbling stone wall, awaiting another order. "The bear," she called to the beasties. "Climb on his back!"

They ran through the battlefield. Cricket whispered her cutting spell to chop off wooden arms before the soldiers could grab them. Hunter Black hung back to hiss the blue-flame spell and set one giant's leg on fire, while the others reached Toblerone and used his branches like a ladder to climb onto his back. Anouk helped Luc climb up and straddle the trunk that formed his spine.

The bear started lumbering toward the château. Anouk wove her fingers into his twiggy bones, holding on with one hand. Toblerone barged straight through the battle, through Goblins casting whispers and wooden soldiers that exploded in flurries of splinters. Anouk tipped her head up, squinting at the bell tower. She was too far away to see Zola's and Rennar's faces, but she hoped they could see hers.

The most dangerous thing in all of France, she thought, *is* me.

"Hunter Black, come on!" Cricket called.

As Toblerone neared the house, Hunter Black climbed up the fountain, frigid water soaking his clothes, and leaped onto the side of the bear next to Anouk. He started to slip but she grabbed his hand, catching him at the last minute. He was soaked. There was a terrible moment when she felt his hand slide out of hers . . . until Luc suddenly clutched him too and pulled him out of his coat, which fell to the ground. Together they helped him climb onto the bear's back.

"Nice of you to join us," Luc said breathlessly.

He only growled, "I liked that coat."

At last Toblerone reached the heavy wooden door of the château. His claws tore at the wood, splintering and shredding it. Behind them, the battle raged on. Every scream made her cringe. She could stop this. Save all the Goblins, put an end to the topiaries. Didn't she owe the Goblins that? But the victory would be short-lived. She had to save her magic for Rennar and Zola. Toblerone reared up on his hind legs and threw his full weight at the door. The boards gave way beneath him. Splintered wood flew everywhere. He fell to his feet, and the whole earth seemed to vibrate.

Petra stood in the entryway as if she'd been waiting for them.

She was casually smoking a cigarette as though enchanted shrubbery often crashed through her front door. But Anouk could see beyond the act. The hand that held the cigarette was trembling.

"You shouldn't have come back," Petra said.

"She's nothing," Hunter Black growled. "A witch's girl. A Pretty. She can't do magic."

Petra put out the cigarette with her boot and then took a rifle from behind her back. "Maybe not, but I can use a gun."

Chapter 36

Nine Hours of (New) Enchantment Remain

P ETRA." ANOUK GASPED. "Put down the rifle. We're not your enemies."

"And yet you've broken into my house and brought an army of Goblins with you. I'd expect something different from a friend. Say, cake." She aimed the rifle. "Now climb down from there."

They descended the topiary bear with no sudden movements.

Anouk dropped to the floor. "I was loyal to a witch too, once," she told her. "I loved her. But she was rotten somewhere deep. The vitae echo eats them away inside. It destroys their minds. It makes them power hungry. They think the Pretties are like livestock, theirs to command, and the same with us and with the Goblins. Do you think you're any different?"

Petra cocked the rifle. "You're the one making this black and white, not me. I helped you before because I like you. And believe it or not, I'm helping you still. I've been around these people my whole life. Zola. Rennar. I know what they're capable of. You have to believe me: there's no way out of this that doesn't end in you begging Rennar for your life."

"You want us to surrender."

"I want you to survive."

Footsteps sounded behind them, and they turned to find Countess

Quine coming down the hallway, lips freshly stained with powder, dressed in an ornate snow-white gown as though to flaunt the fact that capturing them would be so easy that she could do it in formal-wear.

"I can handle it from here," she purred. "Petra, go and tell the prince they've been captured. He'll want the lesser Royals to tie them up."

But Petra didn't lower the rifle. "Not until we get them locked in the cellar. They're smarter than you think."

Countess Quine's expression indicated she doubted that.

Cricket looked at Anouk with a question on her face. They were utterly trapped—Quine behind them, Petra in front. Anouk's mind scrolled through all of Vittora's spells, searching for something small that wouldn't use up much of Viggo's blood . . .

Then, to her surprise, Hunter Black raised his hands in surrender.

Anouk gaped.

Beau elbowed the assassin and hissed, "Did that ice-cold water freeze your brain?"

"You heard her," Hunter Black growled back. "She said she's going to lock us in the *cellar*."

He winked.

Hunter Black never winked.

Countess Quine hadn't seen it, but Anouk had, and though she had no idea what plan was tumbling around in his brain, she raised her hands too. Beau and Cricket stared at her like she'd gone mad, but then Luc raised his hands, following her lead with a trusting nod, and Beau and Cricket warily did the same.

"Excellent." The countess smirked as she herded them down the hallway, with Petra bringing up the rear with the rifle.

Through the narrow windows, Anouk could hear the sounds of the battle outside. Cries for help. Clanking metal. Her stomach revolted as if she'd eaten rotten eggs. How many Goblins were wounded? Dead? Every step she took toward the cellar, she felt more and more despair.

And then, without warning, she didn't feel anything at all.

The cellar stairs had just . . . vanished, as though by magic. There was nothing beneath her feet, and suddenly she was falling. She crashed into Beau in front of her, and Luc slammed into her from behind. She kept sliding, kicking her feet, trying to grab hold of something, but her fingers glanced off every stone, and the whole group tumbled out of the stairwell and through the wine-cellar door to collapse in a messy, painful heap.

Someone moaned. Someone else cursed. She caught a glimpse of a glass shoe attached to a petite foot that must have been Countess Quine's. Saw Luc's face smooshed into Beau's stomach. Smelled cigarette smoke on Petra's breath, just inches from her. Heard the scrape of metal — the rifle!

She and Petra scrambled for it at the same time, but Hunter Black reached it first.

He was standing outside the cell. *Standing*. Not a part of their tumbled mess.

"What did you do to the stairs?" Petra cried.

Hunter Black aimed the rifle in the general direction of the knot of bodies, unable to get a clear shot at either Petra or Countess Quine. "The last time I was locked in this cell I had a lot of time to think, and those wooden stairs are only for scenery. It's an old form of carpentry, constructed with rope and joinery. The rope was all but disintegrated, which meant the only thing holding the entire staircase together was this piece of wood." He held up a wooden pin the length of his thumb. "Pull it out, the rope snaps, it all comes crashing down."

"Since when is an assassin an expert on carpentry?" Petra demanded.

"You'd be amazed how many ways there are to kill someone and blame it on faulty workmanship." He gestured with his free hand. "Anouk. Cricket. Luc. Beau. Come on."

Anouk disentangled herself from Cricket's arm and Countess Quine's silk dress. Hunter Black extended his free hand to help her up.

Beau dusted off his clothes and grinned at Hunter Black. "I think that's the first time I've seen you do something vaguely heroic."

"It's like you're actually almost human," Luc teased.

"Yeah, our hero!" Cricket taunted, ruffling Hunter Black's hair, which elicited the expected growl, though there were no teeth in it this time.

Trapped in the cellar with the countess, Petra scowled at Hunter Black. "You're not a Pretty. You can't fire that gun."

"You don't know what we can do," he answered. "Nobody does. Until two days ago, even I would have laughed if you'd told me we could cast whispers." He cocked the rifle. "Do you want to risk it?"

Petra's expression turned very serious as she faced Anouk. "Listen —you're going to get yourselves killed unless you give this up. There are other ways to stay human." Her voice wasn't unkind.

"By siding with Rennar?" Anouk shook her head. "We're no one's pawns."

Luc and Beau leaned against the heavy wine-cellar door until it slammed shut, and they locked Petra and the countess in. Petra didn't resist, but Countess Quine hurled herself against the door, though the lock mechanism had long ago been secured with Mada Zola's own magic, and no amount of whispering could open it.

Anouk tossed one last look to Petra behind the bars. The witch's girl sat against the wall, legs folded under her, a nasty look on her face —but it was aimed at the countess, as if Quine was the last person she wanted to be imprisoned with. Her eyes shifted to Anouk and softened.

"Good luck, then."

Returning to the kitchen required more than a little skillful shimmying to scale a staircase with no stairs. Once they had made it, Anouk hurried to the kitchen window and stood on tiptoe. Outside, remnants of smoke hung over the gardens. The battle was still raging. Sparks of magic, wielded by the lesser Royals stationed at various windows, sizzled across the gardens. Despite the awful sight of slain Goblins in the grass, it looked like the Goblins might be getting the upper hand. The remaining ones had formed a stronghold near the potting shed and magicked a swarm of termites to go after the wooden soldiers.

Anouk and the others started for the rear hallway, but they hadn't gone three steps before a shadow crossed their path. Lady Metham materialized by the kitchen door. Her fingers sparked with magic; her lips were stained with powder. Anouk and the others scrambled backward.

"My eucalyptus supply is down to dust," Cricket whispered in a rush. "Hunter Black? Your borage?"

"Lost with my coat."

Viggo's blood throbbed in Anouk's body, but she didn't dare use it up on anyone other than Zola or Rennar. "Right. Then run!" she commanded.

The five of them bolted down the central hall. Lady Metham followed. She didn't deign to run; she simply swallowed powder and then projected herself twenty feet ahead, cutting off the beasties. Anouk skittered to a stop just as Lady Metham swiped a silver dagger at her throat, missing by only a hair. Luc grabbed Anouk and they ran down a side hall, but Lady Metham projected herself there too, blocking the exit.

"Don't you know when you've lost, beasties?" Lady Metham taunted.

"Tell the blade in your shoulder that we've lost," Cricket spat.

Lady Metham looked down at her pristine dress with a frown. "What blade—"

Even before she'd finished speaking, Cricket had drawn and thrown a blade. It sank into Lady Metham's left shoulder with perfect precision, and she released a strained cry. Blood poured down the side of her dress, staining the gossamer fabric. She reached for her powder. Anouk got a dark premonition.

"Changa, changa," Lady Metham spat in Cricket's direction with eyes that were blazing with fury, *"a forma verum."*

Anouk recognized the spell with a gasp.

"No—Cricket, run!"

But it was too late. Cricket had nowhere to go. They were penned in by walls on three sides and Lady Metham on the fourth. With a whisper and a twist of her hands, Lady Metham cast out an aura of sparking magic, which floated to surround Cricket. Cricket swatted at the magic glimmers as if they were gnats, clawing at the places where they hit her. But the magic clung to her. Wherever the sparks touched her skin, it rippled and puckered. Her left arm contorted, and she screamed and clutched at it. Long white hairs sprang up from the scratch marks she carved into her own skin. More white hairs sprouted around her neck and spread down her chest. Her curly brown hair was now threaded with white, and her chest contorted too, folding in on itself. Her screams changed to yowls.

Anouk couldn't watch. Clammy sweat poured over her brow, and her mouth was suddenly dry. Her greatest fears—the things she'd not even dared to think about in midnight hours—were happening before her eyes. And she couldn't stop it. With every yowl, she felt an equal pain in her own chest, as though it were her changing too.

And then the crackling magic stopped. Anouk dared to open her eyes, and her stomach plummeted. There it was—the white cat from the painting. Long pearl-white hair, a fluffy tail with a crook at the tip. Her knees buckled. The cat . . . it wasn't Cricket. Not anymore. There was nothing of Cricket's wit or love of Pretty candy. Nothing of her twinkling eyes. At least death was final: This felt somehow worse, a body that continued existing in this awful, twisted form.

Beau caught Anouk in his arms, tried to turn her face away, but her gaze was fixed on the cat. It started to lick one paw. Back in the oubliette, one of the five pelts would be gone now, dissipated into the ether, magically returned to the flesh and bones of its original owner.

Anouk turned on Lady Metham sharply. "You *putain!*"

The lady was slumped against the wall. Her face was pale; there was a light sheen of sweat across her forehead. It had taken much for her to perform such a complex spell—Anouk suspected that somewhere beneath that dress a kidney or her liver had turned to stone—but she wore a grimly satisfied smile.

"That's one little kitty. Soon to be four more animals once Rennar gets hold of you."

Anouk felt a sort of madness come over her as she stared at the cat. In her entire life, short as it had been, she had never experienced such rage, this crackling heat that flushed up her chest and made her whole body shake . . .

"I hope you have some other trick up your sleeve," Luc whispered to Hunter Black.

"He doesn't have to," Anouk answered in a deathly low voice. "I do."

Her anger drew together, concentrating itself somewhere deep within her unbeating heart. She murmured under her breath.

"Anouk, you can't use up Viggo's blood yet," Luc warned.

But she was too angry to stop herself. "Just a few drops," she hissed. *"For Cricket."*

She whispered, low and fierce.

In the next second, Toblerone came charging down the hallway from the foyer, summoned by Anouk's spell. Lady Metham barely had time to register surprise before the bear barreled into her like she was a bowling pin. Lady Metham, already weakened, collapsed, her head knocking against the stone floor with a deadly crack. Blood seeped out. Her eyes were glassy and unmoving. It didn't stop the bear—he began tearing her body with wooden claws until she was nothing but a pile of crimson rags.

"I can't watch this," Beau moaned.

Anouk stared at the blood pooling on the floor, at the bear that tore at Lady Metham's body, and she whispered a quick end to the spell.

Both Beau and Luc looked slightly ill, but Hunter Black gave Anouk an approving nod. "Now there are more of us than there are of them. Good."

Clinking footsteps came from down the hall, interrupting their victory.

"Those are glass shoes. Countess Quine is coming," Luc warned. "She must have gotten out of the cellar."

They took off. Their footsteps were drowned out by the sound of her ragged breath. Anouk darted down a hallway that led past rooms full of more portraits. In and out of interconnecting chambers. Up and down dark staircases where she could barley see her own hands and her mind whirled as though she were trapped in a maze. When she finally reached a quiet alcove near the chapel, she dared a glance behind her. Luc was there, but Beau and Hunter Black were gone. She skidded to a stop.

"The others. We got separated—"

A sound in the distance interrupted her, something between a howl and a yell.

"Did you hear that?" she asked Luc. The howl came again. It was less like a yell now, more of a growl. "That's an animal." She gasped. "Not the cat. Something bigger . . ."

Luc's face turned grim as he grabbed her shoulders and prodded her forward. "Keep going."

They ran down more hallways until they reached a spiral staircase. The steps were narrow and ancient, worn down from countless footsteps.

"This is it." She gasped. "The bell tower."

Luc rested a hand on her arm before she could climb the stairs. He peered up at the turret as though he knew where—and to whom—it led. "Anouk, are you sure about this?"

"It's what we came here to do."

He nodded gravely. "Then let's do it."

"No." She laid a hand on his chest. "There's nothing you can help me with there, but you can help Beau and Hunter Black. Quine must have trapped one of them." She paused. "That howl . . ."

"I know." His tone was somber. He paused a beat before answering the question she hadn't asked. "It came from a wolf."

She closed her eyes, fearing the worst. *Not Beau. Not Beau. Not Beau . . .*

"It's Hunter Black," he said.

Her eyes snapped open. "How do you know that?"

"Three years ago, Goblins dragged in a wolf caught in the Black Forest, and two days later Hunter Black walked out of the attic." He glanced over his shoulder. "Countess Quine must have turned him back."

She felt a stab of anguish. Hunter Black was family, after all, and in some crazy way, she had actually come to care for the sulking assassin.

A wolf.

Cricket had been right. That was two of them turned now. She kept expecting to wake up from this nightmare and be in her bedroom back in the townhouse, tucked snugly beneath a quilt, a book fallen open by her side.

But this was no dream.

"Go," she said. "Find Beau. And Tenpenny and December."

Luc kissed the twin hearts painted on her cheeks and squeezed her tight. "Stay safe, dust bunny."

"You too, Luc."

She climbed one stair, then another, trying to move quietly but deafened by her own raspy breath. She ran her shirtsleeve over her face and it came away with sweat and smeared red lipstick from her cheeks. It made her think of Tenpenny and how the night before, she'd told him that it was their choices that made them human, not their bodies, and he had said that tails had something to do with it too. She almost let out a delirious laugh. Cricket, a cat. Hunter Black, a wolf. No choices they could make now would keep them human.

But *she* still had choices.

"Des forma humana, fiska et skalla animeux," she whispered to herself, rehearsing the words of the contra-beastie spell. She wouldn't let Rennar catch her unprepared this time.

The door to the chamber at the top of the bell tower was made of plain wood, not ornate wrought iron over mahogany like the ones downstairs. There wasn't even a lock, just a simple latch. Press it, and the door would open.

She knew what waited on the other side.

Mada Zola and Prince Rennar, of course, but something else.

She could feel it—that dark thing that she feared looking at too closely, the animal inside her that was always hungry, always awake. For as long as she'd been alive, she'd kept that other self at a distance. But once she stepped across this threshold, she'd have no choice but to embrace it.

She pressed the latch and opened the bell-tower door.

Chapter 37

Eight Hours of (New) Enchantment Remain

THEY WERE WAITING FOR HER.

They stood in the round turret in front of open windows that looked down over the château's gardens where the battle was still being fought. The bell loomed from a ceiling joist, nearly as tall as she was and ten times her weight. Wire cages for Mada Zola's crows, empty now, hung on hooks from the ceiling. The cries of the battle below sounded distant, as though it were happening in some other world. This must be how the Royals always felt in their elevated homes, far removed from the suffering of their people.

Mada Zola had always been beautiful, and she and Rennar together looked like gods out of one of Luc's stories. Those tapeta eyes of Rennar's were swallowing Anouk up once more, regarding her the same way that Luc's had when he'd been freed from the oubliette, as though she had changed in the short time they'd been apart and he was trying to put his finger on exactly what was different about her. She wasn't sure if Rennar liked what he saw — messy hearts painted on her cheeks, the Faustine jacket, wearing determination on her face like the Goblins wore makeup — but he didn't take his eyes off her.

"Where are your friends, little beastie?" Mada Zola asked. "You're all alone."

"I don't need them. Not for this."

The witch smirked. "You were clever to extend your enchantment for an extra day, but you can't buy yourself any more time. Not unless you surrender to us, and then perhaps we can discuss how much each hour of humanity is worth to you."

"I don't want hours," Anouk said. "I don't want days. I want a lifetime, and I'm going to have it."

Rennar folded his arms, looking perplexed. "I cannot understand why someone so bold would refuse to serve her creator. We are the same, you and I."

"You didn't create me," she spat. "Mada Vittora did. And she learned too late what happens when you mistreat a beastie." She took the spell out of her pocket and held it up.

Mada Zola laughed at the scrap of paper—she didn't seem to know what it was, and paper didn't seem like much of a threat.

But Rennar didn't laugh.

"I told you," he said hoarsely. "That spell is useless without one of us to cast it for you. You haven't the Selentium Vox fluency necessary for such a complex spell."

"Not for the beastie spell, that's true," Anouk admitted, "but I'm talking about the spell on the back. The one that is simple enough even for me."

A flicker of confusion crossed Mada Zola's face. She looked for guidance from Rennar, but he ignored her, every ounce of his attention focused on Anouk and the spell.

"What is she talking about?" Mada Zola whispered.

Anouk brandished the spell like a weapon. "One of you is going to cast the beastie spell and keep us human—that is, if you want to stay human too. This is a contra-spell. It will turn anyone, even a witch or a Royal, into an animal. I can't say *which* animal. The spell chooses, not the caster, just as we had no choice what type of humans we'd become." She paced in a slow circle around the bell tower. "If you don't recast the beastie spell on the five of us permanently, I will cast this spell on the two of *you*."

"You haven't the skill," the witch said simply.

Rennar, however, remained quiet.

"I haven't trained at one of the witch academies, no," Anouk said. "I wasn't born into magic, like the Royals. All I've learned are spells overheard from Mada Vittora and a few Goblin tricks. But this spell is simple. It requires nothing but a tremendous amount of life-essence."

Now Mada Zola really wasn't smiling. "You would have to take a human life to acquire that much blood. You wouldn't do that. You're too tenderhearted."

Anouk thought of Viggo and said softly, "Not all life-magic has to be taken by force."

A commotion came from the stairs. Anouk whipped around. Someone was coming. For a second her confidence faltered. Countess Quine appeared with Luc in tow, her hair mussed as though they'd been in a struggle. Luc's hands were bound with twine. A bruise marred his dark cheek.

Anouk sucked in a breath. "Luc, are you all right?"

But he wasn't. Anyone could see.

Mada Zola smirked again, her confidence restored. "Good, he can be a witness to this. Quine, our little dust mop says she's going to turn us into animals if we don't obey her. Go ahead, dust mop. Show us how you'd do that."

Anouk loathed the smirk on the witch's face. It itched at her with blade-sharp claws, just like the sounds of the battle outside.

Rennar grabbed Luc and jerked his head at Quine. "Go. Handle the driver. He's the only one left."

Beau.

Anouk turned and gripped the window ledge, searching the battle. She caught sight of Tenpenny's top hat—he was crouched behind a garden wall near the Goblins' potting-shed stronghold. A dozen or so more Goblins huddled with him, trying to break the spell that locked the shed door. And then a sandy-haired boy in a white chauffeur shirt and black trousers sprinted toward the Goblins, jumped over a fallen wooden soldier, and joined them behind the wall.

A streak of magic tore across the garden, turning the kilted Goblin that Cricket had danced with to stone. Anouk whipped her head around. It was Quine—she was below now, in the shelter of the porte-cochère, eating powder and casting spells.

"Beau, watch out!" Anouk yelled.

He couldn't hear her. He was so far away. He was slamming his umbrella against the lock, unaware that his back was exposed and that Countess Quine was swallowing more powder . . .

"Beau!" Her cry was hoarse. But just as Countess Quine's next bolt hurtled across the garden, Tenpenny heard Anouk's call and spun around to see what was happening. In a few long strides, he got to the shed and shoved Beau out of the way. Beau landed against the stone wall, his shoulder connecting hard enough to make Anouk bristle.

The bolt of magic clipped Tenpenny in the hip. Anouk cried out. It spread from his hip with alarming speed, immobilizing his legs and his chest, swallowing his neck and head, finally reaching the hand that was still outstretched to protect Beau. In only seconds, he was transformed from the leader of the exiled Goblins into a mass of colorless granite.

Anouk gasped.

One of the wooden soldiers wrapped its rootlike fingers around Tenpenny's stone body and, with one swift motion, lifted the statue off the ground and slammed it against the wall.

It shattered into dust and pieces.

Anouk had to steady herself on the windowsill. Her lungs felt robbed of air, like she'd forgotten how to breathe. A statue could be whispered back to life, but there was no returning from rubble and dust. *Tenpenny was gone.* She clutched the ledge hard enough to leave imprints.

"No!"

Below, Countess Quine aimed at Beau again. He was leaning against the stone wall, looking dazed from the fall. He could never get up and run in time.

She's going to turn him to stone too.

In that moment, reason disappeared. She'd never let Beau become a pile of rubble.

She raised her hands toward the window. Luc called out a warning before Rennar could silence him, but she barely heard him. Hot anger was slick between her ears. It deafened her. Controlled her. She channeled every ounce of Viggo's blood, every bit of her love for Beau, no longer needing Rennar's belief in her because she believed in herself.

"Bomba ak ignis bleu," she whispered grimly.

It was quiet. That was the thing about magic. It was best done with whispers, not shouts. And her one whisper, bolstered with the strength of six pints of life-blood, sent a shock wave over the gardens. The lavender in the fields rippled as though a hurricane had passed through; buds, stripped from the plants, rose in the air like a dusky purple cloud. The Goblins fell to their knees from the tremor.

Each of the wooden soldiers, one by one, burst into blue flames. The smell of wood smoke mixed with the lavender as hot flames turned their wooden bones to ash. A hideous scream pierced the air as Countess Quine sizzled along with them.

Just like that, the battle outside was over.

Won.

Rennar and Mada Zola were caught in a stunned silence. Luc too. Zola ran to a window and leaned out over her charred fields and her ashen soldiers, her garden overrun by the surviving Goblins. Her fingers curled into claws on the windowsill as she let out a furious cry.

Rennar, though, didn't seem angered by Countess Quine's death. Instead, he regarded Anouk with something like amazement, and that felt somehow far more dangerous. Goose bumps sprang up from her head to her eight toes.

It crashed down on her then: *a mistake.*

That impulsive burst of anger had saved Beau and won the battle, but it had cost her every drop of Viggo's life-essence.

It felt as though the bones in her legs momentarily vanished, and she had to catch herself on a low wooden beam. A wave of lightheadedness made her see stars. She licked her lips, forcing herself to stand straight. She couldn't let them see how weak it had made her. They had to believe she was still strong enough to carry through with the contra-beastie spell, even though in her hands and her lips, she felt an awful numbness. Her magic was all but gone. And there were no flowers in the bell tower, no butterflies, not even a spider to swallow down.

Zola raked her nails through her hair as she spun away from the window. "Vittora didn't kill your kind soon enough! I won't make that mistake."

Anouk took a shaky step backward. Glanced at the door. Could she make it in time? What about Luc? She couldn't leave him, wrists bound, at the prince's mercy.

Zola raised her hands toward Anouk, but then paused. She saw how Anouk was throwing worried looks at Luc and smiled grimly. She turned toward Luc instead.

Fresh panic thrummed in Anouk's body. *Not Luc!* She bolted around the edge of the bell tower to stop the witch, but she was too weak, too slow. Zola whispered low, and a dark cloud began to surround Luc, crackling and sparking just as it had for Cricket.

Prince Rennar grabbed Anouk's arm and pulled her away from the magic cloud. "Anouk, don't." His voice was quiet in her ear. "Get too close and you'll be caught in the same spell."

But his words felt distant. What did it matter if she sprouted fur or feathers when so many of her friends had already turned?

"Luc!" she cried.

But it was too late. The change had already started. The cloud of sparking light obscured him, but she could make out his limbs shrinking, the twine binding his wrists dropping to the floor. Fine gray fur clouded like smoke around him—the smallest pelt from the oubliette, transported here by magic—and began to weave itself onto his bare arms. She fought against Prince Rennar's grasp, trying to muster enough magic to save Luc, but she was spent. The whispers on her lips had no life behind them.

As soon as the spell was done, Zola cried out, clutching her side. A slash of pain twisted her face. Something had soured in her, just as it had when Lady Metham pushed herself to do the same spell. Maybe her lungs. Maybe her bowels. But not her heart—her heart had turned to stone long ago.

The dark cloud surrounding Luc began to dissipate. Where her friend had been, all six feet of him, there was simply . . . nothing. Confused, she dropped her eyes to the bell-tower floor, and she stifled a cry.

A mouse was left in his place.

First Cricket.

Then Hunter Black.

Now Luc.

And outside, Tenpenny was gone, dozens of Goblins were dead, and Beau—

Anouk glanced out the window, almost afraid to see what might have happened to Beau. Smoke was rising from the smote topiaries. But *there*. Beau was on his hands and knees but moving. *Alive*. He crawled slowly toward the château, one arm streaked with blood.

Despite the pain twisting her features, Zola lurched forward to catch the mouse and stuff it into one of the wire crow cages. "What, no more magic?" She coughed. "Can't you save your friend with all that life-blood you've been bragging about?"

Anouk's gaze fell to the caged mouse. In hours, would she herself be the same? *A dog*, she thought dimly, *or an owl*. There would be no more Anouk. It didn't matter that she'd proven herself to be more than a maid. And her promise to help the Goblins retake London? Worthless. She sank to the floor, her legs like wobbly jam. She felt as weak as Viggo had looked when he was almost drained of blood.

Mada Zola unhooked another of the wire crow cages. "Do you want to do the honors, Rennar, or shall I?" she asked.

Rennar's eyes were flashing again. They held no mercy. A girl in tatters on his floor stirred no pity in him, and yet she wasn't just some helpless girl. He still wore that odd look of curiosity he'd had when she'd cast the spell to stop the battle. Beau's words came back to her: *He's fascinated by you. You have something he lost long ago—youth. Wonder.*

"Yes, I'll handle this," he said simply.

He raised a hand, a gesture as simple as waving away a fly, and cast a spell with a flick of his first two fingers.

Only it wasn't directed at Anouk.

The time she had cast the sleeping spell on Beau, she'd been struck by how instantly it took effect. There had been no yawning, no heavy eyelids, no graceful slump into a chair. No sooner had the whisper left her lips than Beau's head had connected to the floor with an audible crack.

The Mada fell the same way. One moment she was standing, and the next she was lying on her back on the turret floor. No scream. No moan. Just small wisps of dust rising in the air and the vibration from her collapse still traveling through Anouk's ankles. The *thunk* had been heavy enough to cause the crows perched outside to take wing.

The witch's eyes were open. Empty. Her chest did not rise and fall. *Not a sleeping spell this time.*

It was the second time in three days Anouk had seen a dead witch. She'd thought of them as invincible. Next to witches, she had always felt like a fluttery little gnat beside ancient willows—an inconsequential, ephemeral thing. And yet she had outlived both Mada Vittora and Mada Zola. She had mourned the death of the first; the death of the second brought her only a feeling of increasing dread, a tightening hollowness where her pulse should have been, because the crown prince of the Shadow Royals did not take a witch's life and spare hers without a reason.

"Now that it's just the two of us," Prince Rennar said, rolling up his shirtsleeves over sinewy forearms, "I really think you should reconsider my offer."

Chapter 38

THE WITCH'S BODY BLOCKED Anouk's path to the door. There would be no escape; in the time it took for her to move one step, Rennar could send her tumbling to the floor with lifeless eyes just like Mada Zola. A gust of wind blew through the turret windows, carrying notes of lavender and ash.

To be a crow, she thought with a stab of longing. *Able to take wing and fly away.*

But that was impossible too. Even the crows were under Rennar's control.

Rennar clutched at his right leg, wincing. Anouk frowned. She hadn't seen any injury; there had been no bullets or falling objects. But his fingers pressed against his thigh as though something inside were fighting to tear through, and a memory came to her. Once, in a fit of anger, Mada Vittora had used magic to kill a Pretty who'd knocked her over in the street. Almost at once, the vitae echo had doubled back on her, crumpling her body like cardboard, and she'd clutched her side in that same grasping way. Later, Anouk had overheard Luc researching herbs that might reverse a liver turned to clay.

Sweat dripped from Rennar's brow. His breath was coming fast. Slowly, he let go of his leg and straightened, but there was something unnatural to the way he stood now, as though the leg weren't a leg anymore but something heavy and stiff, like stone.

"The vitae echo," she said, realizing what had happened. "Because you took a life."

His only answer was a grimace.

"Why?"

He knelt next to the fallen witch. With a touch of powder on his lips and a whisper, the golden bracelet around Mada Zola's wrist fell to the floor. He picked it up, pooled it in his palm. "Because she isn't the princess I need."

His eyes met hers, and she felt a jolt of dangerous exhilaration.

"You are, Anouk."

She nudged the witch's body with her toe and spat, "No, *merci*, I've seen what you do to your brides."

His lips curved. "Fair enough, but remember that your raw magic is far more powerful than mine. You could kill me ten times over before I'd even get out the first syllable of a whisper. Once you're trained, that is."

Behind him, the caged mouse who had been Luc twitched its whiskers anxiously, its big black eyes fearful. Rennar didn't spare it a glance. Her anger solidified once more. He didn't care about Luc or anyone else but himself.

"Your time is over," she said firmly.

His eyes flashed their dark sheen. "So young you are. The world must seem so clear to you, like black-and-white drawings in a book. I envy that certainty. Don't you think I have asked myself countless times if our time has passed? Each surge of Pretty development, I have watched their ingenuity with respect and thought that, perhaps, at long last, they were ready to stand on their own. And yet each time, I've also been witness to the catastrophic results. Do you know what coincides with each of their advancements?"

She didn't answer, nor did he seem to expect her to.

"*War*. Pretty wars that have nothing to do with us. War between Pretties who have and those who haven't, between those who believe in gods and those who don't, between those who live on the sides of a border they invented. Those wars led to massive deaths, poverty, and inequality that we have been trying to rebalance ever since. But every time we shape a better world for the Pretties, their instinct is to drive it into chaos again. That's their nature. They are like children governed by primal emotions—jealousy, fear, greed. If we didn't control them, they would destroy themselves."

He poured the golden bracelet from palm to palm in a way that made a soft, musical jangle that she found oddly hypnotic—until reason snapped her back to herself.

"The Haute is no better," she spat. "The Goblins live like paupers."

"The witches oversee the Goblins, not I."

"But you command the witches. If you'd ever bother to step out of your penthouse palace, you'd see how unfairly all your lesser creatures are treated. But you care only about maintaining your power."

Abruptly, he stopped toying with the bracelet. "You're right."

It was the last thing she'd expected to hear, and her thoughts hung mid-breath; she sensed that there was a catch.

"As formidable a princess as you'd make, you would also be compassionate, and that is what this world needs. And in return, I'll be whatever you want me to be. The prince from the fairy tales that Pretties tell each other. The prince from those playbills you have pasted to your bedroom walls. I know what you are: a dreamer. I can be a dreamer too." He paused, eyes flashing. "I'm offering you anything you can imagine and more."

He went to the turret window, limping on his right leg, and extended his hand to let the bracelet that had been Zola's shackle fall. Then he came to her, hands open, a bold look in his eyes.

"Say yes. For you and for me. For the Pretties and the Haute."

In that moment, he was once more the boy in the too-big scarf who had stood on her doorstep. Despite all the centuries he had lived, he didn't look much older than her. And maybe that hopeful boy was still in there somewhere, someone not so different from her, caught up in a dangerous world of magic and trying to make right what he could. The arrogant mask he so often wore was slipping now, and beneath it she saw a glimpse of vulnerability. He truly needed her, she realized. He couldn't save his kingdom without her. His eyes were brimming with something that was both soft and wary.

Prince Rennar wasn't so cold after all.

Without warning, a teapot came flying from the direction of the stairs and crashed into the giant bell. She clamped her hands over her ears against the deafeningly loud tolls.

December emerged from the doorway with her golden teeth bared and her yellow braids whipping like serpents. She pulled a pouch from her vest and poured out a shimmery substance, but instead of swallowing it, she blew it into Rennar's face. He coughed, waving it away, and scratched at the places on his arms where the shimmering dust clung to his skin.

"What is this?" he snarled.

"This is a bold and daring rescue, obviously," December cried, and then turned and called to someone, "Now! Release it!"

Two Goblins were in the stairwell—at December's signal, they released something gray that tore out from the stairs, snarling.

Wolf, Anouk thought with a jolt, and then, a half a second later, *Hunter Black!*

A broken chain dangled from the wolf's neck. Anouk felt as though everything was happening too quickly, like time had suddenly sped up. Four strong paws. A snapping jaw. Keen black animal eyes. Tension rippled in the air. The wolf growled low, its hungry gaze going from Anouk to Rennar and back, and she had an awful premonition.

Hunter Black was an animal now. And she was prey.

But then the wolf looked at her—*really* looked at her.

Did a glimmer of him remain beneath that fur? It was impossible, she knew, and yet slowly the wolf's gaze shifted away from Anouk and to the crown prince.

Its lips drew back in a silent snarl.

Still clawing at the mysterious powder on his neck and face, Rennar reacted a second too slowly. He reached for his own powder but the wolf's haunches bunched and it leaped clear across the bell tower. It sank its teeth into Rennar's arm. The prince didn't cry out, didn't flinch. If it weren't for the paleness spreading up his neck, Anouk wouldn't even have known he felt the pain. Rennar dug his fingers into the wolf's neck and tried to wrench it off, but its teeth sank deeper. He couldn't get to his powder. The wolf whipped its head around like it was thrashing a rabbit in its jaws. Any other day,

Rennar might easily have overpowered the wolf, but he wasn't used to the weight of his stone leg. He tripped and fell back against the wall.

Anouk felt the urge to run to the wolf, to help. They were a family and that's what family did. Hunter Black had never been able to fully embrace that fact while human — he was always the solitary assassin, the lone wolf — but in the past few days, she'd seen him change.

December grabbed Anouk's hand. "The wolf won't keep him down for long. Hurry. Out the window."

"The window?" It was a thirty-foot fall. "No! I can't leave him and Luc — the mouse."

Footsteps sounded on the spiral stairs. The two other Goblins drew knives, preparing to hold off the lesser counts and duchesses. The wolf suddenly let out a sharp yip of pain. Rennar had slammed it against the wall. Blood trickled from its left eye. With his free hand, Rennar tore open his vial of powder and swallowed it dry.

"Versik, versik sang . . ."

Anouk stared in horror as blood appeared at the corners of the wolf's mouth like thick crimson drool. Rennar continued to whisper in a controlled voice, pinning the wolf against the wall with all his weight. Life drained out of it in messy wine-colored streaks that stained its beautiful thick fur. The wolf whimpered. Its paws scrambled weakly, uselessly. It gave one final whine.

Anouk couldn't breathe. *No!*

There had to be a trick she could cast . . .

"Leave it!" December dragged her away toward the open window. "It's too late. The wolf is gone."

"No!" Anouk dug in her heels. "We can't!"

"Oh, we can."

December embraced her in a macabre bear hug, pinning her arms so she couldn't fight back, and before Anouk could get another word out, before she could look one last time at Hunter Black dying, the Goblin tipped them both out the window and they were falling, falling into a world that smelled of ash.

Chapter 39

*O*UCH.

For a few breaths, all Anouk could do was stare at the sky and try not to throw up. Waves of pain radiated through her body. She didn't dare move, afraid that she'd discover that her bones had snapped. She could even feel spindly, sharp bones protruding and poking at her legs . . .

Twigs.

She lifted her head and found she wasn't broken at all. She had landed on a pile of branches that had once been a topiary soldier that the Goblins had killed. She sat up, wincing. December was fishing twigs out of her tangled blond braids.

"You shouldn't have done that!" Anouk coughed.

"You're welcome." December brushed leaves off her jacket, pushed herself to her feet, balanced precariously on the pile of hedge clippings, and extended a hand to help Anouk up.

They clambered free of the hedge, and Anouk pitched her head back and looked at the bell tower, hoping for some indication that Hunter Black wasn't dead. But it was awfully, deafeningly silent, and her hopes slipped away. There was no sign of the prince either, but she could feel his presence; it was like knowing you weren't alone in a dark room. He was close. He was coming. Nothing she'd seen so far could stop him, except . . .

"What was that magic dust?" she asked quickly.

December tugged the small bag out of her pocket. "It comes from the Pretty World. I figured the prince wouldn't know what it was and so he'd freak out." She handed Anouk the bag and added, "It isn't magic. We use it for parties."

Anouk squinted at the words on the package. "Glitter?"

December waggled her eyebrows. "It's sparkly."

Voices came from somewhere within the château. Anouk caught a flash of movement behind the curtains of Mada Zola's storerooms. She tossed aside the glitter. Dread built itself around her, stacking up like bricks. All they could do was run.

Movement near the fountain caught her eye. Someone was trying to sit up.

"Beau!"

She and December ran across the garden and crouched next to him. Blood poured from a gash in his shoulder, and his right arm looked unnaturally loose, like it was missing half its bones. A merlot-colored bruise covered his jaw, spreading down the sinews of his neck, as though something had grabbed him by the throat and lifted him clear off the ground.

"I'm okay," he said, though he cringed when he sat up. "At least, I will be. The others?"

She cringed too.

How could she tell him? She could barely hold on to the knowledge herself without shattering like a broken teapot, and then there was the guilt, the awful guilt. *She'd brought them all here. She was responsible.*

"We have to get out of here," she choked out. "Any moment, the lesser Royals are going to throw open those doors and grill us like toast. I've used up all the strength I had from Viggo's blood. We have to run."

"And go where?" he asked.

She paused. "Back to Paris. To Viggo and the townhouse. The spell that protects it is ancient magic, not the kind that dies with a witch. The Royals won't be able to enter. We'll be safe there. The Goblins will too."

"You'll need this." December tugged on one of her brass chains connected to a small pouch. She shook out a vial and pressed it into Anouk's hand. "The antidote to Tenpenny's elixir. You have to drink it before you go from dead-ish to full dead. It will restart your hearts. Slowly—you won't turn back right away. But it can't protect you against midnight."

"And when midnight strikes," Beau said, "without a witch or a Royal to recast the spell . . ." He didn't have to finish.

Anouk handed him the vial. "When that happens—*if* it happens—we'll be together, at home."

He looked as though he might protest again, but then she saw the exhaustion in him. He was hurt. Bleeding. He might be lucky to make it to midnight at all.

He uncorked the vial, drank down a dram, and then handed it to Anouk. It tasted foul—that came as no surprise—and yet it had a subtle, sweet herbal aftertaste that lingered on her lips, making them tingle, and the sensation traveled all the way down her throat.

She pressed a hand to her chest, rubbing life back into her newly awakened heart. "December, spread the word among the Goblins who can still drive. Tell them to carry as many wounded as they can back to Paris and meet us at 18 Rue des Amants. They can take shelter there."

December left to tell the survivors, and in seconds, the first revs of engines began. Anouk rested a hand on Beau's bruised cheek.

"We don't have the Rolls-Royce." He coughed.

"No."

"And my arm . . . I can't steer a motorcycle with only one hand."

"No."

"And you can't drive, and the Goblins are going to be overloaded with the wounded. So what do we do, cabbage? Hot-air balloon?"

She laid a hand on his shirt and smoothed out the wrinkles. "I have a better idea. There's a garage hidden behind the chapel."

He leaned toward her so fast that they almost bumped heads. "Cars?"

She nodded.

"Cabbage, I could kiss you."

"There'll be time for that if we get out of here." She grabbed the lapels of his shirt and pulled him to his feet. His face twisted in a grimace as he hobbled on his left leg, clutching his left arm, which hung too low from his shoulder, the joint protruding unnaturally. Piles of ash billowed columns of smoke that they weaved between, pressing sleeves to their mouths as their eyes burned. Dozens of Goblins rushed in a dizzying mob toward the motorcycles, which roared to life one by one. But it was hard to feel relief for the survivors as they hobbled past dozens more bodies on the lawn, limbs twisted like switches of ivy, and glistening white stone statues of Goblins who had once danced among gravestones beneath the streets of Paris.

She looked up at the bell tower. Empty now.

"What happened to Luc and Cricket and Hunter Black?" Beau coughed out. "It's bad, isn't it?"

She concentrated on the pillars of smoke. On the dirt path to the garage. Anything but those awful animal howls.

"Anouk?"

"Turned." She had to spit the word. "All of them. And Hunter Black . . ." She swallowed back bitter heartache. Ironically—tragically—it hadn't been until he'd become an animal that he'd been his most human. "I don't think he made it."

Beau's feet stopped on their own. A look of surprise passed over his face, and it seemed like he had to force himself to start walking again.

"And we just leave them?"

It pulled at her like tiny little thorns in her skin, scratching her up inside. What would the hero in one of Luc's fairy tales do? Charge back in to save his friends? *This* wasn't a fairy tale. This was a graveyard.

"Rennar put them in cages. If we go back for them now, we'll never get out. But we'll come back for them," she promised. "We'll find a way out of this, I know we will. For us and for them."

Beau didn't remind her that they themselves were only hours away from turning. He didn't have to; it was a noxious, dense cloud over the both of them.

A bolt of light suddenly shot from an upper window. Anouk tugged Beau behind a Goblin statue a second before the bolt shattered against the stone. Dust and pebbles rained over their hair and clothes.

"The lesser Royals." Anouk gasped.

Another ripple of light was lobbed past them, close enough to graze Anouk's arm. She cried out. Heat throbbed in her shoulder.

But when she pressed her palm to the pain, it came back clean. No blood. The metallic threads in the Faustine jacket had deflected the attack.

"Tenpenny was right," she said. "Fashion *is* magic."

Two more flashes of light erupted from the upper windows, shattering the two nearest statues. One after the other, Beau and Anouk darted from shelter to shelter, crouching behind a fountain, then hiding behind the potting shed.

"The garage is just to the left of the chapel," Anouk said, her breath shallow. "We'll have to make a run for it. Are you ready?"

"No. Come on!"

Together they ran across the final exposed stretch of garden between the potting shed and the château. White-hot streaks lit up the grounds like summer lightning. Fountains exploded in spectacular sprays of rubble that clattered on their backs, and for a second she glanced at the château and saw them there, lesser counts and duchesses and baronesses, each one framed in a window, proud and arrogant, like their portraits.

"Anouk, watch out!"

Beau shoved her with his good shoulder as another flash burned the place she'd been a half a second ago. She tumbled to the grass and crawled forward with her heart in her throat until she felt the cool press of stone at her back, the air once more in her lungs.

"There." She indicated a row of garage doors. "That's it."

Beau was already standing on tiptoe and shading his eyes to peer through a window. He made a soft exclamation. *"Ils sont si belle."*

"You're talking about the cars?"

"Well, and you, cabbage."

He pushed open the window and then made a stirrup of his hands to help her up. She climbed ungracefully through on her stomach, swung a leg over, and dropped down into the garage. Beau climbed in behind her, dusting off his hands.

"Which one?" she asked.

In the faint light from the few windows, the cars were like shadowy things from a dream world. His eyes devoured car after car as he ran between them, reverently touching their hoods. "The Aston Martin . . . no, the Bentley . . . *mon Dieu,* is that a Huracán?"

She dragged him to the first car.

"Right," he said. "The Aston Martin it is."

Mercifully, it was unlocked. Beau slid into the driver's seat and, with his good arm, searched for the keys behind the visors. In the passenger side, Anouk checked the glove box.

Beau cursed. "No keys."

"They have to be here somewhere." Anouk rifled again through the glove box, pulling out crumpled receipts and unpaid speeding tickets, and looked under her seat but found only a muddy pair of combat boots.

A knock at the passenger-side window made them both jump.

Petra.

In the dim light, her face looked spectral on the other side of the glass. She dangled a set of silver keys.

Anouk and Beau exchanged a look.

"She could still have the gun," Anouk whispered.

"I can hear you," Petra said, then tapped on the glass again. "These are old '68 pane windows. The glass is not exactly soundproof."

With a held breath, Anouk cranked down the window. "Petra," she said. "If I can just explain—"

"Don't bother." Petra tossed the keys into Anouk's lap. She did it so simply, so effortlessly, that Anouk was left with blankness on her tongue. She'd expected to spend precious minutes they didn't have making desperate bargains, but—

"Take the N Seven along the Rhône," Petra said. "Traffic's awful this time of day on the E Fifteen."

Anouk's thoughts crashed back to her, and she sputtered, "Just like that?"

Petra leaned on the open car window, her eyes hooded. "You put me in a tough place, Anouk. You wanted me to betray my mother for a group of beasties I barely knew. But she's gone now and it's Rennar's fault."

Anouk held up the keys. "So you're helping us escape to get back at Rennar?"

Petra didn't deny it. There was a shadow behind her eyes—she'd lost the person she'd loved most in the world, a particular pain that Anouk knew well. "Revenge is as good a reason as any. And like I said, I like you." She jerked her chin at Beau as Anouk handed him the keys. "Put it in fifth gear on the highway. Purrs like a kitten."

She let go of the car and started to go, but Anouk grabbed her wrist. "Wait. The others."

Petra looked away sharply, and for a second, Anouk saw her mask fall, revealing a well of deep emotion there. "Yeah. I've seen the cages."

"Promise me you'll take care of them."

Petra didn't answer.

"*Promise.*"

Petra's wrist was thin, like Anouk's own, but that didn't mean strength didn't flow through both of them. In the quiet of the garage, Anouk could feel the steady *pulse-pulse-pulse* of the girl's heartbeat.

Petra nodded. "I'll do what I can for them. Now get out of here already."

She tugged on a cord hanging from the ceiling, and the nearest garage door rose. Beau turned the key and the Aston Martin roared to life. He threw it in reverse, then pressed the gas. And then they were tearing out of the garage into the garden. Sparking bolts of white-hot magic hurtled at them from all directions, singeing the hood ornament, cracking against the windshield. As they sped through the dirt path between the lavender fields, Anouk dared one last glance in the side mirror at the château. A figure stood in the bell tower, silhouetted against the fading sun, heavily favoring one leg.

Prince Rennar had survived, which meant that Hunter Black probably hadn't.

He remained perfectly still as he watched them leave, and even long after they were on the highway back to Paris, Anouk felt velvety tapeta eyes on the back of her neck.

Chapter 40

Three Hours of (New) Enchantment Remain

THEY SPOKE LITTLE ON the drive back to Paris. What was there to say, Anouk thought, except *I'm sorry*?

I'm sorry, Hunter Black.

I'm sorry, Cricket.

I'm sorry, Luc, and Tenpenny, and all the Goblins who died.

I'm sorry to you, Beau, and to me—because I can't stop midnight.

That damn black-cat clock was still ticking away on the dashboard, and somewhere around Grenoble, Beau grabbed it with his good hand and threw it out the window. Anouk said nothing. She was glad to see it go. No more clocks. No more ticking. She didn't want to know the countdown to the end. If this was truly it, then she wanted to spend their last night free of the weight of time. She wanted to curl up in an enormous bed full of soft pillows, just Beau and her and Viggo—if Viggo was okay—and drink Mada Vittora's champagne and drape herself in diamonds and kiss Beau and, *oh yes,* kiss Beau. That most of all.

She squeezed the franc-coin necklace, keeping it safe in her fist.

When she'd dropped a coin in the fountain at the end of Rue des Amants, she'd made a wish to keep them safe. Had the coin worked? Or had it been her whisper in the closet that had protected them? Or perhaps simply luck?

But a coin was all she had now.

She leaned forward, looked up through the windshield at the moon.

"We're almost there," Beau said, as though reading her worries. "We'll make it before midnight."

They entered the city, and Paris didn't disappoint. The clouds had lifted, and the night was velvety black and beautiful. The more she saw of Paris, the more dreamlike it was; she wasn't sure where the streetlights ended and the stars began. She leaned her head against the cool window, watching the blocks roll by one by one. Cafés and boutiques. Pharmacies and patisseries. And above the shops, lights were on in apartments where families watched television, and couples snuggled on sofas, and mothers taught their daughters to cook coq au vin.

She pressed the pads of her fingers to the glass, wanting to touch the city, to taste it, to know all there was to know about everything in the world.

They passed a church with a spotlighted spire that drew her eye up, up, to the very top, where a clock presided over the streets.

She jerked upright abruptly: She couldn't help but see the time.

"Beau. It's ten minutes to midnight."

The Aston Martin purred beneath them as he whipped around corners, dodging other cars with an easy grace. And then the houses were more familiar; she recognized that gabled rooftop. That dented mailbox. They were on Rue des Amants.

Beau started to park and Anouk was out of the car before they'd even fully stopped. She ran around to his door, threw it open, and tugged him out, away from the house and toward the far end of the lane.

"Where are you going?"

With her other hand, she clutched her franc necklace. "The fountain."

An odd look crossed his face, and then his eyes fell to the coin and a kind of heartbroken sadness filled them as he realized what she hoped—foolishly—to do. "Anouk . . ."

"It might work, Beau."

"It might not."

"But it *might*."

The street lamp threw a halo of light over his face. A face she knew nearly as well as her own—full lips that were like heaven to touch, his almost too-big nose, sandy hair that had a way of curling in the damp. His features were heavy with doubt. But then, little by little, the doubt melted away. Before her eyes, he became just a boy again.

He grinned. "All right. Screw it. Let's make a wish."

Hand in hand, they ran for the wishing fountain at the end of the lane. Past the townhouses Anouk had stared at dreamily through the windows. Past a tiny bulldog with big ears and an even bigger bark. Their feet skidded as they ducked into the fountain alleyway.

It was darker here, away from the streetlights.

Blue-black shadows encased the fountain; starlight reflected on the tinkling water. The gargoyle spat water into the pool, that mischievous half smile on his face, the one that had once repulsed her but now filled her with affection.

She pulled the necklace over her head. How much time was left? Three minutes? Two?

"Just one coin," Beau said. "So it'll work for only one of us."

"I know," she breathed. "It's for you. You're going to stay human."

Even in the shadows, she could see his expression harden. He reached for the coin, though she held it just out of reach. "No. Anouk, *no*. It's going to be you."

She scrambled back, fiercely guarding the coin. "Forget it, Beau. I couldn't save the others but maybe I can save you."

She extended her arm over the pool, the coin clutched in her hand, but he grabbed her around the waist and pulled her away from the water. *Let him try to stop her.* She'd throw herself into the fountain if she had to. His breath brushed her neck as they scuffled. His arm pressed into her ribs.

He was reaching, but not for the coin.

His fingers closed around one of the few roses still in bloom that hugged the edge of the fountain, and before she could grasp what he was about to do, he popped it into his mouth.

"I know only one spell," he breathed. "But right now it's the only one I need."

An awful premonition struck her. "Beau, no —"

"*Dorma, dorma, sonora precimo.*" For the first time, his pronunciation was perfect. It was quiet. It was powerful. He'd mastered the damn sleeping spell in the one single moment when she *wanted* him to make a mistake.

Blackness came first, crackling like ash.

Then a feeling of falling.

His arms around her, lowering her to the ground, and the smell of roses on his breath.

Lips pressed to her cheek.

And then she heard it — a splash of a coin — followed by the most awful words in the world.

"I wish for Anouk to stay human forever."

In the distance, bells rang out from the church they'd passed on the corner, each chime impossibly loud, impossibly heavy, as though the bells were weighed down by devils.

Bong.

Bong.

Bong.

And then more bells came from more churches on different blocks, tolls that broke the beautiful night with crashing, gnashing, deafening sounds. Twelve chimes. Even long after the bells had stopped, their vibrations traveled throughout the city, straight into the little alley at the far end of Rue des Amants.

Midnight had come at last.

Chapter 41

Time Over

WHEN ANOUK WOKE, THE moon shone bright enough to burn her eyes.

She rolled over, woozy and foggy-headed, to find ivy crumpling beneath her hands. She heard the sounds of trickling water and felt cool night air. Crushed bits of dry leaves clung to her face. For a moment, nothing made sense. Her memory was like an unfinished jigsaw puzzle, missing more pieces than it contained. The fountain . . . a car . . .

Then the impossible happened.

The moon turned *off.*

She blinked in the bizarre sudden darkness, and then her eyes adjusted and she slowly came to make out two people standing in front of her: a young black couple with blue jeans and white sneakers. Americans. The man held a phone to his ear, but when he saw she was awake, he swung it back toward her and shone that bright light again that she'd mistaken for the moon.

They said something in English, but to Anouk's ears it sounded like clunky gibberish.

"What time is it?" she rasped, pressing a hand to her dry throat.

But they shook their heads, not understanding her French, and she tapped on her wrist to indicate her question. The man turned his phone around and showed her the time backlit on the screen: 12:59 a.m.

The woman's gaze shifted to something behind Anouk, and her face suddenly broke in a smile. She crouched down, making a sound like she was calling to an animal. Anouk pressed a hand to her head. She was at the fountain near the townhouse. The cute spitting gargoyle. She'd had a coin, she'd come here with Beau, and . . .

Beau.

She sat up, remembering everything with a rush of panic.

The American woman made that inviting noise again. A shadow came out from the corner, a shadow that changed in the phone's light to two big brown eyes and a wagging tail and sandy-brown fur. It inched forward at the girl's beckoning motion but stopped a few feet away, hesitant and wary.

Anouk found herself staring dumbly at the creature.

Dog.

A dog.

She collapsed backward, her palms scraping on the bricks, but she felt only numbness. The fountain kept tinkling, and the sound was all she could cling to to keep her mind from slipping away.

"Is he yours?"

Another girl, a French teenager in a waitress uniform, had joined the Americans and was peering at her strangely. The girl pointed to the dog.

"Is he yours?" she repeated.

Anouk grabbed for the dog, some instinct making her pull it close and wrap her arms around it fiercely.

"Yes," she said. "He's mine."

Her voice was wild enough that the American couple exchanged a look and then stepped back. The man's phone rang and they used the excuse to walk away at a fast clip. But the French girl knelt down and pressed something cool into Anouk's hand.

"For luck," the girl said. "I was going to throw it in myself, but it looks like you need it more than me."

The girl left, and Anouk stared at the glistening franc in her palm. Still clutching the dog by the scruff of its neck, terrified of letting go, she crawled to the fountain as fast as she could and threw in the coin. It bounced off the gargoyle and plinked into the water.

"For Beau to be human again," she whispered in a rush. "For Beau to be Beau."

She squeezed her eyes closed.

She wished harder than she had ever wished in her life. She wished to see his smile again, to run her fingers through his hair. But the fur beneath her hand didn't change to skin. The breath on her face still smelled of dog. She squeezed her eyes shut harder, wishing and wishing and wishing, but when she at last opened her eyes, the dog was still a dog.

The Pretty girl's coin wasn't magic. It was just an old coin. Besides, it was past midnight. Even if it had been enchanted, it wouldn't have been strong enough to combat the unstoppable force of time.

She sank back onto the bricks, pressed her face into her hands.

If only I hadn't taught him that spell. A wet nose nudged her cheek.

She pulled the dog close and buried her face in its fur, tasting the saltiness of her own tears. She cried because crying was all that was left. But tears could last only so long, even ones as powerful as these.

Finally she sank back on her heels, wiped her sleeve over her face, and did all she could think to do.

"Come on," she said to the dog. "Let's go home."

It wasn't until she had climbed the steps of the townhouse and put her hand on the knob that a thought struck Anouk. She stopped moving.

Cricket was the cat.

Luc was the mouse.

Hunter Black was the wolf.

Beau was the dog.

That left only one pelt. The one that wasn't fur like the others but had long wings and downy feathers over a snow-white body.

The first time they'd seen the pelts, she'd told herself she wasn't curious to know which was hers. That it didn't matter. Cat or mouse or whatever, they were all just animals. She hadn't let herself try to guess the truth in her gestures or reflection in the mirror. But now she knew.

I was an owl.

The truth didn't hurt like she'd thought it would. There was no hot sting of shame. Rather, she felt the opposite. Warmth spread through her freshly beating heart, filling the place where the dark, cold thing had always been. Maybe it hadn't been dark at all. Maybe she just hadn't ever bothered to pull back the curtains and consider it in the right light.

Something rose in her, a sensation beneath her breastbone, like flying. Maybe that was why she was so drawn to the jacket with the gargoyle embroidery—because of the wings and the talons. She had recognized a piece of herself in it even before she knew what she was. Its threads had reminded her of the life she'd once led. She wasn't an owl now, not anymore. But was she really a human?

Maybe not entirely. Maybe she didn't have to be. She could be something both pretty and ugly. Light and dark.

Human and not.

She pushed open the townhouse door.

The dog nudged its way in beside her, wagging its tail as its nails clickety-clacked on the marble floors. She took her time—after all, time had ceased to be her enemy—and listened to the thunk of her shoes on Mada Vittora's marble floors.

Only it wasn't Mada Vittora's house now. It belonged to—

"*Viggo.*" She gasped.

She tore up the stairs.

Fears struck her like the tolling of a clock—that she'd push open the bedroom door to find his eyes closed, his face pale, his body cold. That she'd taken too much blood, and for what? Her plan hadn't even worked.

The dog padded up the stairs behind her, excited by her hurry without understanding why.

She rested a hand on the bedroom door, hesitating. Afraid Viggo was dead. Afraid he *wasn't,* because then she'd have to explain to him what had happened to the others, especially Hunter Black.

"Viggo?"

She entered the bedroom with her heart in her throat. His eyes were closed, just like in her nightmares. His face was pale. She pressed a hand to her mouth to stifle a cry.

Not him too.

She didn't want to be alone. Didn't want the townhouse to herself, all the food in the kitchen, the empty rooms and empty halls. She'd put on an apron again and scrub every last crumb from the floor if it would bring her friends back.

She sank onto the bed. "Oh, Viggo. Oh no."

With a jerk, he sucked in a breath and let out a rasping snore.

She reached for him so fast that she accidentally slapped him. His eyes shot open as he swatted away her hand. "What? Who?"

"Viggo!"

She collapsed on him. She didn't mind the slouchy knit hat that scratched her skin or how he smelled like stale brandy. She squeezed him hard.

"Can't . . . breathe . . ."

"Oh."

She sat up, biting her lip, unable to hide her grin. "I thought you were dead!"

"I almost was. You nearly strangled me."

The dog jumped on the bed, all nuzzling wet nose and big brown eyes. Viggo blinked a few times. "What," he said, "is *that?* And where is everyone?"

Anouk felt the blood drain from her face. She looked away.

Slowly, in halting words, she told him what had happened. The siege of the château, the wooden soldiers, Tenpenny turned to stone, Cricket and Luc changed back into animals. And, of course, Hunter Black too.

To her surprise, when she told him the worst of it, he pulled her into a hug.

"They're still alive," he whispered fiercely in her ear. "Cricket and

Luc, and maybe even Hunter Black. Which means we can turn them back somehow. It isn't over, not while the two of us are still breathing."

She didn't know what to say. Viggo hadn't shown much backbone in his pampered life, but these three days had changed him, just as they had changed her.

"How?" she asked.

He brushed at her lipstick-heart-stained cheek. "You'll find a way. You have so far. And I'll be there to cause convenient distractions when you need them most."

She smiled, but it faded quickly. "There's something else. I told the rest of the Goblins they could come here to tend to their wounded. They're on their way now. Don't be surprised if the house starts to sound like the inside of a discotheque and you find pet rats crawling around."

She scrubbed a hand over her face and realized she was still covered in blood, sweat, ash, Tenpenny's makeup, and even a few errant pieces of glitter. It really did stick to everything.

"I need a shower."

"Use the Mada's bathtub. This townhouse is yours now as much as it's mine. Move your things from your room to the master bedroom, if you like. You've earned a proper en suite."

The dog jumped off the bed when she stood and followed her into the hall. She found herself looking at the house with new eyes. Those cobwebs that had sprung up in the corners? Let them stay. The paw prints on the hardwood floor? Not her problem. The Goblins would make a mess of everything anyway, and let them. It was time things loosened up around the townhouse.

Once in her room, she freed her messy hair from its ponytail and ran her fingers through the tangles. Kicked off her boots one at a time. Peeled off her dirty tuxedo trousers and tossed them onto the floor. Shrugged off her Faustine jacket, brushing a finger over the place where its metallic threads had deflected magic.

And then she carried the jacket downstairs to the Mada's bedroom.

The plush rug tickled her bare feet, and she wiggled her eight toes in the luxurious fibers. The dog plodded straight for the grand master bathroom.

She followed it in, sat on the edge of the tub, and turned on the hot water. Steam rose, easing her muscles. She peeled off the rest of her clothes and then sank into the tub, sucking in a breath at the almost-painful pleasure of the hot bath. Glass bottles of bath salts lined the edge of the tub.

Gardenia. Rosewater. Lavender.

She kicked over the lavender bottle, letting it clatter to the floor. She never wanted to smell lavender again as long as she lived. She chose another, and the scent of gardenia filled the room as she leaned back in the tub, sinking deep until the water tickled her chin.

The dog lay down next to the bathtub, resting its head on its paws.

She closed her eyes and sank even lower, holding her breath, letting the water cover her head. She felt her hair fan out around her like a mermaid's. Like a selka's. What was she going to do now? She didn't even know if Hunter Black was alive. Cricket and Luc were imprisoned by Rennar. He'd take them back to Castle Ides and lock them in those awful cages. He had to know that she'd come for them. They were literally bait.

Would his offer still stand?

If she climbed out of this bath, dressed in Mada Vittora's finest black suit, took a car across town, and rode the elevator up to the penthouse of Castle Ides, would he still agree to the trade he had promised—that if she was his bride, he'd turn her friends back into humans?

It was an intriguing offer. It was also her *only* offer.

And yet she could imagine, like the winding tunnels of the catacombs, where that path would lead. He'd uphold his promise and turn them human—but at a heavy cost. His little monsters. And she would share his table, have a throne by his side, a place in his bed. Bound to him eternally. Princess of a kingdom she loathed.

Underwater, she blew out her breath in a flurry of bubbles, eyes squeezed shut.

The smell of gardenia permeated the water, smoothing over her skin, weaving into her hair. It made her think of Luc and his herbs. There was a lot of life-essence up there in the attic, all of it perfectly cataloged. Even more than in Mada Zola's storeroom. Even more than she'd seen in Castle Ides.

She sat up abruptly, water streaming down her face.

The dog gave her a curious look.

The Faustine jacket lay by the edge of the tub, and she grabbed it and rubbed the fabric between her fingers.

Every witch had two things: a moniker and an oubliette.

She reached into the jacket pockets where she'd stored so many treasures. The coin. The knife. The clock. With the right spell, could these pockets fill the role of an oubliette?

She knew a little of how witches became witches. They started as

373

Pretty girls, as humans, just like her—more or less. There were training academies deep in the Bavarian forests where the girls learned through trials how to call forth and command magic. The girls who survived the initiation ceased to be Pretties and became witches. Capable of performing any spell, even the most complex one she knew of: the beastie spell.

Her fingers curled around the edges of the tub.

She wouldn't stay in the townhouse and drink champagne and sleep in a big bed, not as long as her friends were in cages.

But maybe she wouldn't go to Castle Ides, either.

Maybe—though it was such a dangerous idea, she only dared to whisper it to herself—she would go to a castle in the woods, a place of snow and smoke, a house of girls who all wanted the same thing she wanted and who would kill to get it, and maybe she'd kill too if she had to, and she'd return and find her friends and she'd turn them human again with her own voice.

She leaned over the edge of the tub, looked down at the dog. "Little Beau," she said, toes splashing in the bathwater. "Can I tell you a secret?"

But the words hung unspoken on her lips. She didn't dare even tell the dog. Witches were the enemy. How could she consider becoming the enemy? Cricket—if Cricket were still herself—would kill her for even thinking it.

She sank into the water one more time, submerged in gardenia and bath salts. Once an owl. A maid. A servant. *A little dust mop.* But maybe she could be more.

She had the jacket, an oubliette.

Now she just needed a moniker.

Mada Vittora had been the Diamond Witch.

Mada Zola, the Lavender Witch.

But she was something with talons and wings and magic, something both beautiful and ugly, something gifted and cursed.

"Anouk," she whispered in silent bubbles beneath the perfumed water, a whisper just for her, full of great danger and even greater hope. "The Gargoyle Witch."

Acknowledgments

This book began like many of my others did—with me pestering Carrie Ryan and Megan Miranda to tell me what book I should write next. Of all my ideas, this was the one they leaped on, and for that I am grateful. I never knew I'd have so much fun writing about a maid who might (or might not) have started life with a tail.

As always, big thanks to Josh Adams at Adams Literary for finding the perfect home for Anouk's story. To Cat Onder, Gabriella Abbate, Sarah Landis, Helen Seachrist, Cara Llewellyn, Samantha Bertschmann, Veronica Wasserman, Tara Shanahan, Tara Sonin, and everyone at Houghton Mifflin Harcourt, thank you for your passion, your enthusiasm, and your grace during the sometimes-unpredictable publishing journey. I knew I adored your team when you served champagne and French pastries at the office meet-and-greet. *Merci!*

I'm massively grateful to everyone who helped me get the details right: Victor Dixen, Rishi Chopra, and Ashley Lauren Rogers. This story is much stronger for your knowledge and keen eyes. Special thanks to April Tucholke for her encouragement, and to Courtney Stevens, whose tarot readings helped me find the heart of the story.

Finally, thank you to my friends, family, and to my true lovelies: my readers across the world. *Ne cessez jamais de rêver de plus beaux lendemains.*

Turn the page for a sneak peek at the conclusion
to the Grim Lovelies duology,

MIDNIGHT BEAUTIES

Chapter 1

❧

THERE WAS BLOOD EVERYWHERE, even in her hair.

Anouk tripped through fallen leaves in gold-studded Goblin boots two sizes too small, the laces undone, the novelty tread leaving bloodstained prints in the smeared shape of hearts. Her leather shorts were ripped. Her velvet jacket was punctured once in the sleeve and twice near her ribs. Blood oozed down her side.

The birds were right behind her.

One crow swept down from a lamppost in a flurry of black wings, going for her ear. Its beak sliced her cheek. She swatted at it, but its talons snagged in her hair or, rather, in the blue wig she wore. The wig slid forward over her eyes, blinding her. She pulled it off and threw it — tangled crow and all — into a sewer grate and raced ahead.

Toward 18 Rue des Amants.

The former residence of a witch, the townhouse was now hers. Her home. Her haven. Or, since Prince Rennar had set his winged spies on her, more like her prison. Her hair had become a sweaty mess beneath the wig, clinging to her neck and face. Another crow launched itself at her back. Talons ripped at her clothes. She grabbed the railing to the stairs. *Just a few more steps.* The Goblins were inside, faces pressed against the townhouse windows, motioning for her to hurry.

A crow landed on her shoulder, its talons piercing through the velvet jacket. Pain exploded in her arm. She faltered on the steps. She would have used a spell against it, except that her bag of ingredients was the first thing the crows had gone for, knowing that without it, she was no more powerful than the Pretty tourists strolling down the street, magically oblivious to Anouk's distress.

Gasping, she grabbed the crow by its wing and yanked with all her strength.

"Let *go!*"

She hurled the crow against the steps and, before it could take wing again, yanked open the townhouse's front door, threw herself inside, and slammed it closed behind her.

She collapsed against the door, breathing hard.

The townhouse was protected with a spell so ancient that it hadn't been broken at Mada Vittora's death, unlike most of her other enchantments. It was the only thing keeping Rennar and his crows out, which unfortunately meant that to be safe, Anouk had to stay *in*. Over the past six weeks, she and Viggo and the two dozen Goblins who had survived the siege of Montélimar might as well have been prisoners. The first time she'd tried to leave was two days after the siege; she'd needed baguettes to feed the hungry Goblins. The crows had been waiting in the trees. They attacked her as soon as she crossed the first step. She'd barely made it back inside in one piece.

The second time she'd tried to leave, she waited until night fell, when it was foggy and hard to see more than three feet on either side. That time she made it ten steps before they spotted her. They would have dug in their talons and dragged her all the way to Castle Ides if

Viggo hadn't hurled an empty gin bottle at them and pulled Anouk back inside.

The third time, she'd brought knives. Many, many knives, hidden in pockets and strapped to her belt. But the crows were fast enough to dodge them, their own talons just as sharp.

Today, though, she'd thought she stood a chance, thought that the Goblin disguise—the blue wig, the punk boots, and the velvet jacket—would be enough to conceal her identity from the birds. They were merely Rennar's pawns, after all, just dull-witted spies.

But they'd still known.

She'd made it only five steps this time.

The sound of a *tap-tap-tap* came from the foyer. She opened her eyes. Viggo stood in the hallway. He leaned heavily on a cane. His face was pale. It was a wonder he'd survived at all after losing six pints of blood, but he was tougher than his black eyeliner and slouchy hat made him look. He'd nearly recovered in the six weeks since the siege.

"I take it the disguise didn't fool them," he said.

She slid him a frigid glare.

Blood rolled down her fishnet tights, over her studded boots, and onto the floor. Her tawny hair was knotted. A few blue strands from the ripped wig still clung to the buttons of her jacket. The wounds in her side throbbed. She straightened and took a lurching step forward. Her legs gave out and she started to collapse, but Viggo dropped his cane and grabbed her around the waist.

"Help me to the kitchen," she said, grimacing.

Together they hobbled through the townhouse's grand hallways. They passed the library and the salon, which were littered with signs of her guests—spilled tea, threadbare hats. Goblins peered at her through doorways, their stomachs audibly growling, their faces full of false smiles as they tried to hide their disappointment that she'd failed once again. She narrowly avoided tripping over a butterfly net as Viggo helped her into the kitchen, where she'd spent so many early mornings baking bread and so many late nights scrubbing dishes. She grabbed a dish towel, turned on the hot water, and plunged her hands into the sink. Steam rose around her. She scrubbed the blood and feathers from her arms, revealing fresh wounds and old wounds —now crude scars—from her previous attempts to leave the townhouse.

"Shall I bandage those for you?" Viggo asked, pulling out a roll of gauze from a drawer.

"No, I'll take care of it myself. Just hand me that mint."

He held out the potted mint plant and she crushed a few leaves between her fingers, then swallowed them whole. She ripped off a strand of fake blue hair that was caught in her buttons, laid it over the wound on her left arm, and whispered, *"Attash betit truk."*

Warm magic prickled over her skin in a way that was half pleasant, half unbearably itchy. The sides of the cut started to pull together as the strand of blue hair plunged in and out of her skin, stitching the wound closed. *Attash betit truk* was a spell for fixing loose buttons, not mending flesh, but true healing spells required stronger magic than Anouk was capable of. When she finished, the wound was ugly but it had stopped bleeding. She peeled off her shirt and performed the same spell with the puncture wound on her shoulder. Viggo hobbled upstairs and came back with one of Mada Vittora's robes. It was made of charmeuse silk and worth a small fortune. But what use did a dead witch have for couture?

Anouk pulled on the robe.

She boiled water for a cup of tea to settle her nerves. Not that it would help. Her hands kept shaking. Her stomach growled. She caught her reflection in the curved copper kettle. Goodness, she looked a fright. December had painted full Goblin makeup on her: glittering gold eyeliner, pale pink hearts on her cheeks, black lipstick. Now the blush was smeared and there was glitter everywhere. She scrubbed her face in the sink, then pulled her tangled hair into a ponytail, and she felt a little more like herself.

Viggo stood awkwardly at her side. "We'll try again tomorrow. It's supposed to storm. If it rains hard enough, maybe the birds won't come."

"Rain's never kept them away before." She leaned on the counter and closed her eyes. It had been six weeks of trying to divide every last morsel of stale bread twenty-five ways. Six weeks of living with Goblins who blared the Clash at full volume at first light of dawn. Six weeks of hunger. Six weeks of crows.

Six weeks of a dog by her side instead of Beau.

There had been five of them—five beasties. An owl, a dog, a cat, a mouse, and a wolf, all of whom had been enchanted into people with their own quirks: Anouk, Beau, Cricket, Luc, and Hunter Black. Now only Anouk remained human. The others were cursed to live in their animal forms, and all of them except for Beau were imprisoned in Castle Ides.

She'd tried everything to help them. After the siege of Montélimar, she decided to go to the academy in the Black Forest of Bavaria known as the Cottage where a girl could train in magic and, if she worked hard, possibly transform herself into a witch. She'd be powerful enough to turn Beau and Cricket and Luc and Hunter Black— assuming he was even still alive—human again. Even Prince Rennar would have no choice but to bow before her.

She'd studied maps of Bavaria. She'd learned a smattering of German. She'd squirreled away valuables to trade for money to buy passage. But her weeks of preparation meant nothing if she couldn't get past the front steps.

She sank onto a wooden stool and buried her head in her hands. A cloud of dust rose around her. The kitchen, like everything else, was a disaster. Crumbs everywhere, pantry shelves bare, dirty dishes stacked in moldering piles, blue eye shadow streaked on the stove. (She hadn't bothered to ask about that one.) She felt like the only adult in a houseful of children, never mind that she'd been human for only one year and the Goblins had lived centuries. It was no longer her job to clean, and yet she often found herself with a rag in her hand brushing crumbs into the wastebasket. Frustrating as the Goblins could be, they had no other place to go. They'd been lucky to make it back to the townhouse at all. Not everyone had. The memory of Tenpenny transformed into stone, then exploded into dust, flashed darkly in her mind.

She heard a clicking on the tile, and then a wet snout pushed into her knee. She blinked at the big brown eyes studying her. The dog had tracked in mud and left dirty paw prints all over the kitchen floor. She sighed as she scratched him behind his ears. "You know,

Little Beau, when you were a boy, you were much tidier. Well, not really, but let's pretend."

When Beau was human, his eyes had been blue. There was nothing of the dog to make her think of her friend, except perhaps the way he cocked his head as though he were trying to figure out her thoughts. What would he see now tumbling around in her brain?

The dog licked her nose.

She sighed and looked at Viggo. "We can't go on like this, Viggo. Look at Beau! And Cricket and Luc and . . . and Hunter Black. They're depending on me." Viggo's face paled at the mention of Hunter Black. Last they had seen of him, he'd been in wolf form, bleeding out and left for dead. Anouk looked toward the bare pantry. "Not to mention we're going to starve if we stay here."

Viggo gazed into the pantry wistfully. "I tried ordering a pizza. It never came. Rennar must have even gotten to the delivery boys."

An odd-sounding thump that startled Anouk came from outside the front door. It was heavier than the usual crisp tap of the knocker. Little Beau growled and ran out of the kitchen, barking at the door.

December, the closest thing the Goblins had to a leader since Tenpenny had died, called from the foyer, "Um, Anouk? You might want to see this."

Viggo shifted his cane to his other hand. "Are we expecting visitors?"

"Of course not." Anouk wiped at a smear of blood on the robe's sash. "Everyone we know is either captured or dead."

The dog barked louder. Viggo and Anouk exchanged a look, then Anouk pushed up from the stool and cautiously entered the foyer. A dozen Goblins were at the front window, faces pressed to the glass. The house seemed suddenly very quiet, and Anouk realized that whatever was happening outside was serious enough that the Goblins had shut off the music. And they never turned off the Clash.

December turned away from the window and bit her blue-tinted lips in worry. Anouk's pulse raced. She swallowed her own trepidation and approached the door. The cane stopped thumping as Viggo reached the foyer and joined her.

Anouk pressed her eye to the peephole.

Behind her, Viggo said, "I'm guessing it isn't the pizza."

Read on for a peek at how it all began in the prequel novella

Tricks and Whispers

Chapter 1

❧

CRICKET CLIMBED ONTO A stool and slid a crumpled bill across the bar. "Another one, Gigi."

The bartender wore a pinstriped dress that hugged her youthful curves, though the lines around her mouth hinted at the decades—maybe even centuries—that she'd worked behind the bar. She disappeared into a back room and returned with a martini glass full of glittering pink crystals. She set it in front of Cricket with a wry smile.

"Try this. On the house. For one of my favorite customers." Gigi gave her a wink and pointedly didn't take Cricket's money before turning back to tidy the jars of candy lined up behind the bar.

Cricket eyed the pink crystals suspiciously. Red licorice was her usual order. Chocolate if she was feeling reckless. She'd been coming to Candy Bar every Friday night all winter. She'd first stumbled across it on a blustery November night after she'd finished a job for Mada Vittora. She'd had orders to steal a wristwatch from a wealthy Pretty, and it had meant hours waiting outside his apartment in the cold. The *fichu* cold. Wintry temperatures made her nose chapped and turned her heart into a nasty block of ice. As soon as she'd stolen the watch, she'd stumbled into the first warm doorway she saw, a

1

tiny jewel of a bar in Paris's Latin Quarter squeezed between a youth hostel and a flower shop. It had a Lucite counter, a row of velvet-topped stools, and cozy candlelit seating by the windows, and behind the bar, instead of alcohol, there were vintage glass jars of chocolates and caramels, fruit gummies and sugared nuts. She'd been dazzled at first sight. One look at the bartender's nearly imperceptibly pointed ears, and Cricket had smirked knowingly: a Goblin. Over time, she'd learned that Gigi was one of the most infamous Goblins in Paris, in hiding from the Haute after stealing Royal recipes, which made the transgression of Cricket's secret visits to Candy Bar all the more delectable.

Now Cricket dragged a black-painted fingernail through the pink crystals. "What do you call this?"

The Goblin's eyes glittered. "Pop Rocks."

Cricket grunted, still wary.

Gigi flicked a bar towel at her. "You're such a suspicious creature! You need to trust someone for once, *ma fille*. Try it. You'll see." She winked again, then whispered, and her eyes changed color from green to the same pink as the crystal candy. She went to attend to another customer, a Pretty girl reading a book at the far end of the counter who was oblivious to the magic the Goblin had just performed.

Cricket carefully looked around at the other patrons. Once she was satisfied that no one was watching, she felt underneath her stool and found a piece of paper fastened there with a wad of gum. She grimaced. What did Luc have against glue? Or tape?

She freed the note, wiped her sticky fingers on her pants, then unfolded the paper in her lap.

Male, university student,
black rowing jersey,
La Fourchette Restaurant @ six o'clock

Cricket scanned the bar again—Gigi was cleaning up leftover bonbons and the Pretty girl hadn't taken her eyes off her book. Cricket refolded Luc's note and slipped it into her boot. An athlete. Athletes were difficult marks. Fast, strong, cocky. Maybe she'd be lucky and this one would be drunk, passed out in an alley, and it'd be easy to relieve him of the object.

She checked her phone. It was almost six o'clock. La Fourchette was a block away, down an alley. She could ambush him there, but the thought of waiting even a few minutes in the frigid cold made her shudder. That particular alley had a dead end, meaning he'd have to pass by Candy Bar to get wherever he intended to go. She spun around on her velvet-topped stool, eyed the window. For a frigid mid-February evening, the neighborhood was busy. Couples arm in arm. Romantic music drifting out of the restaurants. Women selling long-stemmed roses on the street corners.

"Come on," Cricket whispered under her breath, flexing her hands.

When her mark still hadn't shown after a few minutes, she anxiously licked a finger and dragged it through the crystals. She popped her finger in her mouth, her eyes never leaving the window. She tasted a burst of cherry and then—*pop!*—a miniature explosion went off. She let out a yelp and clapped a hand over her lips. Her whole mouth was sparkling.

Gigi shot her a devilish grin from the end of the bar. "Good, right?"

Cricket slowly moved her hand away from her mouth. "Amazing."

Her gaze drifted to the window again; she was still dazzled, so it took her a moment to focus on the figure passing by Candy Bar. A young man. Black jersey, number 10 on the back.

"Merde!" She almost fell off the stool. She shoved her phone in her pocket, threw money on the bar, and dashed out into the cold. She scanned the crowds in the street until she saw the black jersey again. He was walking fast, hands in his jeans pockets, hunched against the cold.

She trailed a couple of girls who were walking a few paces behind the boy. He paused at a traffic signal and looked both ways before crossing, so she got a clear view of his face. She raised an eyebrow. Luc hadn't bothered to mention in the note that the boy in the black jersey was *gorgeous*. Skin a few shades darker than her own, soft eyes, generous lips, and the kind of wide shoulders and narrow hips that made half the girls on the street give him a second glance.

A street vendor suddenly shoved a dozen roses in Cricket's face. "Buy one for your valentine, *ma chère*."

Cricket scowled and swatted the woman away, only to have her path blocked by a gaggle of girls wearing pink sweaters. Had the whole city gone mad? Drunk some of Mada Vittora's love potion? She ducked around the flower vendor and managed to shove her way between the girls in pink. She searched the street. No sign of the boy.

She fell back against the nearest building. She had to find him. Mada Vittora didn't tolerate failure. Cricket looked down at her hands, wincing. Her fingertips still hadn't fully healed. Three weeks ago, Mada Vittora had burned off her fingerprints as punishment for not immediately handing over a stolen book.

Next time you fail me, Mada Vittora had said, *you'll lose more than fingerprints. You'll lose entire fingers and toes. Hands and feet. You'll lose every inch of that human skin covering your pretty bones. I'll unmake you back into the clawed thing you crawled into this world as.*

This was the first job since that disastrous one. This was Cricket's chance to prove her loyalty; if she didn't, she'd be turned back into one of those five pelts the witch kept locked in her closet.

Determined, she scaled the base of the nearest building's columns until she stood a few feet above the crowd. The street was packed with couples and groups of students. She'd never find him. She jumped down from the building. *Think.* He was a university student. A rower. Most of the cheap student housing was in the fifth arrondissement, so there was a good chance he was going there. She rejoined the crowd and doubled back in the direction of Candy Bar, where she could take side-street shortcuts to beat him there.

She was passing by an Italian restaurant, momentarily distracted by the couples inside dining over flickering candles, when someone shoved a bouquet of roses in her face again. She growled, twisted toward the flower vendor, and froze. It wasn't the vendor. It was her mark. Before she could react, his eyes met hers. He pressed the bouquet closer and she realized he was using it to hide a knife he had against her side.

Her blood went cold.

How fast could she reach for her own knife?

"Keep walking," the boy said quietly. "The alley ahead."

He nudged her with the hand holding the bouquet. Cricket's pulse raced. Into a dark alley with a boy his size? A boy with a knife? One who was smart enough to know she was following him and then double-back on her?

She made her way to the alley, where he motioned for her to stand by the back door of a restaurant. He kept the bouquet in one hand, shielding the knife from anyone else's view.

"Give me the ring," he said, "and we won't have any problems."

She narrowed her eyes in surprise. "The ring?"

"Don't play dumb. You know what I'm talking about. Prince Rennar's ring."

"Oh, I know the ring," she said slowly, buying time as a million questions ran through her head. But in the end she couldn't think of anything to say but the truth, and she sputtered, "*You* have it. I was given a tip. I'm supposed to steal the ring from *you*."

This made the boy hesitate. Confusion wavered in his eyes until he brandished the knife again and said, "I don't want to hurt you."

She barked a laugh. "I told you, I don't have it." She held up her hands to show she wasn't playing any tricks, then slowly reached into her boot and took out Luc's note, still smelling of bubblegum. She held it up for the boy to read. "See? You're my mark."

"But you're *my* mark."

They stared at each other for the span of a few heartbeats. The wind was merciless. *Merde*, but it was freezing. His lips were chapped. He was still holding the knife, but it was no longer pressed against her side.

"Who gave you your information?" she asked.

"A boy in a café in the Marais. He said I should find a girl with yellow headphones at a place called Candy Bar. That you'd have the ring."

"You got bad intel," she said.

"So you really don't have it?"

"No. And you?"

"No." He studied her for a long time, then cursed and pocketed the knife. He dumped the bouquet of roses in the bin by the restaurant's back door and started past her, back into the busy street.

For a second, she wasn't certain what had happened. She leaned against the alley wall, still tasting the cherry fizz from Gigi's candy. Luc's instructions had come straight from Mada Vittora. She was supposed to steal a signet ring that belonged to Prince Rennar, ruler of the Shadow Royals of the Parisian Court. He always wore it on his fourth finger, but somehow, someone had gotten hold of it, and now this Pretty boy was supposed to have it. She hadn't asked Luc why Mada Vittora wanted the ring. She hadn't asked her anything since the incident with the book. She shuddered to think of her fate if she failed—she'd be plunged back into the darkness of life as an animal.

She banished the thought from her mind. Whatever she'd started out life as didn't matter. She was human now and she would do whatever it took to stay that way.

She balled her hands into fists, pushed back into the crowd, and found the boy in the black jersey. She grabbed his arm, hard.

He turned in surprise, his expression guarded.

"I might have an idea," she said, then paused. She was used to *taking* from random people in the street, not *giving*. She thrust out her hand, though not without a dose of caution. "I'm Cricket."

Hesitantly, he took her hand. "Fabrice."

Chapter 2

T HE MOON WAS HIGH and the throngs were only getting thicker as Cricket led the boy back the way they'd come and through the familiar frosted-pane door. Candy Bar was more crowded now. The girl reading the book had been joined by two friends, and every stool at the bar and all the tables by the windows were taken. Cricket caught Gigi's eye as she was cleaning up chocolate wrappers. Gigi slid a long look up and down the handsome Pretty boy, then kicked out a couple sitting in a private table in the corner.

"For my favorite customer," Gigi said, coming over to Cricket and Fabrice, "and her valentine."

The boy's face slackened in surprise. "Oh, we're not—"

"On the house." Gigi shoved a slice of cake topped with crushed peppermint into his hands, then put two forks on the table.

Cricket gave Gigi an odd look as she pulled out a chair and motioned for Fabrice to do the same. He sat and put the cake on the table. Cricket dropped down into her seat and leaned close to him. "Okay. Here's what I'm thinking."

Fabrice threw glances at the other couples. "You could have picked a less conspicuous place. This has to be one of the most popular haunts in the city on Valentine's Day."

Cricket frowned. "What's Valentine's Day?"

"You're joking, right?"

She shrugged.

He started to explain but got only Cricket's confused expression in response. "Don't take this the wrong way, but you don't know much, do you?"

Cricket's eyebrows shot up defensively. "*You're* the one who doesn't know much. You're just a Pretty."

He was so surprised that he laughed. He had dimples when he smiled. "Um, thank you?"

"No, it isn't a compliment about your looks. Pretties are . . ." She sighed. "Never mind. You'd think I was crazy."

The smile melted off his face. He leaned forward over the candle. The flame's reflection danced in his brown eyes. "You're talking about the Haute."

Her back went rigid. "How do you know about that?"

"Same way I know about Prince Rennar and his ring. The boy in the Marais café? He wasn't . . . normal. He was like that bartender over there. There's something off about her—I can feel it." He dropped his voice. "She isn't human. Neither is Prince Rennar. I don't know if they're witches, but they're *something*. Last year, one of my sister's friends disappeared for months. She came back, but she looked different. She looked healthier, stronger. She told Élodie, my sister, about this secret place in Germany, in the Black Forest. A place where girls walk through fire and come out the other side changed. She did magic—real magic, not card tricks. I saw it with my own eyes. Said she was the only girl at the academy who hadn't burned to death. Well, Élodie got obsessed with finding this place and gaining magic herself. Scoured the internet. She discovered spells. Maps. Most were useless, I'm sure, but she must have come across something she trusted." He paused. "She ran away a month ago. I've been to hell and back to try to find her. I finally came across that boy in the café, the one who told me I needed a magic ring that belonged to a guy named Prince Rennar. The ring permits the wearer to enter areas that are hidden—like that forest my sister went to." He let out a long breath. "That place is dangerous. She could die. I have to go get her back."

Cricket listened to his story in a state of perplexity. For Cricket's whole life, Pretties had been background noise. Strange little distractions in her way. She'd never heard one talk about the Haute. Not all of Fabrice's facts about the Haute were correct, but they were close enough. And the thing that struck her most was that he knew about magic but didn't care. He just wanted his sister back.

"It's called tricks and whispers," she said quietly.

"Pardon?"

"Magic. It's called tricks and whispers."

For a few minutes, they were both silent. The cake sat between them, untouched.

He leaned forward. "Are you a witch?"

She barked a laugh. "Now, *that's* funny." She picked up a fork, stabbed the cake with it. "No. I can't cast tricks and whispers. All I can do is steal things from unsuspecting Pretties like you. Except apparently I can't even do that."

"So what are you?"

She took a bite of cake. "Screwed."

He seemed to sense that she didn't want to elaborate—maybe it was the sharp fork pointed in the general direction of his face—and he folded his hands on the table. "Look, whatever you are, you need that ring. So do I. So what do we do, Cricket?"

She wasn't used to hearing her name spoken outside of a sharp order, and it felt like a sugar rush. She took another chunk of cake and twirled her fork thoughtfully. "Well, my intel said that you'd already gotten the ring from Rennar. But if you haven't, then chances are Rennar still has it. So we'll have to steal it directly from him. Which isn't as simple as it sounds. He's the most powerful magic handler in all of Paris. He lives in a palace shrouded in tricks. Not to mention that the ring is on his *finger*. It's one thing to steal an object out of a pocket, but off a finger? Almost impossible."

"Not always." Fabrice stroked his chin. His fingers were long and nimble, and Cricket wondered if he was more skilled at theft than he was letting on. "I might have some ideas, but I can't do it alone. We'd need each other's help."

She smirked. "Well, there's a problem."

"You mean, what if we succeed? Who gets the ring then?"

"Exactly. I just met you, and I'm not in the habit of trusting Pretties. What's to stop us from turning on each other the second we have that ring? Only one of us can end up with it. And we both need it equally badly."

Fabrice took a big bite of cake, chewed thoughtfully. "That's a problem I'm willing to address when—if—we get the ring." He swallowed, then gave a half smile that made one of his dimples appear. "Until then, partners?" He took another chunk of cake and held up his fork.

She stared at it and then slowly stabbed her own chunk. "Partners now. Enemies later. Deal."

They clinked forks and took their respective bites. His grin made her smile back. Or maybe it was the dimples. Or maybe it was the sheer audacity of a Pretty boy who thought he could steal from the Royals. Then again, maybe she was being foolish too, imagining this would work. Already she was thinking of ways to get that ring from him as soon as they had it—and he was doubtlessly coming up with schemes to do the same thing.

"So when do we start?" he asked.

She laid a hand on her coat. "Right now."

A light snow had started, chasing most of the Valentine's Day crowd off the street and into restaurants and bars. Cricket and Fabrice huddled together beneath her red umbrella on the Champs-Élysées thoroughfare. Across the street stood the gated drive to the imposing Castle Ides, the home of the Parisian Shadow Royals. Cricket had been in it only once, when she and Hunter Black had accompanied Mada Vittora and the witch's adopted son, Viggo, to a party.

Fabrice counted. "Eight floors, ten windows per floor. Just the one entrance, as far as I can see, and no roof access from other buildings."

Cricket gave him an appraising look. "You've done this before."

He shrugged noncommittally. "So how do we break in?"

"We don't." Cricket pointed to the front entrance. "It's protected with far more than locks. There are sentries, keys, invitations—all of it run by tricks and whispers. We'd never get in."

The snow was falling harder. Cricket shivered. Fabrice shifted the umbrella to shelter her shoulders from the worst of it. "We have to. Rennar's in there. With his ring. How are we supposed to get it?"

Cricket gave a coy shrug. "Wait and see."

A slamming door drew their attention back to the front of Castle Ides. Someone had emerged, an Asian girl with a high ponytail. Her youthful look was deceptive—like Gigi at Candy Bar, like all the Haute, she was actually centuries old. She sauntered down the walkway in a sequined dress and fur coat and bare feet, an open black umbrella resting against one shoulder.

Cricket grabbed Fabrice's arm and motioned for him to follow her. She led him down the street, through an alley behind a block of shops, and into a mostly empty parking garage. They hid behind a silver coupe and watched the garage entrance.

Someone cleared her throat a few feet behind them.

Both of them spun to find the girl standing just a pace away, leaning on a red sedan. Fabrice nearly jumped out of his skin.

"*Sacré—*"

"Oh yeah," Cricket said. "I forgot to tell you—Royals can transport themselves with tricks and whispers."

The girl folded her umbrella. Her taste in clothes was sublime; the sequined dress looked straight off the runway. "Are you certain you can trust this Pretty, Cricket?" she asked.

"Honestly, I have no idea. Fabrice, this is Mia. She's a Shadow Royal, a specific type of magic handler. Like Rennar."

"Um, hi." Fabrice seemed uncertain if a handshake was in order or not and he settled for an awkward wave. Cricket snickered. He shot her a glare—it showed off his dimple—and she grinned harder.

"Well, whatever," Mia said with a careless shrug. "It's your funeral." Her eyes widened slightly. "You've got the powder?"

Cricket produced a vial from her pocket, and Mia growled and snatched it. She inspected the contents and then, satisfied, held out an envelope. She didn't take her eyes off the glittering powder. "Our business is concluded?"

Cricket nodded. "For now."

Mia gave a grunt in response, too fixated on whatever was in the vial to care what Cricket said. She opened the umbrella, rested it over one shoulder, then sauntered out into the snow.

Fabrice tapped on the envelope. "And this is?"

"Our way to get that ring." Cricket checked to make sure they were alone, then tore open the envelope and took out a folded piece of paper. She read it closely, eyebrows furrowed, as Fabrice tried to read over her shoulder.

"That looks like a schedule," he remarked.

"It is. Mia wrote down Rennar's business meetings and dinners this week. If we can't get to him inside Castle Ides, we'll wait for him to leave. Ah, look. This is perfect. On Friday night he's meeting with Prince Mavrik of the Hammer Court at a club in the Marais. That's where we're going to steal the ring."

"A club? A dance club? There will be too many witnesses. Better here—" He pointed to the fourth line on the schedule. "On Thursday morning, he's meeting a witch in the Jardins des Luxembourg. Fewer witnesses. In the club, there will be limited ways in and out, and it'll be total chaos inside."

"No. It has to be the club. Prince Mavrik chose that club *because* it's so chaotic. I've walked by it before; the music, the lights, everything is high tech. Royals can't cast magic in a place where there's lots of modern technology—technology and magic cancel each other out. That's why the Hammer Prince chose it, so that they can't use their magic against each other. It's neutral territory. Which means Rennar won't be able to use his magic against *us* either."

Fabrice leaned back on the silver coupe and folded his arms. His eyebrows rose. He gestured to her ripped jeans. "You can't wear that to a club."

She smirked. If there was one thing she loved even more than candy, it was clothes, and as a thief, she considered every department store in the city fair game. "I can manage to get my hands on something appropriate. Can you?"

His eyes glittered. "Wait and see."

Chapter 3

❧

OVER THE NEXT TWO days, as Cricket waited for Rennar's meeting at the club, she found that life was a little boring without Fabrice. When Friday night finally came, she felt a flutter in her chest as she pulled on leather leggings and a corset top. She left her hair in its natural curls and dusted it with glitter. She donned boots with daringly high heels and then grinned at herself in the mirror. There was something fairy-tale-like about this night. Luc and Anouk were always talking in fairy-tale riddles, weren't they? Now it was Cricket's turn to play Cinderella at the ball—though maybe she didn't look *just* like the heroines in the storybooks. But techno and black leather were more her style anyway. All that was missing was a suitable form of transportation. And she knew just where she could get her hands on an enviable ride.

She tapped the brass knocker on the grand door of 18 Rue des Amants and didn't have to wait long before Anouk, Mada Vittora's newest beastie, threw open the door.

Anouk's eyes lit up. "Cricket!"

Cricket responded with half a smile. Six months ago, when Anouk had been made out of some mystery animal, Cricket hadn't been sure what to feel. Anouk had been so wide-eyed that Cricket wanted to roll her own eyes, but the truth was, she liked Anouk. She liked having another beastie girl in the household. She liked having someone smile every time she saw her. And she liked how, behind that naive face, a dark mind pulsed, darker than anyone realized.

Cricket struck a pose. "*Voilà*. What do you think?"

Anouk looked distracted tonight; she chewed absently on her lower lip. Cricket folded her hands over her chest and frowned down at her outfit. "It isn't *that* bad."

Anouk's eyebrows shot up. "Oh no, your clothes are great. Are you going to a party?" Anouk was smiling, but it didn't reach her eyes. Something was bothering her. Something big enough that the maid didn't notice that she was clutching a potato peeler in one hand.

Cricket forgot about her quest for a pumpkin-turned-carriage vehicle and took a step inside. She closed the door and asked in a low voice, "What's wrong?"

Anouk looked away. "Nothing."

Cricket cupped Anouk's face, forced the maid to look at her. There was the ever-present streak of dust on her cheek. Cricket wiped it away with her thumb. "Tell me."

Anouk took a step back and winced. Anouk was almost always barefoot, but today she wore a pair of Beau's wool socks, lumpy and too big for her. Cricket crouched down, suspicious, and tugged off one sock. Anouk's feet were bandaged.

Cricket stood up, her eyes narrowed. "What did that witch do to you?" She ran her thumbnail over her own missing fingerprints, burned off by Mada Vittora to make sure she never forgot who was in charge.

Anouk drew in a breath. That glint of darkness flashed in her eyes. "It's—"

"Look what the cat dragged in!"

Luc came down the hallway, grinning. As the oldest of all the beasties, Luc had always felt to Cricket like a big brother. His wide smile turned into something puzzled when he saw what Cricket was wearing. "*Dieu,* you'd better cover up before Mada Vittora sees you in that. Anouk, fetch her a spare coat, will you?"

"Of course." Anouk headed to the closet in the study, trying to hide her limping.

In the foyer, Luc leaned toward Cricket and said in a low voice, "Listen, Mada Vittora is waiting for you in the library. It's late. Do you have the ring?"

Cricket darted a glance at the library, then pulled Luc over to the stairs, away from the enchanted eyes of the hallway portraits that were always spying. "I'm going to get it tonight. But I need to borrow Beau and the Rolls-Royce . . . and I need you to make an excuse for me. Distract Mada Vittora until tomorrow."

Luc rubbed the back of his neck. "You're in luck. She's been distracted anyway by her new *toy.*" He bit off the final word and jerked his head in Anouk's direction; by the sound of it, she was still digging around in the study closet for a coat.

Cricket's expression darkened. "Those bandages on her feet?"

"Mada Vittora cut off her little toes," Luc said quietly, "so that her feet would fit in shoes for dress-up."

Cricket hissed out a curse. "Luc, we can't go on like this! You know it as well as I do. She burned off my fingerprints. She cut off Anouk's toes. I know what she's done to you, what she still does to you . . ." She trailed off. Luc didn't like to talk about the abuse. "Sooner or later, she's going to kill us."

19

Luc didn't answer right away. A muscle jumped in his jaw. Footsteps told them that Anouk was coming back from the study. Luc leaned in close. "I'll figure something out. Get the ring, okay? Or else she'll burn off more than your fingerprints. Take Beau and the car. He's in the garage." His face twisted into a smirk. "By the way, you look hot."

Cricket smirked back.

Anouk came in holding an expensive silk coat that Cricket had always admired. Cricket took it and, on impulse, pulled Anouk in for a quick hug. "I'll see you tomorrow," Cricket promised.

Outside, she strode around the townhouse to the garage, where Beau was polishing the hood of the Rolls-Royce by the light of the street lamps. He caught sight of her and tipped up his chin. Beau had been made human two years after her, and she'd always felt protective of him.

She rapped on the car's hood. "Not a bad pumpkin." When Beau gave her a quizzical look, she asked, "Can you take me to the Latin Quarter? The end of Rue Saint-Séverin? Luc said Mada Vittora isn't planning on going anywhere tonight. But we need to pick up someone first."

Beau shrugged and started wiping his hands. "A joyride? Sure." He rolled down his uniform sleeves and donned his chauffeur's cap. She climbed in the back and he started the engine, pulled the car into the dark street.

Cricket leaned forward between the front seats. "You know about what Mada Vittora did to Anouk?"

Beau's jaw tightened. "I'd kill her if I could. I really would."

"We can't let this continue."

"You don't have to tell me."

Cricket flopped back and they drove in a troubled silence. Beau glanced at her in the rearview mirror and then opened the glove box and handed back a lollipop.

She took it with a wry smile. "You make a pretty good fairy godmother, Beau."

"Huh?"

"Never mind."

Her thoughts were still troubled when Beau pulled up in front of Candy Bar. Fabrice stood on the street, waiting. He was dressed in black jeans and a black shirt made of some enviable liquid-like material. He'd rolled up the sleeves to show off tattoos that covered both of his arms from biceps to wrists. Leather suspenders gave him a look that was simultaneously timeless and edgy.

Her nostrils flared in jealousy. The bastard looked better than she did!

Beau made an uncertain sound. "*That's* who you're meeting? He's a Pretty. He's possibly the prettiest Pretty in all of Paris." He glanced at Cricket in the rearview mirror. "What exactly are you up to?"

"Don't worry about it."

"He looks like he's about to walk down a runway for a postapocalyptic rave fashion show."

"I *said* don't worry." She reached up to tousle Beau's hair—he hated that—then climbed out of the car. Fabrice straightened as she approached. His eyes glided down the length of her, the leather pants and corset beneath the silk coat, the lollipop in her mouth, and he slowly shook his head.

"You're going to get me in trouble."

21

She felt that flutter in her chest again. She liked trouble. She got the sense that he did too. Maybe they could do another job together after this . . . but as soon as she'd had the thought, her mood turned dark. There would be no *after*. Only one of them could walk away with the ring.

He gestured to the idling Rolls-Royce. "Are you going to explain how you got your hands on one of the most expensive cars in the world?"

"Magic. How else?" She slid on sunglasses even though it was nearly midnight. "We aren't on the club's list, so if we don't show up in style, there's no way they'll let us in." She pointed the lollipop toward the car. "Climb in."

He got in the back seat, and she followed him and gave Beau the address of the club. As the Rolls-Royce purred forward, Cricket ran a finger down the tattoos that covered Fabrice's arm. "These are beautiful." It felt strange to touch someone with her damaged fingers. They were still tender, still extra-sensitive.

"Élodie has the same tattoos," Fabrice told her. "We got matching ones after our parents died. It's a design she drew. She was—is—a great artist."

It was cold outside, but huddled in the back seat with Fabrice, Cricket didn't feel it. She realized she was leaning very close to him when she caught Beau's eye in the rearview mirror. He raised a questioning eyebrow; she cleared her throat, shoved the lollipop in her mouth again. The silence stretched on as Fabrice reached out and took her hand. If anyone else had done that, she would have jerked her hand away. But she stayed like that, her hand clasped in his, the flutter in her chest unbearable, until Beau stopped the car.

"This is it." Beau's eyes went to their clasped hands, but he didn't say anything.

Cricket pulled her hand back and adjusted her clothes. She took a deep breath. It was time to focus, time to work. "You'll wait for us?" she asked Beau.

"I'll park around the corner. Call when you need a pickup."

Cricket and Fabrice exchanged a long look.

"Ready?" Fabrice asked.

She smiled. "Always."

Chapter 4

THE THROBBING BEATS FROM the club made the whole block thump. Cricket and Fabrice approached Club ZouZou, both of them with their sunglasses on, their chins tipped up confidently; Cricket's silk coat billowed behind her. She could feel the music's vibrations running up her high heels and into her ankles, but her hands were steady. This, at least, was familiar territory. The thrill of a job. What *wasn't* familiar was Fabrice by her side. His presence complicated everything—and it also made everything that much more fun.

"I don't have a legal ID," Fabrice whispered under his breath as they neared the bouncer.

Cricket shot him a look. Didn't all Pretties have IDs? What wasn't he telling her? But they were just steps away from the front door. The bouncer looked from them to the Rolls-Royce and back. His eyes widened at the silk coat Cricket wore and the designer logo that indicated it was worth five figures.

"That won't be a problem," Cricket answered.

Without a word about IDs or guest lists, the bouncer opened the door for them. Cricket thrust her arm through Fabrice's with a peal of laughter that she hoped seemed carefree. She pulled him inside the club. It was so dark that it took a moment for Cricket's eyes to adjust. It was large, as far as clubs went. Three balconies, all of them full of people drinking and dancing. The dance floor, in the middle of which sat a horseshoe-shaped bar, took up most of the lower level. The club's dancers performed on platforms at either end of the bar.

Cricket dragged Fabrice to the hall near the bathrooms, where it was quieter. "Be cool, Fabrice," she hissed.

"I am."

"You almost gave us away with that bouncer. He was within earshot when you were babbling about missing IDs." She sent him a sharp look. "We can't mess this up."

He took off his sunglasses, then reached down and took hers off too so he could look in her eyes. "You can trust me, Cricket."

Trust him? What a ridiculous idea. Gigi had also told her she needed to trust someone, but of course, she and Fabrice couldn't trust each other. As soon as they had the ring, it was every person for him- or herself. He'd betray her or she'd betray him. It was only a question of who had the better idea for double-crossing the other.

Whatever his strategy, it couldn't possibly be as clever as hers. She'd thought through every angle. He was risking everything to see his sister again, but he never would because *she* was going to walk away with the ring. She almost felt sorry for him.

She grabbed her sunglasses back from him and put them on. "We stick to the plan we've worked out, we'll be fine."

He held his hands up in mock surrender. "You're the boss."

She shoved his shoulder playfully. He took her hand and they made their way to the dance floor, where they could observe the crowd hidden in plain sight. According to the schedule Mia had given them, Rennar would arrive at midnight. Cricket checked her phone.

Ten minutes until then. She went to the bar and ordered a drink—a double vodka—and handed it to Fabrice. He threw it back, and they took to the dance floor, swaying to the beat, while her gaze scanned the upper levels. On the third balcony, two large men in black suits were standing guard in front of one of the booths. Given their beauty, they had to be lesser Royals. Which meant that the booth was the rendezvous location.

"Turn me around so I can see better," Cricket whispered.

Fabrice pressed a hand against the small of her back, pulled her close. The beat was throbbing. That flutter in her chest stirred at his touch. He was a good dancer, maybe—*maybe*—better than her. She wrapped her arms around his neck and turned him until she was looking over his shoulder at the booth. She leaned in close to him to see better. Her lips hovered next to his ear. "Mavrik is there," Cricket whispered.

Sitting in the booth was a gorgeous man in a black suit; his dark hair was slicked back, and he had a trace of a beard. He was drinking from a crystal goblet. He looked to be in his early twenties, but that meant nothing—everyone in the Haute looked young and beautiful.

"And I'd bet my life that's Rennar who just walked in," Fabrice whispered from his position facing the door. His breath tickled her neck, and she found herself shivering in a not-unpleasant way. He pulled her close as the beat switched to something faster.

"Show me," Cricket said.

He dropped his hands to her hips and guided her in a circle until she was facing the door. She'd seen Prince Rennar only once before, at the party at Castle Ides. He hadn't spared her a glance then. Still, when she'd gotten dressed this evening, she'd been careful to select clothing and makeup that he wouldn't recognize as belonging to Mada Vittora's thief if he happened to give her a close look.

He was dressed in a tailored suit, jacket slung over one arm, as though he were visiting a museum instead of a dance club. He stood out starkly from the clubbers in their black leather and tight dresses, but he didn't seem to care. His eyes scanned the crowd with indifference, even disdain. He shuddered and wiped his hands on his trousers. The loud music seemed to offend him on a personal level.

Cricket watched as Rennar caught sight of the Hammer Prince on the third balcony. He put his head down, went through the crowd to the stairs, and took them two at a time, all the way to the third floor. There he said something to the guards, who nodded and motioned to the man on the couch. The Hammer Prince raised his crystal goblet. Rennar shook his head. Prince Mavrik gestured to the opposite bench and Rennar sat.

"Okay," Cricket said. "Now we wait for them to finish. You should get another drink."

Fabrice did not seem to have heard her. Maybe that double vodka was already working. He had one arm around her back, and his head was pressed to hers. His eyes closed for a moment. "Is this real, Cricket? Are you real?"

If anyone else had said that, she'd have rolled her eyes. But she felt it too, the sense that this was almost a fairy tale come to life. She rested her head against Fabrice's shoulder and closed her eyes. He felt solid beneath her hands. He danced with smooth control. Cricket smiled into his shoulder and swayed with him, letting that delicious flutter in her chest spread to the tips of her fingers and toes. They danced for the next few songs, then took a break at the bar, where she ordered him another double vodka and laughed as he tried and failed to do a card trick with coasters. He was starting to slur his words.

Good.

She motioned for the bartender. Fabrice groaned as she handed him yet another drink. "Come on. Bottoms up."

"This plan of yours to get the ring—it's crazy." He gave her a loopy grin before tossing back the drink. "I love it."

Fabrice getting sloppy drunk was an integral part of the plan that they'd agreed on, but it was also going to make things complicated. Fabrice's hands were already clutching her waist tighter, as though it were the most natural thing in the world for him to pull her close and press his lips against her temple.

His breath was sugary as he said, "That corset, Cricket. *That corset.*"

She gave him a shove, feigning offense. "You're toasted."

"I'm just doing what you wanted."

"Well, now I want to dance."

She pulled him back to the dance floor. He was bolder now, holding her flush against him. It would be scandalous if every other dancer weren't doing the same thing. She leaned into him, giving herself over to the feeling. Anything for a job, right? Then her eyes snagged on Rennar on the third-floor balcony and she went stiff. He was standing up from the booth and reaching across the table to shake hands with Prince Mavrik.

She grabbed Fabrice's shirt. "It's time!"

He blinked as if he were trying to remember why they were there, but his eyes cleared quickly.

Too quickly.

She frowned. "How many vodkas did you have, five?"

He shrugged.

She narrowed her eyes. "You aren't drunk enough. If *I* can tell you aren't totally smashed, Rennar will be able to too. He'll be suspicious. Here—I brought this just in case." She pulled a small bottle out of her pocket and pressed it into his hand.

He read the label and grimaced. "This stuff makes you sick."

"Exactly. We're not taking any chances."

He groaned, but uncorked the bottle and threw back the liquid. Instantly, his face went sallow. His eyes became rimmed in red. His stomach began to gurgle in an unpleasant-sounding way.

She took a step back. "Right. Now split up. Stick to the plan we made. Meet up at Candy Bar once it's done, okay?"

He shook his head. "No. We agreed to meet outside the club entrance."

She scoffed. "Are you afraid I'll ditch you once I get the ring?"

"I *know* you will."

She pressed her lips together. "Fine. We'll meet right outside. Now go."

He was sweating and had one hand clutched to his stomach. The other dancers were beginning to give him worried looks. He stumbled toward the bar, moaning. Dancers cried out as he shoved them out of the way.

With all eyes on Fabrice, Cricket slipped unnoticed through the crowd toward the bathrooms, where she stood in the corridor and pressed her back against the wall. Fabrice was now stumbling toward the exit, looking more ill by the moment. Prince Rennar, also headed toward the exit, didn't notice him until they collided a few paces before the door. Fabrice blocked Rennar's path. Rennar gave him a wary look, sniffed the air, and then grimaced at the reek of alcohol.

Fabrice lurched forward and—exactly according to plan—threw up on the prince. Without his magic, Rennar couldn't move away in time. Vomit coated his hands and arms.

Rennar froze in horror.

Watching from the hallway, Cricket pressed a hand over her mouth, silencing her laugh. There were definitely some perks to this job.

Fabrice wiped his lips with the back of his hand, swaying slightly. He said something to Rennar that she couldn't hear, an apology probably. Rennar lifted a hand as though to keep him from coming any closer. The prince seemed at a loss for words. It was lucky they were in the club, with all its interfering technology, otherwise the Shadow Prince would have turned Fabrice to ash. Rennar looked wildly around the club until his eyes caught on the sign for the restrooms.

Perfect.

Cricket grabbed the bag she'd stashed behind an artificial plant near the men's room and pulled out her supplies. She buttoned a plain black dress over her dance clothes in a hurry, then grabbed a tip jar and a stack of towels and darted into the restroom. It was empty— that was a piece of luck. She set up her props and leaned against the sink counter, trying to look like a bored bathroom attendant. In the next minute, Rennar shoved through the door and rushed to the sink.

Stay calm, girl, she told herself.

She could smell Fabrice's vomit on Rennar's hands and sleeves. Rennar twisted on the hot-water tap, muttering under his breath, but before plunging in his hands in the water, he paused to take off his ring—such things, she had predicted, were too delicate for harsh Pretty soaps. He set the ring on the counter and scrubbed at his hands viciously with soap. Keeping her face carefully blank, she passed him one of the towels.

"Quite a mess, monsieur."

He barely glanced at her. He washed his hands a second time, inspected them, scowled deeply, then wet the towel and dabbed at his shirt. Cricket eyed the ring on the counter, her fingers twitching.

I'll use sleight of hand, Fabrice had said when they'd first discussed this plan. *I've used it before to steal watches.*

Watches aren't rings, Cricket had answered. *The only way to get it off his finger is to convince him to take it off himself.*

Rennar set the dirty towel on the counter and held out a hand for Cricket to pass him a fresh one. He cleaned himself up the best he could, then—all business—replaced the ring on his finger, gave himself a look in the mirror, and made for the door.

Cricket felt the tickle of a grin at her lips, but it froze when Rennar stopped suddenly. Alarm bells went off in her head. He turned around slowly. Her pulse raced. Was Fabrice outside? Would he hear if Rennar attacked her? Rennar reached into his pants pocket and came toward Cricket. She sucked in a breath, prepared to scream. But he only pulled out a hundred-euro bill, dropped it in her tip jar distractedly, and left.

As soon as the door swung shut, she crumpled against the counter. *Ha!* She felt like laughing. Like crying. Her hands were shaking. Had they really just gotten away with it? Really? Her head spinning, she quickly gathered all her props and dumped them in the waste bin, although she fished out the hundred-euro bill first. She wasn't *une idiote.*

She stuffed the bill in her corset, the same place she'd stashed his ring. It had been a simple swap, really. The moment Rennar had laid the dirty towel on the counter and glanced down at his damp shirt, her quick fingers had stolen his ring and exchanged it for a brass-and-colored-glass copy made by a friend of Fabrice's who knew a few things about counterfeit jewelry and could copy it exactly from a small portrait of Rennar she'd stolen from Mada Vittora's townhouse.

She crammed her plain black dress in the trash with the rest of the props and strode back out into the club in her corset and leather pants, silk coat tossed over one shoulder, the ring and the money tickling her skin. She didn't bother to hide her broad smile now.

Chapter 5

CRICKET BURST OUT OF the club's front door, her feet light as air. Every muscle of her body sparkled; it was like feeling the bubbles of Gigi's Pop Rocks everywhere, not just on her tongue, like hearing the first beats of a new song that she knew was about to be her new favorite. She was already imagining recounting the story to Luc and Anouk and Beau. How they'd roar to think of Rennar covered in vomit! She stopped just outside the door, shivering in the sudden cold. Fabrice had insisted on meeting her here to make sure she didn't sneak off with the ring, but he wasn't anywhere in sight.

She pressed a hand over the ring tucked in her corset. If he wasn't here, she could run. The ring was hers. The thrill of it lit a fire in her core, and she glanced up and down the street, ready to bolt. But a worry tickled in the back of her mind.

What had happened to him? Was their partnership over without a goodbye?

Why didn't this feel like a win?

In that moment of hesitation, she heard a whistle.

He was waiting in the shadows of the alley across the street. He motioned her over. She cursed herself—she should have bolted—but a part of her longed to see the smile on his face when she showed him the ring.

As she dashed over, her smile faded. The street lamp lit up his face. He had a fresh bruise on his temple, and his eyes were deeply rimmed in red. He took a step toward her, and she saw he was limping. She bit her lip. *Stupide!* Had she really thought they'd gotten away with it? Just like that? What had Rennar done to him?

"Fabrice!" she cried. "What happened?"

But as soon as she reached for him, concern in her eyes, he shook his head and gave a gruff laugh. "Nothing. I'm fine. The bouncer just wanted to make sure I knew I wasn't invited back. Apparently, it's frowned upon to vomit on the city's wealthiest patron."

The tension in her shoulders eased, but her heart was still thumping. For a moment, she'd been panicked to think of him hurt. She suddenly felt like she was in far more danger here with him than she'd ever been in the club with Rennar. Danger of falling for a pretty Pretty who was destined to betray her.

Fabrice raised his eyebrows. "Well?" There was an expectant hush in his voice, and she swallowed down her conflicted emotions.

She nodded.

His eyes lit up. "Yes? You're serious? You've got it?"

"It's in my corset—don't go reaching for it, eh?"

He threw his arms around her in a hug, swept her off the ground, and swung her around in the alley.

"Ah! You oaf, put me down! You're already limping as it is!" She was laughing.

As soon as her feet touched the pavement, she felt a moment of regret that all of it was over. She clutched his shoulders, reluctant to let go, wishing they could be back in the club again, dancing together.

As if it were the most natural thing in the world, he leaned in and kissed her. It felt like such an inevitable extension of the night—the dancing, their victory. His lips were warm. The alley was cold. She leaned into him. There was something impossibly sweet about the moment, about him. Like candy. But a voice in the back of her mind warned her. Suspicion started to sneak its way back into her thoughts. They had the ring now. This was as far as their partnership went. Fabrice seemed goofily drunk, the way he was wrapping his arms around her and smiling against her lips. It was her idea for him to get drunk enough to throw up on Rennar; that would force Rennar to take off his ring, but it also meant that Fabrice would be like this— dizzy, slow, drunk.

Easier to manipulate.

Fabrice must have been onto her, though. She'd had a ripple of doubt at the bar when she'd ordered him the fifth vodka, and something had felt off in the way he'd tossed it back so easily. His drunken actions hadn't matched the clarity in his eyes, which was why she'd made him swallow the ipecac too. Either he held his alcohol extremely well, or he was acting. It would be so easy for him to slip the bartender a few extra bills to pour water in the shots instead of vodka. Or maybe he'd pulled his famous sleight-of-hand move, swapping the shots out himself when she wasn't looking. Suspicion was like salt in her pudding. She felt one of his hands teasing at the small of her back, distracting her, while the other pressed against her side, where the top of the corset met skin. The kiss turned harder.

She broke it off. Pulled away. "You can drop the act," she spat.

He knit his eyebrows together. "Sorry?"

She hugged herself against the cold. "I know you aren't drunk. I also know you had your jewelry forger make you a *second* dummy ring. He's not as loyal a friend as you think he is. All it took for him to spill everything was the promise of a contract working for Mada Vittora." She paused. "I also know that your wandering hands just swapped out the rings."

She fished out the dummy ring he'd planted in her corset, held it up to the moonlight to see the telltale glass glint, then chucked it into the sewer grate. She leveled a stare at him. "Come on, show me the real one."

What did she want to see in his eyes? A flash of admiration that she'd figured out his double cross? Instead, she saw a flicker of guilt, and it didn't sit well with her. They were thieves. Cons. One was always going to betray the other. What did he feel guilty about?

He leaned against the alley wall, rubbing a hand over his face with a sigh. He seemed suddenly far more sober than he had. "The first two vodkas were real," he said. He reached into his pocket and pulled out a ring. By its sparkle, she knew it was the real one.

"I'm going to need you to give that back," she said. With a sleight of hand of her own, a knife appeared in her fist. What choice had she had? That ring in his hand was going to keep her alive, keep her human. "Sorry, Fabrice. If it helps, I liked you."

He stared at the ring in his palm for a long time, and when he finally looked up, his eyes were softer. "Screw the ring."

She frowned. "Excuse me?"

"I know, I know. Listen . . ." He closed his eyes briefly. "This is going to sound crazy. But I've been thinking. Dancing with you tonight . . ." He sucked in an unsteady breath. "Cricket, what if we didn't do this?"

"Do what?"

"Double-cross each other. What if we didn't go through with whatever schemes both of us have been devising ever since we met? What if we just . . . left together?"

She squeezed her knife. "This is a trick."

"No, it isn't." His eyes were clear. "There's a train to Munich tonight. It leaves in twenty minutes. We're clever, you and I. We can figure out how to change our identities, how to hide from the Haute. We'll stay in trains and hotels and clubs, places with so much technology that the Haute can't use magic to come after us. We'll leave our pasts behind." He swallowed. "Not everything has to be a con."

She stared at him as though he were speaking some other language. "And the ring?"

They both looked down at it in his palm.

He said, "Help me find Élodie with it. I have to help my sister. Then the ring is yours. We'll sell it. Pawn it. Use the money to travel the world. Whatever we want."

She clenched her jaw and felt a muscle jump. The look in his eyes was sober. He was dead serious. This was no lie, no trick. Hadn't he understood the game? How dare he upset her plans by throwing out all the rules on the final toss of the dice.

Her heart was beating fast. He lowered his hand with the ring, and, hesitantly, she lowered hers with the knife. If she closed her eyes, she could imagine them running for that train. Laughing together as they jumped on it a moment before the doors closed, tumbling into a seat together, lips finding each other's.

Her phone buzzed in her back pocket. It was probably Beau, waiting to pick them up, worried the job had gone bad. Luc would be back at the townhouse with Anouk and Hunter Black. Mada Vittora would be waiting for the ring. What did she want it for? So she could gain even greater riches?

"I can't." Cricket regretted the words as soon as she said them. "I can't leave my friends."

Fabrice put the ring in his pocket and took her free hand in his. "What good are you to them as a prisoner? Cricket, I don't want to spend my life working for someone else, and I don't think you do either. Don't you feel like we were meant for more than making someone else richer? This is our chance to leave everything behind."

She hesitated.

If she ran away, Mada Vittora would send all hell after them. She'd call in Rennar for help. Rennar would discover the dupe ring then, if he hadn't already. They'd have all the Haute chasing after them, and if they caught the two of them, they'd kill Fabrice and do worse to Cricket.

"Fabrice, that is the worst idea I have ever heard in my entire life." She sheathed her knife and then shook her head, unable to believe what she was about to say. She closed her eyes and smiled. "Let's catch that train."

Chapter 6

PARIS'S GARE DU NORD train station was nearly empty when they arrived. A sleepy ticket agent yawned beneath a clock that showed it was well into the early hours of morning. They bought tickets and ran for platform four just as the yellow lights on the side of the train flashed, warning of its impending departure. Fabrice jumped on, reached back for Cricket, and tugged her in just before the doors closed. Grinning, they made their way into one of the cars. The after-midnight crowd was a mix of students on holiday and sleepy tourists surrounded by their luggage. Fabrice led Cricket through the first car and into the next one, which was empty except for a gray-haired woman asleep in the rear. He pulled Cricket into a row of seats. As the train lurched forward and glided out of the station, he leaned in for a kiss.

Cricket was a jumble of limbs in his lap. His elbow was shoved against the window. Her head was pressed against the back of the next chair. They laughed as their lips met. Beyond the window, Paris was rapidly vanishing. Cricket didn't mind watching it go. The City of Light could extinguish itself for all she cared. Paris had never been home to her. *This* felt right—making her own home in whatever place her feet led her to with whomever she wanted at her side. She cupped Fabrice's face; her thumb traced his jaw. There wasn't a drop of magic in his veins. His whispers were only whispers, and she loved him for it. She kissed him again. His breath was laced with vodka, but beneath that, he smelled like chocolate. She leaned her head against his. His short hair tickled her cheek and she grinned.

The conductor announced over the loudspeaker that they were approaching Saint-Ambroise Station. Cricket looked out the window at a part of town she'd never been to. In a few more stops, they'd be out of Paris entirely.

Could it really be this easy?

She sank down next to Fabrice, their arms intertwined. "What's Munich like?" she asked dreamily.

He stroked her arm. "It feels like you're walking around in a child's play village. People are friendly. Beer flows like water. There's a youth hostel we can stay at that has movie night every Saturday."

"How are we going to pay?"

"We don't have to give up *everything* about our pasts. I'm sure we can lift some wallets here and there."

She grinned. "I like you, you know that?"

The train stopped at Saint-Ambroise Station; the old woman in the back roused herself and got off, and a few students got on. Cricket rested her head against Fabrice's shoulder, wondering how they looked to the strangers coming and going. Did they mistake her and Fabrice for a couple of tourists? Or lovers? How wonderful life must be when you had nothing to worry about but where to travel to next.

The train pulled into a larger station and the loudspeaker squawked. "Château de Vincennes Station. Last stop in the metropolis of Paris. We'll be paused here for five minutes."

The students tumbled off in a hurry and ran for the nearest vending machine to get coffee during the break. Fabrice gave Cricket a devilish look. "The train car's empty now, you know."

"For five minutes."

"A lot can happen in five minutes."

He pulled her onto his lap for another kiss. Cricket heard someone climbing onto the train, but she ignored the new arrival. Let whoever it was be shocked by a couple of kissing teenagers.

Suddenly, Fabrice's hand was ripped away from her.

Her eyes shot open. It took her a moment to make sense of what she was seeing. Hunter Black was standing in the aisle. He wore his usual black coat, collar pulled up against the cold, his hair a dark mess and his eyes unforgiving.

Dread clawed up her throat.

"Who the hell—" Fabrice started.

Before Cricket could react, Hunter Black grabbed her arm. He dragged her off Fabrice's lap and into the aisle between seats. She cursed and tried to twist out of his grasp. Her pulse was racing. Her mind couldn't string together thoughts fast enough. She had been so close to leaving Paris. Just a few more minutes and they would have been free!

Fabrice shot to his feet and clapped a hand on Hunter Black's shoulder. "Let her go!"

Hunter Black pulled a knife. Fabrice paused, his eyes flashing. If he was as much of a criminal as Cricket suspected he was, he knew how to read the confidence in Hunter Black's grip. This was no petty thief out to rob them.

"Hunter Black, don't!" Cricket yelled.

Fabrice's surprised gaze shot to her. "You know him?"

She nodded darkly.

Fabrice balled his hands into fists. He had nearly a foot on Hunter Black. He was an athlete with the muscles to prove it. But Hunter Black didn't blink.

"He's come to take us back," Cricket told Fabrice.

Hunter Black pushed his hair out of his face and set those dark eyes on Cricket. He pointed the knife in her direction. "No, Cricket. I've come to take *you* back."

Without warning, he slammed the knife hilt into Fabrice's temple. Fabrice had been prepared to dodge the blade, but he hadn't considered the blunt end. He grunted and slumped over. His eyes were dazed. Then he fell forward into the seat.

"Fabrice!" Cricket tried to crawl toward him, but Hunter Black started to drag her down the aisle.

"You didn't have to hurt him!" she cried, kicking.

"Mada Vittora wants a word."

There was an edge to his voice. A *word* wasn't what the witch wanted. She wanted Cricket's neck. She wanted every ounce of Cricket's blood. Cricket would be lucky if the worst thing that happened to her was that she was turned back into an animal.

Cricket clutched the seats on either side of the aisle, dug in her heels, and shook her head. "I'm not going back there."

"It isn't your choice."

She hissed at him and clawed his face. He raised his arm to protect himself, and the knife blade slashed against her arm. She stumbled back, clutching her skin. A thin line of blood appeared by her elbow.

42

"Screw choices!" she spat. "And screw *you!* You've always been her little minion, haven't you? Doing whatever grisly work she won't do herself. This is a new low, Hunter Black, even for you."

He glanced out the window to where the students were still hanging around the coffee vending machine, oblivious. "You don't understand, Cricket. You *can't* leave."

She scowled. "Not with you stalking my every step."

"I'm serious." He sheathed his knife. "Did you think Mada Vittora wouldn't expect us to try and escape? She has safeguards for that. She sent me to find you and bring you back—but it's magic that is keeping you in Paris, not me."

"What are you talking about?"

Cricket had drawn blood on Hunter Black too. It was beading up on his cheek where she'd scratched him. His dark eyes fixed on her. "She has five pelts locked her closet. One for each of us. The skins of what we used to be. As long as she possesses our pelts, she controls us. You couldn't have left Paris even if I hadn't found you. The train would have broken down, or there would have been an accident—it doesn't matter. The spell would find a way to keep you here."

Fabrice was moaning in the middle of the aisle. Blood was trickling down from the gash in his temple. He was lucky Hunter Black hadn't killed him—it wouldn't have been Hunter Black's first kill, or his twentieth. Cricket met Hunter Black's gaze, full of such hatred that she wanted to claw his eyes out. But what she hated more than anything was that there wasn't a trace of dishonesty in his eyes. He was a bastard, but he wasn't lying.

She looked back at Fabrice.

The train's yellow warning lights started flashing. The doors would close in one minute. The students, holding coffee, climbed back onto the train, took one look at Hunter Black in the aisle, and quickly moved on to the next car.

No one was going to help her.

Cricket felt the strength go out of her. As soon as her muscles went slack and she started to fall, Hunter Black pulled her to her feet. She let herself be led along, pausing only to toss a look back over her shoulder at Fabrice, who was clutching his head. Dazed, he looked around as though he didn't know where he was. His eyes locked on hers.

"C . . . Cricket? Wait . . ."

She rested her hand on the last seat, twisted toward Fabrice. "Fabrice, I—"

Hunter Black pulled her onto the platform. The doors closed behind them. She felt tears pushing at her eyes. The train started to lurch forward. She heard pounding on the windows. Fabrice was beating against them, calling her name. She didn't dare look. He'd been the one good thing she'd found in her short life, and now he was gone.

She shut her eyes and kept them squeezed shut until the rush of the train had passed. Until she could no longer hear Fabrice pounding on the windows. Until it was only her and Hunter Black, and all she could hear was her own ragged breathing.

"You're a bastard," she said.

He grunted. "Come on. Beau's waiting."

He didn't have to force her this time. Morosely, she followed him out of the station and toward the idling Rolls-Royce. She felt dazed, as though the world were spinning off-kilter. Hunter Black opened the rear door and guided her in, then climbed into the front passenger seat.

"Drive, Beau," he ordered.

In the rearview mirror, Beau's eyes met Cricket's. His were big and blue and full of pity for her. It stung, that look. She wrapped her arms around herself and wiped away her tears.

"You're an asshole, Hunter Black," Beau muttered to the assassin. He pulled into the street and took the first turn back toward the city center. Cricket stared out the window and tried not to think of Fabrice on that train.

What was Mada Vittora going to do to her this time? Not only had she tried to run away, but she'd stolen her mistress's silk coat and gotten tears and snot and blood all over it. She rested her head against the window. Everyone said how beautiful Paris was, but all she saw were dark alleys and dirty doorways.

"Seriously," Beau continued in a quiet voice to Hunter Black, "you don't think there were better ways to handle that? The girl's heart is broken. Probably a few bones too."

Hunter Black grunted, but after a few moments he cleared his throat and said, "I'm sorry, Cricket. I didn't mean to cut you."

She wanted to tell him to go screw himself. But other than soothing the sharp, angry thoughts poking around in her head, what good would that do? No, she needed to be clever. She needed to be strong. Why was she crying in the back seat of a car, anyway? That wasn't *her*. She wiped her eyes. "Well, don't be sorry," she said to Hunter Black.

In the rearview mirror, Beau's eyes met hers with a question.

She drew in a breath and forced a scowl. "You almost ruined everything, Hunter Black."

He twisted around in his seat. "What are you talking about?"

"The job," she spat. "The con. Come on, you didn't really think I was going to run away, did you? Oof, *quel idiot*. The train ride was all part of the theft."

Hunter Black's eyes narrowed. "The theft was finished. You stole the ring at the club."

She forced a laugh. "That just shows why I'm the thief and you aren't. You got the first part right. At the club, I conned Rennar and got his ring, but Fabrice wasn't about to let me walk away with it. He took it from me and then gave me some sob story about his sister and how he needed the ring and wanted me to run away with him—it was all a lie. He wanted that ring and he didn't want my knife in his belly. He'd have said anything. The only way I could get it back was to promise to run away with him and then steal it from him later, on the train, when his guard was down and he thought he'd won. I was going to get off at the next stop and head straight for Mada Vittora's."

Both boys were quiet, suspicious of her story.

"For someone who was lying," Hunter Black said flatly, "your tears seemed real enough."

She gave a tight smile. "I'm a good actor. Sometimes . . . sometimes I even fool myself. Start believing my own lies. But all that matters is that I fooled *him*. So you can tell Mada Vittora that I was doing exactly as she asked. She doesn't need to burn my flesh. In fact, she owes me a stiff drink for a job well done."

Hunter Black eyed her warily. Mada Vittora trusted him as much as she trusted anyone. If he told their mistress that the escape was all part of the con, she would believe him. It was likely the only way Cricket would make it out of this mess alive. "Prove it," he said.

She motioned to her bleeding arm. "Blood isn't enough?"

"If you're telling the truth, then you'll have the ring. If you're lying, then it will still be on that train with the Pretty boy, on its way to Munich."

Beau's eyes flickered to Cricket's in the mirror. She recognized familiar streets outside. The grand homes that were just a few blocks away from the townhouse.

She reached into her corset. Her heart was pounding. She took a deep breath, clenched her jaw, and thought of Fabrice, of the club, of the youth hostel in Munich that she'd never go to now.

She took out the ring.

Hunter Black snatched it, inspected it, and then grunted in satisfied surprise to find it was the real one. He tucked it into his pocket and then turned to the window as they pulled up to 18 Rue des Amants.

"You *are* a good actor," Hunter Black said. He climbed out of the car and added, "I'll tell Mada Vittora what happened. Clean yourself up and come to the library. She'll want to congratulate you."

After he was gone, Beau cut the engine but didn't get out. After tapping his fingers anxiously on the steering wheel for a few minutes, he turned in the seat to face her. "I don't get it."

Cricket raised an eyebrow. "Get what?"

"I got your text message earlier tonight." Beau pulled out his phone and read, "'I'm sorry but I have to go. You'll never see me again, if I'm lucky. I love you all.'" He held out the phone as proof.

"You sent the same message to Anouk and Luc. You were going to run, Cricket. I know you. You weren't coming back. It wasn't a lie."

She shrugged one shoulder, not meeting his eyes. "So?"

"So then why did you steal the ring back from Fabrice if you were really going to run away with him?"

She looked up at 18 Rue des Amants with dread, at its hard façade, at the rain slapping against the windows. She thought of Fabrice's dimples. How his hair had tickled her cheek. How, when they'd been entwined together in the row of seats, kissing, he hadn't noticed her reach into his pocket and take back the ring.

You're such a suspicious creature, Gigi had said. *You need to trust someone for once.*

"Because I'm a thief," she said quietly, "and a clever thief always hedges her bets." She paused before admitting, "You're right, I wasn't going to come back. But I'm a suspicious creature, and it's saved my life more than once. Trust isn't for people like us, Beau. If the worst happened, I wanted that ring in *my* pocket."

And the worst had happened, hadn't it?

At least she'd saved her own skin. And Fabrice's.

She climbed out of the car, grimaced up at the townhouse, and headed for the door that Anouk was holding open for her. She squeezed her damaged hands tightly and prepared to learn what their mistress would have her steal next.